Paul Klee Notebooks   Volume 1   The thinking eye

Translated by Ralph Manheim   Edited by Jürg Spiller

Paul Klee Notebooks
Volume 1
The thinking eye

THE OVERLOOK PRESS
WOODSTOCK • NEW YORK

Paul Klee Notebooks Volume 1: The thinking eye, edited by
Jürg Spiller, has been translated by Ralph Manheim, with
assistance from Dr Charlotte Weidler and Joyce Wittenborn,
from the original German-language edition *Das bildnerische
Denken* (Schwabe & Co., Verlag, Basel, 1965).

Published in 1992 by
The Overlook Press
Lewis Hollow Road
Woodstock, New York 12498

Library of Congress Cataloging-in-Publication Data

Klee, Paul, 1879–1940
  [Bildnerische Denken. English]
  The thinking eye edited by Jürg Spiller; translated by
Ralph Manheim.
      p. cm. — (The Paul Klee notebooks; v. 1)
  Includes bibliographical references.
  Translation of: Das bildnerische Denken.
  1. Visual perception.   2. Infinite in art.   I. Spiller, Jürg.
  II. Title   III. Series: Klee, Paul, 1879–1940. Form- und
Gestaltungslehre. English; v. 1.
  N7431.5.K4413   1992 vol. 1
  [N7430.5]
                                    92–16536
                                    CIP

ISBN 0–87951–467–1

Printed in Hong Kong

Ingres is said to have created an artistic order out of rest;
I should like to create an order from feeling and,
going still further, from motion.

Paul Klee, September 1914

Publishers' Note

The Preface by Giulio Carlo Argan is a translation by Mrs E. Lewis-Isastid of the Preface to the Italian edition and is reproduced in this edition by kind permission of the author and Giangiacomo Feltrinelli Editore, Milan.

For ease of reference, where there are captions to drawings and diagrams, glossaries are provided wherever necessary. These usually appear on the same page as the captions to which they refer, but to simplify matters the colour terminology which recurs throughout pages 465–511 is treated in a pull-out glossary which appears between pages 465 and 466.

Editor's Note

Klee himself was eager that the articles and lecture notes from his Bauhaus period should be published. His widow, Lily Klee-Stumpf (1876–46), made every effort to help us in carrying out this wish. Her advice was of the utmost help to us in establishing certain of the texts and in deciding between variant readings. We are greatly indebted to the artist's son Felix Klee and to the Paul Klee Stiftung in Berne for the loan of many works and for valuable documentation.

We are indebted to Petra Petitpierre for her shorthand notes 'From Paul Klee's Painting Classes at the Dessau Bauhaus', 'From the Kunstakademie Düsseldorf 1930–32' and 'Klee's Course in Theory'. All these have been used as source material.

Numerous Klee collectors have helped us in our work. Dr Richard Doetsch-Benziger donated a colour chart in memory of his friendship with Klee and placed his collection of reproductions at our disposal. We are indebted to Mr and Mrs Rolf Bürgi for numerous loans, to Dr H. Meyer-Benteli for permission to include the Jena lecture ('On Modern Art'), to the Öffentliche Kunstsammlung, Basle, and to Dr Charlotte Weidler for their helpfulness.

Werner Allenbach, Ida Bienert, Dr E. Friedrich, Susanne Feigel, Fritz Gygi, Daniel-Henry Kahnweiler, the Galerie Rosengart in Lucerne, Hermann Rupf and G. David Thompson have permitted us to make use of originals and reproductions from their collections; we wish to thank them and many unnamed lenders.

Robert Büchler, Christian Overstolz, Kurt Reiss, and a number of friends interested in Klee's work have played a large part in the conception and execution of this volume.

J.S.

Contents

Preface

The writings which compose Paul Klee's theory of form production and pictorial form have the same importance and the same meaning for modern art as had Leonardo's writings which composed his theory of painting for Renaissance art. Like the latter, they do not constitute a true and proper treatise, that is to say, a collection of stylistic and technical rules, but are the result of an introspective analysis which the artist engages in during his work and in the light of the experience of reality which comes to him in the course of his work. This analysis which accompanies and controls the formation of a work of art is a necessary component of the artistic process, the aim and the finality of which are brought to light by it. This explains too how the experience of reality which is acquired in seeking aesthetic value is no less concrete or less conclusive than that which is acquired in scientific or philosophic research.

It is well-known that Klee, more than any other artist of our century, was consciously detached from the main stream of modern art and its theoretical assumptions. In the same way, Leonardo, more than any other artist of the Renaissance, consciously detached himself from the central features of the historical tradition. In their creative thought both Leonardo and Klee are not so much concerned with the art object, as with the manner in which it is produced. They are concerned not with form as an immutable value, but with formation as a process. Both are aware that the artist's approach or creative manner is an independent and complete way of existing in reality and of understanding it; and as they are not unaware that there are other speculative methods, they are led to investigate that particular character which is the distinctive feature of the artistic approach, always bearing in mind, however, that this must develop over the whole field of experience. For this reason Leonardo's mode of thought, like that of Klee, covers every aspect of being; it takes in the entire universe. Since art brings into being, albeit only through what is termed the visible, a cosmic awareness of reality, there is no moment or aspect of being which can be considered foreign or irrelevant to the experience which is acquired in artistic creation.

Historically speaking, Klee's poetics can be linked to what might be called the poetics of contradiction, that is to say, poetics from Mallarmé to Rilke. Klee was a friend of the latter;

and Klee's thoughts on art were linked by at least two sources of common interest to the poetics of Mallarmé: Wagner, whom as a passionate lover of music he knew very well, and Poe, who certainly was one of the sources of his pictorial inspiration.

The fundamental themes are always those of non-positivity, of elusiveness, of the uncertainty of existence, of the emptiness of reality, and the need to fill that void by human endeavour and artistic creation. Nor are these born of an imperious creative will, but of the contradiction which exists between an understanding of the anguished uncertainty of everything and our indestructible awareness of existing, and of existing by necessity in one time, in one space, and in one world.

Everything that we know of reality (and this reality includes ourselves, the clear world of our consciousness and that murky and crepuscular world of the unconscious) comes to us through this tormented paradox. Nor is it a single and grandiose image which imposes itself on us by the logical system of its eternal values, but a hasty sequence of images, often dissociated and enigmatic, and always fragmentary throughout the full cycle of our existence. In turn, our existence is no more in its time-space reality than that self-same succession of images: and there is no moment of our existence which is not an experience of reality. These ambiguous images, then, are formed by ourselves. It is almost as if we evoke them from the darkness of a lost dimension, and reanimate them by the rhythm of our actions, giving them meaning and form. For the threat does not come from the vitality of the unconscious, but on the contrary, from carrying within us something that is dead, which, being corrupted, corrupts us. This endeavour, therefore, and this endeavour alone, is the subject of a speculation on art.

Perhaps, like Mallarmé, Klee too dreamt of the absolute work of art, 'l'œuvre', and did not achieve it; his real work must be found in the mass of evidence testifying to his life of research, in his development by way of a vast number of fragments, in his rapid sequence of paintings, in page after page of sketches and notes, in the restless technical experiments (since every technique is an attempt at 'trying', a 'coup de dés' that may even succeed in eliminating 'le hasard').

The writings which compose Klee's theory of form are, in fact, an attempt to fix the moments of that unaccomplished creative work, which unwinds with the devouring rapidity of time; to give meaning to arbitrary images, releasing them from the changeability of events and from shapelessness. These writings, therefore, more than any commentary, are a live and necessary part of the artist's œuvre. Since they cannot be separated from the drawings which accompany them they cannot be separated either from his other pictorial and graphic works, from the various planes on which his works were being simultaneously developed, from the inevitable irregularity of his progress or from the coherence, no less severe for being full of the unexpected, of his intellectual adventure. Klee's poetics, however, have this special quality, that in a large measure they are born and are formulated as didactics, like a well-prepared course of teaching given in a school with syllabuses and purposes precisely defined, as was the Bauhaus of Weimar and of Dessau. Of all the artists of this century, Klee is perhaps the one who has most purposefully penetrated into the enchanted realm of fantasy. It is as if he were seeking, whilst exploring the unconscious, the manifestation of an absolutely authentic and unique experience in which he would find himself alone in the suffering of the lonely ego, even reaching out to that ultimate and finally truthful manifestation of the ego which only comes to us at the moment of death. It cannot therefore be wondered at that his most constant preoccupation was to be able to communicate his own experience so that it could be repeatable and 'utilisable' and finally productive. Nor is this all: this man who looks upon nothingness with such a candid and dauntless eye, who 'toys' with death like Schiller's artist 'toys' with life, employs his own poetics and his own didactics in a school which not only has a social and somewhat revolutionary syllabus, and sees in technology the new strict spirituality of the modern world, but proposes to intervene effectually in the existing state of affairs by forming a class of technical executives and planners capable of solving problems arising from industrial production and capitalist economy.

Klee always wanted to teach and he dedicated himself to the school with an almost apostolic fervour. Conscious that art should be a means of human communication, he saw in teaching, in the exactness of the didactic method, a strict means of human communication. It is a matter of teaching others how to walk along thin invisible wires, stretched out in the darkness, trying to penetrate an unknown dimension. There can be no other way than that of going forward together along the uncertain road. There is the need not to be alone, to hold hands, to make a human chain: this is still the human basis, sentimental perhaps, of Klee's didactics.

But other and more serious reasons impel his poetics to become didactic and to assume a methodological character. According to Klee, the manner in which the artist creates implies, above all, a didactic requirement, for it is through creation that the artist learns to recognise the world in which he exists and acts, shaping it according to the extent of his own experience. Reading the pages of his theory of form it would appear that Klee desired to penetrate to the very depths of his knowledge of the universe; he speaks of space and time, of forces of gravity, of centrifugal and centripetal forces, of creation and destruction of the being, of the individual and the cosmos. Side by side with strangely happy intuitions, with parascientific propositions, with paradoxical postulates and with a vast quantity of very valuable annotations relating to the daily routine of pictorial work, one finds recollections of readings, passages revealing knowledge (which is neither superficial nor second-hand) of contemporary currents of thought, psychology of form, theory of visibility, psychoanalysis, the philosophy of phenomenology. Certainly all this does not constitute a system, but it does reveal a complicated construction in which everything seems to find its proper place.

Nothing is further from the artist's mind than the assumption that he is producing a scientific work, what is important to him is to specify a dimension or a perspective, to recognise the limits of space and time in which one's own existence manifests itself, to reweave the weft of the universe, from the starting point of one's own ego, with its will to make or to shape.

13

Thus, he thinks, must the world appear to those who do not stand apart from it and contemplate it from outside; to those who see it from the inside, with its infinite prospects, its diverging paths which cross, wheel round, then open slowly along the apparently capricious curves of life's parabola; a world ever eccentric and peripheral, 'irregular', yet nevertheless secretly obedient to certain laws, and ever striving to develop in order to find its path and break through to reality.

Thus space (and here we may note the similarity with the thought of Husserl and Heidegger) will no longer be a logical sequence of planes but above-below-in front-behind-left-right in relation to the 'I' in space; time will no longer be a uniform progression, but in a before and after relation to the 'I' in time; and as nothing is static, that which is now in front, soon will be behind, and that which is now before will be after.

Space and time are simultaneously subjective and objective; for this reason the sequence of values is endless and each value is not permanently bound to the object, but to the existence of the object in this or that point of space and time. It is bound to the recollection of its having been, to the possibility of its future being, under completely different conditions of space and time. The object itself has no certainty; it might have been and might be no longer; it might not be, but might be going to be. Since it is, ultimately, only a meeting of co-ordinate lines, a luminous point in the dark expanse of possible space and time, it could change into another object, whose trajectory may come to pass through that point. Should the unforeseeable parabola of our life pass through that point it could be that we might 'become' that object. Reality is a never-ending metamorphosis; this is a thought Klee had inherited from Bosch, and shared with Kafka.

There is, however, something which differentiates man's being and his actions, which differentiates cyclic changes of history from the unconscious changes and happenings in reality, something which, in the formal instability of metamorphosis, succeeds in isolating and defining forms and in making definite points of light.

It is the aim and the will of humanity somehow to control its own destiny, to know itself and clearly to establish its position in the confusion of chaos. Finally to 'save itself', if this expression still means something when confronted with an empty void. Nothingness, which stretches beyond the horizons of life, impels man ineluctably to find a solution here and now, within the uncertainty of the particular state of his society and of the individual within society.

The main thread which unravels itself throughout the whole of Klee's theory is the search for quality; it is in the search for quality, namely the search for one's own absolute authenticity, that mankind (as Kierkegaard would say) desires desperately to find in order to justify itself, and, perhaps, to save itself.

But it is not enough to desire this; to do or to become is life itself and it is only by acting consciously, and methodically, that one can attain some quality or value, which is also the value of existence, a full consciousness of each moment of it.

14

It may be said that Klee's art and theory represent an attempt to reconstruct the world according to values of quality; and since these values are not given and are embedded in layers of false experience, it becomes necessary to distil these values by a transformation, a 'reduction to quality' of the quantities. In other words, it becomes necessary to reduce progressively the conglomeration of quantitative phenomena which fill the universe and human existence, to the point of that irreducible and immutable minimum, which in fact represents quality, and which is to be found in all things which are real, although revealed only in meditation and in the production of works of art.

Notice how perspective, which is the typical quantitative construction of space, is elaborated in both Klee's painting and theory: or note the almost alchemistic treatment through which the chromatic scores emerge from the quantitative graduation of chiaroscuro, seeking in each note not just purity of tone, but the critical point of the passage from tonal volume to quality of timbre. The true meaning of this unceasing metamorphosis is therefore this: quantities are continually being raised to the level of qualities; and since this level is the level of consciousness, this last transformation can only take place in the mind of man. This is the humanistic foundation of Klee's art and doctrine.

The quality value will only be reached finally when the form produced, or the art object, contains within itself all human experience, the sum of human experience since the beginning of time. The work of art will be, even so, an object closed within its own finality, but it will project itself upon the spatial horizon of the universe and the temporal horizon of humanity. The work of art, since quality possesses individual character, must be elaborated by the individual, but it will acquire a collective meaning; its power will be incommensurable, its active presence will never be erased from the world. The artist's work, though it proceeds according to his own rhythm, will intertwine itself with the work of all mankind. 'We wish to be exact, but without limitations'; limitation is logic and calculation which determine the mechanism of modern productive techniques, the techniques of industry. We do not wish to destroy these techniques which possess almost unlimited possibilities: we want to develop them into more subtle and penetrating techniques harnessing both action and knowledge, manual and mental activity.

The Bauhaus had a definite programme: to restore production, which industrial techniques had developed only in a quantitative sense, to the search for quality values, in this way preserving autonomy, the creative possibility of a real existence, and, finally, the freedom of the individual in a society which was tending more and more to become a compact and uniform mass. But what are these quality values? The attitude of the Bauhaus on this point was ambiguous: in the first period at Weimar, following in the wake of the Werkbund, themes and procedures characteristic of ancient craftmanship were re-elaborated in an attempt to reduce traditional aesthetic values to a schematic system which could be applied to new industrial techniques. In the second period at Dessau, following the example of the Dutch group De Stijl, quality was sought in formal abstract concepts, in a mathematical rationalisation of the form selected as the image of the supreme rational quality of the human being.

Research, however, remained dialectically linked with the question of quantities; in the first instance attention was concentrated on an attempt to preserve certain traditional aesthetic values, whilst increasing the quantity of production; in the second instance, quality was transposed to the level of conceptual abstraction, leaving to production the task of mass-producing the model. It was precisely on this point – whether to conceive quality as a mere model or as a value which manifests itself and remains inherent in the object – that there arose the famous conflict between Walter Gropius and Theo van Doesburg: this was one of the factors which caused the Bauhaus to change its programme to a more constructive level.

Klee was in fact the man who gave the search for quality a completely new basis, and made it a search for an autonomous and absolute value, which, though derived from quantity, is irrelevant to quantity itself. Quality for him was the ultimate product of the individual's unrepeatable and unique experience; one achieves it by descending into the depths and by progressively clarifying the secret springs of one's actions, the myths and recollections lurking in the unconscious which strongly influence consciousness and action.

One must reach out for the point of prefiguration, the agony of death already suffered, without which there can be no completeness of existence or experience. The world we leave behind in this descent (which is also an ascent to superior spiritual forms) is the world of quantities, the dead world of forms already used, the world of logic, of positive science, of the masses, of politics, the three-dimensional world, in which everything assumes proportional and quantitative relations, the world of social classes characterised by degrees of power.

The world of qualities which opens out the more one descends into the unconscious depths, is not the world of forms already dead and established, but the world of nascent form, of formation, of *Gestaltung:* it is the world of unending organic relations which are born of real encounters and are measured by the effective strength which each image develops in its particular condition of space and time.

And since it is no longer admissible to draw any distinction between an object which is real and one which is imaginary, each image, being a moment of experience and of existence, is no longer a fixed and detached representation but preserves almost physical vitality. The transition from lower or passive forms, traditions or habits or remembrances which hamper man's freedom (Husserl calls them 'So-sein'), to superior forms, in which freedom has its highest expression, that is to say creation, is accomplished in the image.

The image will continue to live in the world as a representation of the moment of the individual's authentic existence, of his existence in the world. It will be the password among individuals, a vital link amongst the members of a community.

Klee never loses sight of other men, the community; he always tries to consider society as a single and multiform individual, with its own life story, its own 'Erlebnis'. Unlike Mondrian he does not conceive of an ideal society, which finally and peacefully settles down into a common acceptance of incontrovertible rational truths; he prefers to seek the reasons for common understanding in living experience, in the history and pre-history of humanity, of the 'people', instead of in utopian plans for the future.

In society, individuals appear to him to be bound together by old ties, by the spirit of clan and tribe, by a host of beliefs and terrors, of myths, magical rites, superstitions and taboos; these are the ties which unite them organically to nature and the cosmos.

By understanding his own motives, the individual does not isolate himself in his own monad; on the contrary, he re-discovers in the myths of the unconscious the common roots of man's being and his existence. Not only does he discover the relationship, but the unity of the one with the whole. In the world of quality, the mythical images shed all nocturnal shadows and become as clear as platonic ideas. The passive genesis (as Husserl would say), which collides with memory and matter, becomes active genesis. A new solidarity is established, independent of the objective rationality of certain accepted rules, but dependent on the discovery of a common origin and common ancestors; an origin which renews itself each moment, transmuting death into birth and giving to action a genuine creative meaning.

The vast cosmological vision evolved in Klee's theory does not supply the key to the symbolic or semantic interpretation of the images and signs which appear in his paintings: it rather explains how each one of those images, each of those signs, contains a truth which each man will read according to his own experience and will find a place for in the rhythm of his own existence, and yet retains the same value of truth for everyone. Klee anticipates Adorno's thesis of 'Alienation' and seeks the maximum 'alienation' or 'consumption' of artistic value in a maximum of quality and purity, in the elimination of all formal schemes, in the conquest of value which possesses both clarity of form as well as multiplicity and transmutability of meanings, the vitality, the capacity to associate itself with everyday life, which are characteristic of the image. The association with everyday life, the possibility of the work of art existing on a practical plane: this is another theme which links Klee's poetics with the Bauhaus didactics.

It was Marcel Breuer who perceived the real significance of Klee's teaching at the Bauhaus; to Breuer we owe the fact that Klee's world of images has become an essential component of what is known as industrial design. The tubular furniture invented by Breuer in 1925, thread-like, suspended in improbable yet faultless equilibrium, precise and mechanical gadgets animated by a silent and vaguely ambiguous vitality, as if from one moment to another they might re-enter and dissolve into the space which they do not occupy, is certainly born of Klee's nervous and intense graphics, and the currents of strength which he infuses into his lines. This furniture inhabits man's space like Klee's images inhabit the space of his slanting and oblique perspectives, and of the mobile depths of his tonal layers. This furniture too is born of an invisible dynamic of space, and whilst fulfilling its function with impeccable accuracy, traces a new dimension in which relations are clarified, and values are brought to the purity and transparency of quality.

The capacity of the image or of the object-image (and every image is already an object) in no way contradicts the rational faith of the Bauhaus. If rationality is not an abstract formula, but the character of existence and human action, then the final distillation of experience which is achieved in art, in the ultimate analysis, is the work of a rational being. Klee's didactic aim and, in a wider sense, the exemplary educative meaning of all his work is to show how, through all the meditation and active creation which constitutes artistic activity, experience performs ever widening circles until finally it touches the furthermost limits of the universe and returns to the point of maximum intensity, that is, the point of formation, of *Gestaltung*, where each sign signifies at the same time the individual and the world, the present and all time.

Klee continued teaching at the Bauhaus even after Gropius left, even when, owing to the increasing hostility of German conservative circles already mature for Nazism, life at the school became extremely difficult. Probably he felt that whilst the rationalist utopianism that had inspired the programme at the Bauhaus had already collapsed under the strain of events, his idea of a rationality without formulas, rooted in experience and aimed at redeeming the shapeless contents of the unconscious, could still survive, perhaps might be used as a fighting weapon or a defensive weapon against the outbreak of violent political irrationalism. He himself, it could not have been otherwise, was overwhelmed by events; and if in the presence of historical reality Mondrian's poetics appeared as the poetics of utopia, his own appeared as the poetics of a dream.

This appearance does not correspond to the truth: Klee's poetics are not the poetics of a dream, but the verification, point by point, of an experience which in its fulfilment does not fear to cross the threshold of dreams nor even of death, since death and dreams are still reality. When, after the second world war, the virtues and defects of the previous generation, the vanquished generation, were laid bare, and the rationalist utopia was condemned as one of the factors which had weakened resistance and paved the way for the defeat of European intelligence, it was realised that the germs of a possible 'overcoming' of rationalism were already present in Klee's work and teaching. An 'overcoming', however, which did not imply the denial of rationality nor the disavowal of utopia, but gave ultimate scope to the functions of the rational being, representing him as a continuous process, a continuous redemption from life of lost spaces and times.

Thus even after his death Klee's poetics and didactics continued to operate in times completely different from those in which the artist had so sadly lived and in which he had placed his hopes with so much faith. Perhaps we owe it to Klee's poetics and didactics, to the fundamental humanism of Erasmus and Dürer which pervades them, that at a distance of years Wols was able to temper the ferocity of his despair with a little human pity and Dubuffet to mingle a few notes of tenderness with his social cynicism.

Giulio Carlo Argan

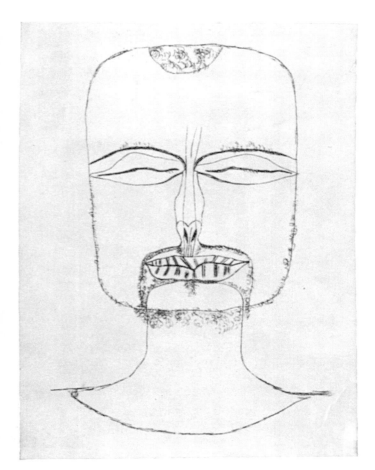

1

2

1919/113: *Meditation* (*self-portrait*)
Lithograph (1).
1932/z 6: *Scholar* (*self-portrait*)
Oil on canvas on wood (2).

'There are some who will not acknowledge the truth of my mirror. They should bear in mind that I am not here to reflect the surface (a photographic plate can do that), but must look within. I reflect the innermost heart. I write the words on the forehead and round the corners of the mouth. My human faces are truer than real ones. If I were to paint a really truthful self-portrait, you would see an odd shell. Inside it, as everyone should be made to understand, would be myself, like the kernel in a nut. Such a work might also be called an allegory of crust formation.'

20

This book is the first full collection of Paul Klee's ideas on form and artistic creation. These copious notes in which he has set forth his thoughts on the pictorial elements, on content and on style, give us new access to his creative work. The theoretical discussions and analyses are accompanied by drawings which illustrate and elucidate the context.

Text and illustrations form an organic whole, revealing the profound harmony between his ideas and his methods of work. Klee himself said expressly that his 'discourse' should not be considered by itself but as a complement to his pictures.

Movement stands at the centre of his thinking about form – from the simple forms to the complex combinations of pictorial elements. The optical foundations of his theory of form, as here presented, provide a remarkable guide to his pictorial world.

Klee's teaching activity – which was always closely bound up with his creative work – helped him become aware of his own way of working. The logic of pictorial thinking is determined by the picture and goes its own specific way. To be an 'abstract' painter meant for him to distil pure formal relations. The aim of his teaching was to promote an 'inner' movement, to encourage the creative disposition.

'We should simply follow our bent . . . Wishing to provide things one can be sure of, I limited myself to my inner being.' What a magnificent blueprint for freedom, given by an artist whose many-sided theory and advice might sometimes suggest a restriction of artistic freedom. Restriction? No, in these meditations he looked more deeply into familiar views of the world, and boldly anticipated a mode of pictorial thinking which then, more than thirty years ago, seemed to lack theoretical foundation.

Creative artists have often felt the need – whether to dispel misunderstandings or to clarify their own ideas by setting them on firmer ground – to formulate their insights in language. A few names may suffice – these are Klee's preceptors, whose writings he studied assiduously during his years of development: Leonardo, Philipp Otto Runge, Delacroix, Feuerbach, Seurat, and not least of all van Gogh (as late as 1918 Klee cited Feuerbach and in his theory of colours he referred to Delacroix).

Already at the age of twenty-three, Klee felt laws to be decisive, and that one should not begin with hypotheses but with examples, no matter how small. 'If I can recognise a clear structure, it gives me more than any high-flown theoretical graphs; the typical will come automatically from series of examples.' Seeing the architectural monuments of Rome in 1902, he was convinced that the relations of parts one to another and to the whole correspond to hidden numerical relations present in other works of art and nature; that these numbers and proportions do not signify something cold and rigid, but breathe life; and that their importance as an aid to study and artistic creation is clear. The *leitmotiv* of the journals from his Italian journey is 'the waking, not the dreaming human spirit'. His visit to Italy brought him the insight that noble style is buried in the perfection of technique. 'A single summit, Leonardo,' he notes, 'drives me back to the noble style, but without the conviction that I shall ever get along with it.'

In this period of the first clarities, he became aware of the fundamental importance of pictorial technique: 'Creative art never begins with a poetic mood or an idea, but with the building of one or more figures, the harmonisation of a few colours and tonalities . . . What uninspiring things, canvas, sizing, underpainting. And nothing much more alluring about line drawing or the treatment of forms – how long will it be until I *experience* these things? (for the present the art of life holds greater fascination).'

His first years of study in Munich and the teaching of Franz von Stuck had not brought him the experience of pictorial dimensions. 'If this teacher had taught me the nature of painting as I later learned to teach it, I should not have found myself in so desperate a situation. 'Apprenticeship is everywhere an enquiry into the smallest, most hidden things in good and evil,' writes Klee in summary. 'Then suddenly one begins to see one's way and the specific direction one must take.'

In his journals from 1900 to 1918, he speaks in brief aphorisms of the artist's specific method and of the dimensions of the picture. In the course of a slow, steady development the relation between thought and creative work grew firm. He resolved to fuse formal expression with his view of the world. In his own words, he built simultaneously on the law and on the work of art – on the foundation and the house.

At exhibitions in Munich from 1908 to 1912, Klee became acquainted with the work of van Gogh, Cézanne and Matisse. After his encounter with Cézanne, he noted: 'This is the teacher *par excellence*, far more so than van Gogh' (1909). He was profoundly impressed by Matisse: 'With the results of impressionism he turns far back to the childhood stages of art and achieves amazing effects.' Klee early recognised the value of children's drawings and in 1912 pointed out that there are still primordial beginnings to art, such as we find in ethnographical collections and at home in the nursery . . . 'The more awkward they are, the more instructive an example they offer us.' (Klee diligently collected the drawings of his son Felix and other children.) 'With the expressionists,' he wrote, 'construction has been elevated to a means of expression'; the skeleton of the pictorial organism, he said, was again receiving due emphasis. He called cubism a school of the philosophers of form. It is nothing new, he said, to think of form in terms of definite measurements that can be expressed in numbers; but now the idea has been extended to the formal elements: all proportions are reduced to forms such as triangle, square, circle. His ideas on cubism and expressionism are set out in an article which he contributed to *Die Alpen* (1912), on the exhibition of the 'Moderner Bund' in the Zürich Kunsthaus (he himself was represented in the exhibit with a few watercolours). In this article he raises the question: is it necessary to do away with the object for the sake of construction? What he had in mind was a union of constructive ideas and 'free breathing'. Art, he held, is not a science, but on the contrary, a world of diversity.

His search was intensified by *Der Blaue Reiter* and the impressions of his trip to Paris (1912) in the course of which he became acquainted with the works of Henri Rousseau and Picasso. Delaunay, whom he met in Paris through Marc and Macke, lent him the proofs of Guillaume Apollinaire's *Méditations esthétiques.* (In anticipation of Klee's visit, Jean Arp had sent Delaunay Klee's article on the 'Moderner Bund'.) Klee was particularly attracted by those of Delaunay's pictures 'which carry on a perfectly abstract formal existence without the benefit of motifs drawn from nature'. For *Der Sturm* (Berlin, January 1913) he translated Robert Delaunay's article 'La Lumière', a short summary of the basic ideas of Orphism. The cosmic phenomenon of multi-dimensional contacts was revealed to him. And indeed Klee held that the actual substance of painting was to be sought in glimpses of harmony between content and colour. His aim of unifying the light relations of several objects in a condensation of colours, was fulfilled in the watercolours done during his trip to Tunisia (1914).

The war found Klee in Germany, spiritually prepared: 'I have had this war inside me for a long time,' he notes in 1915, 'so it does not inwardly concern me. Only in memory – for one does think back sometimes – do I live in that shattered world. What a remarkable destiny, to be the scales between here and there, scales on the frontier between today and yesterday. Today is the flux between the two. The great crucible of forms contains ruins to which one is still somewhat attached. They provide the material for abstraction.'
In 1916, in the midst of a period of fruitful work – a few days after the death of his friend Franz Marc – he was called for military service. He took with him a drawing pencil and painting materials.
Later he wondered whether if he had gone on living quietly, his work would have advanced as rapidly as it did in 1916–17. 'For a passionate drive towards transfiguration seems to be bound up with a great change in one's mode of life.' Looking forward, he made plans for the future; his inner vision attained new depth.

Early in 1917 he was transferred to the finance office of a Bavarian aviation school in Gersthofen. Here he worked as a clerk and led a quiet life from which his artistic activity benefited. He did his painting in the desk drawer – this secured him against surprises. 'Another Sunday in camp. Finance officer suddenly called away on leave. At last I worked hard, painting and drawing, and in the end I didn't even know where I was. In amazement I looked down at my cruel war-like boots . . . Thanks to the absence of the finance officer, I am master of the offices every evening and can spread out comfortably.

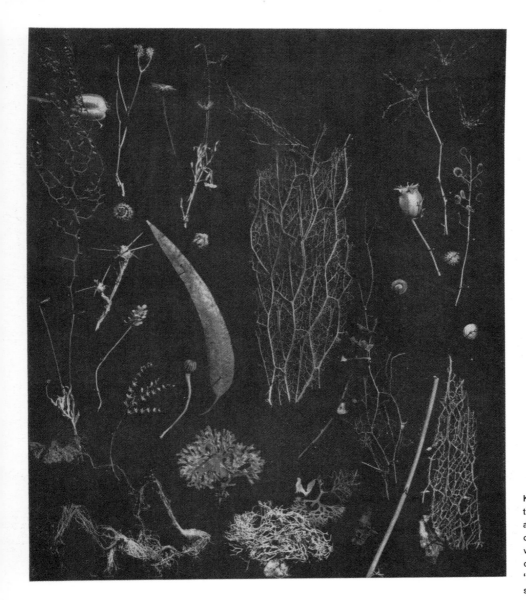

Klee possessed a collection of natural objects that he used in studying the nature, appearance, and structure of the most diverse organisms. He collected algae during visits to the Baltic, pressed them between plates of glass, and entitled the arrangement: 'Baltic forest'. He brought sea-urchins, sea-horses, corals, and molluscs from Sicily and other Mediterranean regions. He collected butterflies and stones – crystals and petrified plants, amber, calcite crystals on coloured sandstone, quartzes and mica. He was interested in stratification, transparency, and colour combinations. The reproduction shows a box from his collection, containing mosses, lichens, dried flowers, seed pods, and leaves from his studio.

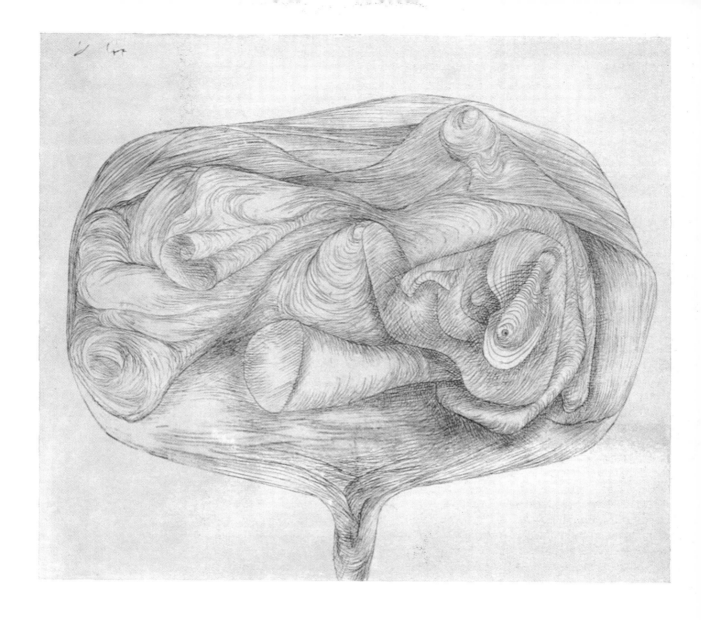

1934/s 11: *Calix abdominis* (*Belly bud*).
Pen and ink.
'Spatio-plastic interpenetration.'

Everything around me sinks away and my work comes into being as if by itself. Ripe graphic fruits fall to the ground. I am planning to enrich my spare time by painting. 'Perhaps I shall pitch camp again in the woods and set up a fine daylight studio and take from nature a little of her spice. How full the impression of timelessness at noon, the knife-edge balance of existence when even breath may hardly whisper. Here all action is purely mechanical, mere appearance. Nothing matters but a long, full glance within.'

Despite outward difficulties (during which his father's house in Berne was always open to him), the war years brought the knowledge that in art it is less important to see than to make visible. 'What an attractive destiny, to master painting at this time; as I think this over, the phonograph grinds on tirelessly. Around it heads are grinning and diabolical masks peer in through the window. New things are in the making, the diabolical is fused with the celestial; the dualism will not be treated as such, but in its complementary unity. The conviction is already present. A simultaneity of good and evil.'

Even before his discharge from the army, at Gersthofen, in December 1918, he completed the first draft of his *Schöpferische Konfession* ('Creative Credo'), provisionally entitled 'Thoughts on Graphic Art and Art in General'. It is a study of form and content from the standpoint of the new methods. With striking clarity he sketched the foundations of a dynamic conception of form. What he had noted spontaneously but in fragmentary form in the *Journals* – his search for a dynamic view of the world – was for the first time expressed clearly and systematically in the 'Creative Credo' (1920).

Here he set down the insights that were to provide the foundations of his work and of his thinking. He was preoccupied with the idea of a duality of concepts joining to form a unity: movement and counter-movement order themselves in meaningful harmony and become functions in pictorial space. Every energy demands its complement through which it achieves a state of self-contained rest, above the play of forces. To this state of rest corresponds the 'simultaneous conjunction of forms'; motion finds its fulfilment in the equilibrium of rest. He was encouraged to write this essay by Kandinsky's article 'Malerei als reine Kunst' ('Painting as a Pure Art') which had appeared toward the end of the war (September 1918) in Herwarth Walden's manifesto *Expressionismus – die Kunstwende* ('Expressionism – Art at the Turning Point'). In the same month he noted in his diary: 'An excellent, outstanding article. It is at once so simple and so full of the light of intelligence. The purest clarity, utterly convincing. And still people clamour for clarification. Why, a maxim such as "The work of art itself becomes the 'subject'" says everything there is to say.'

Freed from the pressure of the war, Klee was filled with an uncontrollable desire to work. In 1919 he was in a position to say in a letter to Oskar Schlemmer: 'Anyone who has seriously concerned himself with art in the last few significant years is bound to know perfectly well who I am.' The statement was justified. The enthusiastic approval of Theodor Däubler, expressed in a number of articles, had greatly encouraged him. Other voices followed. In 1920, Leopold Zahn and H. von Wedderkop published their monographs, in 1921 Wilhelm Hausenstein put out his *Kairuan, oder eine Geschichte vom Maler Klee und von der Kunst dieser Zeit*. These books met with an extraordinary response.

Paul Klee's studio in Schloss Suresnes,
Werneckstrasse, Munich,
where he worked from 1919 to early 1921.

Hausenstein's poetic and highly expressive work in particular attracted the young people to these new worlds of form.

Meanwhile Klee had moved his studio from the Münchner Ainmillerstrasse to the little Schloss Suresnes in the Werneckstrasse. He made music with his friends – Klee's predilection for Bach and Mozart is mentioned several times in our text. Kubin, Carossa, and Wolfskehl came to see him. He was in contact with Rilke who from Soglio in the Bregaglia sent him a print of the 'Ur-Geräusche' with a personal dedication.

Now that Klee was beginning to be more widely known, the question of a teaching position presented itself. Oskar Schlemmer, chairman of the Student Committee of the Stuttgart Academy, backed by a number of friends, members of the so-called Uecht Group, tried to put through his appointment as Hoelzel's successor.

A violent controversy resulted. The students threatened to strike and issued leaflets. One of these, written by Schlemmer and Willi Baumeister, bore the characteristic title: 'Criticism as the Art of Lying'. One of the arguments against which they had to defend Klee was that so dreamy and ethereal an artist could not be a teacher.

Klee's application was unanimously rejected by the faculty on the ground that 'Mr Klee's work as a whole reveals a playful character, in any case not the powerful impetus towards structure and composition that the new movement rightly demands'. The reply was signed by Prof. Heinrich Altherr, director of the Academy.

Paul Klee,
1921 at Possenhofen on the
Starnbergersee.

While his application was still pending, Klee wrote in a letter to Schlemmer (2 July 1919):
'. . . I should like to make it clear at the very start that my willingness springs from the
realisation that in the long run I shall not, with a clear conscience, be able to avoid taking
a profitable teaching position. The essential, it seems to me, is that you insist on the
necessity of appointing an artist whose art is alive and sufficiently in keeping with the
spirit of the times to serve as a guide to youth.'

In October 1920, without preliminaries, Klee received a telegram signed by the 'masters'
of the Bauhaus, Gropius, Feininger, Engelmann, Marcks, Muche, Itten, and Klemm.
'Dear Mr Klee. We unanimously invite you to join us in Weimar as a master of the Bauhaus.' Klee had been attracted to Stuttgart by the student body's support of his appointment. Here again this condition was fulfilled. Walter Gropius assured Klee of full freedom
within the framework of the Bauhaus plans, and wrote him: 'The students are overjoyed
at the idea that you might come to us. All of us are expecting you affectionately. We are
looking forward to a quick Yes. I have been waiting a whole year for the moment when I
could send out this call. Perhaps it would be best if you should come to see us at once, so
that we can talk everything over on the spot. It would be splendid if you should decide to
come. Then we shall be able to develop the strong atmosphere we need, more quickly
than we had thought.'
Two of the masters had just resigned. Gropius confided in Klee: 'It goes without saying
that the blow has produced a kind of fever, but we feel strong, and the government seems
to be with us against the philistines. Now it will be possible for our undertaking to become
something pure and I think great. We must beg you to come soon, because otherwise the
maggots will start digging again, and for a number of other reasons.'
Two days before Christmas 1920, Klee received government approval of his contract with
the Bauhaus. 'I am glad', Gropius wrote, 'that all the difficulties have been overcome.
Your studio will be painted in the next few days, so that we may be ready for you at the
beginning of the New Year.'

At the beginning of 1921 Klee described his first impressions of Weimar to Lily, his wife
(11 January): 'Last night I moved into the "Haus zur Sonne" on the Horn . . . a real
country house on the heights above the park. My way to the studio takes me through the
gardens past Goethe's summer-house, across the Ilm and up to the ruins . . .' (13 January): 'I am pretty well settled at the studio and was able to start painting today. The large
room is still quite empty; it measures 10 by 11 paces and has good walls for pictures. I
have not bought any furniture yet; I have been able to pick up the most necessary items at
the Bauhaus – as in the Army.' Three days later (16 January) he described the atmosphere
of the Bauhaus: 'Yesterday I devoted my time to the Bauhaus and was shown around for
the first time. In the morning one of the masters was working with the preliminary class.
When I went in at 10 o'clock, they were having a break. The master, in a wine-red suit, was
standing with a group of boys and girls who were showing him their work. He gave one
group a written exercise to do on the words of *Mariechen sat on a stone*. They were not to
write until they could clearly feel the spirit of the song. But these were more advanced
students, not the actual beginners.

29

Human movement.
Breakdown into different rhythms. Movement
characterised by varying intensity and
by change of position.

2

1

1930/C 3: *Jumper*.
Varnished watercolour on cotton and wood [1].

Schematic example of change of position [2]:
'Superimposed moments of movement.
Alternate forward and backward movement of
arms and legs in walking.'

'Then the break was over. We went into the next studio, an immense room. One wall
was lined with racks of experimental studies showing the properties of different materials. They looked like hybrids between toys and the art of savages. Along the other
three walls students were sitting on three-legged piano stools, with tables in front of
them. The stools were red, wooden with iron legs. Each student was holding an enormous
piece of charcoal; before him he had a drawing board and a sheaf of scrap paper. After a
few turns round the room the master went over to an easel holding a drawing board and
scrap paper. He seized a piece of charcoal, his body contracted as though charging itself
with energy, and then suddenly he made two strokes in swift succession.
'Two strong lines, vertical and parallel, appeared on the scrap paper. The students were
asked to imitate them. The master looked over their work, had a few of the students do it
over again, checked their posture. Then he ordered them to do it in rhythm and then he
had them all practise the same exercise standing. The idea seems to be a kind of body

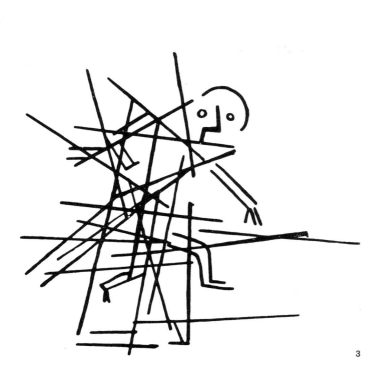

3

4

Schematic detail from 1929/x 1: *Landscape
with fisherman*. Drawing on coloured paper
(fully reproduced in Grohmann, p.397) [3].
Spatio-temporal summation and
intensification of moments of movement.
'The function of a movement can be directed
backward in time, towards the present, or forward
in time. The cardinal question:
"How shall I give form to the movement from here
to there?" embodies a time factor.'

1919/14: *Oh-oh, you strong man!*
Drawing IV for 'Corinth, *Potsdamer Platz*' [4].
'Visible mobility is created by successive
increase or decrease in the quantity or quality
of the energies employed (movement in all
directions – "complicated-offensive").'

massage to train the machine to function with feeling. In very much the same way he drew
new elementary forms (triangles, circles, spirals) and the students imitated them, with
considerable discussion on the why of it and the modes of expression. Then he said
something about the wind and told a few of them to stand up and express the feeling of
being in a storm. Then he gave them their assignment: to draw the storm. He gave them
about ten minutes, then looked over the results and criticised them.
'After the criticism they went on working; one sheet of paper after another was torn off
and dropped to the floor. Some of the students worked with great gusto and covered
several sheets at once. When they were all tired, he let the preliminary students take the
assignment home with them for more practice.
'At five in the afternoon a class in "analysis" was held in a large room resembling an
amphitheatre. It is a kind of lecture hall, except that the audience sits not on benches but
on the steps. In the pit stands a blackboard with a sheaf of scrap paper. Way up on top a
projector. Again the master moved about, getting things ready and loading the projector.
Then he showed slides of formal elements which were intended to lead up to Matisse's

The Dance, which followed. After showing the picture, he had the students draw diagrams of the composition, once he even made them do it in the dark. Then he had them correct their diagrams after the model and do some schematic drawings of single figures. He climbed up and down the steps constantly, watching and criticising. I sat in the corner way up top, smoking my pipe. I'll be back home with you all in another week. Be sure not to put the chain on the door Saturday night.'

That spring, Klee began to work at the Bauhaus. (14 April): 'Tomorrow I am taking over the bookbindery and also posting up a course in practical composition.' Speaking of this class in bookbinding (with only four students) he wrote hopefully: 'Perhaps in time I can put a little life into it. Up to now the work has been good and solid, but I have seen no trace of a new spirit.' Klee began his lectures in May of the same year. His first lecture series attracted forty-five applicants, of whom thirty were accepted.
He reported to Lily at length on his first class (13 May): 'Today I held my first class, and something extraordinary happened. For two hours I spoke freely with the students. First I discussed a few paintings and watercolours by W. and others. Then I passed round ten of my own watercolours and discussed them at length from the standpoint of their formal elements and composition. The only trouble is that I was thoughtless enough to deal with the material so minutely that I shall have to paint some new examples for next Friday. Or perhaps the students will have submitted some more work by then. Just as I was illustrating the relativity of the concepts "light" and "dark" by the excellent example of baths of different temperatures, there was a knock at the door and in came a policeman who gave one of the students a good scolding in Saxon for not reporting to the police. He was greeted with a good deal of merriment as you can imagine, and you can also imagine that as shepherd of a flock so undaunted by the dignity of the law, I found myself caught between two fires.' Klee went on to write that in the same summer semester he would analyse a pair of paintings for their polyphonic style, using four or five examples. 'Perhaps in spite of the Bauhaus Exhibition the students will contribute something; otherwise the course will just have to be a bit shorter this time.'
Klee quickly adapted himself to the ways of the Bauhaus. His schedule (seven or eight hours a week) comprised: his two-hour lectures on theory, the afternoon form workshop – the problems assigned are included in our text – and a class in creative painting, during which he often spoke about his own pictures. In addition, he first taught glass painting and later on weaving.
While the 'Contributions to a theory of pictorial form' were in the making, he wrote to Lily: 'Here in the studio I am working on half a dozen paintings, drawing, and thinking about my course, all at once, for everything must go together or it wouldn't work at all. It is this natural way of doing things that gives me strength. The life and bustle of Weimar do not exist for me. I work and never speak to a soul.'
In 1924 twelve students attended Klee's theoretical course; in Dessau he had over thirty students, although not all of them went to his painting class. In connection with Klee's lectures – a systematic discussion of his experience of painting and life – one student declared: 'His teaching was never instruction in the conventional sense. The full expanse of his thought and experience was accessible only to those who participated in the

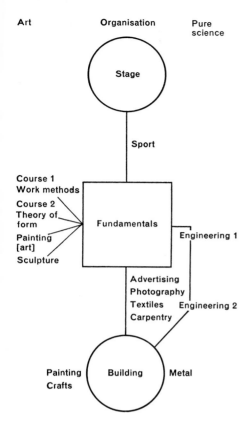

Art Organisation Pure science

Stage

Sport

Course 1
Work methods
Course 2
Theory of form
Painting [art]
Sculpture

Fundamentals

Engineering 1

Advertising
Photography
Textiles
Carpentry

Engineering 2

Painting
Crafts

Building

Metal

Diagram of the organisation of the Bauhaus drawn up by Klee at Dessau in 1928.
The Bauhaus aimed to re-unite all the disciplines in a new form of builders' guild.
The *leitmotiv*: Art cannot be taught but craftsmanship can.

fullest sense.' In his painting class the students had to explain what they were trying to do. Klee would pick up a slate and draw the desired effect.

The aim of his teaching was to reveal the life-giving element in artistic creation, to illustrate it by dynamic arrangement, and to formulate the laws of art as simple rules. 'Education', said Klee, 'is a difficult chapter. The most difficult. The education of the artist above all. Even if one supposes it to be continuous, even if one supposes that there might be a certain number of real educators, many remain within the realm of the visible, because it is enough for them. Few get to the bottom and begin to create. Most stick rigidly to theories because they are afraid of life, because they dread uncertainty.'

In his first years at the Bauhaus, Klee prepared his two-hour lectures in every detail. In November 1921, he wrote to Lily: 'The lecture went quite smoothly yesterday, I was prepared to the last word; this way I don't have to be afraid of saying something that is in any way irresponsible. From the principles of perspective I went on to the sense of balance in man. In the next practical exercises we shall be working with balance, making static constructions with stone blocks, and then we shall work from these models.'

From his notes – he called them 'My contribution to fundamental principles and the theory of form' – we can reconstruct his teaching activity over a period of some two years, with the help of dates and schedules. The backbone of his courses was provided by the lecture notes contained in 'Contributions to a theory of pictorial form', which are published here in their entirety. They cover three semesters, from winter 1921 to winter 1922. Klee himself published a short excerpt from this text in Dessau in 1925; entitled *Pädagogisches Skizzenbuch* ('Pedagogical Sketchbook') (Vol.2 of the Bauhausbücher), it achieved immediate fame. The little volume bore the sub-title: *The Original Foundation of Part of the Theoretical Programme of the Bauhaus at Weimar*. In the present work this partial edition is followed by the complete text of the lectures on theory.

The body of his doctrine of form came into being at Weimar and at Dessau over a period of barely five years (1920–5); it was later amplified to meet new problems and adapted to his teaching requirements; new sections were added. Klee left more than 2500 folio pages of pedagogic notebooks (consisting of memoranda, teaching projects, constructive drawings, and sketches for his pictures) from which it has been possible to collate additional courses of instruction. These are chiefly concerned with amplifications of the theory of perspective, a subjective theory of space, shifting viewpoint, composition, rhythms and rhythmic structures, and static-dynamic synthesis. This material provides us with many new axioms. In editing these complementary sections I have kept to the outlines drawn up by Klee himself. These new methods made it possible to undertake analyses which show the functional process of motion to be the dominant centre of the picture's content.

For the Bauhaus Report that appeared in 1923, Klee wrote his basic *Wege des Naturstudiums* ('Ways of Nature Study'). This publication, the Jena lecture of 1924 and the essay *Exakte Versuche im Bereich der Kunst* ('Exact experiments in the realm of art') 1928 are included in our chapter 'Towards a theory of form-production'. The Jena lecture constitutes a kind of programme for his entire thinking on the subject, which is illustrated here in a wealth of concrete examples.

Paul Klee in 1924
in his studio in the Bauhaus at Weimar.

This juxtaposition of formal examples developing into finished pictures and of theoretical texts is systematically carried out here for the first time. It is in keeping with Klee's plans, many of which were found in his papers after his death. In 1925 he busied himself with the preparation of a *Pictorial Mechanics, or Theory of Style*, which had been several times announced by the Bauhaus.

We have tried to bring out Klee's concern for multi-dimensional simultaneity with the help of typography – that is, by our arrangement of his form studies and creative work. Our intention has been to give the dynamic forms their full expressive value through adequate use of empty space; and thus to guide the reader directly to the pictorial action. In the manuscripts, carefully executed gouaches and pen and ink drawings alternate with quickly tossed-off pencil sketches. Klee's lecture notes include constructive drawings, often geometric exercises serving to elucidate pictorial laws (he drew his illustrations on the blackboard).

For purposes of reproduction it has been necessary to copy certain of the schematic pencil sketches. These copies are easily distinguished from Klee's original sketches and constructive drawings with their delicate calligraphic line.

From year to year Klee modified the subject matter of his lectures. In connection with his pictures he wrote: 'Whenever, during creation, a type outgrows its genesis and I arrive at the goal, intensity disappears and I have to look for something new. In production it is the way that is important; development counts for more than does completion.'

And just so for his thinking.

In working out new lines of thought, one requirement was crucial for him: not to fixate one point but to leave his mind's eye absolutely free. This accounts for the corrections and additions to his manuscripts.

Marginal notations and subsequent deletions are indicated in our notes. The peculiarities of language due to his oral delivery and Swiss dialect have not been changed.

In the course of his formative years, Klee noted: 'Busy as a bee collecting forms and perspectives from nature'. At the Bauhaus his nature studies underwent a change: the emphasis was now on the observation of functional processes and motion. 'First give space and form to the smaller living functions, and only then build houses round them, as in the apple, the snailshell and the human house.'

He tried to find out how form arises in nature. The honeycomb or the water cycle served him as a theme for variations. Simple crafts such as plaiting, weaving, sowing, masonry showed him the 'original, primordial roads to form', and answered his question of how form comes into being.

While still in Weimar he wrote to Lily (1924): 'I am looking forward to the herbarium and am surprised that these treasures of form didn't reach me long ago'. He made use of all sorts of structures, such as seed pods and flowers, to investigate the relations between kernel, inner space, and actual shell. In longitudinal sections and cross sections, in the interpenetration of base and elevation, he explored their structure, combined many aspects of the material world, and blended them into new form. From fragmentary insights into the world of form, intricate new organisms developed. Klee wrote: 'When several aspects interpenetrate, the structures must be capable of life. The harmony between

Nolde, die uralte Seele, den Erdhaften als Menschen aus Fleisch und Blut sich vorzustellen fällt weniger schwer, als bei den paar Anderen. Und wenn man ihn sieht, ist man mehr als nicht enttäuscht: ein wahrhaftiger Nolde, wie er sein kann, sein muss, bleiben soll.

Erdferne oder Erdflüchtige (Abstrakte) vergessen manchmal dass Nolde ist. Nicht so ich, selbst auf meinen weitesten Flügen nicht, von denen ich immer wieder zur Erde zurück zu finden pflege, mich auszurasten in wiedergewordener Schwere.

Nolde ist mehr als nur erdhaft, er ist auch Dämon dieser Region. Selber anderswo domiziliert, fühlt man stets den Vetter dort der Tiefe, den Wahlverwandten. Man legt +

Man legt sich nicht schlafen bei Daemonen, dazu ist die Spannung ihrer Nähe zu gross. Der Ferne schätzt die Spannung nach der Nähe. Er fühlt sich gegenseitig mild durchleuchtet Die verkehrte Richtung ist sein besonderes Genuss, seine Erholung im Wachsein.

Ihm, Nolde, geht es wohl ähnlich bei uns. Wir rasten gelegentlich durch die Lust zu ihm. Manches Mitgebrachte, was Mächte auf unsern Ausflügen als unser Werk registrierten, machte, vor ihm ausgebreitet, Spass.

"War dabei auch Menschenhand im Spiel? mochte er sich zuweilen wohl fragen. Hand aus Fleisch und Blut? oder nur Nerv?"

Denn bei ihm schafft Menschenhand, eine Hand nicht ohne Schwere in einer Schrift nicht ohne Flecken. Die geheimnisvollblütige Hand der unteren Region.

Jede Region formt und färbt ihre Geheimnisse, und sehr unterscheiden sich die Hände, die sie zeitigen, je nach der Sphaere ihrer gemeisterten Meister. Das Herz der Schöpfung aber speist, für Alles pulsend, die Regionen.

Paul Klee.

(Januar 1927)

Facsimile of Klee's handwriting
(on the occasion of Emil Nolde's sixtieth
birthday, January 1927).

inside and outside is not a formal problem, but a question of psychic unity of spiritual content.' In Klee's teaching the transformation of forms is revealed part by part, step by step. Interpretation and creative activity remain closely linked.

In considering a work of art, he asked whether it reflected the essence of the object or only its outward, optical manifestation. A reference to human movement or plant growth may suffice. The complex development from seed to flower raises the question of how growth as a texture of dynamic occurrences can be represented 'in its essence'. Dynamic processes assume increasing importance in his thinking about form. Human movement passes from walking (taken as a norm) to jumping, hopping or sliding, ending in the violent inner agitation of overall spiritual activity.

In the type of mobility (statics and dynamics) Klee saw the stylistic criterion by which to differentiate forms (he investigated the general laws of motion on earth, in the water, in the air). These insights considerably changed his feeling for form and space. Balance and statics gave way to a dynamic ordering of the pictorial elements. Colour in its most violent tensions and subtlest dynamic relations became the vehicle of the dynamic unfolding of space. In his late work extremes of action are held together by brilliant fundamental chords. 'Contrasts exist only in relation to the formal part; unity is restored by means of the colour values.' In his creative work statics and dynamics are consciously emphasised as the core of his artistic method.

In the course of his ten years at the Bauhaus, Klee applied well-nigh endless knowledge to his investigation of the laws of painting. For him everything that happens in a picture must have its logical justification. He termed his exercises in planimetry and stereometry 'constructive ways to composition'. He applied his understanding of growth and motion, won during nature study, to the realm of geometry. He investigated basic forms from the same point of view as plants and living creatures: according to their faculty of motion, their behaviour, and their essence. As a result of kinetic changes, simple forms assume a variety of personalities – for example: 'the death of the triangle'. In his thinking geometrical abstraction is humanised.

An active exchange goes on between the two fundamental modes of experience, the constructive-geometrical and the metaphysical. 'The possibilities become numberless and infinitely variable.'

The Bauhaus faced increasing opposition in Weimar. In November 1924, Klee wrote to Lily: 'We are engaged in feverish activity to cope with the great crisis, expected in about a week . . . Possibly the "gallows birds" will climb down the ladder to catch their breath; and possibly they will be sent back up again. No decision. The affair seems to keep dragging on.' At length plans were made to move the Bauhaus to Dessau in 1925. Meanwhile Klee had his first exhibition in New York (1924) and participated in a surrealist group show in Paris (1925). Aragon, Crevel, and Eluard translated his pictures into surrealist poems and spread his name far beyond the sphere of influence of the Bauhaus. In the course of his years at Weimar and Dessau, Klee travelled a good deal and gained impressions that exerted a lasting influence on his work and his sense of form. Noteworthy are his experience of the Ravenna mosaics (1926), of the prehistoric hieroglyphic inscriptions of Carnac (Brittany, 1928), and his famous trip to Egypt in the winter of 1928/1929.

1923/79: *Assyrian game*. Oil on cardboard on wood.

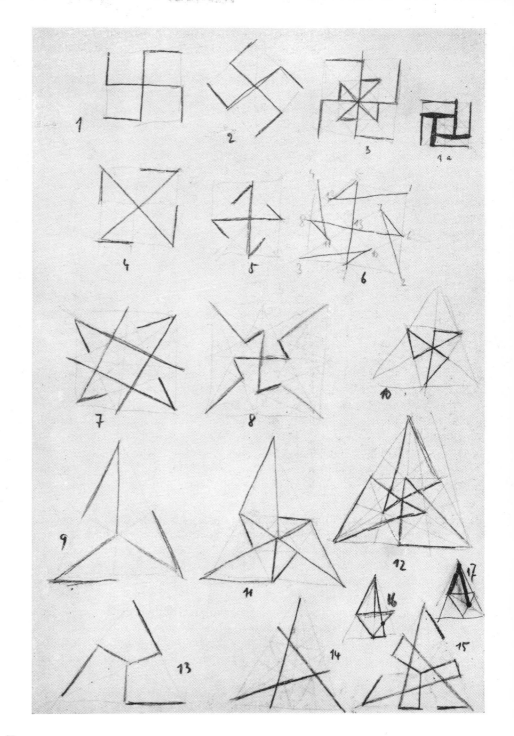

'Dynamics based on the square and the triangle, in part related to the circle.'
(Klee's note:
[1] 'Static interpretation of the swastika.'
[2] 'Best position of the swastika from the dynamic point of view.')

He visited Segesta and Agrigento in Sicily several times. On his return to Dessau (1929) he wrote: 'Nothing is happening to me here and I don't want it to; I bear within me the mountains and the sun of Sicily. These are all I can think of – in terms of abstract landscape – and now something is beginning to take shape. For the last two days I have been painting again. Everything else is savourless. The German November is the preparation for the great northern festival, full of promise, but itself quite without direction.

In Dessau, Klee often admitted that it was difficult for him to go on combining creative work with his Bauhaus teaching. In 1929, he entered into negotiations with the Düsseldorf Academy, which bore fruit the following year. W. Kaesbach wrote to Klee that he hoped with Klee's help to save a professorship for the Academy. 'In the forthcoming reorganisation it will be borne in mind that three of my teachers of painting have had no students for years . . . The outcome rests with you. The freer, the happier you feel, the better it will be, in my opinion, for the institution at which you teach.'

The call to take over the class in free painting at Düsseldorf reached Klee in the summer of 1930, just as he was leaving for the Engadine.

On the occasion of Klee's departure from Dessau, Kandinsky wrote in the *Bauhaus* magazine (1931): 'My colleagues have asked me to put out this issue; I wish it were for the opposite reason, not departure but return . . . His words and acts, his own example, have done much to develop positive aspects of the students' character. We can all of us learn from the example of Klee's tireless devotion to his work. And indeed we *have* learned.' At the Düsseldorf Academy, Klee devoted himself chiefly to correcting the work of his painting class. His new works and the efforts of his students were discussed and criticised at informal gatherings in his studio. From this time on, written comments on the creative process became infrequent. His spoken comments based in part on analyses of his own pictures, were taken down in shorthand by Petra Petitpierre (Klee himself made considerable use of these theoretical notes in the last years of his life, in Berne). We have worked up parts of these notes that clarify Klee's ideas and used them to round out two sections of the theoretical introduction. Klee's statements on his own works – dealing with content and creative method – are inserted in small print and in quotation marks.

Klee was dismissed in April 1933. The explanation given him was that it was necessary to restore the indigenous character of the art schools. In December he gave up his studio; since his dismissal he had not set foot in the Academy. It was an eventful year: his house was searched by the police; his works were exhibited as examples of 'degenerate' art; he visited Porquerolles, met Picasso in Paris; and before Christmas he returned to Switzerland.

He went to Berne, where his father, Hans Wilhelm Klee, and his sister were living in the family house in the Obstbergweg. 'Berne was my true home and attracted me as such,' Klee wrote: 'It was clear that I would return to it'. He lived on the Kistlerweg, in a quiet suburban quarter, surrounded by gardens. Here began the magnificent development of his Berne period.

The events – illness and the work that brought deliverance – are reflected in letters from the Bauhaus painters. 'Dear friend,' wrote Kandinsky in 1936, 'it seems to be your turn and

Style group A
above: static
below: dominant gravity

Statics and Dynamics [1]:
In the realm of the static 'steady' means attached to the vertical. In the realm of the dynamic it refers to the controlled harmony of free movement. The circle is the epitome of the dynamic, the straight line the epitome of the static.

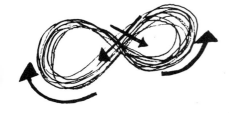

1
Style group B
above: dynamic
below: dominant energy

2

3

1930/R 2: *Planes measured by their heights*.
Pastel with paste. Colour on paper [2].
1929/y 2: *Propagation of light I*. Watercolour [3].

The opposition between static and dynamic.
'The static is checked or fettered mobility
the dynamic is accentuated movement
or free spiritual mobility.'
Purely static emphasis: *Planes measured by their heights*.
Dynamic emphasis and polyphonal transparency:
Propagation of light I.

I am glad of the opportunity to wish you the very best of everything from the bottom of my heart. And above all a speedy return to perfect health. Otherwise there is little you need wish for. You have always got ahead wonderfully with your work; the fame of your art is spreading irresistibly from country to country and across the big oceans. I only hope that you will soon, very soon, recover your full physical powers . . . We often think of the days when we were neighbours, how we watered the flowers together and battled each other at *boccie*, and complained together about the Bauhaus meetings. How far away it all seems.'
As a young man Klee had written: 'Death . . . puts right whatever did not fulfil itself in life. I consider the yearning for death not as a renunciation but as a struggle for perfection.' These words are borne out by the vast scope and great stature of his last works.

Those who, looking through this book, try to track down the source of its visual energy, will recognise more and more fully the miraculously complicated interaction of Klee's basic precepts: the eternal dialectic between static and dynamic, the 'multi-dimensional simultaneity' first formulated by the cubists; the relation between active and passive elements; the connection between quantity and quality; the parallelism between accented and unaccented functions . . . all of them meet to form fascinating patterns of thought. With their help he put together his last views on painting, his final grasp of its autonomy. Klee himself once said: 'I would like to draw upon those parts of the creative process which are carried on, largely in the subconscious, while the work is taking form'. Largely in the subconscious? Like Oedipus, he set out to solve the riddles of the world.

With sovereign restraint he said of his theory: 'It is a device for achieving clarity'. The main thing, he said, was not to inculcate constructive or schematic foundations (these must spring from the student's own equipment, his insight), but to keep the creative process alive. A living art must break away from theory and achieve new order in organic fulfilment.

'Don't learn this by heart. Everyone is bound to feel at home in some part of this chart,' said Klee not without irony in 1922, as he expounded one of his philosophic-artistic tables to his students. He warned them of the impoverishment that can come from rules, and explicitly condemned 'formalism – the new academy'. The sovereign aim of his teaching was to disclose the right extent of freedom. He summed up his vision in the words: 'Man is not finished. One must be ready to develop, open to change; and in one's life an exalted child, a child of creation, of the Creator.'

Paul Klee's signature.

In the outside columns Paul Klee's
texts and lectures are printed in
large type. The inside columns contain,
in smaller type, written and spoken
remarks of Klee in quotation marks,
and notes by the editor.

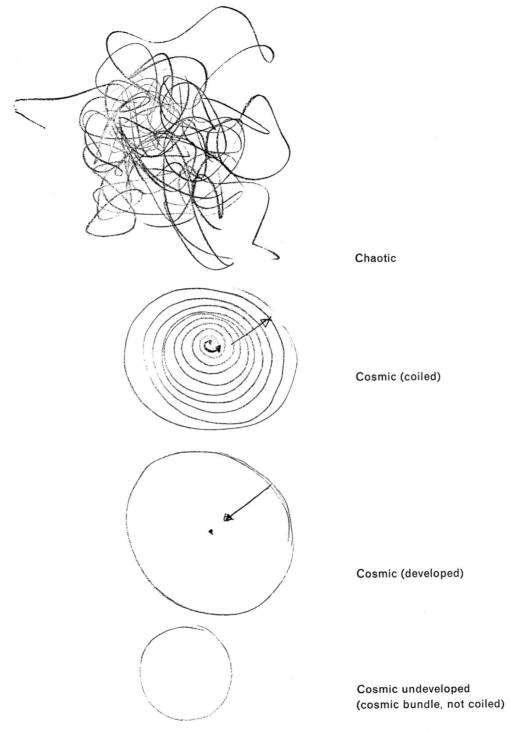

Chaotic

Cosmic (coiled)

Cosmic (developed)

Cosmic undeveloped
(cosmic bundle, not coiled)

2

Cosmos-Chaos

Cosmos	Chaos
Order	Disorder

Chaos as an antithesis is not complete and utter chaos, but a locally determined concept relating to the concept of the cosmos. Utter chaos can never be put on a scale, but will remain forever unweighable and unmeasurable. It can be Nothing or a dormant Something, death or birth, according to the dominance of will or lack of will, of willing or not-willing.

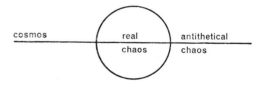

The pictorial symbol for this 'non-concept' is the point that is really not a point, the mathematical point. The nowhere-existent something or the somewhere-existent nothing is a non-conceptual concept of freedom from opposition. If we express it in terms of the perceptible (as though drawing up a balance sheet of chaos), we arrive at the concept grey, at the fateful point between coming-into-being and passing-away: the grey point. The point is grey because it is neither white nor black or because it is white and black at the same time.

It is grey because it is neither up nor down or because it is both up and down. It is grey because it is neither hot nor cold; it is grey because it is a non-dimensional point, a point between the dimensions.

The cosmogenetic moment is at hand. The establishment of a point in chaos,[1] which, concentrated in principle, can only be grey, lends this point a concentric character of the primordial [1]. The order thus created radiates from it in all directions [2].

When central importance is given to a point: this is the cosmogenetic moment. To this occurrence corresponds the idea of every sort of beginning (e.g. procreation) or better still, the concept of the egg.

[1]Klee notes elsewhere:
'A point in chaos: Once established the grey point leaps into the realm of order'.

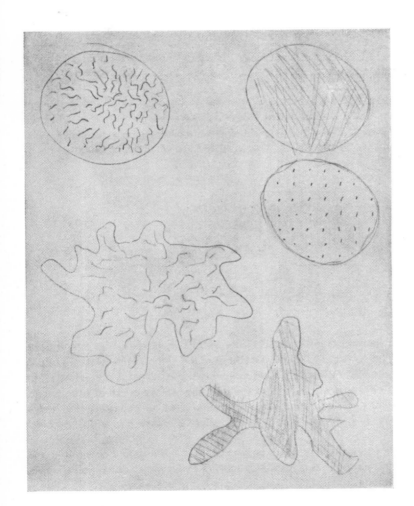

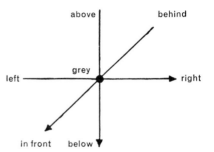

The idea of all beginning, procreation: the primordial cell, set in motion by fertilisation (discharge of tension with a complementary) and growing. The mobility can have a 'formal' accent: this means rest in the large form, mobility in the small. Or the accent may be on 'value': then we have a mobile greater form with a static small form inside (in the sense of filling). Or the two as a synthesis (of the part and of the whole); then both the great and the small forms are mobile.

4

In bold outlines the whole, and, in between, the earthly man

1940/From Klee's estate (Untitled).
Paint mixed with paste, on paper.

[1]Added: '...but not to be overlooked on pain of suffering grave injury'.
The pictorial reversal of man's natural structure produces, as a side effect, the risk of 'grave injury'.
Cf. 1939/LM 18: *Accident*, p.40.

Everything (the world) is of a dynamic nature; static problems make their appearance only at certain parts of the universe, in 'edifices', on the crust of the various cosmic bodies. Our faltering existence on the outer crust of the earth should not prevent us from recognising this. For we know that, strictly speaking, everything has potential energy directed towards the centre of the earth. If we reduce our perspective to microscopic dimensions, we come once more to the realm of the dynamic, to the egg and to the cell. Accordingly, there is a macroscopic dynamic and a microscopic dynamic. Between them stands the static exception:[1] our human existence and its forms. In other words 'we' – an episode within the whole, an episode subject to strict and compelling necessity. We are constrained by the plumbline, an imperative that crumbles in the directions of egg and death. The static imperative of our earthly being.

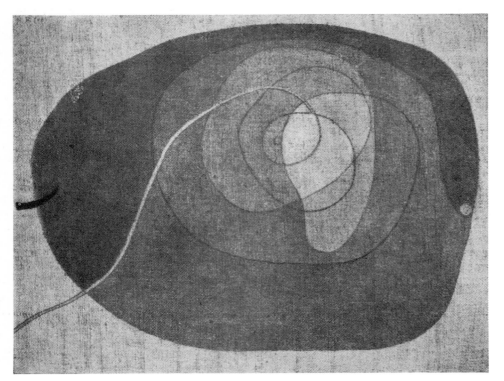

Outer space

Body, fixed limit **(shell)**

Inner space

Primordial
point

Outer space

'Ab ovo' – spatio-corporeal:
Parts: 1. The primordial cell set in
motion by fertilisation (discharge of
tension with a complementary) and
growing.
2. Inner space (in the egg, broken into
yolk and white).
3. Limit of the thing-concept (shell),
body.
4. The surrounding space (outer space).
The whole: spatio-corporeo-spatial.[1]

[1]That is: a spatial body in space.
Cf. 1917/130: *ab ovo*, Grohmann p.145
and 1932/Ae 2: *Woman's mask*. Oil.
Illustration No.16 in Courthion:
Klee, Hazan, Paris 1953.

6

1925/c 9: *Profile of head.*
Relief-like painting.
Oil on plaster.

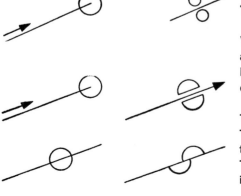

The protogenesis of form

When a linear form is combined with a plane form the linear part takes on a decidedly active character and the plane a passive character in contrast.
If this is carried back to the first genesis of form it leads to the phenomenon of cell division.

Taken productively the same process signifies growth, and taken destructively, death. Taken abstractly, i.e. detached from life, pictorial events should be evaluated according to their productive capacity.
The active part, the line, can accomplish two things by its impetus: it may divide the form into two parts, or it may go still further and give rise to a displacement.

7

1 Natural order: Concept of illumination in nature (light form).
The natural unorganised crescendo or diminuendo. The innumerably subtle tones between white and black. The natural confluence of light and dark tonalities, a vibrato between light and dark. Opposites merge with one another (light form). Only in movement is richness of shade possible. To attain greater precision you must become the poorer.

2 Artificial order: Analytical sub-division to make light and dark measurable.
Sub-division of light-dark movement on a scale of a regulated tonal mixture.
The middle steps of the scale need latitude if they are to become perceptible and measurable. The ends stay apart of their own accord. 'The peaceful character of compromise.'
*Cf.*1922/79: *Separation in the evening*, p.11.

Chaos, Disorder　　　　　　　**Cosmos, Order**　Natural order-Artificial order

Chaos (Disorder)　　Grey in Chaos:　　　　Cosmos (Order)　　Grey in Cosmos:

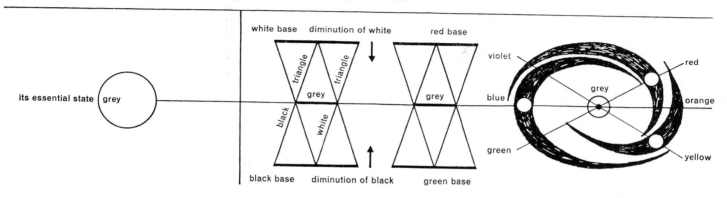

I begin logically with chaos, that is the most natural. And I am at ease, because at the start I may myself be chaos.

Chaos is an unordered state of things, a confusion. 'Cosmogenetically' speaking, it is a mythical primordial state of the world, from which the ordered cosmos develops, step by step or suddenly, on its own or at the hand of a creator.

[1]From red to green in the second example.

Natural movement from white to black[1] is not unregulated, but unarticulated. It is regulated by comparison with chaos, in which light and darkness are still undivided. It has the natural order of an unbroken flow from one pole to the other.
This movement or distribution of tension is infinitely subtle. The minute particles can scarcely be distinguished. A definite orientation is not possible. Position cannot be sharply fixed, because the flux, the subtle flow, takes certainty, gently but surely, away with it.

9

Natural order in the cosmos, i.e. the natural balance of nature. The partial field from light to dark moves up and down between the poles of white and black. In nature it is assuredly white that can lay claim to the most primordial activity. White given in nature is light itself. In the beginning resistance is dead and the whole is without movement or life. We must bring black and summon it to battle against the formless strength of light. Thus we use offensive and defensive energies together or in turn. A living balance between the two poles – this is the task we cannot avoid. The penetration of nature based on black and white [1]. The concept of balanced opposites.

In the 'natural order' white and black are opposite poles. One may also say that the tip of the black base (darkening) extends into the white base (source of light) and conversely. Illumination (maximum brilliance) and darkening are subject to continuous interchange in nature; the rhythm of day and night. Their order and interpenetration are of a natural kind.

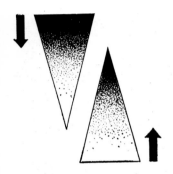

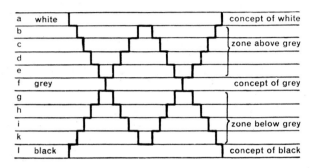

a	white	concept of white
b		
c		zone above grey
d		
e		
f	grey	concept of grey
g		
h		
i		zone below grey
k		
l	black	concept of black

1   **2**

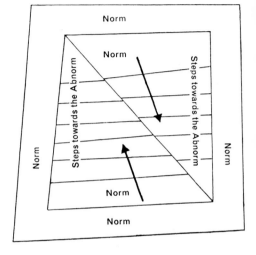

Movement and countermovement
as a process of compensation between opposites

Artificial order. Impoverished, but clearer and more comprehensible. Articulation of the movement from light to dark in measurable passages from pole to pole.
What first interests us in the scale of tone values is the abundance of tonalities between the two poles. Rising from the bottom towards the source of light, we feel an increase of unparalleled intensity and breadth between the poles. Below, dark subterranean rumbling, in between, the half shade of under water, and above, the hiss of brightest brightness.
On the scale the middle steps may be distinguished by weight or critical evaluation. The practical task is this: to fix them in the scale by mixing them or glazing them [2].

In the 'artificial order' the different degrees of white and black (from darkness to extreme brilliance and elevation or conversely) are analysed for their augment or diminution in black and white. The intervals are equal in measure but different in weight: brilliant = lighter, dark = heavier. The scale divides the light-dark tonalities artificially, to make them susceptible to measurement. Artificial measurement attaches exact numerical values to the steps and so gives us a synthetic method of representing the scale of tone values.

10

1922/79: *Separation in the evening.* Watercolour.

Movement and countermovement (rise and fall) bring a clash of opposites. The gradations of tone value lead to confluence 'in a silvery vibrato between black and white. Then broad repose may be a deviation from the norm.' In *Separation in the evening,* 1922 the accent is on the upper of the dark base norms. The darkness moving down is dominant.

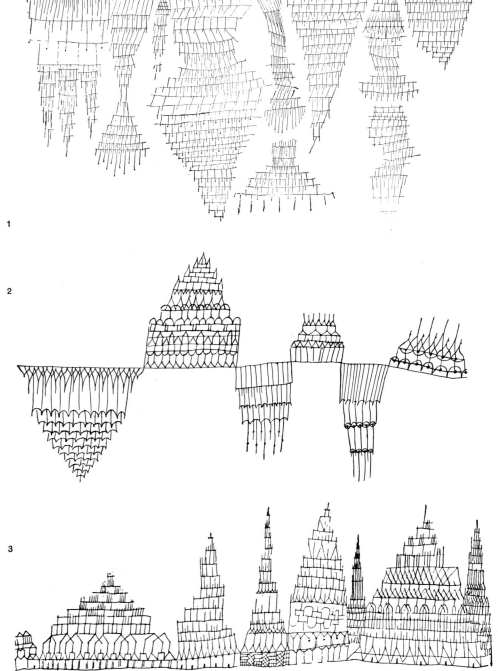

Natural and artificial measurement

1

2

3

Examples of the artificial
measurement of increase or decrease:

[1] Base on top: *Rain*, pen-and-ink, 1927/o 9.
[2] Base in the middle: *Pagodas by the water*,
pen-and-ink, 1927/m 9.
Rhythmic change: increase and decrease on
the same base.
[3] Base underneath: Excerpt from pen-and-ink
drawing: *City of Cathedrals*, 1927/o 8.

Natural measurement

Increase and decrease
between them, culmination

Increase or decrease

Artificial measurement

Increase or decrease

Simultaneous increase
and decrease

Increase or decrease

 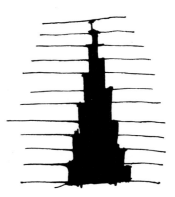

Crescendo and diminuendo
between the poles of white and black
striving up and down
with accelerated tempo
or slipping on and off
with retarded tempo on the scale

13

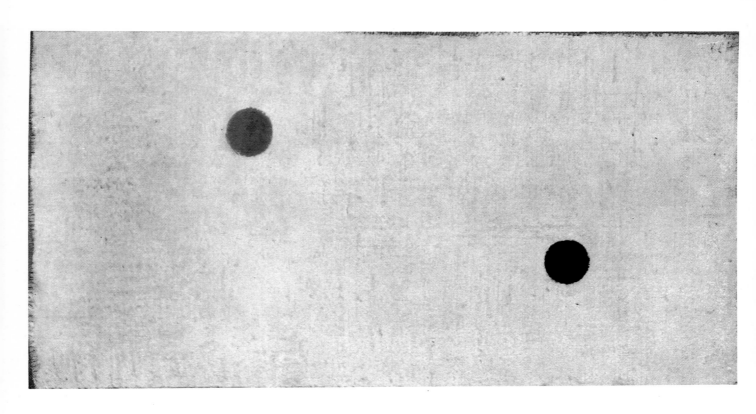

1938/T 19: *Le rouge et le noir*. Oil.

Pictures illustrating the concept of polarity:
1917/26 *Growing form and rigid form*. Watercolour.
1921/76 *Male and female plant*.
Colour on paper.
1926/p 3: *Static-dynamic opposition*. Watercolour.
1926/m 2: *Constructive-impressive*. Oil.
1930/x 6: *Mountain and air, synthetic*. Watercolour.
1932/y 8: *Mobile meets the immovable*. Oil.
1933/s 19: *Spiritual and worldly*. Drawing
1936/w 10: *Heavy and light forces*. Colour on paper.
1938/R 13: *Below and above*. Drawing.
1938/B 14: *Coarser and finer*. Pen-and-ink drawing.
1940/K 6: *Topsy-turvy*. Red and black colour
pigment with paste, on paper.

14

**On the whole idea of concept
The polarity of concepts**

A concept is not thinkable without its opposite. The concept stands apart from its opposite. No concept is effective without its opposite.

On contrasting concepts (pairs of concepts):   Chaos————Cosmos
                                            Disorder   Order

There is no such thing as a concept in itself; generally speaking, there are only pairs of concepts. What does 'above' mean if there is no 'below'? What does 'left' mean if there is no 'right'? What does 'behind' mean if there is no 'in front'?

Every concept has its opposite, more or less in the manner of:

Thesis ——————— Antithesis; the line between them is long or short according to the extent of the opposition.

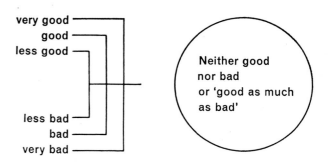

The opposing positions are not fixed; they may slip past one another. Only one point is fixed, the central point in which the concepts lie dormant.

Relatively fixed (in relation to the central point) are opposing points of equal intensity.

Good and evil. Concept and counterconcept. Thus I would supply a particle and then, over and over again, another particle, nothing more: for of course I know quite well that the good must always come first, but that it cannot live without the bad. In every individual I would therefore order the relative weight of the two parts in such a way as to provide a certain degree of compatibility.

Dualism is treated not as such but in its unity. Rest and unrest as the alternate elements in the painter's procedure.

'The creation of a definite movement and countermovement from the centre of a plane. The norm in the centre.' [1]
'If the norm is acentric, it becomes isolated and non-normative.' [2]

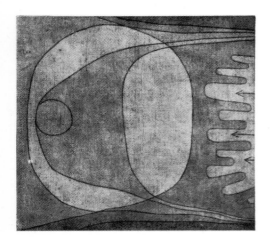

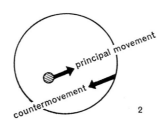

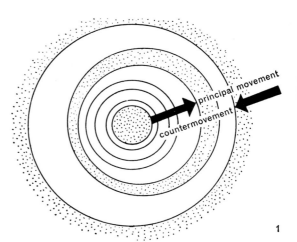

1934/U 2: *Fear*. Oil on burlap.

The tension between rest and incipient motion as alternate elements in painting.
The opposites may be combined or contrasted; the two intrinsically connected groups may be put side by side or one over the other. The characteristics of 'here and there' are intensified by the contrast.

16

The concept of artistic creation

The study of creation deals with the ways that lead to form. It is the study of form, but emphasises the paths to form rather than the form itself. The word *Gestaltung* suggests as much. 'Theory of form' (*Formlehre*), as it is usually called, does not stress the principles and paths. 'Theory of formation' (*Formungslehre*) is too unusual. Moreover, *Gestaltung* in its broader sense clearly contains the idea of an underlying mobility, and is therefore preferable.

For another thing, 'Gestalt' (over against form)[1] means something more alive. Gestalt is in a manner of speaking a form with an undercurrent of living functions. A function made of functions, so to speak. The functions are purely spiritual. A need for expression underlies them.

Every expression of function must be cogently grounded. Then there will be a close bond between beginning, middle, end. They will be joined by necessity, and there will be room for nothing doubtful, since they fit so tightly.

The power of creativity cannot be named. It remains mysterious to the end. But what does not shake us to our foundations is no mystery. We ourselves, down to the smallest part of us, are charged with this power. We cannot state its essence but we can, in certain measure, move towards its source. In any case we must reveal this power in its functions just as it is revealed to us. Probably it is only a form of matter, but one that cannot be perceived by the same senses as the familiar kinds of matter. Still, it must make itself known through the familiar kinds of matter and function in union with them. Merged with matter, it must enter a real and living form.

This freedom in nature's way of building form is a good school for the artist. It may produce in him the same profound freedom, and with it he can be relied on to develop freely his own paths to form.

Genesis as formal movement is the essence of the work of art. In the beginning the motif, the harnessing of energy, sperm. Work as form-making in the material sense: primordial feminine. Work as form-deciding sperm: primordial masculine.

[1] According to a note by Klee: Gestalt = Living being. Form = 'nature morte'.

The choice of means should be undertaken with great restraint. This, more than profusion of means, makes for orderly intelligence.[2]

Material means (wood, metal, glass, etc.): massive use of material means is above all to be avoided here.

Ideal means (line, tone value, colour): ideal means are preferable.

They are not free from matter; if they were, it would be impossible to 'write' with them. When I write the word wine with ink, the ink does not play the primary role but makes possible the permanent fixation of the concept wine. Thus ink helps us to obtain permanent wine. The word and the picture, that is, word-making and form-building, are one and the same.

[2] A note by Klee: 'Do not use material means: wood, metal, glass, but ideal, intangible means such as line, tone value, colour.' *Cf.* Contributions to a theory of pictorial form, pp.362–5. The ideal and material concept of a function.

3. Genesis of form. Motion is at the root of all growth

1940 From Klee's estate No.034 (Untitled).
Pigment mixed with paste, on paper.
Example of 'Will – tension
and discharge'.

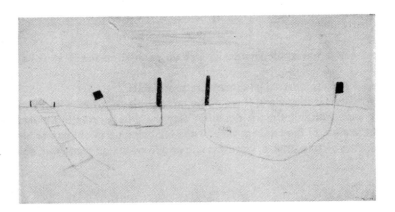

1927/T 7: *Two boats near path*. Crayon drawing.

What was in the beginning? Things moved so to speak freely, neither in straight nor crooked lines. They may be thought of as simply moving, going where they wanted to go, for the sake of going, without aim, without will, without obedience, moving self-evidently, in a state of primal motion.

There was just one thing – mobility, the prerequisite for change from this primordial state.

I can't prove that this is how it was; I hope it was; at any rate it is conceivable, and what is conceivable is fact and useful. It is useful as a counterconcept, the opposite of what seems to have happened afterwards, change, development, fixation, measurement, determination.

Moreover, it can be used because it can be formally expressed in terms of contrast.

The point is not dimensionless but an infinitely tiny elemental plane, an agent that carries out no motion; in other words, it is at rest [1].
Apply the pencil and shortly a line is born [2].

1   2

3   4

The point as a primordial element is cosmic. Every seed is cosmic. The point as an intersection of ways is cosmic [3].
As a point of impact the point is static [4].
Tension between one point and another yields a line [5]. Not yet discharged (abstract) [6]. Discharged [7]. The universal cause is therefore reciprocal tension, a striving for two dimensions.

5
6
7

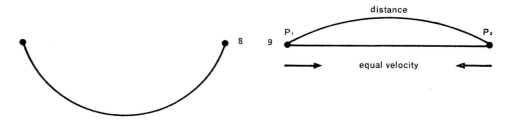

8   9

distance

P₁   P₂

equal velocity

Two points ideally related in tension to a line. Result: an arc [8].
Given equal velocities, the propagation of points along a line results in a meeting in the middle [9].

1927/ue 2: *Ardent flowering.* Watercolour.

How a reality is generated by causality

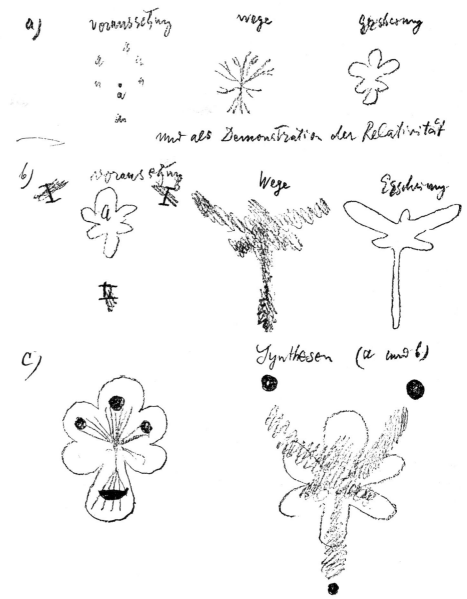

The point sets itself in motion and an essential structure grows, based on figuration.¹ The end is only a part of what is essential (the appearance). True essential form is a synthesis of figuration and appearance.

Starting from an origin *a)* (seed), ways are laid out under influence from outside and in, *b)* and *c)*.

The point, seen dynamically, as agent: the growth of energy concentrated on one side
determines the direction of motion. When a point is given central value – this is the
cosmogenetic moment. This event encompasses the whole concept of beginning.
Suns, radiation, rotation, explosion, movements of fireworks, sheaves.

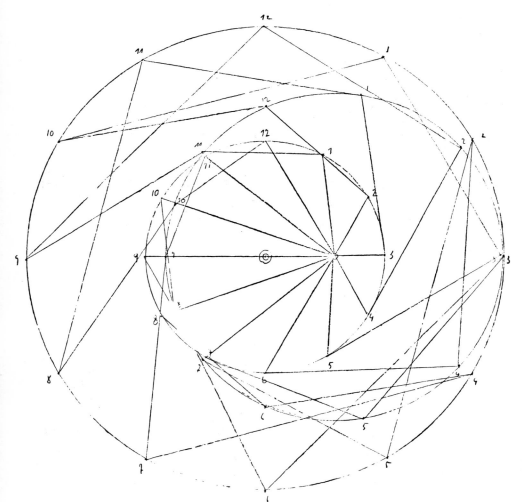

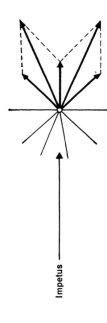

Impetus

'Rotation at different velocities, on a combined base.
The rotation is based on a variety of centres and
circles.'

**Synthesis of figuration
and appearance
Centrally irradiated growth
Growing in partial cross
section and in longitudinal
section**

Centrally irradiated growth.
It grows as if along a single dimension, on all sides at once; it grows according to the size of the former whole (primary motion).

Plants: growing in partial cross section [1].
Growing in longitudinal section [2].
Plant growth in longitudinal section is partial and centripetally oriented.[1]
Might be called 'feminine' [3].
Plant growth in diametrical section is wholly and centrifugally oriented.
Might be called masculine [4].
Syntheses of plant growth in cross section and longitudinal section [5, 6, 7].

[1]centripetal: striving towards the centre.
centrifugal: striving away from the centre.

1

7

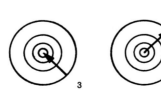

2

3

4

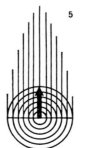

5

6

I begin where all pictorial form begins: with the point that sets itself in motion.

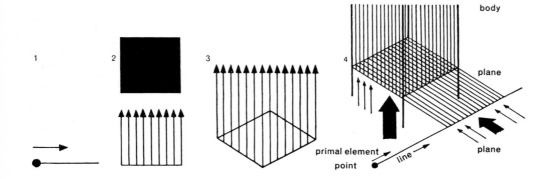

The point (as agent) moves off, and the line comes into being – the first dimension [1]. If the line shifts to form a plane, we obtain a two-dimensional element [2].

In the movement from planes to spaces, the clash of planes gives rise to a body (three-dimensional) [3].

Summary of the kinetic energies which move the point into a line, the line into a plane, and the plane into a spatial dimension [4].

1929/o 8: *Huts,* pen-and-ink drawing.
1925/T 4: *The last village in the valley of Ph.*
Colour on paper.

25

Detail from 1927/3h 4: *About to take a trip.*
Pen-and-ink drawing.

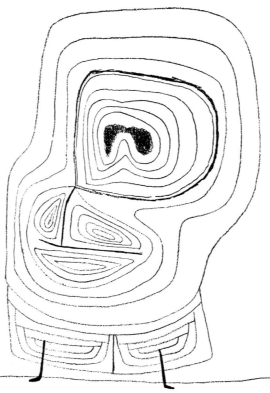

1934/qu 10: *Heavily fructified*. Pencil drawing.

Graduated accentuation of the line (lines made stronger or weaker).

Productive growth of selected line with graduated accentuation (flux) [1].

Productive growth of the point (concentric waves). Two-dimensional structure emanating from nuclear strata [2].

Linear accent on nerves, or incarnation of the line (the linear body becomes broader in growth).

Incarnation: the middle line as skeleton [3].

The line as limit: for progressive growth, flow, inner content [4].

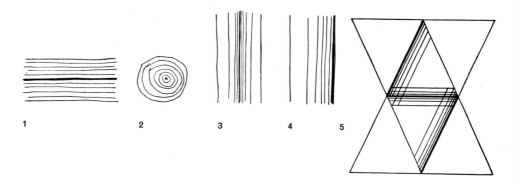

1   2   3   4   5

Incarnation represented in terms of causal reality. The constructive propagation of lines strictly adjusted to the threads of construction [5].

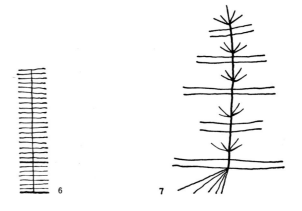

6   7

The line articulated in terms of measure or time (growth, motion, divisibility) [6].
Structure classified in its essentials [7].

1927/om 9: *Variations* (*progressive motif*).
Oil on canvas.

'Progressive stratification is characterised by the pull from outside in.
In spatio-temporal terms the density and extension of the progressive motif indicate the 'road travelled' by the sum of the endotopic and exotopic accents. Variation of accent, which may be progressive-inward, progressive-outward (limiting), or spatial.
Note in the Appendix.

Dynamic density:
Discharge of tension from within or additive
(harmonised progression of a dimension of motion,
enrichment by spatial emphasis).

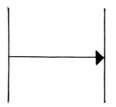 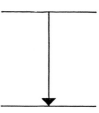 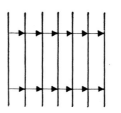 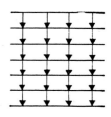

The tension spreads
in two directions

Motion, regular or irregular
(progressive)

Result:
Diagram of dynamic density in two directions.
Inwardly progressive, marching in the directions
up-down and left-right.
(Harmonised progression of two dimensions,
simultaneous outward and inward pull.)
Thing or body – active, locality or space – passive
(tensions between bodies and space).

'Progression always has spatial effects.
The rule in progression is: movements of
extension and contraction of tone value
accompanied by measurable movement of area,
enlargement and diminution.'

Corporeo-spatial tensions

Diagram of the dynamic formation
of the circle.
The radius grows from the inside out
in pure progression

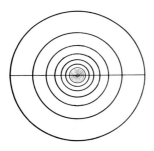

Another diagram of the dynamic
formation of the circle by radiation.
Radiation comes from the centre
and is related to the innermost point

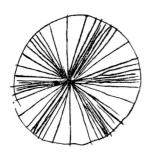

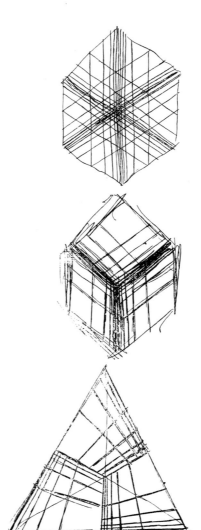

Illustrations:
Variant on 'towards the innermost'.
Inner dynamic density

Variation of rotation
extension into space

Diagram of the dynamic formation
of the triangle in a variation
with rotary movement

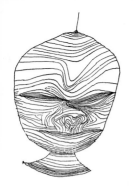

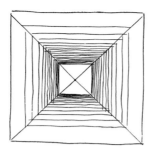 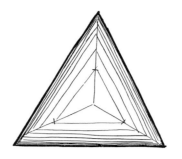 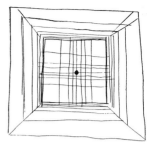

1   2   3

Detail from 1928/k 9: *Overtones*.
Pen-and-ink drawing.

Progressively spatial [1].
Progressively pushing from the centre to the limits [2].
Outside and inside in corporeo-spatial combination
(progressively inward and medial) [3].

Stratification is defined by the relation
that outer bears to inner.
Inside and outside, as concepts, are
either relative or limiting.

1928/k 5: *Horn perceived in tent*. Pen and ink.

The basic forms, their tensions and inner relations (The basic forms from the point of view of their causal determinants)

In this representation, which is necessarily based on a consideration of the inner essence, the circle is the encompassing, the universe, the cosmos. The square is an exception, based on the horizontal-vertical. The triangle is closer to the circle, a part of it, and the diagonal relates the two. From here there might well be a bridge to a theory of style.

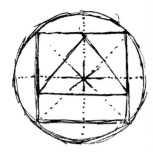

The tensions underlying the basic forms considered according to their inner coherence (inside and out).
How did it come about?
What is the 'cause'?
The universal cause is reciprocal tension, a pull in two directions at once.

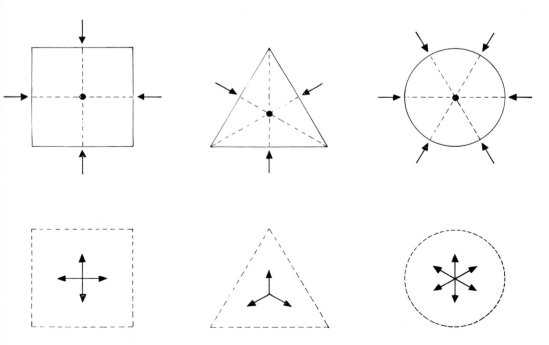

Discharge of tension
from outside
or subtractive

Discharge of tension
from within
or additive

A straining from all sides: exertion

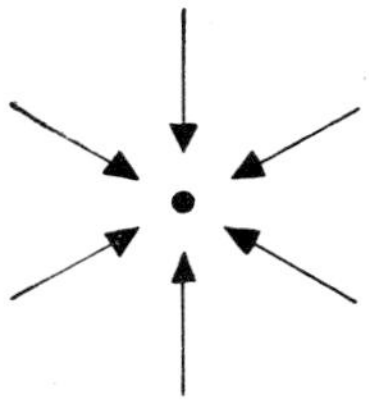

Centripetal: Inward pull

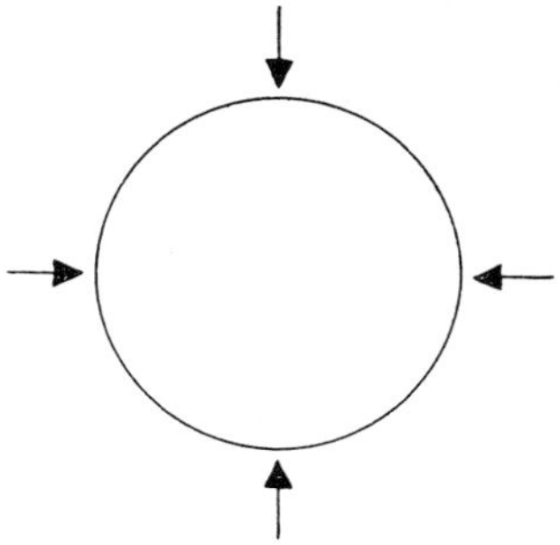

The tension discharged, accomplished

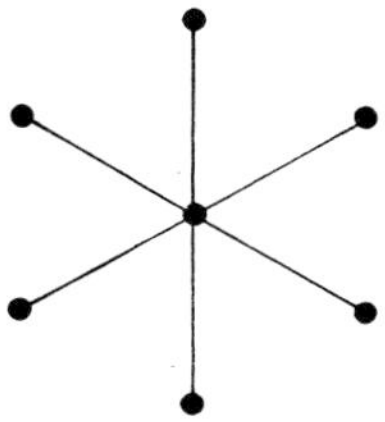

Basic movement of domination

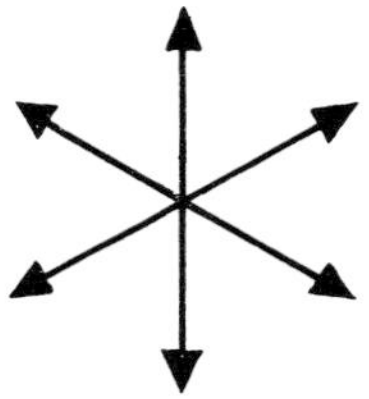

The centre as point of culmination. The intensified inner relations are directed towards the centre

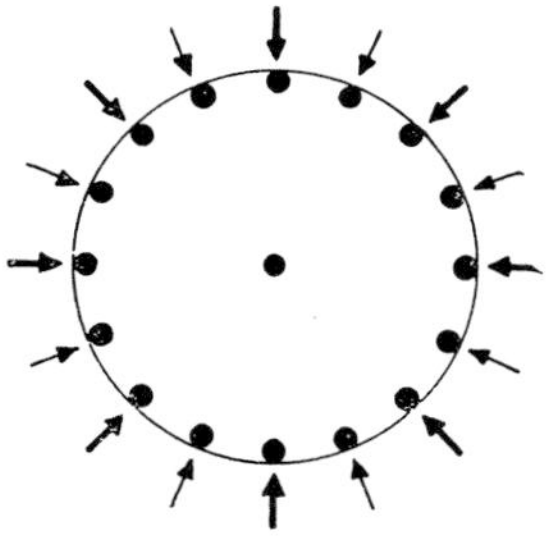

Movements starting from one's own being can be enhanced by suggestions of counter-movement. Synthesis of movement and counter-movement

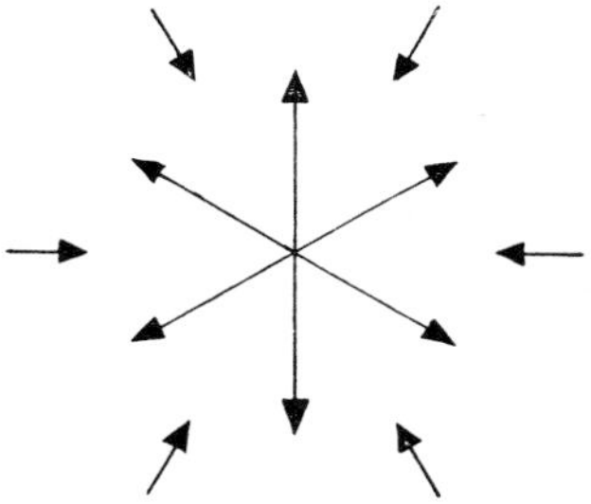

Centrifugal: Outward pull

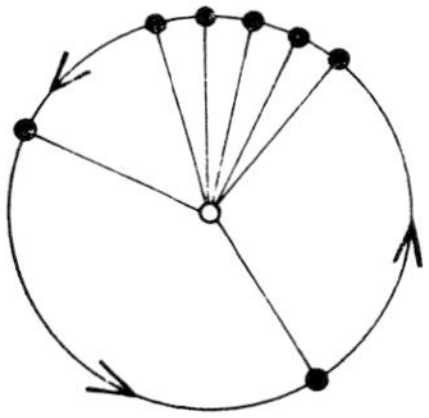

↑

The articulating energies and impulses illustrated by the example of a leaf (growth in several directions). Union of material tension and ideal tension (i.e. simultaneous presentation of essence and appearance).

Adjustment between progressive forms of motion (Combination of rigid and free rhythms)

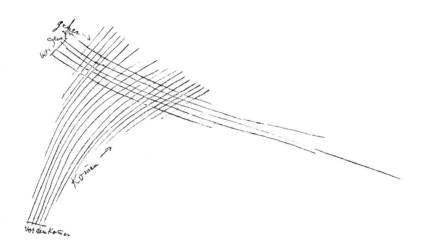

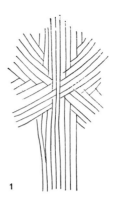

1

Coming and going represented by increase and decrease. Each dimension grows in relation to the other. (Two-dimensional relation of growth.)

A change in the direction of parallel rays may be considered as a repeated deflection of the centres (shifting centres) or, in the case of elementary forms, as a compromise (interlock). Compromise between straight, broken, and bent lines. The movements in the example should be defined mechanically as discharges of tension between fixed and moving points.
The compromises yield series of forms whose movement is intermediate between the movements of free and strict form. The union between rigid and free rhythms produces hybrid forms. These hybrid forms may be perfectly harmonious or they may incline towards either parent.

Progressive trend towards the centre. Outside diminishing, inside increasing. The progressive multiplication at the centre brings about a proportional decrease as the movement approaches the periphery. Increase towards the centre.

Progressive interlocking of multi-dimensional growth:

Constructive-impressive combination. i.e. 'causally real and merely real' (simultaneous genetic and phenomenal presentation).

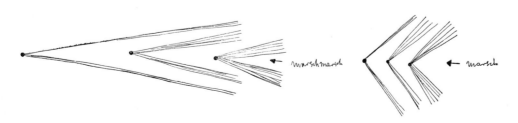

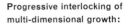

1925/y 1: *Exotic bird park.* Pen-and-ink.

Several forms of motion, starting from a guide line (in parallel). The formal extension results from 'shifting centres' and their influence on the normal radiation. Interpenetration of endotopic and exotopic treatment, of essence and appearance moving in rhythm, suggests the focal movement.

Compromise between free and strict form.
The combination of relaxed and rigid rhythm results in hybrid forms. Rays are defined by their relation to the centre, to the point.
Stratification is defined by the relation of outer to inner.

Stratification employed genetically
(dynamic proximity)

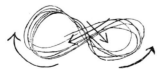

Representation according to essence
(movement, growth)

Synthesis of essence and appearance
(interpenetration, interlacing)

Boundaries of different value for inside and outside

Boundary line of
the outer areas.
Boundary line of
the inner areas.
Boundary line of
the innermost areas

Example showing
formation of differentiated
boundaries.
Space and form
transparent in a
three-dimensional body

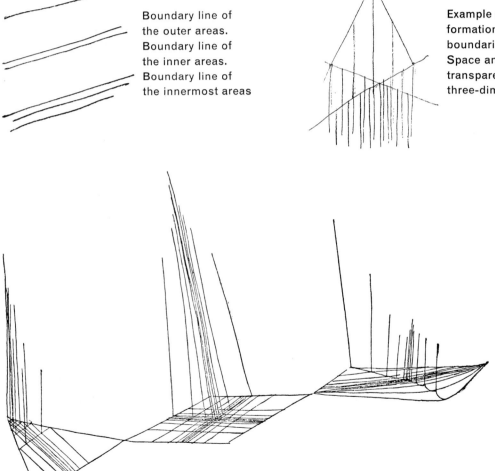

1928/k 2: *Three phantom ships.*
Pen-and-ink drawing.

36

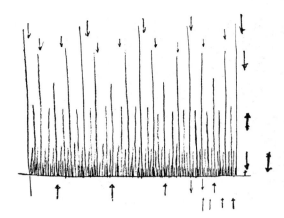

Boundary resistance to the
vertical, that is, parallel deflection.
Boundary resistance:
deflection through an angle

Illustration of the power of boundaries to deflect
motion of varying density and acceleration.
Pen-and-ink drawings:
1927/v 4: *Severities in motion*.
1931/R 4: *Atmospheric-sharp*.
1931/R 4: *Space formation by degrees in motion*.
1931/qu 20: *Severities of space*.

1931/M 1: *New things on old soil*. Colour.
The traditional concepts of linear perspective:
foreground, middle-ground, and background are
replaced by determinations of position:
top-bottom, left-right.

**Dimensions on the surface
and in space**

Orientation on the surface. The scene is the surface, more precisely the bounded plane. Two questions must be asked: What enters and where does it enter?[1]

The regular division yields the proportion to right or left, above or below. Point P is spatially-determined in two dimensions, first by its position with regard to above and below, second with regard to left and right.

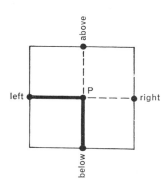

The dimensions on the surface always turn up in pairs on either side of the centre. Polarities are present as in the case of good and evil.

The form produced on the surface is based on a function. A spiritual function requires expression.

This expression is based on the elements. Dematerialised elements. The required expression is obtained not by material but by ideal means. The ideal elements liberate the expression and fix it clearly on the plane.

[1]Notation in manuscript:
'To paint well is simply this: To put the right colour in the right place.'

1939/LM 18: *Accident.* Tempera and crayon on white underpainting.
Exchange of the dimensions that govern our natural sense of up and down.

40

In the dimensions of the plane: Determination of position by means of co-ordinates.

Co-ordinates

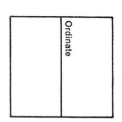

Here the position of P is given by its position above (below) the abscissa and its position to the left (right) of the ordinate [1,2].

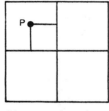
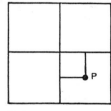

Above and to the
left [1]

Below and to the
right [2]

Orientation in space. In fixing a point in space, we must consider the dimension in front – behind as well as the two above-mentioned dimensions; in this case, the point P is fixed with respect to three dimensions.

From the spatial point of view, P is also localised by its position in front of or behind the co-ordinate plane.

In front   Behind

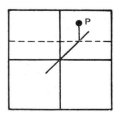

1928/P 6: *Italian city*. Watercolour.

Summing up these directions, we obtain the following picture in space:

In this case the point P is fixed with respect to three dimensions

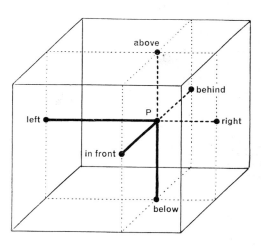

The three dimensions combined in cube

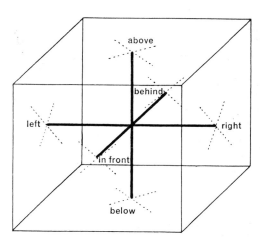

The 'I' orients itself in space according to three dimensions [1]. It judges its position in this space according to the concepts:

above   → below
left hand → right hand
in front → behind

Synthesis of objective body and subjective space

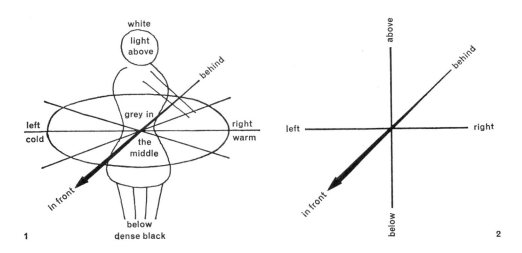

1

2

Transposed to the surface, our spatial picture looks like this [2]. For the sake of precision we take a cubic space with fixed boundaries. On the left → right line the position is computed according to the distance from the left- or right-hand bounding plane or from an intermediate point. On the horizontal plane the distance to the front or back is also measured (estimated). The position in space is also computed by reference to the upper and lower plane. In above → below, the downward direction predominates; the upward drive operates only as a corollary to the downward pull ↓ (attraction of the earth). This is the real force: the upward drive is secondary.

In left → right (attraction of heat), the direction is free and the drive towards heat may predominate (accent on the direction from left to right).

In behind → in front the forward direction is also free, and the forward drive may predominate (accent on the direction from behind to in front).

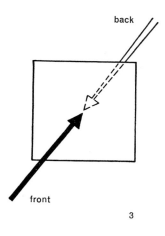

back

front

3

If we consider direction or movement, we obtain the following result:
1. Dimension: left-right, movement each way
2. Dimension: above-below, parallel movement
3. Dimension: front-back, movement and countermovement [3]
Movement and countermovement (in which a clash is possible).

In answer to the question 'Where does it enter?' we measure: height, width, length or depth, and displacement (in relation to the norm).

The forward drive, combined with direction

striving forward

heat

attraction of earth

Dimensional directions in the 'I'

line of sight

feeling of warmth

stance

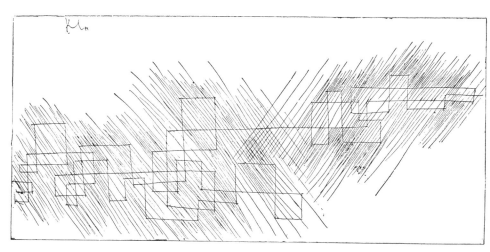

1929/p 6: *Village in the rain*. Pen-and-ink drawing. Two directions of movement overlap in a rhythmic combination of forms.

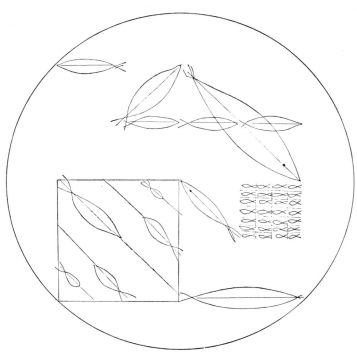

1

2

1926/E zero. Reworked in 1936. *Fish in circle*.
Oil.

The relation of the pictorial components to
one another and to the whole:
[1] *Fish in circle, 1926* – Example
of the problems of articulation in pictorial space.
Balance between directions of movement, in a circle.
[2] Example of articulation in a circle.
(Applied exercise from 'Diagrams within
square and circle' 6/15.)

46

Questions of articulation in pictorial space. In painting, 'the picture' should be regarded as the object. The picture is the whole; the parts should be evaluated in relation to the whole, that is, in relation to the picture. This makes format of foremost importance.

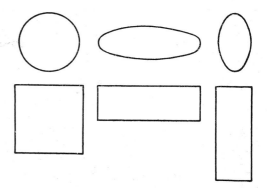

But it does not exclude the so-called object in the traditional sense. And even in the good old masters objects must always be judged as parts of the whole picture. This fish is an 'object' in the old sense, while from the modern point of view it is part of the picture.

I. Picture body (format)

1. Fish body   2. Fish space

Parts of the fish   Four outer
body a, b, c   pictorial
                       limits of space
                       d, e, f, g

Or four corners of space, the inner
boundaries of the fish body, h, i, k, l

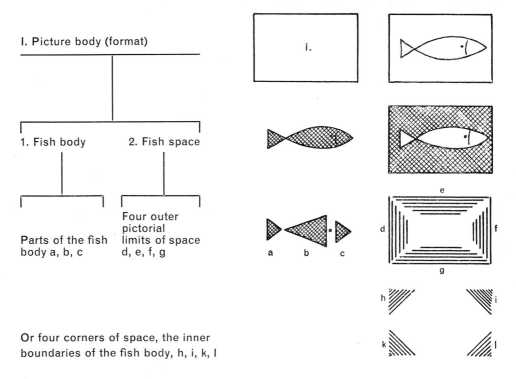

47

1930/y 1: *House, outside and inside*. Watercolour. Transparent-polyphonic interpenetration of the inside and outside. Overlapping of simultaneous representations of ground-plan and elevation.

Orientation in pictorial space

Practical considerations in regard to space: the spatial character of the plane is imaginary. Often it represents a conflict for the painter. He does not wish to treat the third dimension illusionistically. Today a flat effect is often sought in painting. But if different parts of the plane are given different values, it is hard to avoid a certain effect of depth. If everything remains perfectly flat, we might under certain circumstances have a good carpet. If it does not remain flat, we come to the formal problem of the third dimension. One of the artist's basic problems is how to enlarge space.

We do it by means of overlapping planes. In this way we can create the illusion of larger and smaller planes in depth. Side by side, one behind the other, overlapping, interpenetrating. If we compare the steps, we tend to see differences in them. The mere facts of a side by side and one behind the other, argue the presence of 'behind-in front'. Here even boundaries are spatial, and progression always produces an effect of depth.
Ever after the Renaissance, perspective was used in the enlargement of space. It is an intellectual device.

There have been other experiments with exact method in art. Exotopic and endotopic treatment, by flooding and tapering off of colour.
All this is a struggle for space. The struggle is not determined by outward necessity, the aim is inward. It encompasses a number of things, including the ultimate problems of space. Instead of problems we might say: a certain mystery. Simple things can also present a problem. We must ponder a great many factors that all culminate in the problem, the mystery.
Once extension in one of the two dimensions is brought out sharply, we have the impression of a plane. It brings with it a tendency to orient oneself by this dimension. Major-minor, large or small components, brilliance-darkness, behind-in front. And so the desire or need to bring in a third dimension gives rise to very simple artistic contrasts. If what we designate as the main object is not in the foreground but in between, and similar things lie in front and behind, as regards the third dimension we shall have three different frontal planes. Then the main action takes place in the middle, through its relation to the frontal planes 'behind and in front'.
There is a conceivable bridge between the foremost and the hindmost: so the middle is not free. We see that there is an element of unclarity in the dimensions. The notion of fluid space with a fourth imaginary dimension, 'time', makes nothing clearer.
These intellectual constructions require exact clarification if they are to serve as an artistic law.

1929/m 1: *Houses at crossroads*. Watercolour.

Endotopic and exotopic treatment with a view to simultaneous interpenetration.
'The movement of boundary contrast',
says Klee, 'is brought out in different ways.
Sometimes we have an endotopic treatment
aimed to produce contrast on the boundary,
and sometimes an exotopic treatment. Sometimes
the endotopic centre receives a special new
emphasis. A conflict arises between endo- and
exotopic. Then we have a sort of
mesh of forms.'
The simultaneous treatment of inside and outside
points to the concept of simultaneity, i.e. of
contacts between many dimensions (p.86).
Cf. the interpenetration of ground-plan and
elevation in *House, outside and inside* (p.48) in
contrast to the increased emphasis on the ground-
plan in *Houses at crossroads*.
For the mesh of forms, i.e. the simultaneous
treatment of ground-plan and elevation, *cf.* the
frequently reproduced pictures:
1919/156: *Composition with windows*, oil.
1919/232: *The full moon*, oil.
1919/97: *Façade, brown-green*, oil on paper.
Öffentliche Kunstsammlung Basle, and
1919/199: *Inside of house* (p.154), with main
emphasis on endotopic elevation.
Cf. 1930/b 9: *Vase*. Watercolour.
'Positive-negative plane formation as
interpenetration of form and space.'
Colour reproduction in *Dokumentarmappe
Klee-Gesellschaft*, Benteli, Berne 1949, and
Grohmann, p.236.
1925/v 1: *Still life with fragments*. Oil.
'Simultaneous treatment of base and elevation,
inside and outside.'
1930/s 8: *Plan of a castle*. Drawing with accent on
light and shade. Sprayed watercolour.
'Endotopic and exotopic plan.'

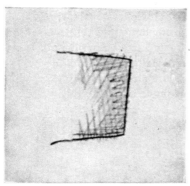

Endotopic
treatment

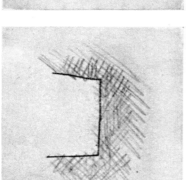

Exotopic
treatment

Endotopic – exotopic

These two principles of the positive-negative treatment of relief, applied to linear figures containing intersections.
Rule: in handling boundary contrast, always stay on one side of the line.

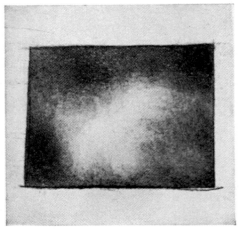

1

2

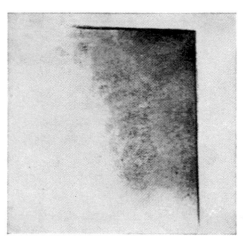

4

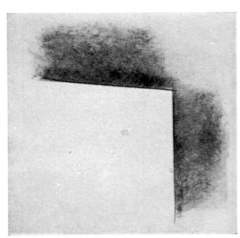

5

3

Square, endotopic treatment [1]
Square, exotopic treatment [2]
Square, treated as a body without
reference to inside or outside [3]
Corner, endotopic treatment [4]
Corner, exotopic treatment [5]

If we call to mind Klee's statement: 'The depth of our surface is imaginary', it follows that without a perspective viewpoint in space, 'the relations on the scene' have to be organised. This proves necessary if we wish to indicate clearly the directions of motion.
We have a three-dimensional space when tone value or colour is added to a linear plane figure. Here Klee's conception of the third dimension differs appreciably from the generally held notions of space and dimension.

It is based on the space-time unit which covers completely every movement.

Movement from black to white

Schematic representation

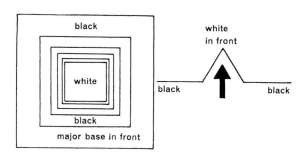

Countermovement from white to black

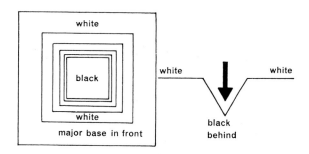

The step that the eye takes from a lighter inner point of the surface to a darker outer one presupposes motion from inside to out (or vice versa): from fore to rear.
Examples of space generated by tone value: *House, outside and inside*, 1930/y 1 (p.48) and *Polyphonic setting for white*, 1930/x 10 (p.374). Motion is attained through the depth that tone value and colour give. Klee designates depth in a non-perspective space by using motion, 'from fore to rear'. This is the spatial expression of inside-outside in terms of motion and countermotion.
(*Cf.* Diagram 3, p.45, and the section: The succession or the temporal function of a picture. Active and passive motion in form, p.369.)

The two movements taken together

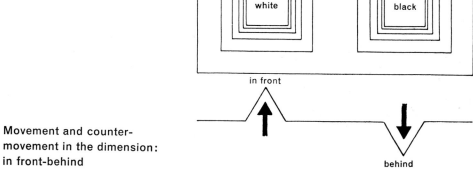

Movement and counter-movement in the dimension: in front-behind

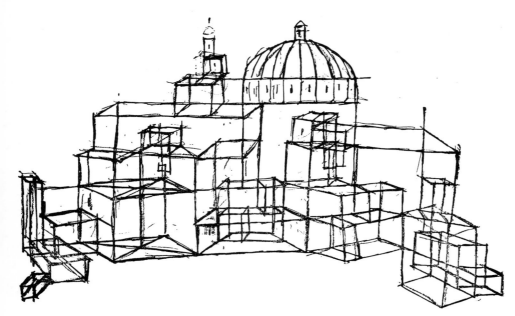

1929/g10: *Santa A at B.*
Pen-and-pencil drawing.

These different treatments – the endotopic and the exotopic – are diametrically opposed to one another.

Expressions of energy are based on contrast: this contrast between endotopic and exotopic treatment applies not only to the way it actually works but also to the function that is set in motion. What is treated exotopically on the picture-plane tends to stand out. What is treated endotopically tends to recede.

This brings us to the third dimension. But there are exceptions to all general principles. Sometimes, it becomes impossible to say that something really goes back or comes forward. The third dimension asserts itself, but still operates with flat values that stand a little farther back or forward. This is the relief style. Through it is expressed slight movement in the foreground. The endotopic and exotopic activation lessens the objective element and brings up the possibilities of boundary contrast.

A work is three-dimensional when its outside and inside can be clearly differentiated. When height, width, length, or depth may be measured on the basis of a norm.[1]

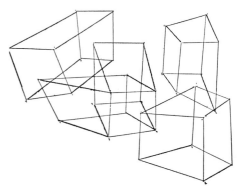

1930/U 9: *Spatial study (rational connections).*
Pencil drawing from the series
'Studies in three dimensions'.

[1]In a plane the norms are co-ordinates, in cubic space the norm is distance from the centre. *Cf.* p.43.

[1]The diagrams relating to the orientation of the 'I' in pictorial space start from an ideal centre, common to the 'I' and to the 'work'. Every movement in 'illusionistic flat space' stands in relation to the natural sense of direction of the 'I' and to the centre of the work. The resulting relations are significant, especially for an exact description of the directions of motion, and replace the concepts of foreground, middle ground and background, which are not applicable to a non-representational picture. Compare the directions of motion in 'Illustrations to a Theory of Pictorial Form', p.297 (and also pp.369–420). The examples indicate that in a predominantly dynamic process – for example, spiral movement from the inside out – the concept pairs left-right (reciprocal motion) and up-down (parallel motion) are not adequate. If we wish to establish the direction of motion, we must also use the concept in front-behind.

Orientation in pictorial space is achieved through the idea that the work is a mirror image of the 'I'; and moreover an upright image of an 'I'[1] that stands.

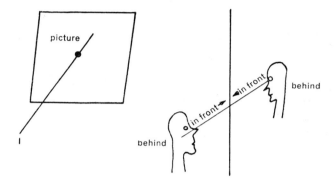

The upright 'I' and the work look each other in the face. Because the 'I' is assumed to be upright, the dimension above ⟶ below remains the same both in the 'I' and in the work. If the mirror, for example, were not upright, but fixed horizontally to the floor or ceiling, the dimension above ⟶ below would seem the wrong way round according to the mirror image.

The next dimension left ⟶ right appears in the same direction in the work (the mirror-man). But if I raise my left hand, the mirror-man raises his right; if I advance my right leg, the mirror-man responds with his left. This logical reversal becomes important on the stage[2] where real human beings face us, though they seem reflected in a mirror. When the stage script says 'left', it has to make clear therefore whether it means to the left of the audience or of the stage.

[2]The stage on which the play takes place.

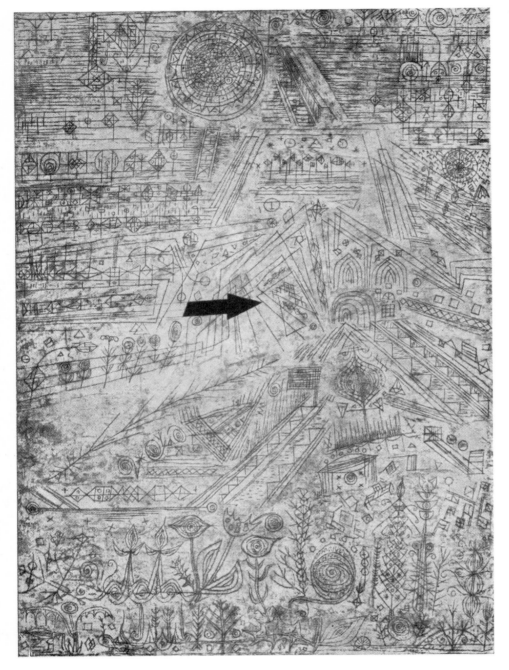

1929/s 7: *Arrow in garden*. Oil.

It is possible to single out the unique by normal means, by way of movement or articulation.
The dynamic is in the action. It moves, it is not static being, but process. Relatively predominant being and relatively recessive being. By way of contrast, the fixation of developing motion in a precise moment.
'If localities tend towards the centre, there is a psychological reason for it. The rational and the less rational are mixed. The meaning of this law is that a simple natural scene is given and that in this natural scene one particular thing is emphasised.
The weight on the centre stresses the deviation from the norm.'
The arrow as active agent in the many-sided motion of the total space.

The third dimension in front ⟶ behind, corresponds for the 'I' and for the mirror-man both in fact and in appearance, but the directions are opposed.

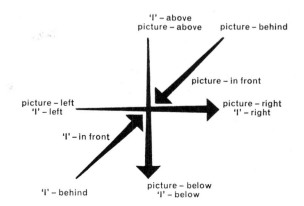

To sum up: the beholder of the picture should imagine that he has his mirror image before him. Then he can assume that the dimensions above ⟶ below and left hand ⟶ right hand in the picture run in the same direction as his own dimensions, but that as far as the dimension in front ⟶ behind is concerned, the directions are reversed; in a manner of speaking they meet him halfway.

The picture as mirror image of the creative artist; the dimensional concepts are made to fit him.

'I' and the picture look each other in the face.

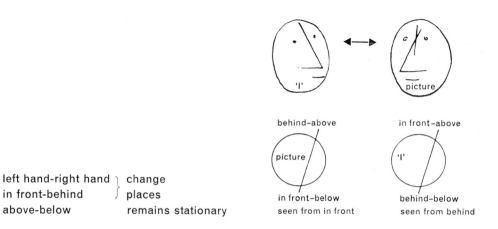

left hand-right hand ⎱ change
in front-behind ⎰ places
above-below   remains stationary

57

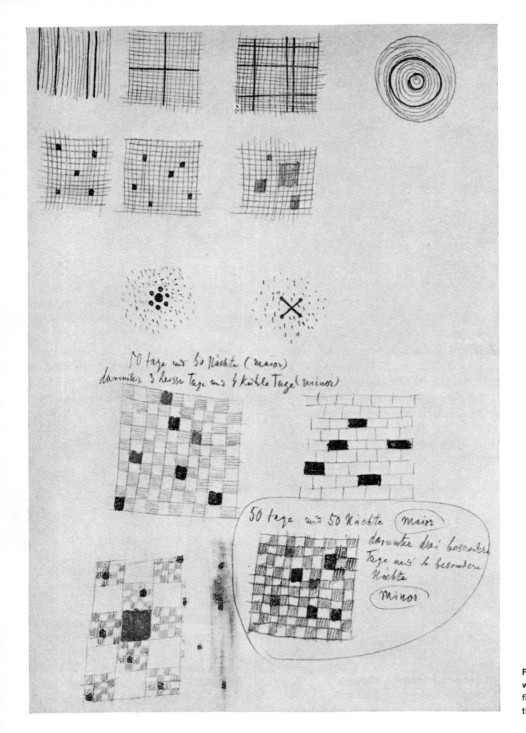

Facsimile page from the 'Theory of Articulation'
with stress on the major–minor function:
fifty days and fifty nights (major); among them
three hot days and four cool days (minor).

58

6. Objects in nature investigated in regard to their inner being. Essence and appearance

What we are after is not form but function[1]

We shall try to be exact but not one-sided. This is quite a task but we shall try just the same. Knowledge tries to be as precise as possible. The imaginary is indispensable.
What we are after is not form, but function. Here again we shall try to be precise: the machine's way of functioning is not bad; but life's way is something more. Life engenders and bears. When will a run-down machine have babies?
The fundamental things of life are theoretically present of themselves; their essence is exact function, with 'God' so to speak (as one is still entitled to say). Human judgement yields certain approximations. According to our standard, it has 'come a long way', or 'still has far to go'. In any event limits soon make their appearance.[2]
The formula of the function is far away, but it is somewhere, the source and origin.[3]

[1]This text is the first version of the article 'Exakte Versuche im Bereiche der Kunst', which was later considerably reworked and published in the *Bauhaus Zeitschrift für Gestaltung*. The first version bears no date, but was most probably written several years before the revision and publication. In the first version the emphasis is on the problem of 'function' and the 'creative'. In the second version, the accent is on a harmonious balance between exact knowledge (the educational factor) and intuition. The editor has taken the title from the text.

[2]Crossed out in the text: 'boundaries begin in cyclical regularity, where the captive point moves with the finest precision'.

[3]Crossed out in text: 'The hair anchor is far away, but this primal point is somewhere'.

'As creation is related to the creator, so is the work of art related to the law inherent in it.' The work grows in its own way, on the basis of common, universal rules, but it is not the rule, not universal *a priori*. The work is not law, it is above the law. As projection, as phenomenon, it is 'for ever starting' and 'for ever limited'; but it does match the infiniteness of the law in this: even in its limited sphere, the reckoning does not come out even. Art is a transmission of phenomena, projection from the hyper-dimensional, a metaphor for procreation, divination, mystery. But let us investigate further.
Consider the actual with benevolence; the present should not be deprived of its rights. But measure it by the eternal that is preserved throughout the changing times, periodically stirred up or, quite frequently, taken back to the womb, yet immensely fruitful even in the latent state. Measure everything by the natural process and its law. That prevents obsolescence, for everything is in flux and flows fast today. Do not define today, define backwards and forwards, spatial and many-sided. A defined today is over and done for.

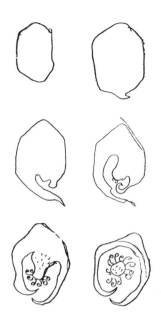

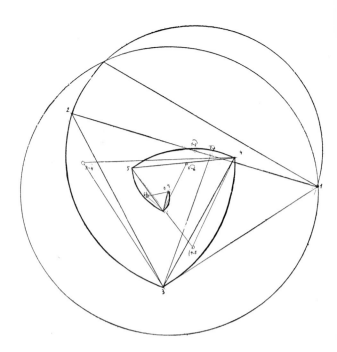

Formalism is form without function. When we look round us today, we see all sorts of exact forms; whether we like it or not, our eyes gobble squares, circles, and all manner of fabricated forms, wires on poles, triangles on poles, circles on levers, cylinders, balls, domes, cubes, more or less distinct or in elaborate relationships. The eye consumes these things and conveys them to some stomach that is tough or delicate. People who eat anything and everything do seem to have the advantage of their magnificent stomachs. They are admired[1] by the uninitiated formalists. Against them the living form. The initiate[2] divines the primordial living point; he possesses a few living atoms; he possesses five living, ideal elements, the pictorial pigments, and he knows of a little grey spot whence one can leap successfully from chaos to order.

He has a presentiment of procreation. He has a certain knowledge of the first action, can move things into being and make even their motion visible. His motion leaves traces in them and there you have the magic of life. And for the rest there is the magic of experience.

Metalogic is concerned with the smile, the gaze, the scent, all the seductions between good and evil. The investigation of functions never ceases, and yet there are still, even today, plenty of obstacles, thank God perhaps. For in the face of the mystery, analysis stops perplexed.[3] But the mystery is to share in the creation of form by pressing forward to the seal of mystery.

'Objects in nature investigated in regard to their inner being.'
Cross-sections of a calla lily, studies on the synthesis of essence and appearance.
'Cut fruit.' Constructive drawing illustrating the progression within the normal tensions of elementary forms. Cf. 1927/m 5: Cut fruit. Oil.

[1]Crossed out: 'envied'.

[2]Crossed out: 'The wise man'.

[3]Crossed out: ' . . . analysis "blushes" and stands still'.

An organ investigated with a view to its inner being (The transformation of a formal theme and its amplification as a synthesis of outward sight and inward vision.)

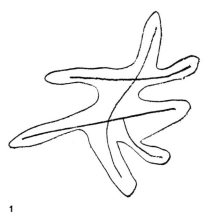

1

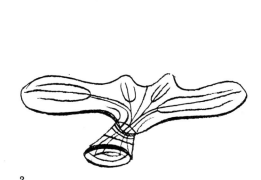

2

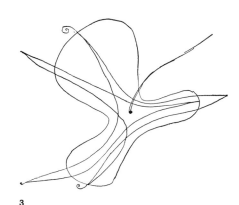

3

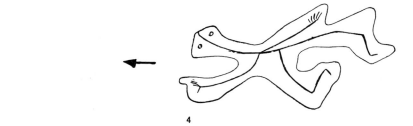

4

An organ investigated with a view to its inner being:
[1] Articulation 'according to essence', studied on the basis of a simple example.
[2] Nature study; spatial-transparent articulation 'according to manifestation'.
[3] Dynamically accented study of articulation from a flower.
[4] Detail from 1930/I 9, *Spirits of the air*, pen-and-ink drawing.
[5] Organic co-ordination in a composition: Detail from 1929/Omega 8: *Group under trees*. Wash and ink drawing. Polyphonic interpenetration of organs.
[6] Detail from 1930/z 8:
Dynamised starfish. Pencil drawing.

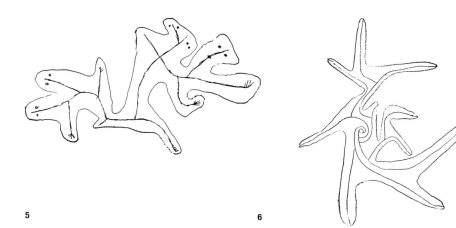

5

6

Study of a higher organism and the interlocking
responsible for its total function. 'Polyphonic
synthesis with a linear-active subject' – emphasis
on points of impact.

[1]'Wege des Naturstudiums', first printed in 'Staatliches Bauhaus Weimar 1919–23'. Published by Staatliches Bauhaus in Weimar and Karl Nierendorf, Cologne. Bauhausverlag, Weimar/Munich 1923.

7. Ways of Nature Study[1]

For the artist, dialogue with nature remains a *conditio sine qua non*. The artist is a man, himself nature and a part of nature in natural space.
But the ways that this man pursues both in his production and in the related study of nature may vary, both in number and in kind, according to his view of his own position in this natural space.

The ways often seem very new, though fundamentally they may not be new at all. Only their combination is new, or else they are really new in comparison with the number and character of yesterday's ways. But to be new as against yesterday is still revolutionary, even if it does not shake the immense old world. There is no need to disparage the joy of novelty; though a clear view of history should save us from desperately searching for novelty at the cost of naturalness.

Yesterday's artistic creed and the related study of nature consisted, it seems safe to say, in a painfully precise investigation of appearance. I and you, the artist and his object, sought to establish optical-physical relations across the invisible barrier between the 'I' and the 'you'. In this way excellent pictures were obtained of the object's surface filtered by the air; the art of optical sight was developed, while the art of contemplating unoptical impressions and representations and of making them visible was neglected.
Yet the investigation of appearance should not be underestimated; it ought merely to be amplified. Today this way does not meet our entire need any more than it did the day before yesterday. The artist of today is more than an improved camera; he is more complex, richer, and wider. He is a creature on the earth and a creature within the whole, that is to say, a creature on a star among stars.

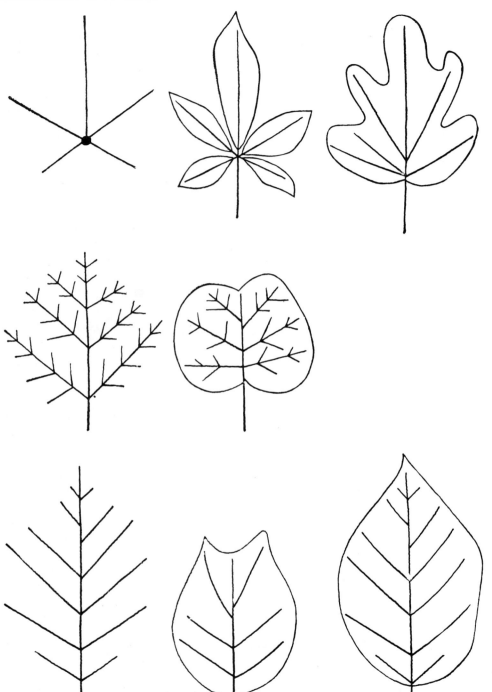

Study of the complementary effect of ribs and leaf shapes with identical inner form and changed outer form. 'The plane form that comes into being is dependent on the interlocking lines.
And where the power of the lines ends, the contour, the limit of the plane form, arises.'
Theoretical knowledge of the energies that create and articulate forms in nature serves as a basis for the creation of free and composite forms.

1929/OE 4: *Illumined leaf.* Watercolour.

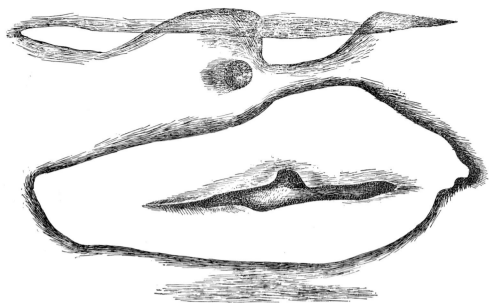

Accordingly, a sense of totality has gradually entered into the artist's conception of the natural object, whether this object be plant, animal, or man, whether it be situated in the space of the house, the landscape, or the world, and the first consequence is that a more spatial conception of the object as such is born.

The object grows beyond its appearance through our knowledge of its inner being, through the knowledge that the thing is more than its outward aspect suggests. Man dissects the thing and visualises its inside with the help of plane sections; the character of the object is built up according to the number and kind of sections that are needed. This is visible penetration, to some extent that of a simple knife, to some extent helped by finer instruments which make the material structure or material function clear to us.

The sum of such experience enables the 'I' to draw inferences about the inner object from the optical exterior, and, what is more, intuitive inferences. The optic-physical phenomenon produces feelings which can transform outward impression into functional penetration more or less elaborately, according to their direction. Anatomy becomes physiology.

But there are other ways of looking into the object which go still farther, which lead to a humanisation of the object and create, between the 'I' and the object, a resonance surpassing all optical foundations. There is the non-optical way of intimate physical contact, earthbound, that reaches the eye of the artist from below, and there is the non-optical contact through the cosmic bond that descends from above. It must be emphasised that intensive study leads to experiences which concentrate and simplify the processes of

Auge	eye
Centrum	centre
Du (Gegenstand)	thou (the object)
Dynamik	dynamics
Erde	earth
Erscheinung	appearance
Ich (Künstler)	I (the artist)
metaphysischer Weg	metaphysical way
nicht optischer Weg	non-optical way
gemeinsamer irdischer Verwurzelung	of shared terrestrial roots
kosmischer Gemeinsamkeit	of cosmic community
optisch-physicher Weg	optical-physical way
sichtbare Verinnerlichung	visible intensity
Statik	statics
Welt	cosmos

which we have been speaking. For the sake of clarification I might add that the lower way leads through the realm of the static and produces static forms, while the upper way leads through the realm of the dynamic. Along the lower way, gravitating towards the centre of the earth, lie the problems of static equilibrium that may be characterised by the words: 'To stand despite all possibility of falling'. We are led to the upper ways by yearning to free ourselves from earthly bonds; by swimming and flying, we free ourselves from constraint in pure mobility.

All ways meet in the eye and there, turned into form, lead to a synthesis of outward sight and inward vision. It is here that constructions are formed which, although deviating totally from the optical image of an object yet, from an overall point of view, do not contradict it.

Through the experience that he has gained in the different ways and translated into work, the student demonstrates the progress of his dialogue with the natural object. His growth in the vision and contemplation of nature enables him to rise towards a metaphysical view of the world and to form free abstract structures which surpass schematic intention and achieve a new naturalness, the naturalness of the work. Then he creates a work, or participates in the creation of works, that are the image of God's work.

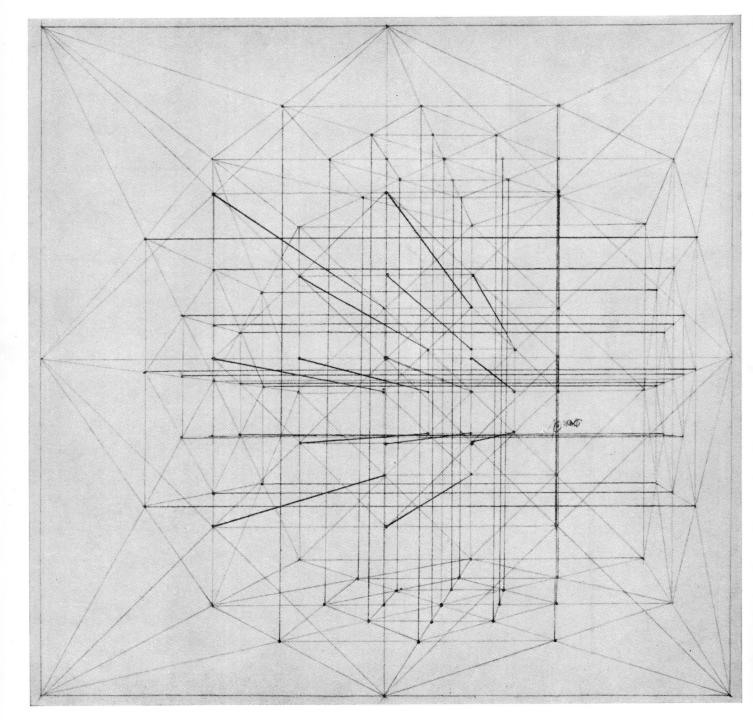

8. Exact experiments in the realm of art[1]

[1]'Exakte Versuche im Bereiche der Kunst', first published in *Bauhaus, Vierteljahrzeitschrift für Gestaltung*, vol. 2, No.2, Dessau 1928. The complete text reprinted in the prospectus, 'Junge Menschen kommen ans Bauhaus', Bauhaus Dessau, Hochschule für Gestaltung, under the title, 'Paul Klee spricht', Dessau 1929.

The manuscript shows certain slight deviations from the printed version. Those which may clarify the thought are cited here.

[2]'do a good deal but can awaken no true artistic life. To no work of art whose conception is significant.'

[3]'Exact research winged by intuition surges powerfully forward.'

[4]Mechanical problem: i.e. in reference to statics and dynamics.

[5]In place of 'what flows beneath': 'the law that flows beneath'.

Constructive drawing from 'Nodal points in space'. The outer surfaces and their inner nodal points linked in pairs (nodal points in cubic space).

We construct and keep on constructing, yet intuition is still a good thing. You can do a good deal without it, but not everything.[2] Where intuition is combined with exact research it speeds up the progress of research. Exactitude winged by intuition[3] is at times best. But because exact research is exact research, it gets ahead even without intuition, though perhaps not very quickly. In principle it can do without intuition. It can be logical; it can construct. It can build bridges boldly from one thing to another. It can maintain order in the midst of turmoil.

In art, too, there is room enough for exact research, and the gates have been open now for quite some time. What was accomplished in music before the end of the eighteenth century has hardly been begun in the pictorial field. Mathematics and physics provide a lever in the form of rules to be observed or contradicted. They compel us – a salutary necessity – to concern ourselves first with the function and not with the finished form. Algebraic, geometrical, and mechanical problems[4] are steps in our education towards the essential, towards the functional as opposed to the impressional. We learn to see what flows beneath,[5] we learn the prehistory of the visible. We learn to dig deep and to lay bare. To explain, to analyse.

We learn to look down on formalism and to avoid taking over finished products. We learn the very special kind of progress that leads towards a critical striving backward, towards the earlier on which the later grows. We learn to get up early to familiarise ourselves with the course of history. We learn cogent truths on the way from causes to facts. We learn to digest. We learn to organise movement through logical relations. We learn logic. We learn organism. As a result the tension between us and the finished product eases. Nothing exaggerated – tension inside, behind, underneath. Passionate only deep within. Inwardness.

All this is fine but it has its limits: intuition remains indispensable. We document, explain, justify, construct, organise: these are good things, but we do not succeed in coming to the whole. We have worked hard: but genius is not hard work, despite the proverb. Genius is not even partly hard work, as might be claimed on the ground that geniuses have worked hard, in spite of their genius. Genius is genius, grace; it is without beginning and end. It is creation. Genius cannot be taught, because it is not a norm but an exception. It is hard to reckon with the unexpected. And yet as leader it is always far ahead. It bursts ahead in the same direction or in another direction. This very day, perhaps, it is already in a place we seldom think of. For from the standpoint of dogma, genius is often a heretic. It has no law other than itself.

The school had best keep quiet about genius; it had best keep a respectful distance. The school had best lock up the secret and guard it well. For if this secret were to emerge from latency, it might ask illogical and foolish questions.

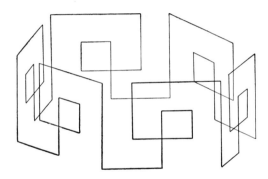

It would stir up a revolution. Surprise and perplexity. Indignation and expulsion. Out with the total synthetist! Out with the totaliser! We're against![1] And the insults would fall like hail: Romanticism! Cosmicism! Mysticism! In the end we should have to call in a philosopher, a magician! Or the great dead (who are dead?)[2] We should have to hold classes on holidays outside the school. Out under the trees, with the animals, by the side of brooks. Or on the mountains in the sea.

We should have to give assignments such as: construction of the secret. Sancta ratio chaotica! Scholastic and ridiculous. And yet that would be the assignment if construction accounted for everything.[3]

But we may as well calm down: construction is not absolute. Our virtue is this: by cultivating the exact we have laid the foundations for a science of art, including the unknown X, making a virtue of necessity.[4]

[1]'We, the over-analytical, are against.'

[2]'Not a word about the great dead. They're dead.'

[3]'Here we should need a philosopher whom people could understand.'

[4]Note at the end of the manuscript: 'Line of reasoning. What exact research can do with and without intuition. What it cannot do without intuition. (Genius). The necessity that becomes a virtue: Advantages for science and the school.'

70

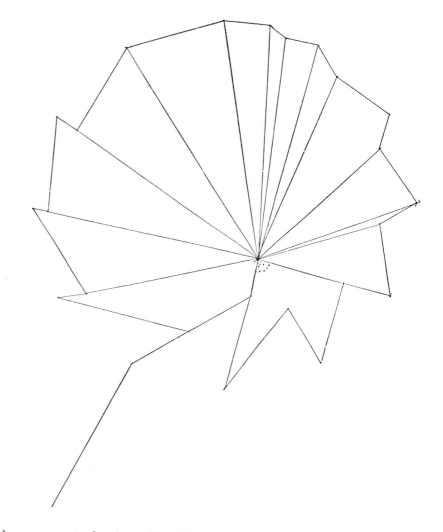

'The truth about a palm-leaf umbrella.'
Construction on the basis of progression and
regression of angles. Progression of radii in a
24-part circle. Connections: 24–2, 1–4, 2–6, 3–8,
4–10, 5–12, 6–14, 7–16, 8–18, 9–20, 10–12.

[1] Irregularity as a deviation from the
constructive norm.

Irregularity[1] means greater freedom without transgressing the law.

The conflict between universal and restricted application. The partial choice has expressed itself as an absolute structure (omission of the universal) or as a relative structure. Accented, but at the same time susceptible of being measured by the law which forms a part of it.

All figuration relates the general to the particular. It is more personal or less, according to the nature of the relation.

But if the priests ask sternly: 'What is this shocking anomaly you are producing?' – the absolute structure makes it possible to prove after the fact that the law has been observed, while the relative structure includes the proof, rejects the question, and makes the proof unnecessary. Thus the absolute is more free in its gesture, but not in its essence. Many

9. Purity is an abstract realm

1915/83: *Blossom*. Pen-and-ink drawing.

things are free without showing it; others are free only in a very limited sense but present a free appearance in the freedom of this gesture.

To be an abstract painter does not mean to abstract from naturally occurring opportunities for comparison, but, quite apart from such opportunities, to distil pure pictorial relations. Example of opportunities for comparison:

What is represented looks like a woman, a cat, a flower, an egg, a cube.

Pure pictorial relations: light to dark, colour to light and dark, colour to colour, long to short, broad to narrow, sharp to dull, left-right, above-below, behind-in front, circle to square to triangle.

'Abstract?'

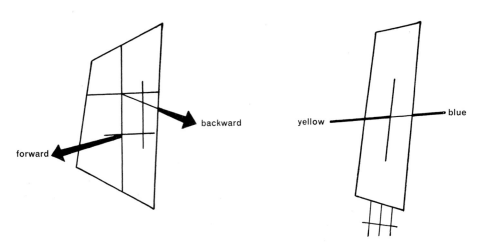

In regard to the question 'Abstract?' the treatment of direction is crucial. If you set the yellow forward and the blue back, then that is abstract.

Cf. 1923/62: *Architecture*. Oil.
Colour reproduction: Grohmann, p.201.
1927/k 9: *Plant and window* – still life Oil.
Colour reproduction in *Dokumentarmappe Klee-Gesellschaft*, Benteli, Berne 1949.

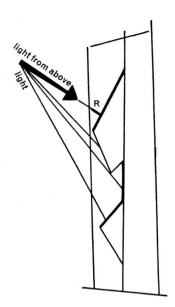

But if you use lighting to emphasise or underemphasise in front-behind then that is representational. According to the angle at which it falls on the picture, the beam of light produces forward and back. You are imitating a plastic object with the help of a light source that lies outside the picture plane and cannot strike the plane as such.

This kind of representation that gives the illusion of an object (whether known in nature or not) can be particularly unpleasant if the painted light, for example, comes from the left while the window in fact stands to the right.

The crucial point in evaluating such a picture is not whether dog, cat, etc. or 'nothing' (which does not exist) is represented, but whether the representation makes use of means that belong to picture-making, or do not.

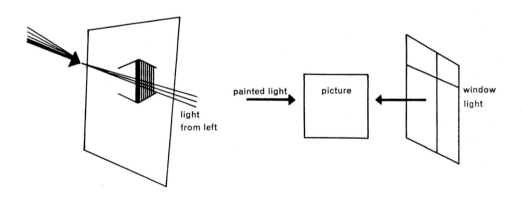

Purity is an abstract realm. Purity is a separation of elements pictorially and within the picture. Nothing may be added that comes only from outside. If, despite the pure separation of the elements, extraneous concepts like 'catdog' establish themselves pictorially and in the picture, they are permitted.

Thus from an abstract point of view the outcome cat or dog is not to be condemned if it occurs along with (or in spite of) a pure use of the pictorial elements. What is to be condemned is blurring introduced by extraneous concepts. Where the action of the elements is purest, effects of behind and in front are: a) usually inevitable, b) a considerable problem, c) permitted.

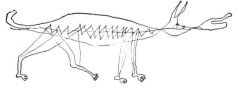

1930/e 10: *Ad marginem* (in the margin).
Oil.

The light can contribute to the representation if it does not come from outside but is formed in the picture. In other words, its source must be in the picture both as regards position and function.[1]

A schematic example of pictorially pure use of light:

[1]Cf. p.65, watercolour 1929/OE 4: *Illumined leaf,* and p.48, 1930/y 1: *House, outside and inside.*

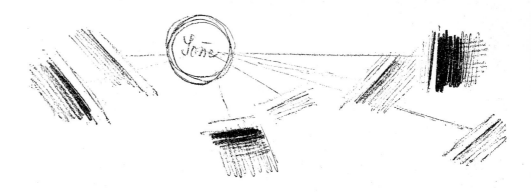

Examples:
1919/169: *Growth in an old garden.* Watercolour.
1930/e 9: *Sunset.* Oil.
1932/x 14: *Ad Parnassum.* Oil.
Giedion, p.132.

In contrast to the rest of the picture, the source of light must be shown by extraordinary and extremely powerful means (cause and effect). The light may be bright on a medium contrast, e.g., normal grey; the middle zone makes fine gradation possible where obstacles to unlimited diffusion occur. The light may also be warm (a source of heat).

10. Creative Credo[1]

[1]The 'Creative Credo' was first printed in *Tribüne der Kunst und Zeit*, edited by Kasimir Edschmid: Erich Reiss Verlag, Berlin 1920. The little volume contained contributions by various writers, painters, and composers. In the order of the table of contents: Schickele, Pechstein, Unruh, Grosman, Klee, Toller, Benn, Hoetger, Beckmann, Scharff, Becher, Schönberg, Kaiser, Felixmüller, Sternheim, Hölzel, Marc, Däubler.

Various notes added to Paul Klee's private copy indicate that he made use of the text, begun in 1918, in his early teaching at the Bauhaus. For example, a note under Section V, referring to the grasp of form through nature study in Section II as 'elementary building material' (in the pictorial sense). These additions to the manuscript have been taken into consideration.

I. Art does not reproduce the visible but makes visible. The very nature of graphic art lures us to abstraction, readily and with reason. It gives the schematic fairy-tale quality of the imaginary and expresses it with great precision. The purer the graphic work, that is, the more emphasis it puts on the basic formal elements, the less well-suited it will be to the realistic representation of visible things.

Formal elements of graphic art are: points, and linear, plane, and spatial energies. A plane element which is not composed from subordinate units is, for example, an energy, produced by the stroke of a broad-edged pencil, uniform or modulated. A spatial element, for example, is a misty, cloud-like spot made by a full brush, usually uneven in its intensity.

II. Let us develop: let us draw up a topographical plan and take a little journey to the land of better understanding. The first act of movement (line) takes us far beyond the dead point. After a short while we stop to get our breath (interrupted line or, if we stop several times, an articulated line). And now a glance back to see how far we have come (countermovement). We consider the road in this direction and in that (bundles of lines). A river is in the way, we use a boat (wavy motion). Farther upstream we should have found a bridge (series of arches). On the other side we meet a man of like mind, who also wants to go where better understanding is to be found. At first we are so delighted that we agree (convergence), but little by little differences arise (two separate lines are drawn). A certain agitation on both sides (expression, dynamics, and psyche of the line).

We cross an unploughed field (area traversed by lines), then a dense wood. He gets lost, searches, and once even describes the classical movement of a running dog. I am no longer quite calm either: another river with fog (spatial element) over it. But soon the fog lifts. Some basket-weavers are returning home with their carts (the wheel). Accompanied by a child with the merriest curls (spiral movement). Later it grows dark and sultry (spatial element). A flash of lightning on the horizon (zigzag line). Over us there are still stars (field of points). Soon we come to our original lodging. Before we fall asleep, a number of memories come back to us, for a short trip of this kind leaves us full of impressions.

All sorts of lines. Spots. Dots. Smooth surfaces. Dotted surfaces, shaded surfaces. Wavy movement. Constricted, articulated movement. Countermovement. Network and weaving. Brickwork, fish-scales. Solo. Chorus. A line losing itself, a line growing stronger (dynamics).

The happy equanimity of the first stretch, then the inhibitions, the nervousness! Restrained trembling, the caress of hopeful breezes. Before the storm, the gadflies' attack. The fury, the murder. The good cause a guiding thread, even in the thick of twilight. The lightning shaped like the fever curve. Of a sick child . . . Long ago.

1919/115: *Landscape with gallows.*
Oil on cardboard.

The ideas underlying *Landscape with gallows,*
1919, point to the 'Creative Credo', begun in 1918
and published in 1920. In the landscape the
'forms suggested by nature study' become
elementary symbols of experience. Section II, with
its 'topographical plan', points to the relation
between landscape and the experience of forms.

III. I have mentioned elements of graphic representation which should be visible in the work. This must not be taken to mean that a work should consist solely of elements. The elements should produce forms, but without losing their own identity. Preserving it.

Usually several of them will have to stand together to produce forms, or objects, or other secondary things. Planes produced by lines entering into relations one with another (e.g. as one sees stormy watercourses) or spatial structures produced by energies related to the third dimension (swarming fishes).

Through such enrichment of the formal symphony the possibilities of variation, and with them the ideal opportunities for expression, grow beyond number.

In the beginning is the act; yes, but above it is the idea. And since infinity has no definite beginning, but is circular and beginningless, the idea may be regarded as the more basic.

In the beginning was the word, as Luther translated it.

IV. All becoming is based on movement. In Lessing's *Laocoon*, on which we wasted a certain amount of intellectual effort in our younger days, a good deal of fuss is made about the difference between temporal and spatial art. But on closer scrutiny the fuss turns out to be mere learned foolishness. For space itself is a temporal concept.

When a point turns into movement and line – that takes time. Or when a line is displaced to form a plane. And the same is true of the movement of planes into spaces.

Does a picture come into being all at once? No, it is built up piece by piece, the same as a house.

And what about the beholder: does he finish with a work all at once? (Often yes, unfortunately.)

Didn't Feuerbach say: For the understanding of a picture, a chair is needed? Why a chair? To prevent the legs, as they tire, from interfering with the mind. Legs get tired from long standing. The space in which we move belongs to time, character belongs to movement. Only the dead point is timeless. And likewise in the universe, movement is the basis of everything. (Where do they get the energy? That is the idle question of a disappointed man.) Peace on earth is an accidental congestion of matter. To take this congestion as basic is mistaken.

The Biblical story of Creation is a good parable for motion. The work of art, too, is first of all genesis; it is never experienced purely as a result.

A certain fire flares up; it is conducted through the hand, flows to the picture and there bursts into a spark, closing the circle whence it came: back into the eye and farther (back to one of the origins of movement, of volition, of idea). What the beholder does is temporal too. The eye is so organised that it conveys the parts successively into the crucible of vision, and in order to adjust itself to a new fragment has to leave the old one. After a while the beholder, like the artist, stops and goes away. If it strikes him as worth while – again like the artist – he returns.

In the work of art, paths are laid out for the beholder's eye, which gropes like a grazing beast (in music, as everyone knows, there are channels leading to the ear – in drama we have both varieties). The pictorial work springs from movement, it is itself fixated movement, and it is grasped in movement (eye muscles).

V. Formerly, artists depicted things that were to be seen on the earth, things people liked to see or would like to have seen. Now the relativity of visible things[1] is made clear, the belief expressed that the visible is only an isolated case taken from the universe and that there are more truths unseen than seen. Things appear enlarged and multiplied and often seem to contradict the rational experience of yesterday. An effort is made to give concrete form to the accidental.[1]

The inclusion of concepts of good and evil creates an ethic. Evil should not be an enemy who triumphs or who shames us, but a power contributing to the whole. A part of conception and development. The primordial-masculine (evil, stimulating, passionate) and primordial-feminine (good, growing, tranquil) together producing a state of ethical stability.

To this corresponds a simultaneous union of forms, movement and countermovement, or to put it more naïvely, of objective contrasts (the use of disjunct colour contrasts, as by Delaunay). Every energy requires its complement to bring itself to rest outside the field of force. Abstract formal elements are put together like numbers and letters to make concrete beings or abstract things; in the end a formal cosmos is achieved, so much like the Creation that a mere breath suffices to transform religion into act.

VI. A few examples: A man of antiquity sailing a boat, quite content and enjoying the ingenious comfort of the contrivance. The ancients represent the scene accordingly. And now: What a modern man experiences as he walks across the deck of a steamer: 1. his own movement, 2. the movement of the ship which may be in the opposite direction, 3. the direction and velocity of the current, 4. the rotation of the earth, 5. its orbit, 6. the orbits of the moons and planets around it.

Result: an interplay of movements in the universe, at their centre the 'I' on the ship.

An apple tree in blossom, the roots, the rising sap, the trunk, a cross section with annual rings, the blossom, its structure, its sexual functions, the fruit, the core and seeds. An interplay of states of growth.

A sleeping man, the circulation of his blood, the measured breathing of the lungs, the delicate function of the kidneys, in his head a world of dreams, related to the powers of fate. An interplay of functions, united in rest.

VII. The relation of art to creation is symbolic. Art is an example, just as the earthly is an example of the cosmic.

The liberation of the elements, their arrangement in subsidiary groups, simultaneous destruction and construction towards the whole, pictorial polyphony, the creation of rest through the equipoise of motion: all these are lofty aspects of the question of form, crucial to formal wisdom; but they are not yet art in the highest sphere. A final secret stands behind all our shifting views, and the light of intellect gutters and goes out.

1927/d 10: *The ships set sail.*
Oil on canvas on wood.
Development of energy moving in a definite direction.
Cf. p.79, Section VI: 1. 'his own movement,
2. the motion of the ship', etc.

We can still speak rationally about the salutary effects of art. We can say that imagination, borne on the wings of instinctual stimuli, conjures up states of being that are somehow more encouraging and more inspiring than those we know on earth or in our conscious dreams.

That symbols console the mind, by showing it that there is something more than the earthly and its possible intensifications. That ethical gravity coexists with impish tittering at doctors and priests.

For, in the long run, even intensified reality is of no avail.

Art plays in the dark with ultimate things and yet it reaches them.

Fellow man, arise! Learn to appreciate this *villégiature*: a change of air and viewpoint, a world that distracts you, and gives you strength for the inevitable return to work-a-day grey. And that is not all. Let it help you to shed your shell; try, for a moment, to think of yourself as God. To look forever forward to new holidays when the soul will sit down to feed its hungry nerves, to fill its tired veins with new sap.

Let yourself be carried to this life-giving ocean along broad rivers and delightful brooks – like the branches of concentrated graphic art.

11. Survey and orientation in regard to pictorial elements and their spatial arrangement

Lecture delivered on the occasion of an exhibition at the Jena Kunstverein, 26 January 1924[1]

[1]First appeared in 1945 under the title: Paul Klee, *Über die moderne Kunst*. Benteli, Berne. English edition: *On modern art* translated by Douglas Cooper, Faber and Faber, London 1947

Ladies and gentlemen:

As I prepare to address you here, in the presence of my work which should really speak for itself, I cannot help wondering a little whether I have sufficient grounds for saying anything and whether I shall be able to do it right.

For while as a painter I feel quite in command of the means to move others in the direction in which I myself am driven, I feel that it is not within my powers to map such paths so surely through the word.

Still, I comfort myself with the thought that my words will not stand alone; their aim is merely to complement the impressions gained from my pictures and to add some definition that may be missing.

If I manage this at all I shall be content and consider that my aim in talking to you has been achieved.

It is often said that a painter should paint and not talk. I should have been glad to dodge this reproach by concentrating on the parts of the creative process which are carried on largely in the subconscious while the work is taking form. Quite subjectively, I believe that this would justify a lecture by a painter, for it would involve a change of emphasis, a new approach. It would mean a partial shift of accent from the formal aspect, which has been consciously overemphasised, to the question of content. A compensation of this sort would appeal to me and might enable me to express my thought in words.

But were I to take this course I should be thinking too much of myself and forgetting that most of you are much more at home in matters of content than of form. So I won't be able to avoid saying something about form.

First I shall give you a look into the painter's workshop and after that I'm sure we shall understand one another.

There must, after all, be some common ground between laymen and artists, where they can meet half-way and the artist will no longer look like a mere eccentric, but like a creature set down unasked, as you were, in a world of innumerable forms, and who, like you, must get his bearings in it as best he can. Who differs from you only in that he manages by his own specific means and methods, and that sometimes, perhaps, he is happier than the uncreative man, who cannot achieve release through art.

You will surely grant the artist this relative advantage, for he has it hard enough in other respects.

Let me use a parable. The parable of the tree. The artist has busied himself with this world of many forms and, let us assume, he has in some measure got his bearings in it; quietly, all by himself. He is so clearly oriented that he orders the flux of phenomena and experiences. I shall liken this orientation, in the things of nature and of life, this complicated order, to the roots of the tree.

From the roots the sap rises up into the artist, flows through him and his eyes. He is the trunk of the tree.

Seized and moved by the force of the current, he directs his vision into his work. Visible on all sides, the crown of the tree unfolds in space and time. And so with the work.

No one will expect a tree to form its crown in exactly the same way as its roots. We all know that what goes on above cannot be an exact mirror image of what goes on below. It is clear that different functions operating in different elements will lead to sharp divergencies.

And yet some people would like to deny the artist the very deviations that his art demands. They have even gone so far in their zeal as to accuse him of incompetence and deliberate distortion.

And yet all he does in his appointed place in the tree trunk is to gather what rises from the depths and pass it on. He neither serves nor commands, but only acts as a go-between. His position is humble. He himself is not the beauty of the crown; it has merely passed through him.

Before I begin to discuss the realms that I have likened to crown and roots, I must own to certain qualms.

It is not easy to orient yourself in a whole that is made up of parts belonging to different dimensions. And nature is such a whole, just like art, its transformed reflection.

It is hard to gain an overall view of such totality, whether it be nature or art, and it is still harder to communicate the view to others.

The answer lies in methods of handling spatial representation which lead to an image that is plastically clear. The difficulty lies in the temporal deficiency of language.

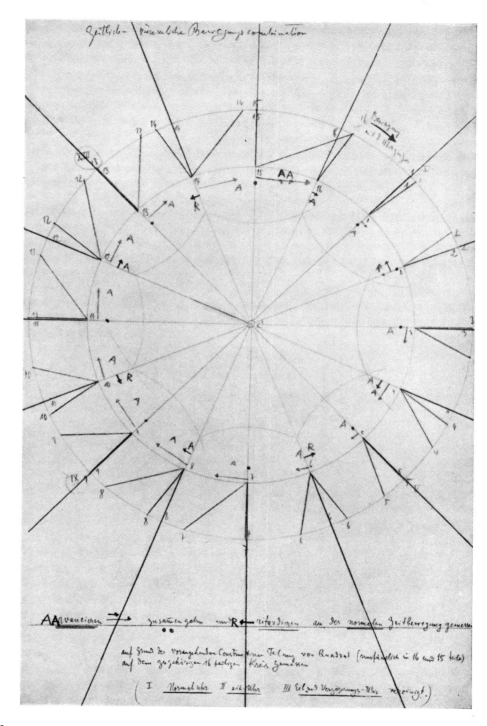

'Movement combining space and time:

A: Fast

•••: Convergence and

R: Slow, measured by the normal standard.
Measured on the 16-part circle on the basis
of the preceding constructive division of the
related square (peripherally into 16 and
15 parts)

I: Normal clock

II: Clock that runs fast   } combined.'

III: Clock that runs fast and slow

83

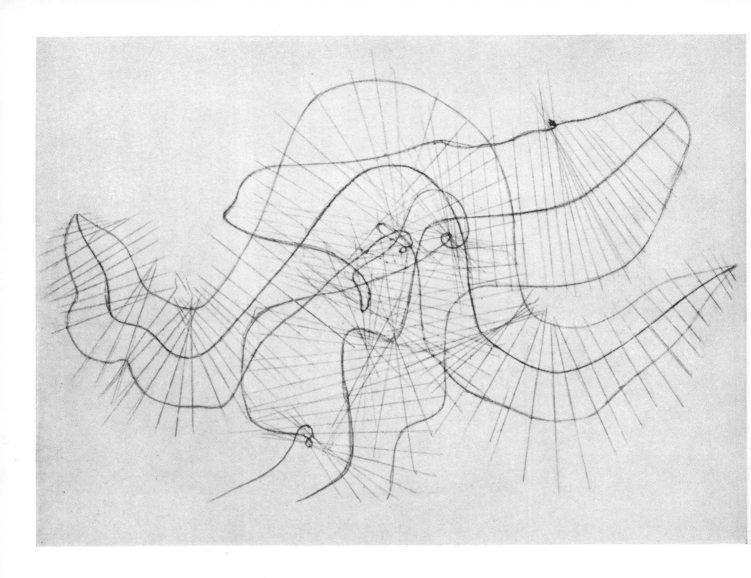

The interlocking towards total function in a free-formed polyphonic organism. The rhythmic progressions are determined by successive increase and decrease, both quantitative and qualitative, of the energies used. In the present example the direction and character of the movement result from the density and spacing of the linear tensions and nodes.

84

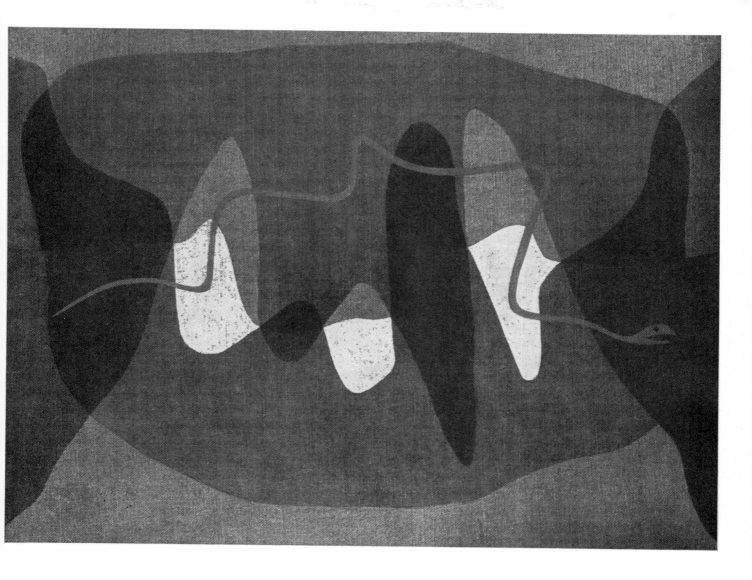

1934/U 17: *Snake-paths*. Oil.

Rhythms in nature become 'truly individual
in the figurative sense when their parts take on
a character that goes beyond the rhythmical'.
Where there is an overlapping of planes,
as in *Snake-paths*, two other dimensions enter in;
tone value and colour (multi-dimensional contacts
between means). Polyphonic interpenetration
is based on an unequal progression of planes,
'attenuated by a dynamic adjustment of

progressive proportions (displacement of
movement)'. The surface is activated (contrast
between light and dark) and is contrasted across
the centre with free movements (body of snake
and boundaries between planes).

85

For in language there is no way of seeing many dimensions at once.

In spite of this deficiency we must consider the parts in great detail.

But with each part, regardless of all the problems it presents, we must not forget that it is only a part. Otherwise our courage may flag when we encounter a new part leading us in an entirely different direction, to new dimensions, to a distant realm where our memory of previously explored dimensions may give way.

To each dimension as it seeps away in time, we ought to say: You are becoming past, but later on perhaps, at some critical – perhaps fortunate – juncture, we shall meet again and once again you will be present.

And if, as more and more dimensions turn up, it becomes increasingly difficult for us to visualise the different parts of the structure all at once, we must simply be very patient. Unfortunately, what the so-called spatial arts have long succeeded in accomplishing, what even the temporal art of music has achieved so eloquently in polyphony, this simultaneous view of many dimensions which is the foundation of the great climaxes of drama, is unknown in the realm of verbal explanation. Contact between dimensions must be made outside this medium; and afterwards.

And yet perhaps I can make myself well enough understood to help you to experience interdimensional contact when you look at pictures.

As a humble go-between, who does not identify himself with the crown of the tree, I think I may promise you a radiant light.

And now to the point, to the dimensions of the picture.

I have spoken of the relation between root and crown, between nature and the work of art, and explained it by the difference between earth and air, and the correspondingly different functions of depth and height.

In the work of art, which we have likened to the crown, we enter specifically into pictorial dimensions, which demand distortion of the natural form.

For such is the rebirth of nature.

What, then, are these specific dimensions?

First of all there are more or less limited formal factors, such as line, tone value, and colour.

Most limited of all is line, for it is a matter of measure alone. Its use depends on length (long or short), angles (obtuse or acute), radial and focal length. All these can be measured.

Measure is the hallmark of this element, and wherever the possibility of measurement is in doubt, line has not been treated with absolute purity.

Of a rather different nature is tone value, or chiaroscuro as it is also called, the many degrees between black and white. In this second element we deal with questions of weight. One degree has white energy more densely or more loosely packed; another is more or less weighted with black. One degree can be weighed against another. And further, the black can be related to a white norm (on a white background), the white related to a black (on a blackboard), or both together related to a middle grey.

Thirdly, colour, which obviously has still other characteristics. For we cannot fully define it by measure or weight: where scales and ruler reveal no difference, for example, between a pure yellow surface and a pure red surface of the same extension and the same brilliance, an essential difference remains – which we designate by the words yellow and red.

Just as we can compare salt and sugar in every respect – except in their saltiness and sweetness.

I should therefore like to call the colours qualities.

Accordingly, we have three formal factors, measure, weight, and quality. Despite their fundamental difference, there are certain relations between them.

The nature of these relations will be seen from the following brief analysis.

Colour is first of all quality. Secondly it is weight, for it not only has colour value but also light value. Thirdly it is measure, for in addition to the above-mentioned values, it also has its limits, its area and its extension, which can be measured.

Tone value is first of all weight, while secondly, in its extension or limits, it is measure.

But line is only measure.

Thus we have applied three lines of reference, which all intersect in the realm of pure, cultivated colour; two of which meet in the realm of pure tone value; and only one of which extends to the realm of pure line.

Each according to its contribution, the three reference lines characterise three realms which in a way resemble three boxes, one inside the next. The largest box contains three reference lines, the middle-sized box two, and the smallest only one. (It is perhaps in this light that we shall most readily understand Liebermann's remark that drawing is the art of omission.)

We see that the three realms fit together in a very special way; thus it is no more than logical to handle them all with the same precision. The possibilities of combination are already rich enough. Blurring is justified only when there is a special inner need; such a need might account for the use of coloured or extremely pale lines, or of opalescent tints ranging from yellow-grey to blue-grey.

The distinguishing symbol of pure line is the linear scale with its innumerable variations of length. The symbol of pure tone is the weight scale stepped between white and black.

But what is appropriate to the nature of pure colour? What symbol best expresses its character?

Line movement from 1934/M 12:
Carrier for a shield.
Pen-and-ink and watercolour.

The complete circle – this is the form which best expresses the essence of colour relations.

Its definite centre, the possibility of dividing its circumference into six arcs and of drawing three diameters through the six intersections, these make it possible to picture the chief scenes in the drama of colour relations.

These relations are first of all diametric; and just as there are there three diameters, so there are three main diametric relations, which are:

Red-green, yellow-violet, and blue-orange (or the principal pairs of complementary colours).

Along the circumference a primary colour alternates with one of the main mixed or secondary colours, so that the mixed colours (three in number) are situated between their primary components: green between yellow and blue, violet between red and blue, orange between yellow and red.

The complementary pairs connected along diameters destroy one another's colour when they mix across the centre to make grey. This is true for all three pairs, as we see from the fact that all three diameters bisect one another in the same point, the grey centre of the colour circle.

Furthermore, a triangle can be drawn through the points of the three primary colours; its corners are the primary colours themselves, while its sides are given whatever colour comes from a mixture of the two corresponding corner colours. Accordingly, the green side lies opposite the red corner, the violet side opposite the yellow corner, and the orange side opposite the blue corner.

This gives us three primary colours and three main secondary colours, or six main adjacent colours, or three pairs of related colours (colour pairs).

Leaving the formal elements, I come to the first constructions using the three kinds of elements just listed.

This is the heart and core of our conscious creative effort.

This is a critical juncture.

Mastery of these elements gives us the power of creating things so strong that they can reach out into new dimensions, far removed from conscious associations.

This phase of artistic endeavour has the same crucial importance in a negative sense. This is the point where one can miss the greatest and weightiest content and fail in spite of the finest sensibility. Just for lack of orientation on the formal plane. As far as I can say from my own experience, it is the artist's momentary disposition that decides which of the many elements will emerge from the comfort of their natural order to rise together in a new order.

To produce a figure which one calls form or object.

1933/D 20: *Bust of a child.*
Oil.

In a very limited sense, this choice of formal elements and the way in which they are combined is analogous to the musical relation between motif and theme.

As the figure grows little by little before our eyes, an association of ideas may easily tempt us into an objective interpretation. For with a bit of imagination every complex structure lends itself to comparison with familiar forms in nature.

The associative properties of this structure which, the moment it is interpreted and named, already deviates to some extent from the artist's direct purpose (or in any case from his most intense preoccupation) – these associative properties have become a source of impassioned misunderstanding between artists and laymen. Whilst the artist is bending every effort to group the formal elements so purely and logically that each has to go exactly where it does and none trespasses on its neighbour, a layman, looking over his shoulder, will utter these devastating words: 'That's a very poor likeness of Uncle.' If the painter has control over his nerves, he will think: 'Bother Uncle. I must get on with my building . . . This new stone', he says to himself, 'seems a bit heavy, it's pulling things to the left; I'll need a sizable counterweight on the right to restore the balance.'

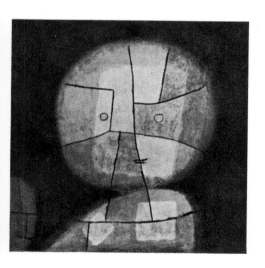

And he adds a bit first on one side and then on the other, until his scales are balanced. And he will be overjoyed if he has had to upset his original pure construction no further than to make sure that those tensions and contrasts necessary to a living picture are present. But sooner or later the association may occur to him even without the help of a layman, and nothing then prevents him from accepting it, if it introduces itself under a really appropriate name.

This acceptance and formulation of the object may suggest additions which can be put in necessary relation to it, objective motifs which, if the artist is fortunate, may fit into a slight gap in the formal structure as though they had belonged there to begin with. Thus the issue concerns not so much the presence of an object as the kind of object, what it looks like.

I can only hope that the layman who keeps looking for some favourite object in pictures, will gradually disappear from my surroundings, and that when he does come from time to time he will be no more than a ghost which can't help what it does. For a man knows only his own objective passions. And sometimes admittedly we are very pleased when a familiar face, as though of its own accord, emerges from a picture.

Why not?

I have admitted the justification of an objective concept in a picture and so obtained a new dimension.

I have named the formal elements singly and in their special context.

I have tried to show how they emerge from this context.

I have tried to explain their appearance in groups and their combination into figures, limited at first, then somewhat widespread.

Figures which may be called constructions in the abstract, but which may be named concretely: star, vase, plant, animal, head, man, etc. according to the association they have conjured up.

I began with the dimensions of the pictorial elements, such as line, tone value, and colour. Then the first constructive combination of these elements brought with it the dimension of form or, if you prefer, of the object. Now a further dimension is added, the dimension occupied by questions of content.

Certain proportions of line, certain combinations of tone values, certain colour harmonies always bring with them very definite and distinctive modes of expression.

The linear proportions, for example, may involve angles: for instance, angular zigzag movements, in contrast to a smooth horizontal line, strike resonances that contrast correspondingly.

From this ideal viewpoint, two linear figures, one characterised by firm cohesion, the other by loose dispersion, will produce a similar contrast.

Contrasting examples of expression in the realm of tone value are: broad use of all the tones from black to white, which suggests strength and full deep breaths, or limited use of either the upper light half of the scale or of the lower deep dark half,

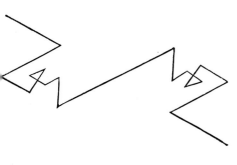

or of the medium shades round the grey – all of them weak from too much or too little light –

or hesitant twilight shades around the middle.

Again great contrast in content.

And what possibilities for variety of content are provided by colour combinations.

Colour as tone value, e.g. red in red, in other words the whole scale from no red to too much red, extended, or the same scale bounded.

Or the same in yellow (something quite different), or the same in blue. What contrasts!

Or: diametrically opposed colours, that is, changes from red to green, from yellow to violet, from blue to orange:

Each a subworld of the world of content.

Or: colour changes towards the segments of the circle, not touching the grey centre, but meeting in warmer or cooler greys.

What subtle variants on the above-mentioned contrasts!

Or: colour changes towards the circumference of the circle, from yellow through orange to red, or from red through violet to blue, or right across the whole circle.

How many steps there are between very slight shading and full-blooded colour harmony! What a perspective on the dimension of content!

Or, finally, passages through the whole of the colour order, including diametric grey, and even making use of the black-white scale.

Only in a new dimension can we go beyond these last possibilities. So we might now consider where to put the assorted colours. For every assortment has its own possibilities of combination.

And every figure, every combination, will have its particular constructive expression, every form its face, its physiognomy.

The pictures of objects look out at us, serene or severe, tense or relaxed, comforting or forbidding, suffering or smiling.

They look out at us in all the contrasts of the physical-physiognomic dimension; they can extend from tragedy to comedy.

But this is far from the end of the matter.

The forms, as I have often called these object figures, also have their own postures, which result from the way in which the selected groups have been put in motion. If an attitude of firm repose has been achieved it means either that the construction has provided for broad horizontals without elevation, or, where the elevation is appreciable, that the verticals have been treated conspicuously and consistently.

While retaining its repose this firm posture can also be somewhat more relaxed. The whole action can be transposed into an intermediate realm such as water or atmosphere, where there is no longer any vertical to dominate (as in swimming or gliding).

I say intermediate realm to contrast it with the first, wholly earthbound posture.

In the next example a new posture appears, which moves impetuously, and so transcends itself.

Impetuous gestures of this sort point clearly to the dimension of style. This is the beginning of roma ticism in its especially crass grandiloquent phase.

This gesture tries fitfully to rise above the earth; the next one succeeds, rising under the impulse of energies that triumph over the force of gravity.

If, finally, I can carry these earth-shunning forces onward, as far as the cosmic sphere, I shall be graduating from the stormy-pathetic style to the romanticism that opens up the universe.

Thus the static and dynamic aspects of pictorial mechanics provide a close parallel to the opposition between classicism and romanticism.

By this time our figure has gone through so many dimensions and dimensions of such importance that it would be inappropriate to keep calling it construction.

From now on we shall allow it the resounding name of composition.

As far as the dimensions are concerned, we shall content ourselves with these rich possibilities.

I should now like to consider the dimensions of the object in a new light and try to show why the artist often arrives at what seems to be an arbitrary 'distortion' of natural forms. First of all, he does not set such store by natural forms as do the many realists who criticise. He sets less store by these realities, because it is not in these finished forms that he sees the crux of the natural creative process. He is more concerned with the formative powers than with the finished forms.

He is a philosopher, perhaps without exactly wanting to be one. And while he does not optimistically declare this world to be the best of all possible worlds, or believe it to be so bad that it is unfit to be taken as a model, he nevertheless says to himself:

In its present form it is not the only world possible!

Accordingly, he looks inside the finished forms that nature sets before his eyes.

The deeper he looks, the easier it becomes for him to extend his view from today to yesterday. And in place of a finished image of nature, the crucial image of creation as genesis imprints itself on him.

It dawns on him that the process of world creation cannot, at this moment, be complete.

He extends it from past to future, gives genesis duration.

And he goes further.

Standing on earth, he says to himself: This world has looked different and in time to come it will look different again.

And saying this he means: Entirely different forms may well have arisen on other stars. Such journeying along the paths of natural creation is an excellent school of form.

It can move the artist profoundly and, once moved, he will be sure to care for the free development of his own form production.

In view of all this, the artist must be forgiven if he looks on the present stage of his particular phenomenal world as accidentally caught in time and space, if it strikes him as absurdly limited compared to the more profound, more mobile world of his vision and feeling.

Is it not true that even the relatively tiny step of a glance through the microscope discloses images that we should all declare to be fantastic and far-fetched if, unequipped to understand them, we ran across them by accident.

If Mr X were to see these same images reproduced in a popular magazine, he would cry out indignantly: 'You expect me to believe that such forms exist in nature? Why, it's just bad art!'

Does the artist concern himself with microscopy? History? Palaeontology?

Only for purposes of comparison, only with a view to mobility. He is not interested in a scientific check on fidelity to nature.

But only in freedom.

A freedom that does not lead to set phases of development, exactly as they once occurred or some day will occur in nature, or as they might (one day demonstrably perhaps) occur on other planets,

but rather a freedom that demands to be mobile in the same way that great nature itself is mobile.

From prototype to archetype.

It is the presumptuous artist who gets stuck somewhere along the way. The chosen artists are those who dig down close to the secret source where the primal law feeds the forces of development.

What artist would not like to live where the central organ of all space-time motion, call it brain or heart of creation as you will, activates all functions? In the womb of nature, in the primal ground of creation, where the secret key to all things lies hidden?

But it is not the place for all men. Let each man go where his heartbeat leads him.

Our antipodes of yesterday, the impressionists, were perfectly right to live with the trailing vines and underbrush of everyday appearances. But our pounding heart drives us down, deep down to the primordial underground.

What springs from this journey downward, whether it is called dream, idea, fancy, shall be taken seriously only if it ties in with the appropriate means to form a work of art. Then curiosities become realities, the realities of art, which make life a little wider than it ordinarily seems to be. For they not only put a certain amount of spirit into reproducing things seen, but make secret vision visible.

1924/1934/U 19: *Botanical theatre*.
Oil on wood.
Example of a work of broad scope extending
through the dimensions of 'elementary object, in
content and style'. This work was produced
over the period from 1924 to 1934, which includes
the highly productive years at the Bauhaus and
at the Düsseldorf Academy.

**'Energies of form-creating nature. Natural
growth.'** (Schematic representations.)
'Growth is the progressive movement of matter,
accreting round a nucleus.'
[1] unilateral progressive growth of a line.
[2] influence of the line: impulsions in one or two
directions. Broadening with different
structure and density.
[3] Productive increase. Influence of the line as
metamorphosis (change of form) of the linear
limit. Inner or outer energies, according to accent.
[4] Productive growth of the line in the sense of
bilateral amplification or progressive
refinement of the representation of movement.
Regular or irregular broadening of the line,
growth, extension.
[5] External, spatial emphasis. Productive increase
of energies starting from the linear limit.
'Growth is not only a quantitative striving for
elevation, but a spread of energies and
transformation of substances on all sides.'
[6] Energies in two directions (movement and
countermovement combined). Graduated density
of movement or distension (rejuvenation) with
graduated accentuation.

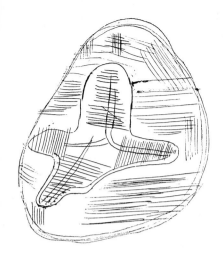

Example, showing the cross-section of a plant.
Cf. the cross-sections of a calla lily on p.60.
In contrast to the study from nature, we have
here a spatio-plastic interpenetration of two
different scales (projection of two forms into a
higher unity).

'With the appropriate pictorial means', I have said. For this is the point where it is decided whether pictures will be born, or something else. And here the character of the pictures is also determined.

Our tormented times have no doubt produced a good deal that is confusing, though we may still be too close to judge. But among artists, even the youngest, one effort seems gradually to be gaining ground:

The cultivation of these pictorial elements, their purification and their use in the pure state.

The legend about the childishness of my drawing must have started with those of my linear compositions in which I tried to combine a concrete representation, let us say a man, with a pure use of the linear element.

If I had wished to represent the man 'as he is', I should have required so bewildering a tangle of lines that a pure treatment of the element would have been out of the question; there would only have been an unrecognisable blur.

Besides, I have no desire to show this man as he is, but only as he might be.

In this way, perhaps, I am able to benefit from an association between philosophy and pure craftsmanship.

And this applies to the use of all the formal elements, including colour; we must avoid the slightest trace of blurring.

So much for the supposed untrue colouring of modern art.

As you can see from this 'childish' example, I engage in the partial processes: I also draw.

I have tried pure drawing; I have tried painting in pure tone values; in colour I have tried all the partial operations suggested by my exploration of the colour circle. Thus I have worked out a number of different types of painting: in coloured tone values, in complementary colours, in many colours, and in full colour.

Always combined with the more subconscious dimensions of the picture.

I have also tried every possible synthesis of two types. Combining and again combining, but always, as far as possible, cultivating the pure element.

Sometimes I dream of a work of vast scope, spanning all the way across element, object, content, and style.

This is sure to remain a dream, a vague possibility, but it is good to think of it now and then.

Nothing can be rushed. Things must grow, they must grow upward, and if the time should ever come for the great work, so much the better.

We must go on looking for it.

We have found parts, but not the whole.

We still lack the ultimate strength, for there is no culture to sustain us.

But we are looking for a culture. We have begun in the Bauhaus.

We have begun with a community to which we give everything we have.

We cannot do more.

1940/x 1: *Eyes in the landscape*. **Oil.**
Variable point of view combined with
static-dynamic synthesis.

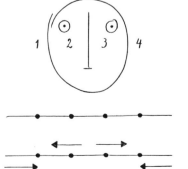

'Shifting standpoint and viewpoint.

Several viewpoints and connection between
stages 1, 2, 3, 4 (*ad lib.*)

Given: 'an "active harmony" (off-centre) and
balance through countermovement.'

96

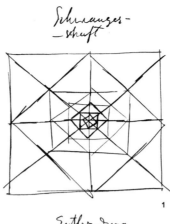

Schwangerschaft

Entbindung

1

The 'product' in the centre
(Internal construction) = Pregnancy [1].
Subtraction from the whole, or 'delivery'
$(1 - \frac{1}{4} = \frac{3}{4})$ [2].

2

In subtractive configuration the complete form with its internal construction is the minuend. The part emphasised as internal construction is the subtrahend. The difference is what is left of the whole.

The delivery, identical with the movement of an internal part, is a sporadic axial movement determined by the outside of the basic form [2].

Subdivision of the child on the basis of the complete construction of two compensating generative circles [3].

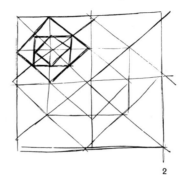

3

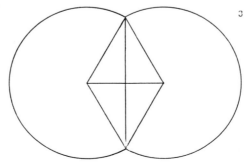

4

Subdivision of the child [4]:

1 Elementary components of the left-
   hand circle
2 Elementary components of the right-
   hand circle
3 Secondary components of both circles

I shall begin with a brief clarification of concepts. First, the meaning of analysis. The term is most frequently applied to chemical analysis. A certain compound, for example, is widely sold because of its excellent effects. The manufacturer's commercial success arouses the curiosity of other manufacturers and they send a sample of the product to a chemist for analysis. He must proceed methodically in order to break the product into its ingredients. To solve the riddle.

In another case a food or beverage is harmful to the health. Again the chemist is called in to disclose the harmful ingredients. In both cases the given is a whole consisting of various unknown parts; the problem is to find the ingredients.

In our business the motives for analysis are naturally different. We do not undertake analyses of works because we want to copy them or because we suspect them. We investigate the methods by which another has created his work, in order to set ourselves in motion. This approach should save us from regarding a work of art as something rigid, something fixed and unchanging. Exercises of this kind will guard us against creeping up to a finished product hoping to pick off what is most striking, and to make off with it.

One particular kind of analysis is the examination of a work with a view to the stages of its coming-into-being.[1] This kind I call the analysis of 'genesis'. The first book of Moses, concerned with the creation of the world, is called Genesis. It tells what God created on the first day, on the second day, etc. The total world that surrounds us is articulated in terms of history.

We are artists, practical craftsmen, and it is only natural that in this discussion we should give priority to matters of form. But we should not forget that before the formal beginning, or to put it more simply, before the first line is drawn, there lies a whole prehistory: not

*Pictorial analyses in the text:
Towards a theory of formation, see p.21.
Correct functional emphasis on the organs: pp.343–55.

only man's longing, his desire to express himself, his outward need, but also a general state of mind (whose direction we call philosophy), which drives him from inside to manifest his spirit in one place or another.

I emphasise this point to avoid the misconception that a work consists only of form. But what must be stressed even more at this point is that the most exact scientific knowledge of nature, of plants, animals, the earth and its history, or of the stars, is of no use to us unless we have acquired the necessary equipment for representing it; that the most penetrating understanding of the way these things work together in the universe is useless to us unless we are equipped with the appropriate forms; that the profoundest mind, the most beautiful soul, are of no use to us unless we have the corresponding forms to hand.

Here we must forget about the isolated stroke of luck which may enable the dilettante just once to produce a successful work which puts the professional to shame. After these general preliminaries, I shall begin where pictorial form has to begin; with the point that sets itself in motion.

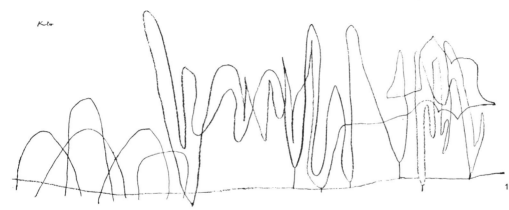

1934/N 17: *Avenue with trees.* Pencil.

11. Ways to form, how form comes into being, ways to the basic forms
Survey and orientation in regard to ideal formative elements
Essence and appearance of the formal elements

Regular and irregular projection
Measure and weight. Structural formation
Elements of a theory of structure. Rhythms and rhythmic structures

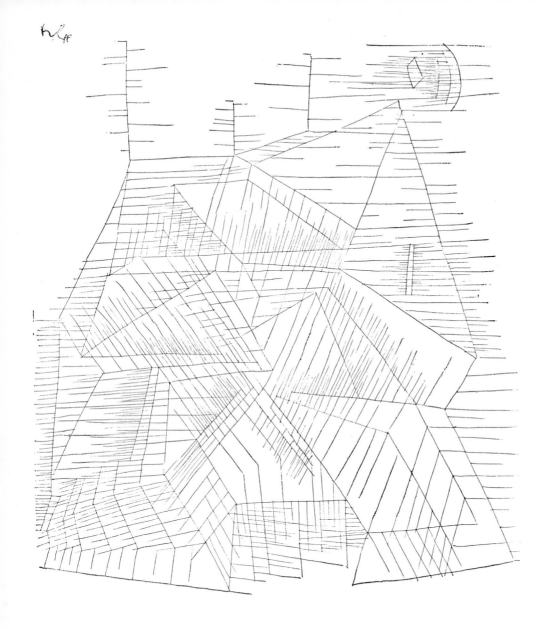

1929/o 4: *Rock*. Pen-and-ink.

102

1. Line: active, middle, passive

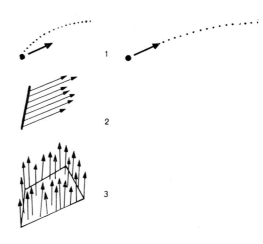

From point to line
The line as element
Linear and planar character

Shortly after application of the pencil, or any other pointed tool, a (linear-active) line comes into being. The more freely it develops, the clearer will be its mobility [1].

But if I apply a line, e.g. the edge of a black or coloured crayon, a plane is produced (at first and when the freedom of movement is very limited) [2].

If we had a medium that made it possible to move planes in a similar way, we should be able to inscribe an ideal three-dimensional piece of sculpture in space [3].

But I am afraid that is utopian.

For the present then let us content ourselves with the most primitive of elements, the line. At the dawn of civilisation, when writing and drawing were the same thing, it was the basic element. And as a rule our children begin with it; one day they discover the phenomenon of the mobile point, with what enthusiasm it is hard for us grown-ups to imagine. At first the pencil moves with extreme freedom, wherever it pleases.
But once he begins to look at these first works, the child discovers that there are laws which govern his random efforts. Children who continue to take pleasure in the chaotic are, of course, no artists; other children will soon progress towards a certain order. Criticism sets in. The chaos of the first play-drawing gives way to the beginning of order. The free motion of the line is subordinated to anticipation of a final effect; cautiously the child begins to work with a very few lines. He is still primitive.
But one can't remain primitive for long. One has to discover a way of enriching the pitiful result, without destroying or blurring the simple, intelligible plan. It becomes necessary to establish a relation between things of first importance and those which are subsidiary.

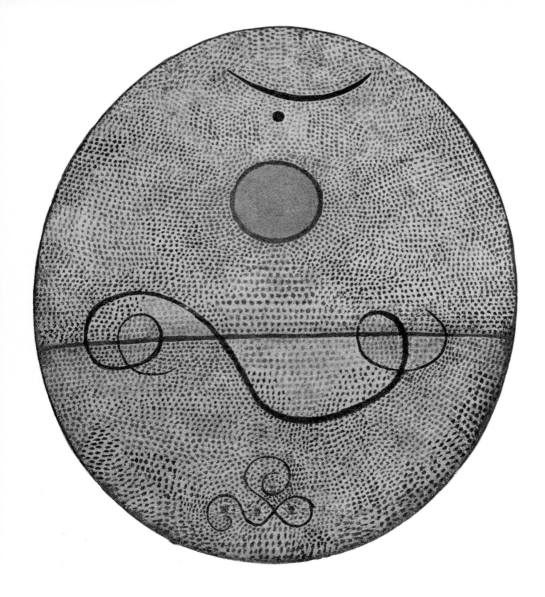

1932/k 9: *Tendril*. Oil.

Linear-active

From point to line. The point is not dimensionless but an infinitely small planar element, an agent carrying out zero motion, i.e. resting. Mobility is the condition of change. Certain things have primordial motion. The point is cosmic, a primordial element. Things on earth are obstructed in their movement; they require an impetus. The primordial movement, the agent, is a point that sets itself in motion (genesis of form). A line comes into being. The most highly-charged line is the most authentic line because it is the most active.

In all these examples the principal and active line develops freely. It goes out for a walk, so to speak, aimlessly for the sake of the walk.

● Dynamic repose Dynamic movement. The point seen in dynamic terms, as an agent.

1

Simple linear motion, self-contained. Free line a–b [1].
Free line a–b, companion line a_1–b_1. (The melody in Fig.1: accompanied) [2, 3, 4, 5].

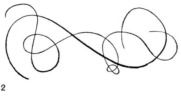

2

3

4

5

Free line making detours [6, 7, 8, 9].

6

7

1927/D 9: *Difficult journey through O.* Pen-and-ink.

8

9

Two 'interpenetrating' lines

Two secondary lines, moving round an imaginary main line [10, 11, 12, 13]

10

11

12

13

Dividual-individual, connected by rhythmic articulation

107

1937/R 11: *Harbour with sailboats*. Oil.

Active line

This new line on the other hand

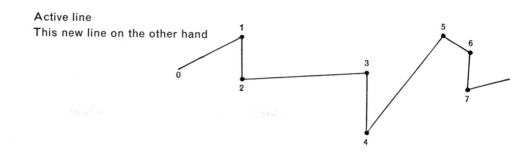

is short of time, wants to get to 1, then to 2, then to 3, etc. as quickly as possible. More like a series of appointments than a walk. This is shown by the straight stretches. But both the free and the hurrying line are purely active types.

The linear tension of the straight stretches (most active line) is discharged between the points of tension lying on the path. (Dualism = static. •————————• The straight lines are the quintessence of the static.)

Linear-medial

Neither line nor plane, but some sort of middle thing between the two. At the beginning it is linear, the movement of a point; it ends by looking like a plane. A medial line: planar effect obtained by circumscribed lines.

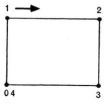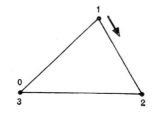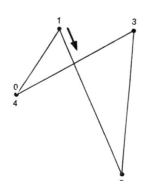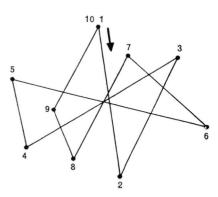

The line determined by few points. Time is of the essence.

In these examples the hurrying line circumscribes plane figures like the triangle and square.

The energies that move a line are the result of forces working in different directions. Tension is connective.

Cf. p.368, 1927/i 1: *Many-coloured lightning.* Oil.

Variation on 1926/A 4: *Embraced*. Drawing.

Plane formation with medial lines in a structure
of a higher order.
Point-line movement = planar impression.
The concentric design (Fig.3, p.111) is taken
as a norm.
'In displacements representing deviation from the
norm the centres move apart, the elementary
forms multiply and change, evenly or unevenly.'

A square stood on its corner moves into the dynamic realm, the tensions are diagonal.

The line circumscribes a circle
and an ellipse

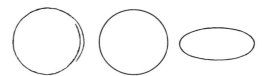

Taken as a line it has a soothing character and is without beginning or end. In an element-ary sense (taken as an action of the hand) it remains a line, but when it is completed the linear impression inevitably gives way to a planar impression. The mobile character disappears (no one looking at the disc of the moon will take it for a merry-go-round and want to go for a ride). It is replaced by a sense of perfect rest, especially in the case of the circle.

Linear-medial, planar-medial
in amplified,
composite examples

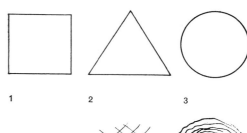

1   2   3

The straight line (as a progression
of points), quintessence of
the static [1, 2].
The circle (as a progression
of points), quintessence of the
dynamic [3].

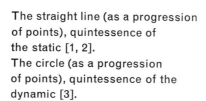
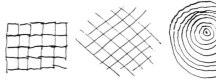

In this case the character
of the lines is wholly passive

We still see lines, but not linear acts; what we see are linear results of planar actions.
The line is not made but suffered.
What is this? a square.
How did it come into being? What are the underlying tensions?

Linear movement displaced 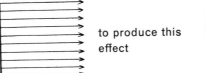 to produce this effect

It came into being when a line entered into a relation of tension with a parallel line and discharged this tension. The most general cause therefore is a reciprocal tension forced into two dimensions.
Result: a square, without accent, without emphasis. With horizontal emphasis, the square becomes

a recumbent rectangle

The linear movement rotated 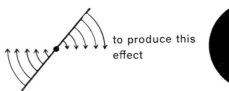 to produce this effect

Plane formation by progressive linear rotation round a point. In linear-passive development the line operates as a planar element; and the impression therefore is planar. Any suggestion of a line is a left over, and is suffered (passive lines, active plane formation).

The triangle came into being when a point entered into a relation of tension with a line and, following the command of its Eros, discharged this tension.
The tension between point and line is characteristic of the triangle.

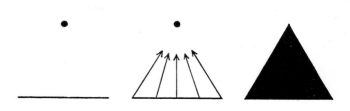

In a contrary direction to this brief account of the line runs the account of the plane contained in it. When the line was active, it created divisions into imaginary planes. Meanwhile the planar character thrust itself forward and became active when the line was designated as passive. The plane is pure bred, the tranquil element.

[1]Note in the manuscript: pictorial examples of 'linear-active', 'linear-passive', and 'lines of both characters':
Linear-active: 1921/112: *About the fate of two girls*. Transfer drawing. Grohmann, p.392.
Also: *Precursors* and *Mass prayer*.
Linear-active painting: Jawlensky: *Head of Christ*.
For linear-passive: 1919/68: *With the three* (*three part time*). Watercolour. Giedion, p.105, Grohmann, p.389.
With elements of both characters, linear-active and planar active:
1919/156: *Composition with B*. Oil.
Colour reproduction: Giedion, p.97, Grohmann, p.390.
Similar example: 1919/235: *Picture with rooster and grenadier* (*Gallus militaricus*). Oil.
The picture titles were written in the margin at a later date as visual aids for the students.

But if it becomes mobile,  it takes on a linear character.

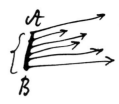

The farther the line A–B progresses, the thinner becomes the plane it describes in relation to its length, until in the end we may think of A and B as coincident, which takes us back to the active line.[1]

113

1938/g 10: *Dancing from fright*. Watercolour.

Energies of both characters: linear-active and
planar-active (linear-passive) in equilibrium.
Linear and planar fields clearly separated. The
lines dynamise the accented motion of the planes
(dynamic accentuation by rotation).

114

The basic formal differences: active, middle, passive. We must distinguish three characters:

I. a linear character:

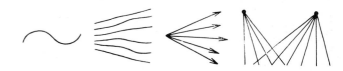

Linear-active – planar passive.
In 'active' the point goes to work, and the effect is linear in keeping with the point progression. Linear energies (tensions between active lines) result in passive planes, as side effects.

II. a middle character:

Middle character: point-line progression, planar impression.
In linear-'medial' (middle) the point progression leads indirectly, by way of the contour to a planar impression. Linear energies, 'medial' (middle) lines and planar effect.

III. a planar character:

Planar active – linear-passive.
In linear-'passive' the line works as a planar element. Active plane, linear side effect (passive lines).
I. and III. are main, primary characters; II. (the middle ground) is intermediate, a hybrid.

1930/x 4: *Six species*. Watercolour.

Analysis and synthesis of differences

In connection with the synthesis of active, middle, passive.
cf. 1932/z 19: *The Step*. Oil on burlap, p.434.
1932/13: *Poison* Watercolour. Giedion, p.162
Grohmann, p.399.

From the linear standpoint this character is   active

this one middle

this one passive

From the planar standpoint this character is   passive

Thus the standpoints are
diametrically opposed
to one another, meeting only in
the medial zone.

this one middle

this one active

116

The genesis of composite forms (interpenetration or mesh)
A new type of structure arises when the parts do not lie side by side but overlap.
The nature of such structure is characterised by the word interpenetration. One part penetrates the other, or the two parts penetrate each other.
The relation between the parts: no contact, or contact in point, in line, in plane, in space.
The situation of the parts: apart, grouped but separate, touching, or interpenetrating.

Side by side, or individual [1].
Circular planes with linear interpenetration (variant: interlocking) [2].

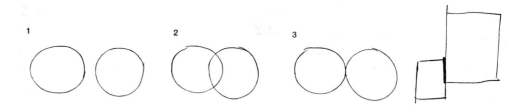

One-dimensional contact (contact in point or line, balanced or unbalanced) [3].
Composite form with planar contact. Two-dimensional contact in the plane. More or less interpenetration (planar penetration). The same loss from both sides [4].

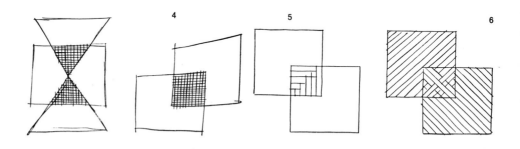

Interpenetration and division of the common territory on the basis of the inner constructive relations and elementary formal factors [5].
Overlapping or mixture in the passive realm. Interpenetration as organisation of differences to form a unity [6].

117

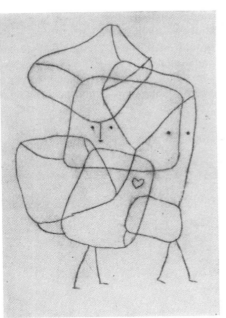  

1930/a 7: *Twins*. Drawing.
1930/w 8: *Twins*. Oil on canvas.
1930/e 8: *Brother and sister*. Oil on canvas.

Result of several partial actions:
1930/w 8: *Twins*. Oil on canvas.
Here Klee notes: 'Additive relations: twins, triplets, etc.
Productive relations: mother and child.'

Studies in movement:

1   2

Planar results from both kinds of linear progression [1].
Movement in one direction on the basis of a norm [2].
(Examine the way. Follow it back to the gentle start. Compare the action with the scene of action.)

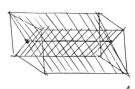

3   4

The mesh of the planes indicates the body-content. Diagonals suggest intermediate positions [3, 4].
The mesh should be interpreted as a summation of all three kinetic processes (in the three directions). Tension between plane and counterplane is the quickest way to form bodies.
We must also consider the transparent representation of tone values. They suppress the values of frontal planes, so eliminating them and letting us look in freely. Then space is formed in space.

Analytic representation as partial action.

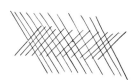

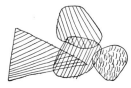

Tension between two directions of motion, plane and counterplane.
The greater energy wins out.
Further possibilities:
Penetration as polyphonic intersection of different planar structures and directions of motion.
Structures of similar or dissimilar form, which stand close together, touch, interpenetrate, or intermesh, while one absorbs the other.

Active, middle, passive: Summary[1]

[1]*Cf.* pp.435–441.

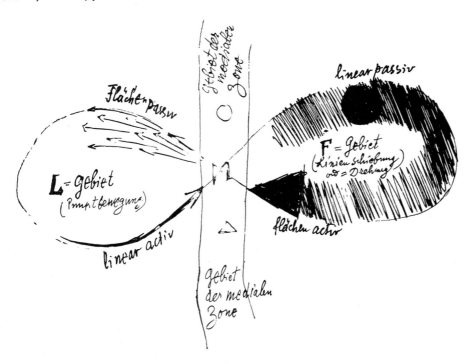

Linguistic analogy:

Active: I fell: The man felled the tree with the axe.

Middle: I fall: The tree fell with the man's last stroke.

Passive: I am felled: The tree lay felled.

At the end of the exercise: Attempts at composition with these three elements.
L (linear territory) and P (planar territory) – here clarity prevails.
M (middle territory) blurred.

Crossed-out footnote: 'ML (medial-linear) and MP (medial-planar), new hybrid, secondary blurring'.

Preliminary remarks: The violin as finished form, as a work of art, as an independent personality (not a machine). The interpretations, for example, of Picasso, Braque, and the present-day Paris school.

Analytic beginnings suggested for those who are not too sure of themselves; afterwards, free composition with the acquired forms.

"More emphasis on violins as violins' means: their structure, their inner nature, their essence rather than their visual appearance.

Tacit wish: the freest possible compositions, more emphasis on violins as violins.[1] Results at first predominantly analytic.

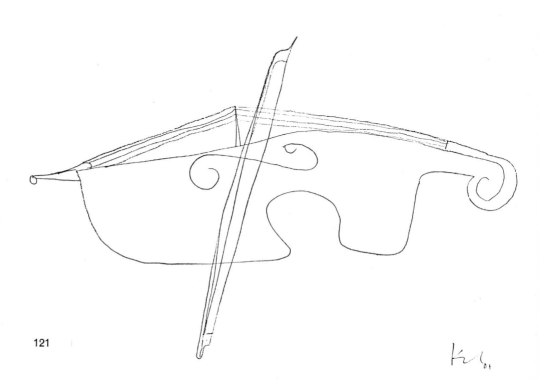

1939/w 11: *Violin and bow*. Pencil drawing.

1937/P 17: *Peach harvest.* Colour.

**Converging and
diverging lines
The dimensional signs
Perspective construction
of space**

Convergence: Two weeks ago we took up, among other things, the free line. I chose as an example a kind of line suggesting a restful walk without definite aim or purpose. This line had something restful, harmonious about it; if used as a theme in a composition, it would have favoured a treatment with accompanying forms. In musical terms, it would then have suggested a folk-song rather than a more elaborate form. And actually we added only companion forms or substitute forms to this resting line:

Companion forms, of an absolute converging character [1]
of an effective converging character [2]

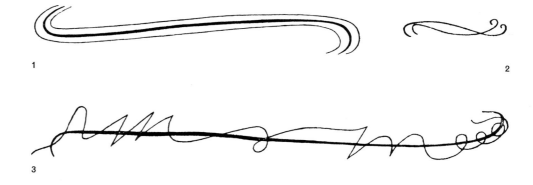

1   2

3

or effectively converging, while the companion line retains its independence [3].
Rather like the path of a man with a dog running free.

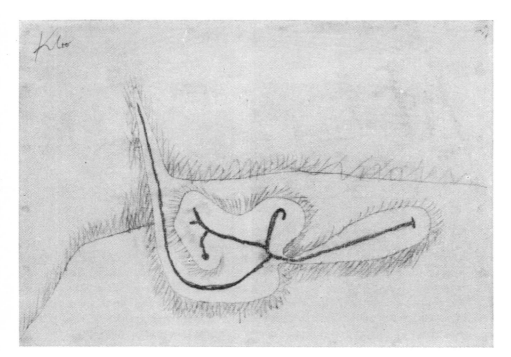

1937/N 3: *Germinating.* Pencil drawing.

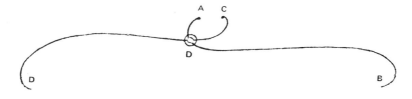

Two diverging lines **A–B** and **C–D** with a point of intersection **D**.

Divergence

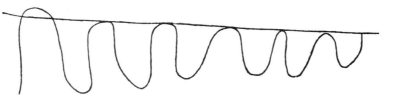

Two diverging lines with two points of intersection

The best way to illustrate the essential difference between this new structure and the previous examples of convergence is to consider each line as the path of a man. In the previous examples we may speak of friendship; the companions never part. But in this new, divergent example we see the companion only once, running briefly across our path at point D.

124

The dimensional signs

Concerning the development of a point into a line, of a line into a plane, of a plane into a body

Point. The point as primordial element, all-pervasive.

Line. A point discharges its tension towards another point. The causal principle is the will inherent in reciprocal tension. Essence of a dimension. One-dimensional element.

Plane. Tension between line and line results in a plane. Essence of two dimensions. Two-dimensional element.

Tension

Discharge of tension

from point to point = line

from line to line = plane

Body. The line moves and produces the plane; the plane moves and the body comes into being.

Essence of three dimensions. Three-dimensional element.

The cube is a balanced synthesis of three definite dimensions and as such the normative symbol of corporeality.

The movements summarised:

Characteristic of the dimension behind-in front (the third dimension) is the increasing progression of points, lines, and surfaces. In the point the opposite ends of the pictorial elements are still effective; less so in the intermediary stages. They need more room before they can be weighed or measured by the eye, or critically appraised.

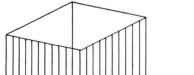

Body, three dimensions

Plane,
two dimensions

Primal element

Line, one dimension

125

Body

Body
two-dimensional,
marginal or middle
(body-limit)

Body
two-dimensional.
External-material,
active-planar
(outer surface
of a body)

Body
three-dimensional
(body-outward)

Spatial

Spatial
two-dimensional
encompassing
(activated passive)

Exotopic
encompassing
(without body)

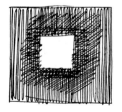

Spatial
three-dimensional
and transparent

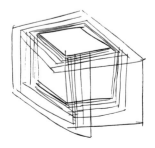

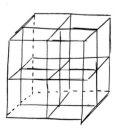

126

Inward

Inward
two-dimensional
(content)

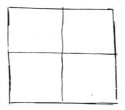

Most-inward
(centre)

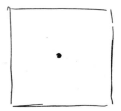

Inward
two-dimensional,
inward
representation
of outer planes

In contrast
to the inside and
outside of a body

Inward
three-dimensional,
body inside

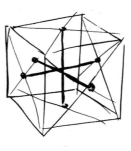

Purely inward,
body innermost

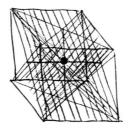

The inward
plays the dominant part
The whole inward territory
designated by the word 'content'

127

1923/179: *Landscapely-physiognomic*. Gouache.

Notation by Klee: 'Physiognomics:
a) Pure function of vision
b) Connection with the cerebral functions
of feeling.'

The combination of the bodily, spatial and
inward factors of the basic forms leads to
synthesis, that is, an interpenetration of space,
body, and thing. The influence of the lines and
planar forms suggests productive increase and
decrease, outer and inner energies, growth and
change. Interpenetration of endotopic and
exotopic factors.

On exotopic interpenetration, of space and body, *cf*
1923/176: *Cosmic flora*, p.350.
1924/1934/U 19: *Botanical theatre*, p.94.
1926/R 2: *Spiral flowers*, p.377.
1930/e 10: *Ad marginem*, p.74.
1931/m 7: *Figure*, p.383.
1931/w 18: *Landscapely-physiognomic*, p.66.

A theme treated in different ways

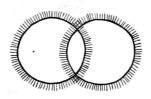

Interpenetration with exotopic

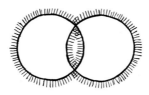

and endotopic accent

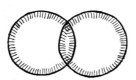

The common ground
treated endotopically, the individual
ground with exotopic accent

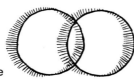

Interpenetration with alternating
endotopic and exotopic
accent (in relief)

 outside-inside   outside-inside

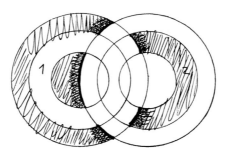

Interpenetration of space and volume:
(Variations on the treatment of relief)
Variants: 'Meshed or intertwined'.
Organisation and unification of
variations:
Reciprocal interpenetration, equal
parts unequally accented

129

1927: *Little jester in trance*. Oil print, one of three versions, 1927/169–171.
1927/i 3: *Figurine 'The jester'*. Oil on canvas.
1929/n 6: *(Little) jester in trance*. Oil on canvas.

Klee in a remark to his students:
'The jester in a state of trance might be taken as an example of superimposed instant views of movement.'
When an independent movement is added, the elementary forms change and multiply evenly or unevenly. The accent of their space-body interpenetration changes accordingly.

Concentric mesh
in harmonious interpenetration.
Forms generated by the superimposition
and mixing of 1 and 2.
With displacement
(shift of centre)
or change of position
the mixed forms are modified

Alternating
endotopic and exotopic accent
on 1 and 2

Inner linking of the two in free variation.
Interpenetration of space and body.
Basic possibilities:
Combinations of identical forms,
which are related,
touching,
which interpenetrate,
which are meshed with one another,
one of which absorbs the other,
a) in constructive-logical connection,
b) in a partly free selection.
(Metalogical, sometimes psychological,
allowing deeper spiritual reaction)

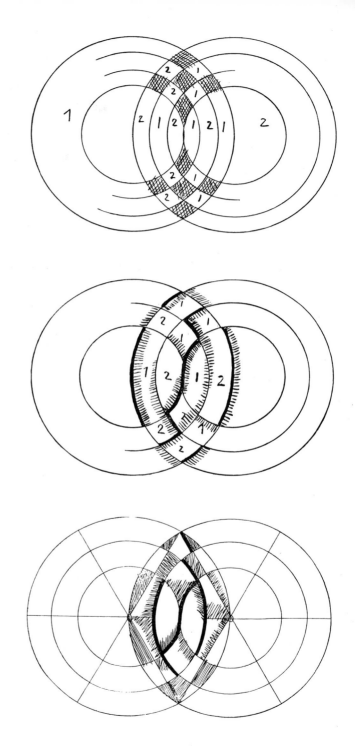

131

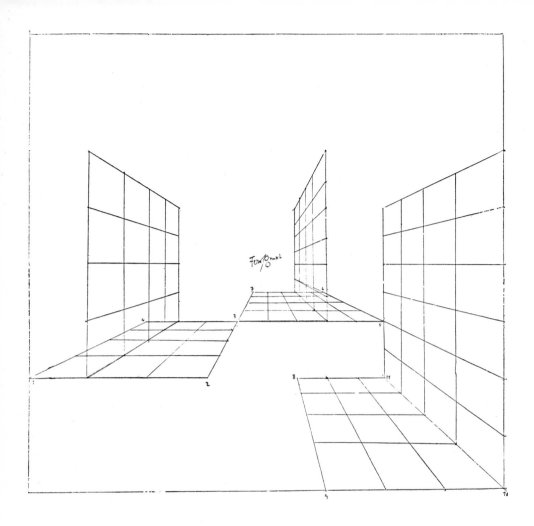

Combined operations on horizontal planes of different heights and on vertical planes variously oriented as to left and right.

Perspective

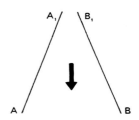

Let us imagine two railway tracks [1]. There is something very misleading about this (?) For in reality these lines are quite divergent. If the rails keep moving farther apart, the train is bound to jump the track. Or suppose they take the opposite direction [2].

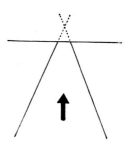

Rails that are going to cross somewhere up ahead are almost more alarming (?)
What is going on? Well, the fact is we have suddenly passed from the planar to the spatial realm, to the third dimension. We are doing perspective.
In our last meeting we observed to our regret that we have no three-dimensional script, that although we can move points into lines,

or lines into planes

 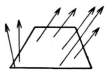

we cannot, with any visual effect, move planes to form volumes.
Consequently we must help ourselves with perspective.
But this will not be complicated or difficult if we stick to the essentials, and it is well worthwhile to clarify the underlying phenomena.

133

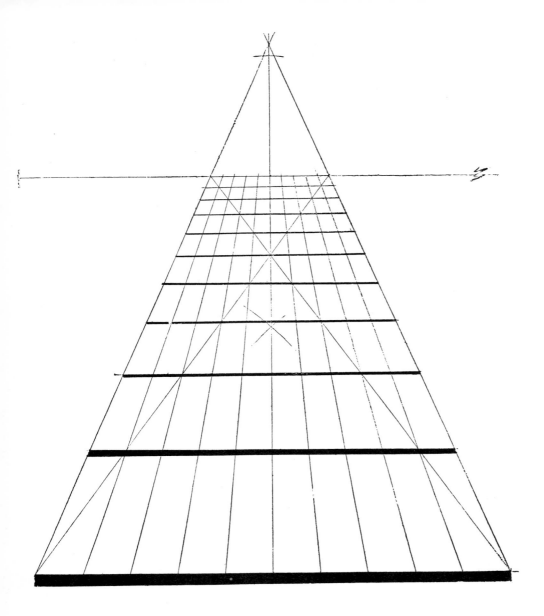

Construction of a natural progression that depends on length and thickness of lines and the spaces between them.
(Possible amplification: scramble the lines while preserving their length and thickness.)

So these are railway tracks. Railway tracks lie on sleepers. How shall I represent this? If I were a surveyor or a map-maker, and I had to draw tracks on a plane, my picture would show two parallel lines.

Two parallel lines seen at right angles.

Cross-gradation. The sleepers would have to be placed at regular intervals.

The two parallel lines shift with a change in our visual angle. If the form of the space between two lines is left open, something else happens.

With cross-gradation.

Seen laterally from above with perspective progression towards the horizon (intermediate position).

Represented in spatial terms, this diagram looks quite different. As most Europeans know, the distance between the sleepers increases perceptibly towards the viewer.

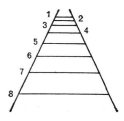

Natural progression, seen frontally.

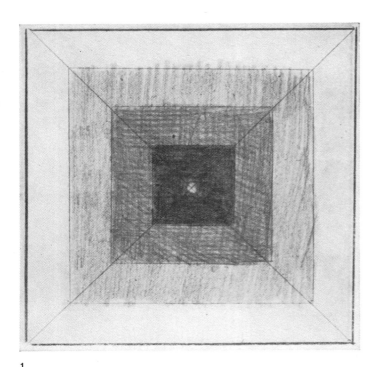

1

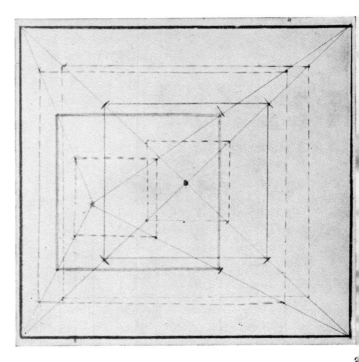

2

3

Construction of a space with displaced centre

Normal relations between centre and nuclear strata (density) [1].
Displaced centre and effects on the nuclear strata (density) [2].
(The abnormally divided square, dominated by the abnormal centre, presents entirely different proportions.)
Every change is based on extension or density and results in functional changes. The displacement of the centre brought out by tone value [3].

136

The front of the locomotive is at right angles to the plane between the rails [1] (thus at the start we have projected the greatest spatial elevation). We can now imagine new angles and planes in this new, third dimension (thus, for example the new plane in Fig.3 is at right angles to the plane in Fig.2).

In the end we manage to construct a space into which we can march erect [4, 5].

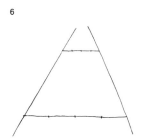

1

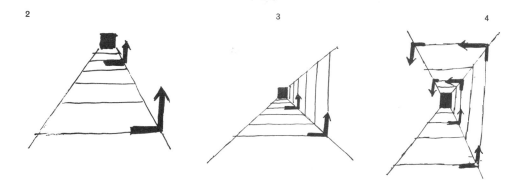

2   3   4

Construction in three dimensions

Lengthwise gradation: Let us start once again from the notion of the rails but restricting ourselves to one sleeper lying far back and another that is close to us; in other words, to just two sleepers. We divide these sleepers into a number of equal parts; here for example, we intersect them at three points. A nearby and a distant sleeper divided into equal parts seen from the front [6].

In this way we pass from crosswise to lengthwise gradation; we see before us the perspective of a ground-plane with five parallel lines on it [7].

Now which line is most conspicuous? The middle line of course (from two to two). And in what capacity? As the **vertical** [8]. (Perspective progression with emphasis on the direction perpendicular to the sleepers.)

What does this vertical mean? It means that we ourselves have stood where it stands. (The frontal plumbline.)

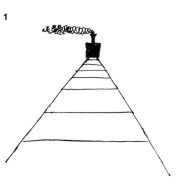

5

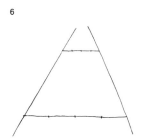

6   7   8

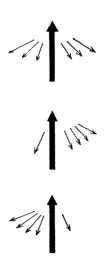

1927/m 7: *Church and castle.* Pen-and-ink drawing.

The shifting vertical, with shift of viewpoint (position of the eye) from left to right.

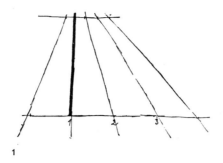

1

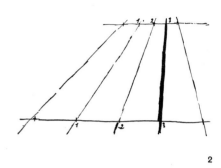

2

3   4   5

If we now take a step to the left, the vertical will shift to Point 1 and the ground-plane will take on this form in projection:
Position of the observer shifted leftward [1].
Whereas if the observer situates himself at 3, this new diagram will result.
Position of observer shifted to the right [2].
In material or terrestrial statics the shortest way runs vertically from an original 'front' position to a definitely marked-out horizontal line in the distance. The vertical (as plumb-line) means the correct way.

6

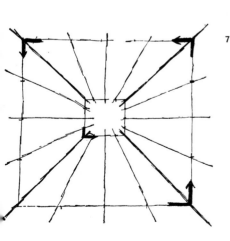

7

If I travel over a plane of this kind ↑ the vertical stays vertical as long as I do not leave the line, while the other lines radiate towards me [3].
But if I leave the line, the picture runs off in the opposite direction [4, 5].
This brings us, incidentally, to the phenomenon of countermovement.
Now let us stand still and proceed as before in connection with the crosswise gradation [6]. The following diagram results [7].
Again we have a space into which we can enter. I should like you to pay special attention to the side walls. On the ground-plane it was the vertical that assumed special importance; here it is the horizontal.

Figs.3, 4, 5 (p.139) refer to the movement of the 'I' deviating from the vertical. The position of the 'I' changes to left and right, thus displacing the visual point. Seen from the vertical, this shift of the visual point results in movement [4] and countermovement [5].

Klee used his conclusions from the problems of perspective as a basis for the figuration of movement. In those of his pictures that seem to work with a central perspective, he does not content himself with one visual point (i.e. a single axis of symmetry and a simple horizon).

There is a shift of visual point, a 'shifting viewpoint'.

The straight lines have different lower terminal points, some of which are situated outside the picture. In regard to this Klee notes: ' "I" far away, "I" not so close. "I" very close.'

The eye follows various stimulus points, on the basis of which the space is limited by points of varying distance. 'The shifting viewpoint', he notes elsewhere, and the connection between stages 1, 2, 3, 4. In the end let the viewpoint pass out of the frame.'

In *Uncomposed objects in space*, the upward and downward views of bodies do not follow central perspective, but are shown in motion from the bottom upward by means of a shifting viewpoint. At the same time there is a deviation from the vertical axis, both to left and right. Through this compensation of movement and countermovement, a compositional balance, i.e. a symmetrical impression, is created.

From the standpoint of central perspective (taken as a norm) movement produces a distortion which is compensated by a countermovement.

Cf. 'The Receptive Process', Theory of Pictorial Form, pp.357–365.

A prolongation of the straight lines to their points of intersection shows that several viewpoints are present. Concerning this specific picture, Klee notes: 'The further down the imaginary projection lines touch higher dimensions, the better.' The points of intersection should lie outside the pictorial space.

1929/c 4: *Uncomposed objects in space*.
Watercolour.

The horizontal. What does this horizontal mean? The answer will soon be apparent.

This also explains the following remark about central perspective (p.149): 'The value of the whole process lies solely in the possibility of checking: there is no merit to drawing in proper perspective; anyone can do it.' In the light of the rules for symmetrical composition *Uncomposed objects in space* is a deviation from the 'norm' (or canon). 'Composed objects' would strictly follow the norm, the constructive rule. *Cf.* 1921/24: *Perspective of room with occupants* (p.144) in which three main visual points can be found.

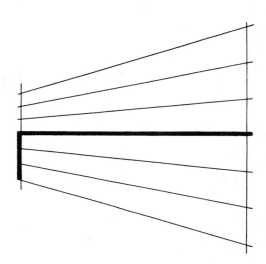

For a more detailed treatment of the problems see: J. Vonderlinn: *Parallelperspektive. Rechtwinklige und schiefwinklige Axonometrie.* Göschen Collection, 1914. Fully worked-out examples may be found in: G. Wolff: *Mathematik und Malerei*, 2nd edition. Mathemat.-physikal. Bibliothek, Vol.20–1. Teubner, Leipzig 1925. Walther Lietzmann, *Mathematik und Bildende Kunst.* Ferd. Hirt, Breslau 1931. All these works were in Paul Klee's library.

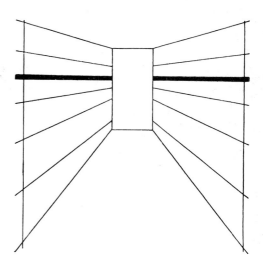

1928/p 7: *Little week-end house*. Oil.
The perspective viewpoints are rhythmically
arranged and the volumes are transparent.

'The deviation of the constructive-impressive
modes which take the place of ordinary
construction is based on a logical process.'
Subjective theory of space: combined operations
(multi-dimensional simultaneity of projections).
Projections in different positions, deviating from
pure central perspective (multi-dimensional
contacts and highly articulated structures).

Shifting viewpoint:
Contrasting viewpoints due to movement of
spectator [1].
Change in the relation between height and
horizon means:
lifted horizon, widened horizon [2].
Varying subjective height.
Alternation of downward and upward views.

Summary: Change of subjective height, visual
point variable to left and right. Movement and
countermovement lead to a balance of movement.
For amplification *cf.* the organic connections
between the principal forms of perspective and the
basic possibilities, pp.151–159.
Examples, see p.159.

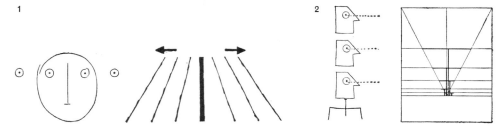

1

2

Within the space already known to us I have here built a second space whose upper surface is visible to the eye [1]. Hence we may speak more appropriately of a body than of a space contained within our visual field. For real spaces go beyond our field of vision (we are in them).

We have then a body that lets the eye look down on its upper surface.

The horizontal plane that our eye sees from above lies lower than our eye, below us [1].

In this case the body yields no view of its upper surface [2]. If we suppose it to be made of glass, it will permit a view of this surface from below. But a horizontal plane that can be seen from below is situated higher than our eye, it is above us [2].

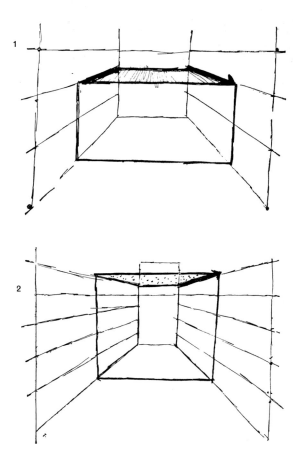

1921/24: *Perspective of room with occupants.*
Watercolour.

144

But in this third case something special happens. The eye cannot discern this surface as a surface either from above or below; it looks to us like a horizontal line.

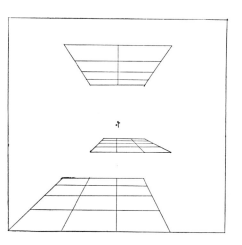

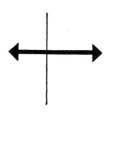

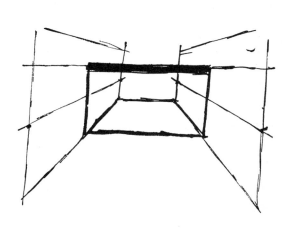

Operations with horizontal planes at different levels. (None in full width. One plus ¾ high, front section in symmetrical position. A second minus ¾ below, rear section displaced to right. A third minus ¾ below, front section displaced to left. Progression broken by cardinal limits.)'

This means that the body is exactly at the height of our eye. The horizontal is exactly at eye level. (If we want to be meticulous, we may add that the lengthwise and crosswise gradations coincide.)
But what is true of this horizontal plane, is also logically true of the connected horizontal line of the two side walls. These horizontal lines at eye level appear again as horizontals in perspective projection.

So we have the answer. 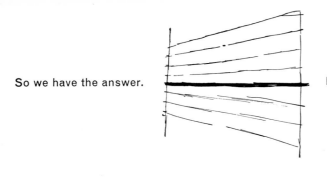 It is called 'eye level'.

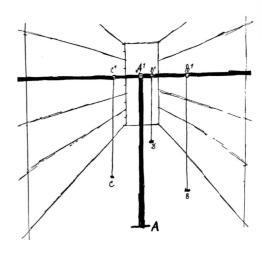

The man or possessor of the eye may now stand forward at A or farther back (at B, C, D); from any of these positions the phenomenon of the horizontal will develop (A^1, B^1, C^1, D^1). The horizontal is the connection between the points in space situated at eye level on the line of sight.

1929/m 3: *Evening in Egypt*. Watercolour.

146

We can conceive of a large plane defined by all these points from A^1 to D^1 (as shown above, we can never see this plane), the plane of the horizon. Or limiting ourselves to A^1, we can conceive of a large disc.

Horizontal: the horizon as appearance. Material (earthbound) statics or pure statics. 'Seen.'

Horizontal: 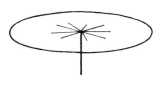 the horizon as idea. Ideal (cosmically conscious) statics or idealised statics. 'Conceived.'

Vertical and horizontal: This horizontal disc separates all visible space into an upper and a lower part. As if we were in a great round tin, consisting of the tin and of its cover.

This sign (vertical and horizontal) corresponds also to the human frame in reference to the attraction of the earth. We have an acute sense of the vertical that keeps us from falling; and if need be (in an emergency) we extend our arms to correct and counter-balance a mistake. In special cases we prolong the horizontal, as a tightrope walker does with his pole.

The vertical is the direct path from a frontal viewpoint to a distant horizontal laid out 'behind'.

The horizontal means eye level.

In material (earthbound) statics the relation between height and horizon varies. A 'raised horizon' is an extended horizon.

The raising of the eye level brings with it a raising of the horizontal:

standing

sitting

lying down with head raised
foot = horizon

147

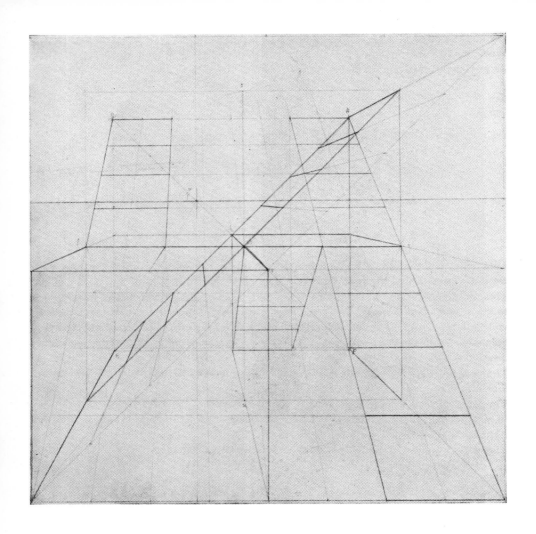

The scaffolding by the sea.
Transparent-perspective interpenetration of the horizontal and vertical planes and of planes in intermediate positions. Example from the section: 'Cubic plane combinations in intermediate positions.'

148

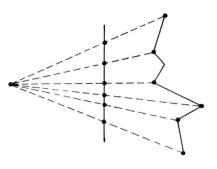

The questions of perspective we have broached and everything else that seems worth knowing on the subject can be checked or investigated with the help of a very simple apparatus. Fasten a glass disc in a vertical position and place it at eye level in front of the object to be projected. You observe with one eye, which must remain in a fixed position. You draw the essential lines of the object on the glass disc with ink or crayon.

If the glass is not vertical the lines will look distorted. Similar distortions are created by photographers who direct their cameras upward at an object whose perspective can easily be checked, e.g. a house.

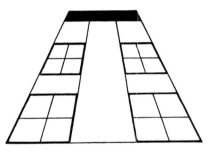

Such images are not even objectively or logically wrong; the lower windows are closer to the eye than the upper ones, hence broader, which for purposes of perspective means larger.

But at this point the human being puts in his veto, because he wants his horizontal and vertical fixed; otherwise he will totter and grow dizzy. It is not logically but physiologically wrong. The value of the whole process lies solely in the possibility of checking; there is no merit to drawing in proper perspective; anyone can do it. Additional examples: Van Gogh's perspective instrument. Hodler's 'carré'.

5 December 1921

Exercises:
Examples of balance in
drawing and tone value,
according to balanced structures in the
plane.[1]

'Balanced structures in the plane': planar composition of formal elements in a balanced relation to vertical and horizontal. Perspective elements may be used *cf.* 1924/39: *Houses in landscape*, p.186.

1932/v 11: *Small town*. Colour.

'The main tensions go from plane to counterplane;
the shortest way suffices for body formation.
The inside of the bodies remains amorphous.
The connection between the centres of a plane and
counterplane yields an inner body line
(a dimension); repetition of this connecting
movement ultimately results in three analogous
lines representing the body's three dimensions.'
Cf. the linear and planar interpretation of the
balance of forces, p.201.

3. Synthesis of spatio-plastic representation and movement

Irregular projection
Subjective theory of space
Shifting viewpoint
Ideal and material statics

Internal volumes, two-dimensional.
The broadening of the lines
corresponds to gradations from
far to near or: rear to front

The same volumes seen from
the side (rotation)

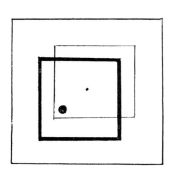

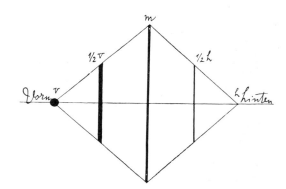

Theory makes for clarification, but in the concrete instance there are such complicated influences at work that we cannot proceed consistently with theory alone; we must again digress a little.

We need mechanical function. This means working on the basis of a law, not in order to demonstrate the law, but in order to create a freer form, based on the rules.

In leaving the realm of rules, we upset theory. This departure from law and rule is something we must do morally, so to speak. Always bearing in mind the need for harmony, for sensitive organisation of the individual component parts, so that a satisfying result is achieved.

151

In art the essential is to create movement according to rules, to create deviations while bearing the rules in mind. If you adhere too strictly, you get into barren territory.

There is no need to demand absolute conformity. It is only recently that we have been free to deviate from the rules. What do we gain by it?

We gain possiblities of spatio-plastic representation and movement that were limited under earlier methods.[1] With constructive dexterity such effects might be obtained from one position. But that is only one way and not the direct way of showing different things at once. This possibility was seriously discussed only after it had been used by artists who knew how to unify and combine organic processes.

[1] Central perspective with motionless visual point.

152

1923/11: *Town square under construction.*
Watercolour.
Note in Klee's diary:
'Even from the church tower the activity on the
square looks funny. But imagine how it
looks from where I am.'

We must work our way back to unity. This can be done in the pictorial field by bringing disparate things together harmoniously. Here the links are important. And the scale depends also on the distance from the beholder.

The first step is a regular deviation based on projection. Projection means here that the viewpoint is not strictly static; it is displaced a little and the object moves along. We can also remain stationary and displace the object.

The irregular consists in the accentuation of parts or the omission of certain parts.

In any case this introduces freedom into movement and movement into freedom.

153

1919/199: *House interior*. Watercolour.
Interpenetration of endotopic and exotopic.
Main emphasis on endotopic elevation.

Forms react on us both through their essence
and their appearance, those kindred organs of
the spirit. The line of demarcation between
essence and appearance is faint. There is
no clash, just a specific something which
demands that the essential be grasped.

154

Linear sketch from:
1923/11: *Town square under construction*, p.153.
Simultaneity of perspectives in plan of picture.
Front and side view and perspective elements
of ground plan combined.

1. 'Material, terrestrial horizon.
2. Ideal horizon, widened.
3. Synthesis.'

Linear sketch from:
1922/150: *Plan of garden*. Watercolour.
Simultaneous projection with interpenetration of
base and elevation. Representation according
to essence and appearance.

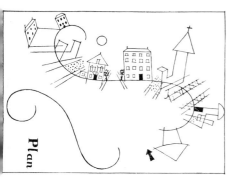

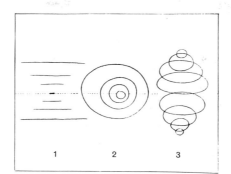

Multi-dimensional simultaneity of projection,
with temporal succession.

Examples:
1925/E zero: *Village in relief. A game*.
Colour drawing. Grohmann, p.177.
1927/Y 5: *Partial view of G*. Watercolour and oil.
Colour reproduction in Grohmann, p.269.

Irregular projection

Combined operations and projection in different positions, deviating from pure central
perspective.
Organic combination of the main forms of perspective:
interpenetration of space and body, simultaneous inner and outer form. Representation
according to essence and appearance.

Points to be considered:
Simultaneous, multi-dimensional phenomena.[1] Multi-dimensional contacts. More complex structures.

In deviation from pure central perspective:
(a) deviating progressions;
(b) deviating position of the vanishing point (P zero);
(c) deviating perspective (and building boxes and building blocks).
Slight deviations are playful movements round the normal paths of construction. Pronounced deviations are movements contrary to the normal paths of construction.

155

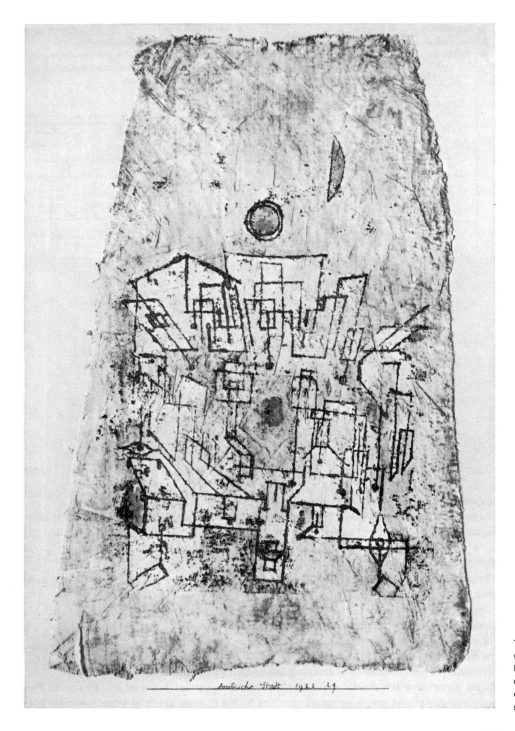

Arabische Stadt 1922 29

1922/29: *Arabian city*. Watercolour and oil on gauze prepared with plaster.
Interlocking of perspectives. Simultaneous downward and upward views obtained by combination of several viewpoints. (Balanced synthesis of several positions.)

156

Succession, interpenetration, or interlocking of perspectives.

(a) The shifting or variable viewpoint. Several viewpoints combined.
(b) Representation.
   1. of the surface (superficial),
   2. transparent-spatial,
   3. analytically and plastically reunited in 'transparent polyphony'. (Cubical volumes and volumes related to the cube interpenetrate in plastic transparency, sometimes producing a deviating, mobile structure which plays round the fringes of the law.)
   Body, inner and outer space combined[1] (e.g. cubic volume, cubic inner space, cubic outer space).

Most of these forms are combined. To understand the combined forms, we must break them down into their component parts.

[1] i.e. 'transparency of volume and space' or 'interpenetrated'.
Cf. 1928/P 6: *Italian city*, p.42.
1928/p 7: *Little week-end house*, p.142.
1929/g 10: *Santa A at B*, p.54.
1928/D 7: *Perspective of city*. Pen and watercolour. Grohmann, p.219.

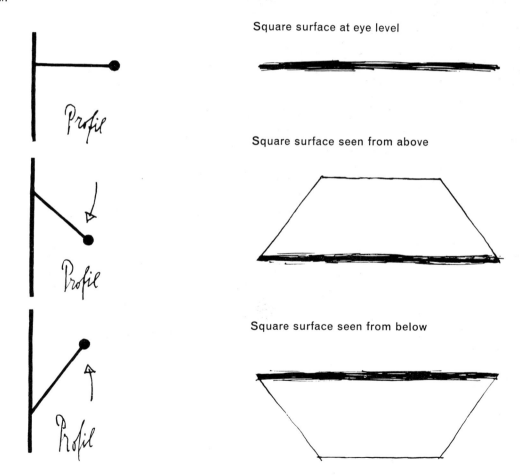

Square surface at eye level

Square surface seen from above

Square surface seen from below

1929/s 6: *Castle hill*. Oil.
Rhythmic articulation of planes, spatio-plastic
accentuation of elevation. Recombined by
plastic analysis. (*Cf.* accentuation of ground plan,
pp.252–253.)

Combined operations with basic forms of perspective (perspective variations). Shifting viewpoint and interpenetration of space and volume.

A theme with accompaniment or several themes. Single and combined articulation. Intermediate positions:

> neither purely frontal
> nor purely vertical
> nor purely horizontal

The deviations singly and combined

Examples:

1914/180: *Church under construction.* Pen-and-ink.
1918/93: *With the net fisherman.* Watercolour. Giedion, p.89.
1919/193: *Newly constructed fortress.* Colour drawing. Grohmann, p.389.
1919/157: *Architecture with window.* Oil.
1920/160: *Ascona.* Watercolour.
1921/25: *City in limbo.* Watercolour.
1921/50: *Transparent perspective I.* Watercolour.
1921/55: *Transparent perspective with pavilion.* Watercolour.
1921/104: *Climbing houses in autumn.* Watercolour.
1921/120: *Transparent-structural architecture.* Watercolour.
1921/183: *Revolving house.* Oil.
1922/103: *Building of the Z. corporation.* Pen and watercolour.
1925/d 2: *Perspective figuration.* Oil.
1925/6: *Perspective scherzo.* Watercolour.
1925/T 1: *Idyll in garden city.* Oil.
1927/L 7: *Excavation.* Oil. Colour reproduction in Grohmann, p.261.
1928/o 6: *Little houses rhythmically in gardens.* Watercolour.

Rules made to be broken:

Divisive formation	(pictorial division)
multiplying formation	(pictorial multiplication)
form as addition	(pictorial addition, combined by summation)
form as subtraction	(pictorial subtraction, definitely separative)

Synthesis of spatio-plastic representation and movement:
Six viewpoints can be unified and combined into a single median collective viewpoint.

The formal elements singly and as they are related.
Their appearance in groups, their limited synthesis. Then amplified to become forms or constructions. The balanced synthesis of different positions.
Phenomenology of apparent position and ideal position.

One need only imagine an object in space in order to appreciate the difficulties in the analytical approach.
But how else are we to arrive at an orientation in space? I do not know. All these divisions, even the most commonplace, have a meaning if we keep in mind the value of the part without forgetting the whole. If we remember that every such pair of statements is only an analytical operation and therefore partial, our procedure remains meaningful. Each pair of statements moves on a particular plane, and ultimately the different planes, taken together, produce a spatial synthesis, the summation that forms the whole.
Because I cannot do what I should prefer, namely, deal at one stroke with a whole comprising many of these elements (each in its place), I must resign myself to analytic methods.

Note in appendix:
Survey of examples according to the basic aspects of irregular projection.

1

2

1939/M 8: *Houses close together*. Colour [1].
Irregular projection on an uneven surface.
Accent on plan.
'Here one might bring in still another category:
it seems as if we were looking down from above.
Like looking into a jar. Then the concept
above–below disappears, as it were.'

1932/x 16: *Little cliff town*. Oil [2].
Simultaneous ground-plan and
elevation. (*Cf*. 1940/N 14: *Churches*, p.194.)

Dimensional operations combined into a higher structure

Two-dimensional partial analyses
of the four operations:
One pair of lines in like direction
lineally expressed

Another pair of lines in like
direction lineally expressed

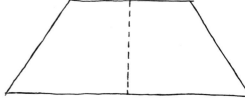

One pair of lines in different
directions lineally expressed

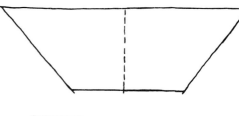

Another pair of lines in different
directions lineally expressed

The four operations
combined

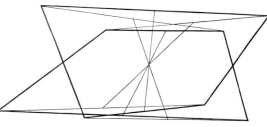

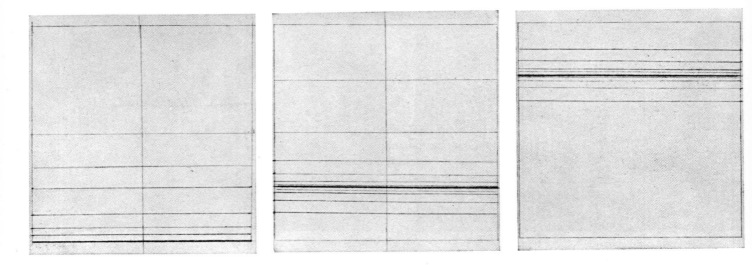

1   2   3

The natural possibilities of width
in all natural positions:

The single horizontal on the ground [1]
The single horizontal lifted [2]
Width accentuated
  at its uppermost natural position [3]

Static narrowness. The perfectly static direction of gravity is one-sided and does not
end in a middle position, but at the bottom. Crucial for the bottom-most position is the
distance of the object from the 'I'. When there is identification, the 'I' is the object and
the gravitational pull ends at the soles of the feet. This object (the 'I') can be sensed but
not seen, or seen only very approximately, if one is lying down. Lifting the viewpoint or
point of departure also raises the given horizontal.

Examples:
1929/m 7: *Church and castle*, p.138.
1929/m 3: *Evening in Egypt*, p.146.
1929/R 10: *Main path and side paths*. Oil and plaster
on canvas. Giedion, p.129.
1930/r 2: *Individualised altimetry of planes*.
Colour drawing. Colour reproduction
Grohmann, p.277.
1932/a 8: *Raised horizon*. Oil.

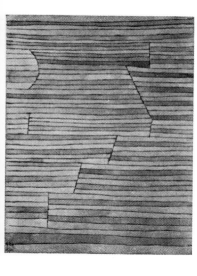

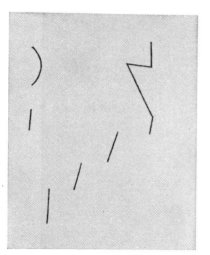

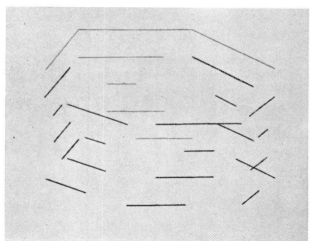

4

5

6

1929/M 4: *The sun grazes the plain*. Watercolour [4].
(Title cited in œuvre catalogue:
The light grazes the plain.)

Linear analysis from 1929/M 4:
The sun grazes the plain [5].

1931/u 15: *Variation on 'Circuit through 6 planes'*.
Coloured ink on paper [6].

The horizontal in itself, purely as form, is perhaps already movement. However, it gives an impression not of movement, but of rest. Perhaps the form is mobile, but it is rest that is suggested.

In discussions of statics, 'lying' means to be inactive. Lying and working are not easily compatible. Movement can be situated within a certain tendency towards rest.

The single form sleeps, but many sleepers together produce action.

163

1930/s 1: *At seven over rooftops*.
Tempera and watercolour, varnished.

'The fluctuating definition of the foreground
and background (varying with the sharpness of
our depth perception) might suggest distance.
This indeed is what happens in the actual
optics of space.'

164

Mechanics of subjective height [1]. For the 'I', height and horizon are the essential factors. Slight elevation gives a good upward view, a poor downward view. Slight cover from above (important), good cover from below (unimportant). The result: an upward drive.

Great height gives poor upward view, good downward view. Good cover from above (important), poor cover from below (unimportant). Increased well-being.

Increased height, ascendency, positive. The horizon rises, the view of the ground-plane increases, the view from below diminishes, the upward drive is appeased. Dangers are reduced if you go to meet them.

Decreased height, retrenchment, negative. Height, cover from above, downward view diminish. Pathological complexes of oppression arise (as a result of too much space and weakness above).

Mechanics between above and below ↑↓
in relation to height.
Constructive movement

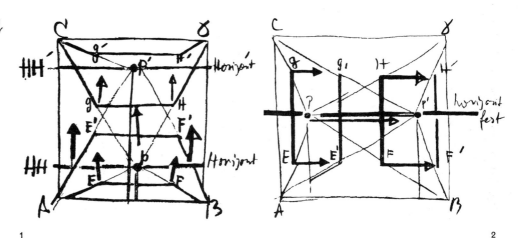

1

2

Mechanics of width [2]. The left-right movement is less significant. The horizon, whether high or low, stands fast. Even a critical situation in respect of left and right is not of fundamental importance.

In the mechanics of width, the 'correct way' is formed by this movement ⇆. Correct ways to the background lead rather to the left or to the right of space. There is either more cover from the left or from the right. Either more danger or more of a view to the right, or vice versa.

1937/qu 17: *The way to the city castle*. Oil.

'One must have the main features of a picture from the very start and then add the secondary features, so much so that one always gets something out of looking at it. Often the battle is already won with the ground-plan.'

Actual planes and perspective planes
by themselves and combined
(Frontal, horizontal, and vertical planes)

Actual plane: frontal or actual vertical plane
as it appears from the front

Perspective horizontal planes

Perspective vertical planes

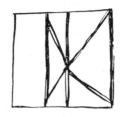 

The three cardinal planes
in their relation
to the linear dimensions.
The oppositions are only apparent.
In series of planes
friendship appears

1. Frontal plane from
both sides

2. Vertical plane from
left and right

3. Horizontal plane from
above–below

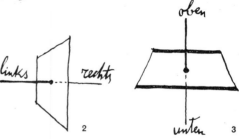

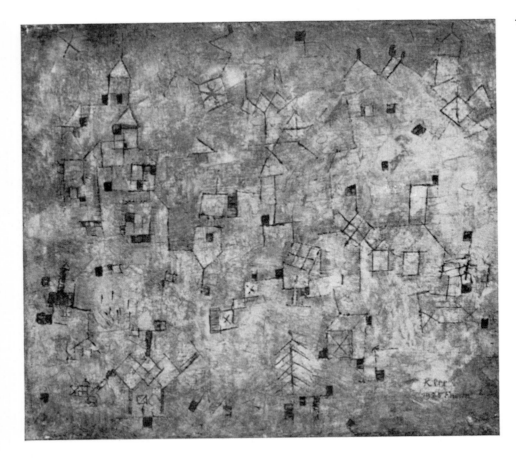

The shifting viewpoint. Active, operative movement. Centres of meaning. Identity of way and work.

The word 'stimulated' says everything necessary for the beginning of action. The word 'stimulated' suggests the prehistory of an incipient act, its connection with what has gone before, its bond with the past.

The affective possibility of going beyond a beginning is further characterised in the concept, which, extended from beginning to end (not only to the beginning), produces a cycle – where motion is the norm so that the question of its beginning disappears.

Under the impact of this normative motion a creative disposition takes form within us. Since we ourselves are moved, we find it easier to set things in motion.

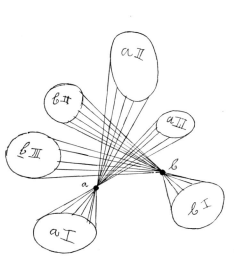

The shifting viewpoint,
operating from two centres: a and b.
From a I to a II, a III;
from b I to b II, b III.

The initial movement in ourselves; the active movement from us to the work; the communication of the work's mobility to others, the beholders of the work: these are the main divisions of the creative whole, pre-creation, creation, post-creation.

If we follow the gradual unfolding of a primitive simple work, we shall obtain a closer view of two things: first the phenomenon of formation, formation in relation to impulse, formation bound to the conditions of life, formation as development from mysterious mobility to purpose. This phenomenon was discernible in the very earliest craft, when form in the smallest sense (structure) first made its appearance.

The relation between formation and form, which we discern even in the smallest things, retains its fundamental character in later stages, because it is determined by a principle. I think the nature of this relation can be stated in one sentence: the way to form, dictated no doubt by some inward or outward necessity, is higher than its own end and goal.

The way is essential and determines the conclusive or concluded character of the work. Formation determines form and is therefore the greater of the two.

Thus form may never be regarded as solution, result, end, but should be regarded as genesis, growth, essence. Form as phenomenon is a dangerous chimera.

Form as movement, as action is a good thing, active form is good. Form as rest, as end, is bad. Passive, finished form is bad. Formation is good. Form is bad; form is the end, death. Formation is movement, act. Formation is life.

This was the first thing we saw as we followed the gradual unfolding of a primitive, simple work. Then a second revealed itself.

As the creative process continued, as the way grew longer, the danger of monotony became apparent. For the way, as an essential part of the work, should not tire us. It must rise higher, branch out excitingly, rise, fall, digress; it must become by turns more or less distinct, broader or narrower, easier or harder. And the sections must fall into a definite structure; with all their widening development, one must be able to encompass them at a single glance; they must enter into an intelligible relationship with one another. Through the identity of way and work, the work becomes structured 'along the way'; the first even rhythm develops into several rhythms. The different segments of the way join into an articulated whole. The interaction between the general structure of the whole and the natural structure of the parts forms the core of an elementary theory of proportion. The different modes of interaction produce works of different kinds.

Subjective horizon:
For at eye level every plane
appears as a straight line.
The perspective foci
are always at horizon level.

Objective horizon:[1]
The right way of the 'I' recedes
from the marked-off space with
vanishing point outside to the right
and to the left.
Then the space, too, is objectified.

[1]Objective horizon: with several changing
viewpoints the result is a natural deviation from
static relations, giving greater freedom
and mobility.

Horizont subjectiv ———— *Horizont objectiv* ◯

Subjective theory of space. Wandering viewpoint. Irregular projection with free
application of the principles of perspective.

Different viewpoints with change of place:
Shifting vertical with viewpoint moving from left to right. The subject changes his basic
position.[2]
Change of subjective level.
Change of the relation between height and horizon means raised horizon = widened
horizon. Change of downward and upward view.[3]
Subjective height and subjective distance:[4] I, far away
                                             I, not so close
                                             I, very close
Summary: change of subjective height; viewpoint moving across the left–right horizon.[5]

Several viewpoints and several subjects in space:
Possibility of connecting paths. Paths of various subjects in space.
Persons with varying eye level.[6]

Three persons see a frontal plane from three different points.
Thus the synthetic viewpoint (or collective viewpoint) sees three planes.[7]

Several viewpoints combined. The shifting viewpoint and the connection between stages
1, 2, 3, 4.[8]

Where the viewpoint is shifted several times, different projected images appear simultaneously. In the subjective theory of space, movements and countermovements produce
a balanced movement.[9]

[2]*Cf.* p.139.

[3]*Cf.* p.147.
[4]*Cf.* p.171 [1].

[5]*Cf.* p.142.

Cf. p.171 [2]

[7]*Cf.* p.173.

[8]*Cf.* p.171 [3].

[9]*Cf.* the static-dynamic synthesis, p.96.

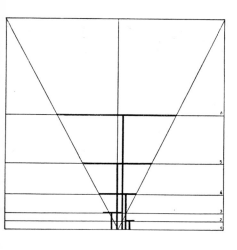

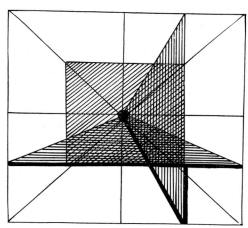

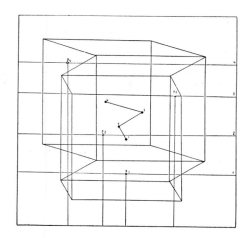

1

2

3

1. Subjective height and subjective distance: Possibility of a connection between view-point and base-point (Stages 1–6).

The quickest path from an original viewpoint 'front' to a fixed horizontal 'behind' runs in a vertical direction. The vertical is the right way. To designate height and a horizon extended upward, the limits must remain rigid.

2. Ways of several subjectives in space.

Vertical plane of the lady on the right or her right way

Middle horizontal plane of the child or his eye level

3. Several viewpoints combined. The shifting viewpoint and the connection between stages 1, 2, 3, 4 (differences in height: p_1, p_2, p_3, p_4).

171

1930/s 10: *Hovering before rising*.
Oil on canvas.
'Three-dimensional body, transparent.'

In the realm of the static there are also movements; these movements, however, are not free but bound to the vertical. Movements of this restricted kind are not only
1. construction,
2. balance, but also
3. movement
of the whole static structure.
Balance is a movement away from the vertical, to which a corresponding countermovement is always opposed. This countermovement annuls the one-sided deviation from the vertical. In the movement of the static structure the whole static organisation moves. The vertical and the movements of balance change their place together.
(On the parallelogram of forces, rise and fall, see pp.410–413,
on phenomena of balance, pp.207–213.)

Examples:
1930/w 5: *Surfaces in tension*. Oil.
Grohmann, p.400.
1930/T 10: *Sailing city*. Watercolour.
Colour reproduction in *Dokumentarmappe Klee-Gesellschaft*. Benteli, Berne 1949.
1932/t 10: *Glider flight*. Oil on canvas.

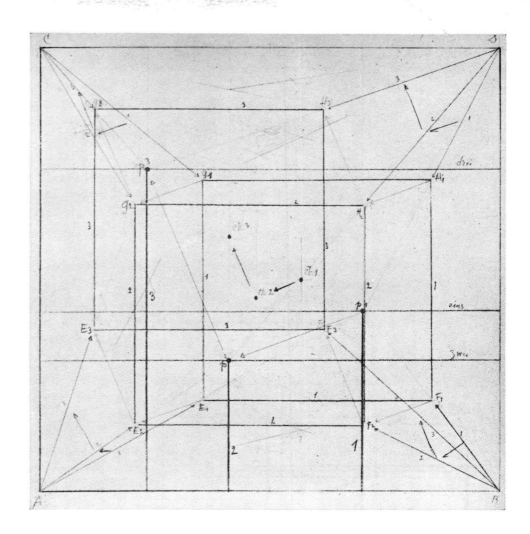

Note by Klee: '2 July, 1929. Stereoscopy. Part and whole. The whole moved quadratically in variations.'

Similar motion of the centres:
ctr 1 → ctr 2 → ctr 3.

Shifting viewpoint. Three men see a frontal plane from three positions; the synthetic viewpoint sees three planes. We have discovered one of the roots of spatial vision.[1]

Variable viewpoints: Stages of movement from 1 to 2 to 3 ($p_1 \rightarrow p_2 \rightarrow p_3$).
Shift of point p and consequences:[2]

	12		14		15
from p_1	14 + 6	to p_2	8 + 12	to p_3	5 + 15
	8		6		15

173

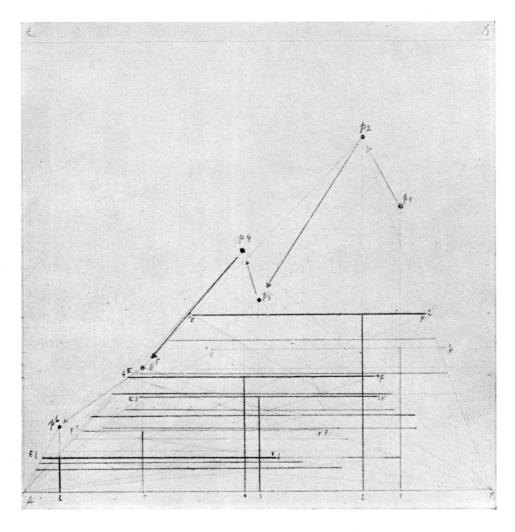

Six viewpoints: E_1–F_1, E_2–F_2, E_3–F_3, E_4–F_4, E_5–F_5, E_6–F_6. The same and summed up in a median collective viewpoint.[1] Differences in height $p_1 \rightarrow p_2 \rightarrow p_3 \rightarrow p_4 \rightarrow p_5 \rightarrow p_6$, represented by the right way from AB to EF. Operations on horizontal planes of varying heights with related depth sequence. Unification achieved through the median height and width of the right ways.

[1]Median collective viewpoint.
E_4————————————F_4
Median height 4·6
Median width 9·43

Median height:	$6\cdot3 + 7\cdot19 + 4\cdot2 + 5\cdot1 + 2\cdot7 + 1\cdot4 = \dfrac{27\cdot6}{6} = 4\cdot6$
Median width: (measured from A)	$16\cdot1 + 14\cdot4 + 10\cdot1 + 9\cdot4 + 5\cdot1 + 1\cdot5 = \dfrac{56\cdot6}{6} = 9\cdot43$

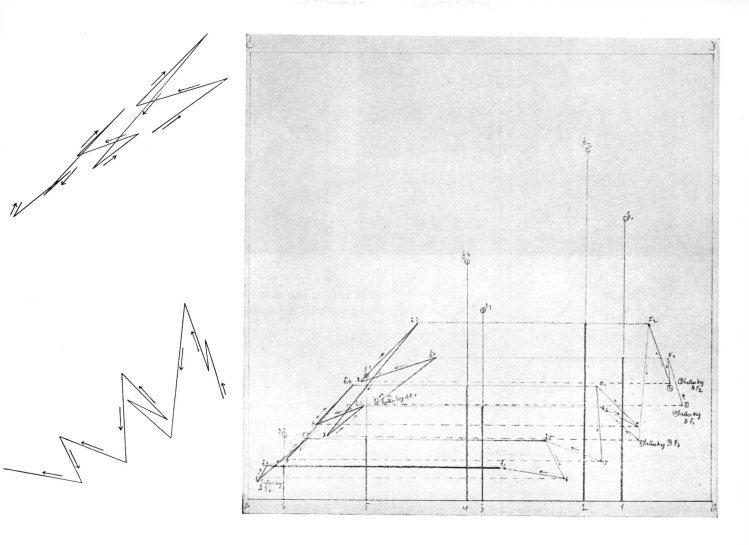

The subjective way. The viewpoints descend from right to left, but not without intermediate rises (from 1 to 2, from 3 to 4). The points from 1 to 6 on AB are the base points of the 6 viewpoints. The mid-points on the lines from these base points to the corresponding viewpoints are in every case the right ways from AB to EF, hence the bisectors of the principal section in various positions. Points E_1 and F_1 are situated at a height of $\dfrac{1 \longrightarrow p_1}{2}$; Points 1 (half-way from A to E_1) and 1 (half-way from B to F_1) are situated on the lower half of this lower section at the height of $\dfrac{1 \longrightarrow p_1}{2}$. Then comes the double zigzag to the outside right and left: $1 \longrightarrow E_1, 2 \longrightarrow E_2, 3 \longrightarrow E_3, 4 \longrightarrow E_4, 5 \longrightarrow E_5, 6 \longrightarrow E_6$ and $1 \longrightarrow F_1, 2 \longrightarrow F_2, 3 \longrightarrow F_3, 4 \longrightarrow F_4, 5 \longrightarrow F_5, 6 \longrightarrow F_6$.

175

1

2

Static and dynamic balancing movements. Lateral shift of weight is movement within the horizontal plane. And in tune with the symbol of the pair of scales the lateral shift of weight is connected with an ultimate effect of balance.

Movements that lead to balance and end in balance are not free; the vertical imposes certain conditions on them. Subject to these conditions, movements belong character-istically to statics, provided they do not contradict the fundamental principle of balance. It is incorrect to say that 'static' means 'at rest' and that 'dynamic' means 'in motion'. For 'static' can also mean 'in conditional motion' or 'becalmed motion', while 'dynamic' can mean 'in unconditional motion', in other words 'under its own motion' or simply 'moving'.

1933/L 4: *Dominated group*. Watercolour [1]. Fluid balance. 'Horizontal, vertical, and diagonal factors are gathered together. Oppositions. The horizontals produce a more tranquil effect, the verticals and diagonals have something active about them.
'Standing adds something further to the sense of action. Standing takes the vertical into consideration; in contrast to lying, it builds.'

1929/3 H 26: *Collapse*. Watercolour [2]. Exaggerated shift of the horizontals and verticals leads to disturbed balance = collapse.

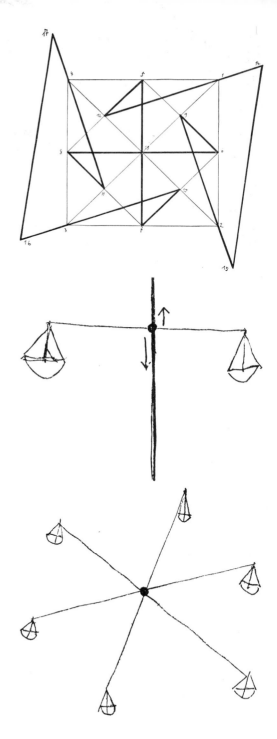

The feeling here expressed is the
dynamic shifting of a
static premise

Balance in static style.
The vertical puts
the fulcrum in motion

Balance in dynamic style.
The fulcrum
is fixed at the centre

177

Static-dynamic tension and position of balance

Statics: The terrestrial norm is rest. Terrestrial tension on earth is the prerequisite for motion.

Dynamics: From the cosmic standpoint, motion is the norm. There are static factors that lead to immobility and others that are themselves immobile (rhythm and balance). There are dynamic factors that are in motion and others that are ready for it.

Mechanical elements of statics:

verticals: primary
horizontals: secondary
diagonals: tertiary within the rules of statics

Fundamental mobility of the tertiaries (diagonals)

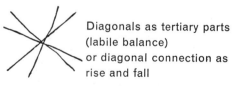 Diagonals as tertiary parts (labile balance) or diagonal connection as rise and fall

1937/U 6: *Harmonised battle*. Pastel.
'Dynamic shifting of a static premise. Stress on partial viewpoints, connected with changing position (central motion).'

Cf. 1937/T 5: *Overland*, p.504.
From the point of view of line, more or less static: the movement of the coloured forms, dynamic.

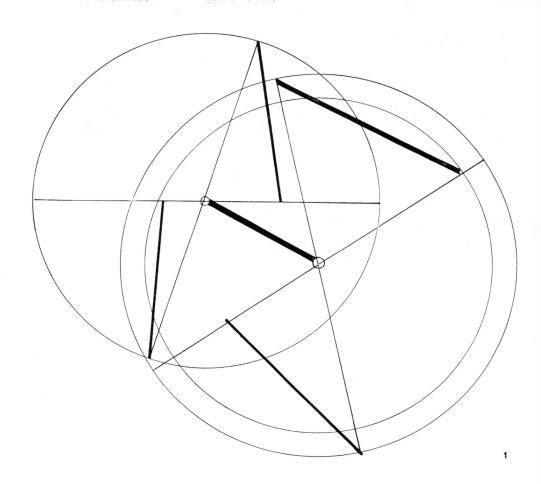

1

Diagonal synthesis of dimensions. In diagonals every point and its inverse point at the other end of the diameter must disclose a balance of the (two) dimensions. In every case we have a rotation of the centre but there must be a balance between left and right, between above and below (reciprocal motion). Two pairs of lines with different centres: hence movement of centre [1]. The moved centre can fall, lie still, or rise.
The synthesis of several component movements tending towards a centre suffices to give an idea of the innermost essence of an irregular form of this kind. The centre is in motion; not only along the line, but also two-dimensionally, within the plane.

Analytically, according to component viewpoints. Part construction: not all lines are emphasised; (a) certain lines stressed, the rest unaccented; (b) the unaccented lines omitted (productive-destructive method).[1] In the space between the lines mediating actions occur, which stand for the structure of the relations between them. Successive emphasis on parts of the total form. Representation of the line as distinctive or unifying.[2]

Where a part is singled out the process can also be interpreted as divisive formation: 'Composite form without contact'.

Disjunctive = opposition, struggle.
Unifying = harmonisation.

179

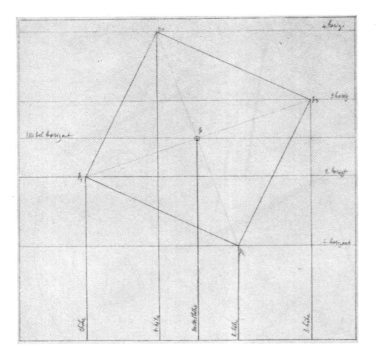

1

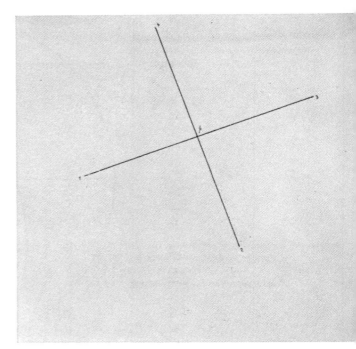

Basic dynamic principle: Avoidance of static rules, gravitation, the plumbline: hence no distinct verticals, horizontals, or diagonals. Feasible through mobility.

Static-dynamic tension:[1]
The causal principle is a
reciprocal tension
between purely terrestrial
statics

and ideal statics
(terrestrial-cosmic tension)

[1]Static-dynamic tension:
the tension is undischarged, the opposition remains (Cf. p.393). Static-dynamic balance or static-dynamic synthesis: concrete and discharged Harmonisation of opposing means of expression or dynamic shifting of a static premise. Cf. 1927/E 9: *Sailboats in gentle motion*, p.276, and 1937/U 11: *View in red*, p.291. 1938/T 5: *Harmonised locality*. Colour drawing.

The forces that move lines are gravity, evasion of gravity, or the result of forces moving in different directions.
(*Cf.* Gravity and momentum, p.395 and the pictorial schemata of the first, second and third laws of statics, p.414.)

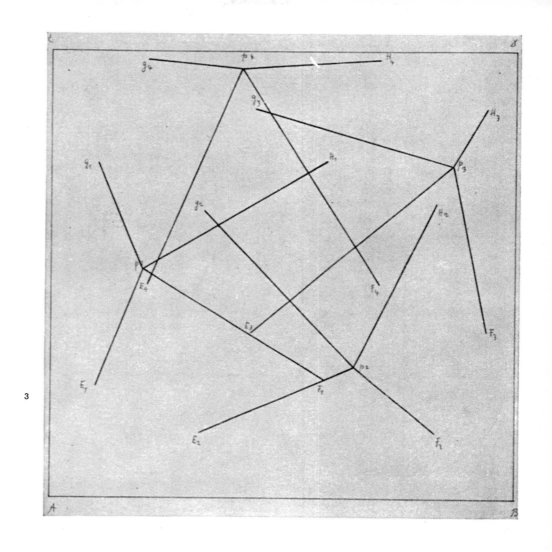

3

¹The four viewpoints p_1, p_2, p_3, p_4 are situated on the same diagonal cross as in [1] and [2], p.180. On the diagonal synthesis of dimensions, *cf*. 1937/U 6: *Harmonised battle*, p.178.

Constructive principle: four viewpoints p_1, p_2, p_3, p_4 arranged in a square (first second, third, and fourth horizon) meet in a single point p (median horizon) [1] (p.180). The four viewpoints (1, 2, 3, 4) in another version [2] (p.180). A variation. Constructive emphasis on diagonals [3].¹

Ideal statics. Pure dynamics (energies)

Area of the rules of ideal statics, first, second, and third degrees.

From the cosmic point of view verticals are never parallel; and horizontals are arcs. Cosmically speaking, tangents are unreal. Cosmically speaking, the area of the 'I' is a point.

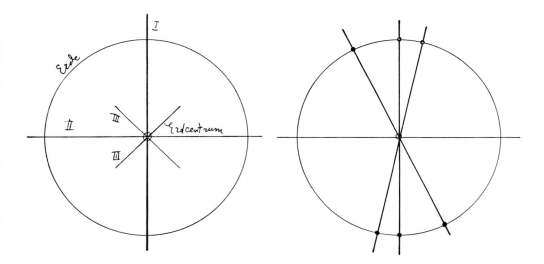

Ideal and material statics. Ideal (cosmically conscious) statics or idealised statics. Material (terrestrial) statics or pure statics.

In the static realm stable means rigidly bound to the verticals. In the dynamic realm stable means settled harmonisation of free mobility. Marked deviations in the static realm are deviations from the normal position of the verticals and horizontals, but are still verticals and horizontals.
Marked deviations in the dynamic realm are essentially shifts of centre and shifts of the localities dependent on the centre; the plumbline and the forces closest to it are ignored.

Material statics. (Gravitationa forces in one direction)

Area of the rules of material or terrestrial statics

From the terrestrial point of view the parallelism of verticals and horizontals (really tangents) is an illusion caused by the enlargement of the area of the 'I'.

The centre of the earth is the centre of gravity

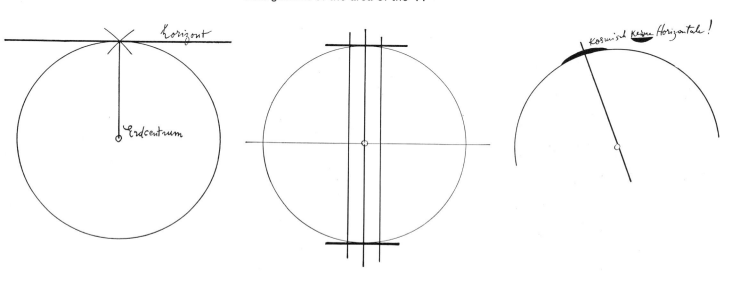

Dynamics is the great, the principal area, the endless area of the cosmos.
Statics, by comparison, is an exception, where gravitation kills motion by subjugating it to an alien law. The suction of the stronger. This stronger power is itself dynamically moved and carries the vanquished along in its orbit. But the vanquished does not perceive this directly; he must accustom himself as best he can to the new power and gradually carve out a sphere of motion where, if he manages it skilfully, he can attain a kind of independence.
This is how the plant grows, how man and beast walk or fly.

From a terrestrial point of view: Statics   = gravitational forces in one direction
                                    Dynamics = energy
From a cosmic point of view: Only gravitation
                                    The forces of gravity come together from all sides

1937/qu 18. *Architecture in the evening.* Oil.
'In the three-dimensional world a simple rotation
produces a two-dimensional effect.'

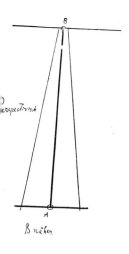

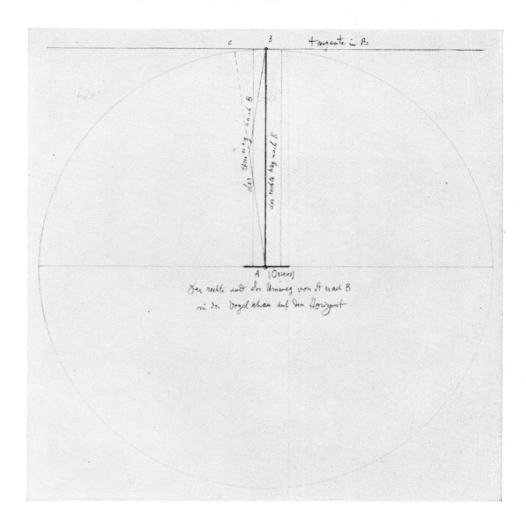

Deviation from the rules of material or purely terrestrial statics (gravitation) makes possible an ideal statics or earthly-cosmic synthesis. (*Cf*. diagram p.67.)

Ideal and material statics: the earth, from a cosmic point of view, provides the basis for a static-dynamic synthesis. Starting from here, earthbound man arrives at a cosmically ideal-static view of the world and an earthly-cosmic one.

Theory of style. The questions are these: Are verticals or horizontals present? Right angles? Centres? Peripheries?[1]

Theory of composition. The questions are these: are the inner-constructive relations of form and format observed?

185

1924/39: *Houses in landscape*. Colour.
Analysed on pp.188–191.

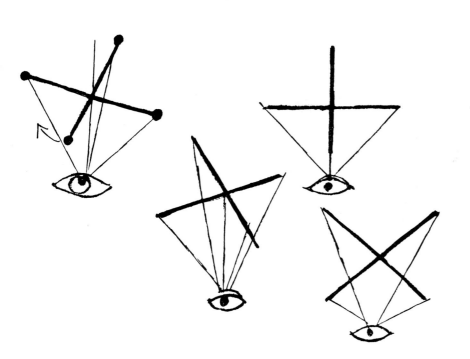

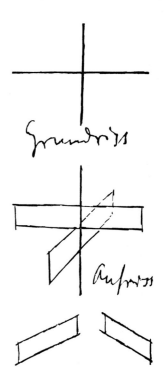

In a three-dimensional experiment with motion the moment when one plane is perceived only as a vertical is especially critical. Far less significant are foreshortened planes. Hence the apparent irregularity of pace.

Contingent and free movement. It seems very likely that there is no such thing as a purely dynamic architecture, and here we must attach importance to the slightest hint leading in that direction.
It would be well to take the appearance for the reality.

Our means of investigating natural structures by means of cross-sections and longitudinal sections is no doubt applicable to architectonic structures, but we should never find an example in which ground-plan and elevation were not fundamentally different. Which again means that there is no example of the purely dynamic in this field.
Consequently we must situate architectural works in the purely static sphere, though there may be a certain inclination towards the dynamic. At best we shall find an intermediate sphere somewhere between the static and the dynamic.
In more ideal realms of art, such as painting, the greatest mobility of all is possible, an actual development from the static to the dynamic.

Examples:
1921/208: *Dynamisation of the P. house.* Drawing.
1922/42: *Castle in the air.* Oil.
1924/75: *Relations between landscape and houses.* Oil.
1928/p 7: *Little week-end house.* p.142.

How to overcome static narrowness
Analysis of 1924/39: *Houses in landscape*, p.186.

Change of subjective elevation, viewpoint movable from left to right, dynamic shifting of static relations. Dynamic in the sense that the subject is free to move in space.

'The eye like a grazing animal feels its way over the surface, not only from top to bottom but also from left to right and in any direction for which the occasion presents itself. The eye moves, grazing from the values that attract it, towards values that draw it on after the first values have been grazed bare.' (p.359. *Cf.* also pp.357–367.)

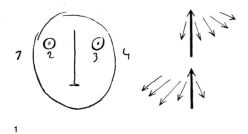

1

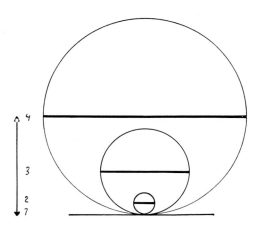

[1] The shifting viewpoint connects stages 1, 2, 3, 4. Several viewpoints, with eye moving from left to right.

'Change of subjective height and subjective distance: "I" very close. "I" not so close. "I" far removed.' The combined foundation of the viewpoints 1, 2, 3, 4 provides alternating upward and downward views.

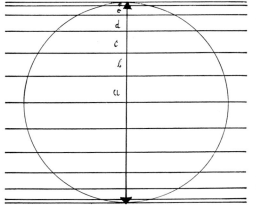

'Ideal and material statics: combined foundations or composite form.

Mobile progression (on the basis of the 24-part circle). From the centre of the earth outward. Eccentric condensation.

188

Converging horizontals joined by diagonals.

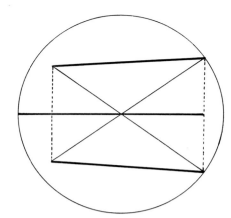

Horizontals sensitised by means of displaced
centre. Road travelled from **A–B** to **C**.

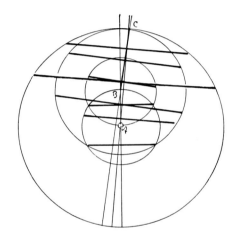

Operation on horizontal planes of different height.
'The raising of the viewpoint brings with it a
raising of the horizontals.' A mobile viewpoint
results in a projection. Mesh of
alternating upward and downward views.

The shift of centre brings with it changed relations
between height and horizon. Sensitisation of
horizontals by upward-downward motion
and the reverse.

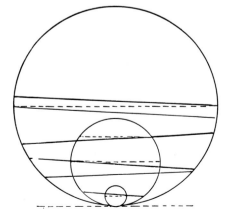

Syntheses of material and ideal statics (i.e. static
and dynamic relations) by setting in
diagonals. Connections between viewpoints
, 2, 3, 4. Dynamic shifting of static relations.

189

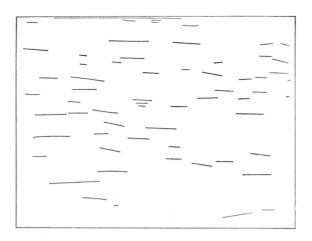

Linear analysis of converging horizontals from:
1924/39: *Houses in landscape*, p.186.
Shift of static relations with deviation from normal eye level.

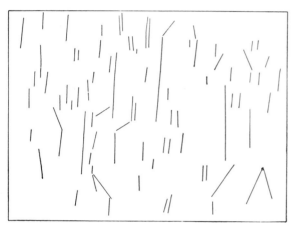

Shifting verticals and deviations from the vertical with viewpoint moving left to right.
Linear analysis from:
1924/39: *Houses in landscape*, p.186.

Static-dynamic synthesis, deviating from purely terrestrial statics. Connection between several viewpoints or stages. Simultaneous front view and profile, i.e. projection through space and time.
Linear analysis of:
1924/39: *Houses in landscape*, p.186.

'In the static realm stable means rigidly bound to the vertical. In the dynamic realm it means calm harmonisation of free mobility.'

Without combined foundations. More
frontal emphasis:
1924/21: *Village in blue and orange.*
Oil on paper prepared with chalk.

'These are highly favourable conditions in which
to create a dominant proportion if the general
local relations are treated in different ways. Now
factors treated quite differently enter in. Some
are taken fully into account, some partly, some
scarcely or not at all. Now is the time to say something very special. Thus we achieve
the possibility of spatio-plastic representation and
movement, which was limited in the former method
(central perspective, Ed.).'

To sum up:
Organic combination of the principal forms of
perspective with the process of motion.
Multidimensional simultaneity of projection with
temporal succession (several viewpoints
combined). Synthesis of movement and
three-dimensional representation.

[1] Immanent: statics; transcendent: dynamics.

Pure dynamic action within a limited sphere is only possible on the spiritual plane.
Fundamentally, style is the human attitude towards these questions of the immanent and
the transcendent.[1] Accordingly, the field of style has two main parts. In the first, the static
concept and the classical resemble one another; in the second, there is a kinship between
dynamics and romanticism.

Between the two meeting-places, the static-classic and the dynamic-romantic, there is
an intermediate realm, where statics yearns for dynamic freedom. Pathos is expressed in
art as a motor impulse off the vertical, or as denial or disruption of the vertical.

There are also more peaceful syntheses of the two realms; where what is static, well-
balanced and, often, quite symmetrical, is given a touch of the dynamic.

1938/D 16: (*Landscape*) *with the two who are lost*.
Gouache on newsprint.
Cf. 1919/115: *Landscape with gallows*, p.77.

Note on p.193:
The style-forming tensions of the 'I' relate to
gravitation (inhibited individual energy) or
momentum (free individual energy or free
mobility). Height and width are static in nature.
Equal tension on all sides points to the dynamic
sphere (the natural dynamics of the circle).
Unequal tensions belong to the special sphere of
static-dynamic syntheses.

The style-forming tensions of the 'I'

Originally the 'I' too is a point

Tensions make their appearance;
for example, the one-sided tension
of height.
Consequence: the 'I' grows upward

Tension in different dimensions:
height and width.
Consequence: the 'I' grows upward
and at the same time spreads out

Equal tension on all sides.
Consequence: the 'I' spreads outward
radially

Unequal tensions round about

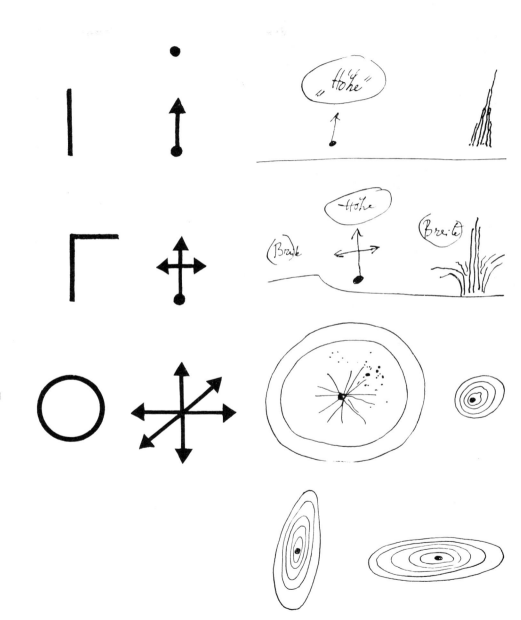

1940/N 14: *Churches*. Colour.

'Synthesis of movement and spatio-plastic
representation.' Simultaneous projection of
ground-plan and elevation while the subject
moves in space. 'But through the identity of
way and work the work is organised along the
way, and the segments of the way are joined
to form an articulated whole.'
Cf. Irregular projection on uneven surface, p.253.
City castle of KR, pp.232 and 234.

All figuration is movement, because it begins somewhere and ends somewhere. In general the paths of the groping eye are free in space and time; that is, the eye is not compelled to begin at a definite place, to proceed to definite places, and to finish in a definite place. Such constraint is imposed only by a particular pattern of movement, which lays down very definite paths in a very definite order.[1]

The cardinal question: How shall I represent the movement from here to there? involves a factor of time.

[1] Cf. 1937 qu 17: *The way to the city castle.* p.166

Representation with change of place and moving picture plane

1. Different viewpoints as the subject moves in the landscape: change of place and shifting viewpoint.

Locality, object: passive
Subject: active

2. Irregular projection on an uneven surface.
Where the basic surface moves, a shift of the schematic relationships (contraction, extension) occurs, making the whole picture more dynamic (*cf.* p.253).

Place, object: in active motion
Subject: passive

3. Combined operations. Multi-dimensional movements.
The basic image (2) is in motion, or both dimensions move (1 and 2) in different ways. Where there is tension from two directions, the elementary forms multiply and change evenly or unevenly (unevenly, in motion; evenly, at rest).
Movements against one another or reinforcing one another. Communication to and fro, or interwoven countermovements. Where there are two factors of mobility, reciprocity between them gives rise to symmetry. Movement and countermovement result in balance. Multi-dimensionality consists in a combination of movements. Two-fold (two-dimensional) or three-fold (three-dimensional) main movement.
Where the main movement is three-fold (three-dimensional):

What has moved? Everything.
What has not moved? Nothing.

The relation between object and subject can be reversed, that is, the main action can be in the landscape, or the main action can be in the artist. Conflict between the subjective and the objective yields perfect unity.

195

1923/138: *Tightrope walker.* Lithograph.

4. The sensation of weight as a formative element.
The balance of forces. Weight and counterweight.
Quantity, quality, and their relativity

We were speaking of a tightrope walker as the extreme example of a symbol of the balance of forces. The tightrope walker with his pole as 'symbol of the balance of forces'. He holds the force of gravity in balance (weight and counterweight). He is a pair of scales.

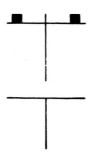

From our study of the elements of perspective we derived this symbol as an indication of the meaning of vertical and horizontal. The extension of the seen horizontal line to the horizontal plane or simply to the horizon gave us the spatial form of this symbol:

Sentence crossed out:
'Thus the scales will be as useful to me as they are to the shopkeeper.'

Today I should like to investigate the balance of the forces on either side. By this I mean the forces resulting from the gravitational pull of the earth. Thus we shall speak of gravitational balance.[1]

1935/M 17: *Signs on the field*. Watercolour.

'The balancing of the forces on either side,
the gravitational balance may be seen
in the structure, where it is reflected in
modifications and shifts of weight. Every deviation
from symmetry is based on active energies.'

1

2

3

Forces of this kind seem closest to us, because we ourselves are physically subject to the same laws of gravity. For the present let us presuppose the solid ground on which we stand, and let us not, as we do in exceptional cases, take to the water or the air.

In this weighing, scales will be useful as to us as they are to the grocer in his shop.

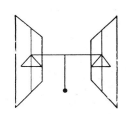

4

The scales

Symbol of the scales is the balance of vertical and horizontal [1, 2, 3]. This is more or less what scales look like. Scales weigh two weights against one another; because there are only two, the weights can operate in a plane. For I can always situate two points, wherever they may lie in space, in a single plane.

If we assume that the one plane has been correctly weighed, we can move our scales into a new position and weigh a second opposing plane against it [4].

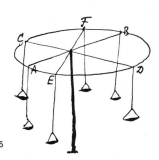

5

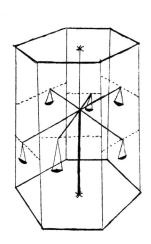

6

Fully spatial scales would look like this:

In this case we have spatial scales on three axes; A–B, C–D, and E–F [5]. With this device we might measure the weights on the walls of a hexagonal room [6].

It would not be wise to carry out our first experiments with this little machine, which has already ceased to be simple. You will agree that we had better stick to a single plane.

It does not matter whether these plane scales stand or hang [1,and 2]; all that matters is the cross formed by the horizontal and the vertical. This is the spirit of the scales and we can safely omit the pans [3].

199

1937/qu 14: *Little seaport*. Oil.

If we disturb the balance by overloading one side, the picture changes like this:

If we correct the imbalance by counterweight and counter-effect, it looks like this:
The new element is this cross. The diagonal cross representing the re-establishment of symmetrical balance.

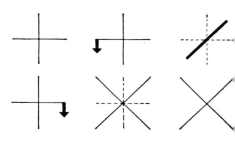

Now let me remind you of the complementary relation between lines and planes that we discussed in the lesson before last. The planes on which such plays of forces occur are usually limited. For example:

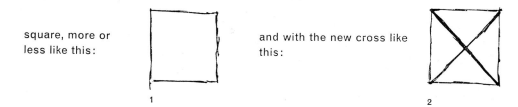

square, more or less like this:

1

and with the new cross like this:

2

If we take into consideration the complementary relationship between two views, this figure [2] may be interpreted as linear or planar. From a linear point of view, it is a square with two diagonals; from a planar point of view, it is a square divided into four triangles. These four triangles arrange themselves, especially if our square is not quite perfect, into two sets of opposite triangles [3, 4].

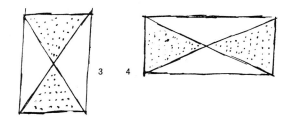

3   4

It is characteristic of their position that they strike each other with their points; the direction of the thrust is vertical-horizontal [5, 6]. Here we have the scales again [7, 8].

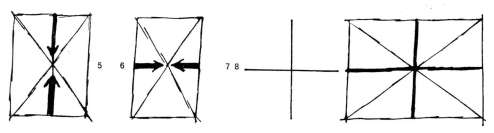

5   6   7 8

From Klee's estate No.028 (Untitled).
Watercolour mixed with paste on burlap.

The primitive simplicity of this particular handling of equilibrium has enabled me to use a kind of symbolic treatment. The result is symmetrical, because the weights on both sides are the same.

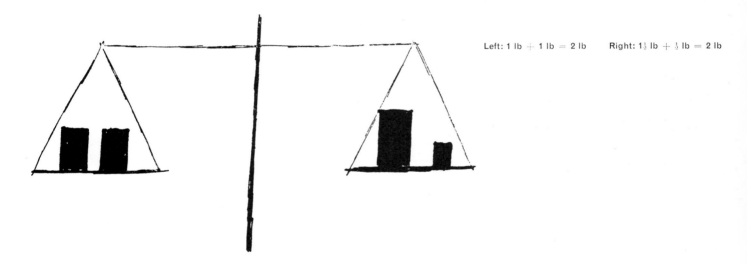

Left: 1 lb + 1 lb = 2 lb   Right: 1½ lb + ½ lb = 2 lb

A state of balance deviating from symmetry might be illustrated with the image of the scales: in one pan, for example, two pound weights, in the other a weight of one and a half pounds and one of half a pound.

Asymmetrical balance

But there is more to it than that. We must operate with pictorial elements that can serve as a basis for a discussion of the sense of weight. First, a few cases in which there is surely no question of balance.

203

Difference in extension,
more energy
on the right side through addition
surface = measure

Difference in tone value,
right hand side weighed down
with black energy

Difference in coloured tone-value,
right hand side weighed down
with colour energy

Difference in colour value
left hand side weighed down
by colour character

Now for correction:
In Fig.1a
we reach into the line compartment of
our box of elements[1] and put in what is
missing on the left
(Correction to Fig.1)

In Fig.2a we reach into the black
tone compartment and add a little
square of black to the grey square[2]
(Correction to Fig.2)

In Fig.3a
we reach into the red tone compartment
and proceed in the same way
(Correction to Fig.3)

In Fig.4a
we reach into the pure colour
compartment and weigh down the
blue side which is too light, with a bit
of yellow perhaps (Correction to Fig.4)

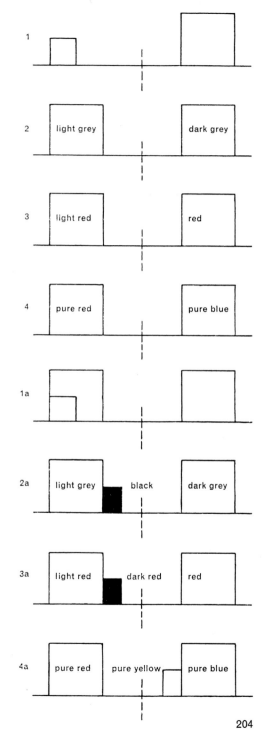

[1]'Box of elements' refers to the pictorial elements:
line, tone value, and colour. In the examples from
1a to 4a, line, tone value (in this special case black)
and colour are taken successively from the
box.

[2]Complementary variant of the sentence: 'Now for
correction: in Fig.2a we reach into the black tone
compartment of our box of elements and add a
little square of black beside the light grey square
(Bringing Fig.2 in balance).'
Instead of 'line', black (tone value) is added as a
counterweight. The complementary variant to the
colour corrective in Figs.3a and 4a is the same.

If the question of balance is formulated in terms of the three basic pictorial elements, the following schema results.

Disturbed balance   Balance restored

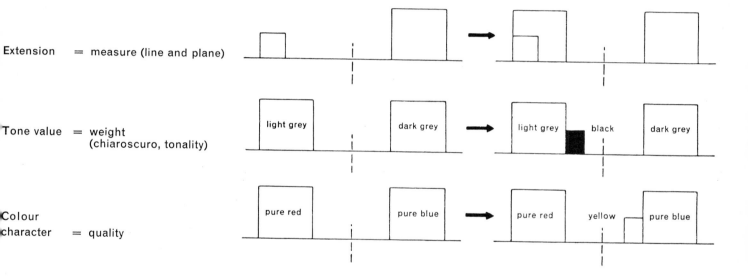

Extension = measure (line and plane)

Tone value = weight
(chiaroscuro, tonality)

light grey   dark grey   light grey   black   dark grey

Colour
character = quality

pure red   pure blue   pure red   yellow   pure blue

With accurate dosage on both sides we may regard the balance as restored; but this balance will no longer be identical with symmetry. But, of course, something more than this crude illustration will be needed for a complete and conclusive characterisation of 'this side' and 'that side'. To situate them definitely as part and counterpart, we shall need a hard and fast local imperative. A cogent example is a good deal more than a loose comparison.

205

1935/qu 15: *Will you be seated?*
Charcoal and red chalk.

206

Here a local imperative of this kind has been added, i.e. a particular idea governs the situation of the centres of gravity [1].

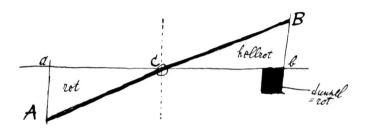

Schematic compositions related to our studies of balance [1] and [2]

The A–B axis overheavy with red has fallen to A and risen to B. Originally it was horizontal (a–b). These two axes, the original a–b and the new A–B have a single point in common, point C. C is therefore the fulcrum. The result of the axial rotation is that the red on the left is now lower than the light red on the right. Now dark red is added as a correction; it will restore new balance.

A little drama of horizontals interpreted in human terms: I have begun to lean leftward and I have reached out with my right hand for something to hold on to, to stop myself falling. Or, transposing the action to the vertical:

207

The top of my body is too heavy, the vertical will topple to the left unless a correction is quickly made below. By spreading my left leg I broaden my base [2]. The character of these two schematic compositions is centric, i.e. they depend on a centre.

If we conceive of a number of such compositional actions repeated from the bottom upwards, we obtain a series of such centres one above the other; and can no longer speak of a centric arrangement. This series of C points begins to look like a backbone, as you will see.

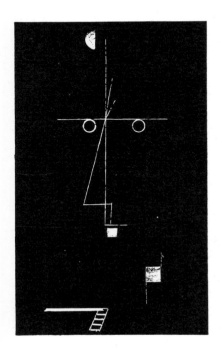

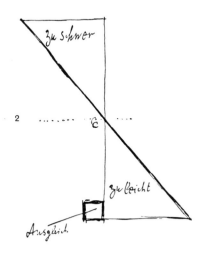

1927/k 3: *Artist's portrait.* Oil.

3

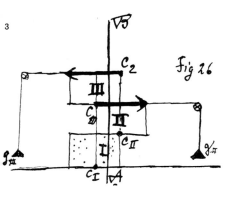

Suppose I to be a pedestal. II is a stone set on the pedestal in such a way that it barely escapes from toppling over. The energy that would make it topple is expressed by the arrow → and is measured in terms of weight g. Now if we continue this type of structure alternately on the left and right, nothing will actually topple. Each stone clings as it were to the vertical axis, each one would like to make the horizontal rotate at its point C_I, C_{II}, C_{III}.

The basic pattern of this construction provides the following structures (though there are other possibilities) [4, 5].

4   5

Figs.3, 4, and 5 represented as a layout, taking account of the forces which are directed away from the vertical axis [6, 7, 8], p.211.

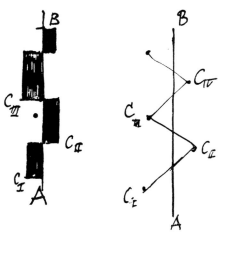

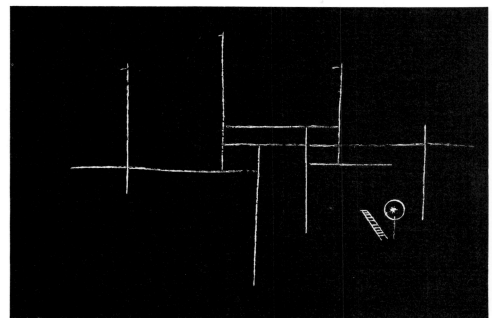

1930/N 1: *Scaffolding of building under construction.*
Colour.

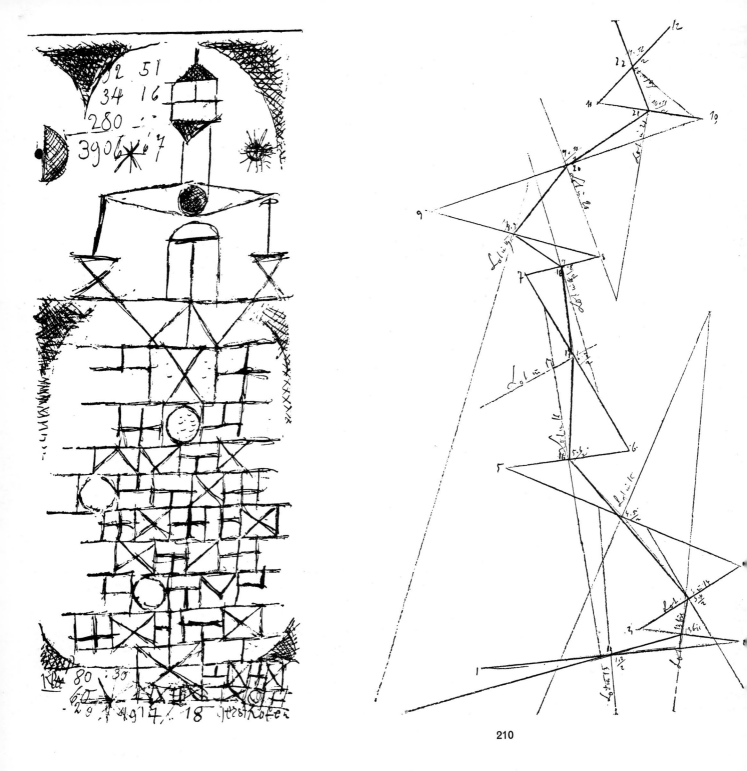

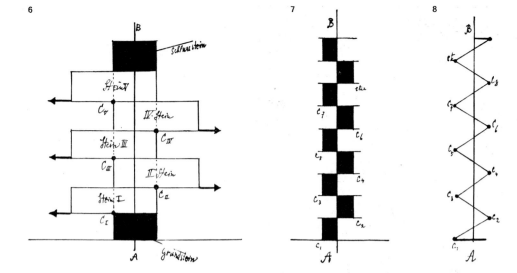

6   7   8

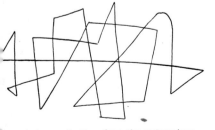

Linear balance structure from the watercolour
1933/L 4: *Dominated group*, p.176.

C_1, C_2, C_3 are fulcra. The series of C points looks like a backbone. Or if they were joined by lines, a zigzag about the vertical axis [8] would appear as a further possibility.
Such structures (a little like towers) may be compared with a standing man. Whenever the effort of keeping his balance becomes too arduous, he sits down and reduces it by approximately half. If he goes farther and leans on something, only a vestige of balancing activity remains, but still a vestige. For when a man faints, he usually falls off his chair. The vestige vanishes completely only when he lies down. Then the man becomes a block of stone.
Compositions of a horizontal character have something restful about them, compared with vertebral structures [7 and 8].

211

The base broadens and with it the horizontal at the expense of the vertical.

An appreciable relaxation sets in, an epic tempo as against the dramatic of the vertical, though, of course, this does not exclude the balancing of both sides. The vertical is still with us.

Balance is excluded only when the diagonal disappears, when the scales congeal, e.g. in the most primitive of structural rhythms, where there are only horizontal or vertical lines.

1930/y 4: *Daringly poised*. Watercolour.
Note in appendix.

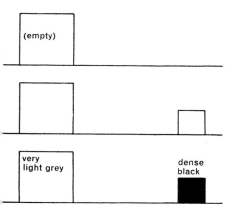

Now we come to the question of weight as it applies to the pictorial elements.
When I ask: Do you consider this square heavy or light? – there is no definite answer.
For if the answer were 'light', and I added a second, far smaller square

your hasty answer would be invalidated. For now the square makes a definitely heavier impression. Now we can say, the big one is heavy in comparison to the little one and the little one is light compared with the big one. Relativities.

But what now? Don't the weights tend to equalise each other, and why? The one is lighter in energy but much larger, the other is extremely heavy in energy, but small.

213

Now it is harder to decide which one is really heavier. In such a case our indecision implies a feeling of balance.

The effect of weight on the left is more a question of quantity, while on the right it expresses itself more qualitatively. Relativities! The notion that black is heavier than white applies only while we think of a white surface. In this case, if we disregard colour, black is the means of developing energy. The blacker the energy, the greater the impression of weight in comparison to the white surface. Another relativity.

But in the case of a black surface, black energy cannot express itself on it, if only because its heaviest development, the deepest black, would not stand out on such a surface. In this case, if we disregard colour again, white is the developer of energy, and the strongest effects are produced by the brightest white.

On a grey surface of medium tone, black and white can vie with one another as energies. Out of doors, that is, in the landscape, we can say that a white surface is present if the weather is foggy. The closest things, hence the heaviest, look particularly dark, while farther back things lighten progressively, merging at length with the background. On a dark night, light objects, such as lighted windows, produce the heaviest and strongest effects. And on a normal day we can observe the interplay of dark and light on a middle background. In physics we speak of specific gravity compared to water; for us there are different kinds of specific gravity: in comparison with white, with black, with medium (and with every intermediate tone).

The colour world brings in still other values, colours on a red background, colours on a violet background, etc.

'Lighting in nature is largely a matter of free space and atmosphere.'

'Darkening in nature is more a matter of hill and dale, it is discerned mainly in the artificial inner space, where air and light do not exert their power of dissolution, but where darkening, in cubic space, modulates distinctly in steps.'

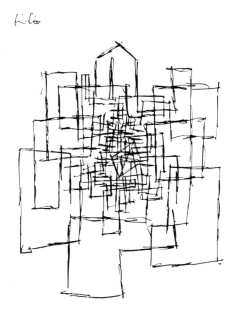

1930/A 1: *Abundance in village.* Pen and ink. Linear-active polyphony.

214

The examples illustrating the exercises show letters in balance as linear-active polyphonies: in solemn static construction and in dynamic position, with one or more subjects interpenetrating.

a) Letters by themselves, balanced, as for example, H A M etc. b) Unbalanced letters, such as P F etc. Plan the composition to be solemnly static, or in a dynamic position.

Linear-active polyphonies

A subject E, purely static

Two subjects, E, B

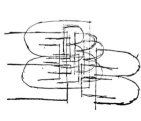

Three subjects, Z E T

A higher subject, P A M

P R I in dynamic position

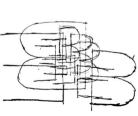

E I L in dynamic position

Note in Appendix

1931/y 3: *Chess*. Oil.
For analysis, see p.218.

5. Structural formation. Individual and dividual characters
Measuring and weighing as a pictorial procedure
Measurements of time and length   **16 January 1922**

Structure (Dividual articulation)

In our last lesson we noted the contrast between compositional and structural character. The most elementary structural rhythms made their appearance. Numerically they were expressed in small numbers, the sum of simple units: horizontal and vertical lines as the most primitive structural rhythms [1].
Linear addition of simple units [2, 3].

from left to right   from top to bottom

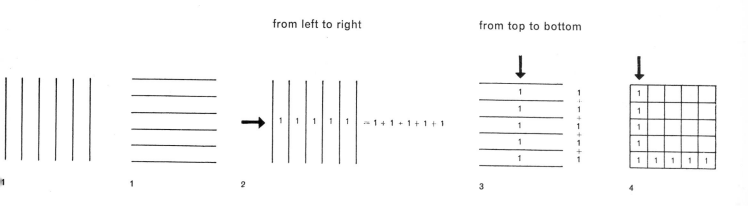

Repetition of the same unity in the directions from left to right and from top to bottom.
A combination of the two directions produces the following structural design [4], which may be described as an addition of units in two dimensions. Though amplified by its two-dimensional direction, this picture still occupies the lowest rank in the structural scale.
The most primitive structural rhythm in the directions from left to right and top to bottom.

217

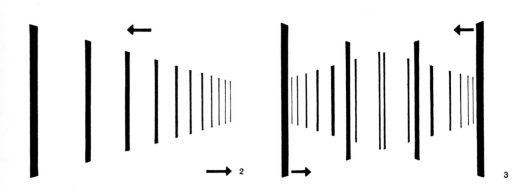

1

Analysis of movement in connection with 1931/y 3: *Chess*, p.216.

Measured by the norm, the movement increases in relation to the fixed dimension [1].

2

3

The natural progression of the lengths and thicknesses of lines and of their intervals[1] [2].

The same progression coming and going, interwoven [3].
(Interpenetration of progression and regression. 'From the constructive point of view not a result in itself but an expression of function.')

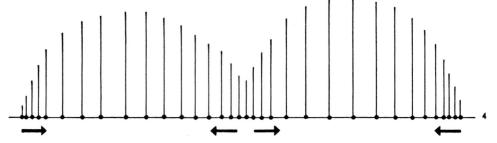

4

'A regular, double progression (twice there and back) looks like this (intermittent progression, interwoven countermovement)' [4].

[1]*Cf.* the construction of a natural progression, p.134. On the same page: 'Possible amplification. Mix them up while preserving the thickness and length of the lines'.

218

the course of the movement and
countermovement in Fig.3 is changed by free
choice, the progression of steps changes to a
progression of 'leaps' (free choice of elements).
'The chronology of the situation' deviates from
strict symmetry and changes according to the
movement through space and time. The series of
lines serving for visual articulation should be
thought of as shifted in space [Figs.2 and 3].'

f. the 'receptive process', the
space-time problem, p.357.

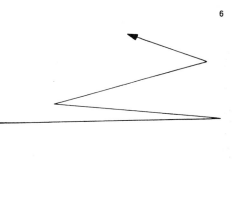

Regression

Progression

this local change of position in *Chess* leads to the
following analysis of movement [5]:
'The proportions of the lines characterise the
varying progress of the movement; the intervals
indicate the measure of time.
Each progression results in a spatial factor.'

'The movement takes on a definite character [6]
when the basic design is both visible and
locally defined as the measure of
structural repetition' [7].

In a pictorial representation of progression in
two directions, the movement, despite its agitation,
achieves balance; where the values are
equal it comes to a standstill.'

In *Chess* there is a visual division given, while
in *Superchess* it should be thought of as the
basis of measurement or function.

f. on the analysis of motion: Movement and
countermovement, treated as a duality, p.16.
The dimensional concepts:
Line   = what can be measured
Tone value   = questions of weight
Colour   = quality
Towards a theory of form-production, p.86.

6

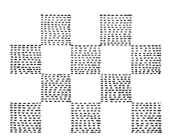

7

219

In the use of measure and weight: This new structure is one step higher. Its unit is one plus two: 1 + 2.

In terms of measure

1

$1 + 2 + 1 + 2 + 1 + 2 + 1 + 2 + 1 + 2 + 1 +$
represented in numbers

Or this structure:

In terms of weight

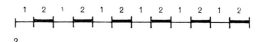

2

$1 + 2 + 1 + 2 + 1 + 2 + 1 + 2 + 1 + 2 + 1 +$
represented in numbers

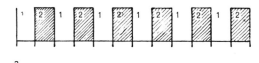

3

The two structures (Figs. 1 and 2) are exactly alike if we compare their numerical expression. The difference lies only in the choice of pictorial elements. The first structure makes use only of a 'single unit of distance' and 'a double unit of distance' (quantities) as measurements; the second makes use of the weights light and dark (qualities) [2 and 3]. Measure on one side, weight on the other, one might also say.[1] Or in one case a force which does the increased work 2 without extra strain, simply by taking twice as long; and in the other case, a force which works towards its higher goal by doubling its energy.[2]

[1] The original version of this sentence had 'quantities' and 'qualities'. Klee crossed them out in pencil and substituted 'measures' and 'weights'. This accounts for the repetition of 'measure' and 'weight'.

[2] The concepts of measure and weight and their movements: 'Movements of measure: broadening–narrowing, expansion–contraction. Movements of weight: thinning–thickening, stretching–tightening. 'Theorem: Weight is the degree of density of an element compared with another element. The rule is: extension and contraction of tone value connected with measure, the enlargement and diminution of surface content.' (*Cf.* p.235.)

Wishing to attach a hook to a picture frame, I measure the top most carefully to find the centre. I fix my hook exactly in the centre and feel sure that everything will be all right. But in the end my picture slants. Why does it slant? Because the wood is not of the same density throughout, or perhaps because the glass is thicker and heavier on one side. In short, I have made the mistake of measuring rather than weighing. In another case I wish to cut a long wooden pole exactly in two. It seems to me that the simplest way is to balance the pole on something with a knife-sharp edge. Delighted at my cleverness, I cheerfully apply my saw. The result: two parts of entirely different length. How so? Here again the wood must have been uneven in thickness and weight, and I have made the mistake of weighing rather than measuring.

So we have measure on the one hand, weight on the other. I return to our two structures that we have called one step higher, and consider the numerical series that is common to them:

$$1 + 2 + 1 + 2 + 1 + 2 + 1 + 2 \text{ etc.}$$

Nothing changes in this series if I represent it like this:

$$(1 + 2) + (1 + 2) + (1 + 2) + (1 + 2) \text{ etc.}$$

And this too will be the same:

$$3 + 3 + 3 + 3$$

and this is a regular repetition of a kind of unit (made up of three parts), hence a pure structural matter.
The following diagram gives a picture of this algebraic manoeuvre:[1]

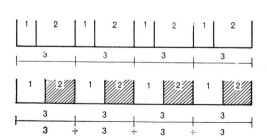

Thus $3 + 3 + 3 + 3 + 3 = I + I + I + I + I$. The Roman one stands for a higher unit.

1937/R 1: *Superchess*. Oil.
Œuvre catalogue: *'Über Schach'* (About chess)
instead of *'Überschach'*. Analysis, p. 224.

Weight structure in two dimensions

second dimension
horizontal sums
(weight of the strips)

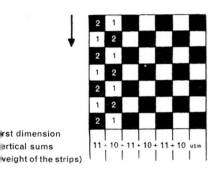

first dimension
vertical sums
(weight of the strips)

11 + 10 + 11 + 10 + 11 + 10 usw

2

3

The chess-board. If we expand Fig.3, p.220 (weight structure) in two dimensions, the vertical sum of fields [1] is:
11 + 10 + 11 + 10 + 11 + 10 = (11 + 10) + (11 + 10) + (11 + 10) =
21 + 21 + 21 = I + I + I etc.
The horizontal sums present the same picture, that is, I+I+I etc. in a horizontal direction [2].

4

Two values of different weight added to form a rhythm which when repeated produces a diagram of linear two-part time [4].
Extended in two dimensions in the simplest synthetic order, the diagram becomes a chess-board:
The two dimensions combined (the actions in Figs.1 and 2) [3].

223

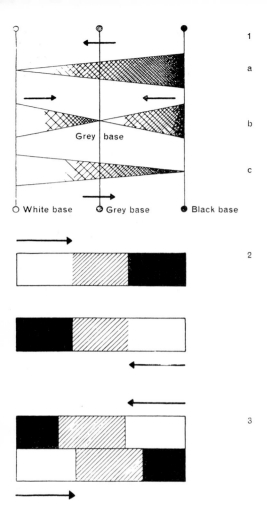

1

a

b

Grey base

c

○ White base   ◑ Grey base   ● Black base

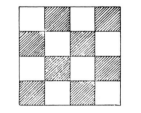

2

3

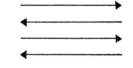

4

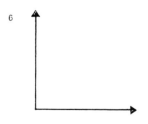

5

6

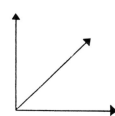

7

Analysis of movement in connection with 1937/R 1: *Superchess*, p. 222.

Light-dark movement [1]:
(a) Progression towards a primary contrast. Black base.
(b) Progression towards two secondary contrasts. The grey base in the middle is the norm.
(c) Progression towards a primary contrast. White base.

Regularly stepped movement from white to black and back again ('light-dark movement on a static surface') [2].

The individually structured movement from light to dark (irregular and displaced base planes) [3].

'Even structure makes for continuity without progression and without the stimulus of increase or decrease. The individual forms at any rate, are motionless. I myself go forward, but despite their multiplicity the resulting forms are unproductive. Regularly measured multiplication is stagnant.' [4].

In principle, a new dimension of movement is added to the simple movements of measure and tonality from left to right and back again (displacement and change) [5].

'The crossing of light and dark: progressive movement from left to right (horizontal) and progressive movement from bottom to top (vertical)' [6].

Where the two structures are combined, the diagonal direction from lower left to upper right determines the path of movement [7].
'This is the path of pure squares, forms corresponding to the initial form. In this case subdivision in the direction of increase is positive. Already enough to make up the mind of the optimist.'

224

'The basic predynamic form by which to appraise the direction of movement and determine its nature as increase (crescendo) or decrease (decrescendo).' [8, 9]

'With a change in the relation between progressive intervals, the progression no longer advances in steps but in jumps (free choice of elements).' [8, 9]

Progression ↗

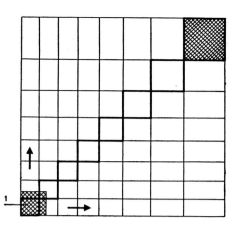

8

'1 = $\frac{1}{64}$ square as the regular surface unit.'

Regression ↘

9

Summary:
The movements in the dimensions 'left–right', 'top–bottom', 'before–behind' are measured simultaneously in several dimensions by the local norm. The structural parts differ in measure (quantitatively) and in colour (qualitatively). Structural parts in ultramarine and red serve to stress the diagonals, increasing and decreasing towards the centre of the plane. Visible mobility arises in relation to the quantity and quality of the energies. 'The centres of the progressive parts are intuitively established in such a way that the progressive movement persists from part to part.' The irregular measures are filled out with progressive energy values. The organism of its movement may be measured against the regular rhythmic structure 1/2 (black-white) – the lowest link in the chain of development (Fig.3, p.223) – or, in other words: movement and countermovement may be measured by (or operate 'through') the structural rhythm of *Chess*. (*Cf*. multi-dimensional contacts: 'Towards a Theory . . .' p.86.)

Progression ↗ and regression ↘ add up to the diagonal cross [10]:
(The main directions, given by the parts, make this the symbol of spatial dimensions.)

10

225

The two directions add up to: Light and Heavy.

Light, considered by itself □ □ □ □   Heavy, considered by itself ■ ■ ■ ■
　　　　　　　　　　　　　　□ □ □ □　　　　　　　　　　　　　　　 ■ ■ ■ ■
　　　　　　　　　　　　　　□ □ □ □　　　　　　　　　　　　　　　 ■ ■ ■ ■
　　　　　　　　　　　　　　□ □ □ □　　　　　　　　　　　　　　　 ■ ■ ■ ■

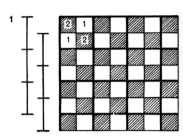

Consequently this entire square breaks down horizontally and vertically into pairs of neighbouring fields [1]. The result is a cluster of square units each having four parts and a value of six.

The combination of the two dimensions produces this composite unit

    or | 1 | 2 |
　　　　　　　　　　　　　 | 2 | 1 | A single unit of Fig.1, whose value is 6.

The same spatial unit of a two-dimensional composite six repeated. The repetition of units is the basis of the rhythmical beat [2].

Numerical representation of the six-part unit.

VI	VI	VI
VI	VI	VI
VI	VI	VI

or

```
6 + 6 + 6        I + I + I        I  I  I
+   +   +
6 + 6 + 6   or   I + I + I   or   I  I  I
+   +   +
6 + 6 + 6        I + I + I        I  I  I
```

This regular repetition of a higher unit is again characteristic of structural form.

226

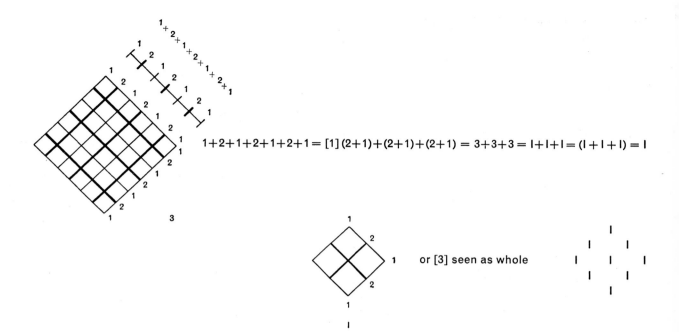

$$1+2+1+2+1+2+1 = [1] \, (2+1)+(2+1)+(2+1) = 3+3+3 = I+I+I = (I+I+I) = I$$

or [3] seen as whole

A different view of this chess-board structure with stress on the diagonals gives us a linear structure with two lines of different quality, which can be read reciprocally[1] as a rhythm of four-part units [3]. These units take the form of squares standing on their corners. In this way we might invent more complex and highly captivating structural motifs. As soon as any repetitive rhythm can be continued, its structural character is determined.

$$I + I + I + \big| I + I + I + I + \big| I + I + I + I + I + \big| \text{ etc.}$$

3 units   4 units   5 units   as structural type

All these series of figures are suborganic in character. Parts can be taken away or added without their rhythmic character, which is based on repetition, being changed. Thus the structural character is dividual, i.e. divisible.

227

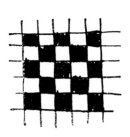 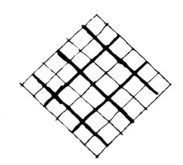

Conceived as a mesh, this rhythm is at the same time structural (i.e. simply repetitive).

In linear terms 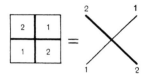 hence  purely linear, without weight

Linear variants

 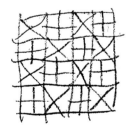

Further variations at will, by repeating composite units designed for the following kinds of repetition: reversal, displacement, reflection, and rotation.

The centre clearly
marked

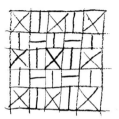

The centre obscure

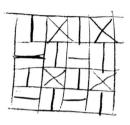

Such rhythms cannot be said to have an organic character. This is evident from a glance at the corresponding number series. Every organism is an individual, that is to say, cannot be divided. In other words, one cannot take anything away without changing the character of the whole, or in living creatures, without disturbing or even destroying the function of the whole. Nor can anything be added.

Our series and complexes of numbers keep their individual character,

if instead of $1+1+1+1$ instead of: $6+6$ we write: $6 + 6 + 6$ or: $6 + 6 + 6 + 6$
  we write: $1+1+1$ $+$ $+$ $+$ $+$ $+$ $+$ $+$ $+$ $+$
    or: $1+1+1+1+1$ $6+6$ $6 + 6 + 6$ $6 + 6 + 6 + 6$
                                     $+$ $+$ $+$ $+$ $+$ $+$ $+$
instead of: $3+3+3+3$ $6 + 6 + 6$ $6 + 6 + 6 + 6$
  we write: $3+3+3$ $+$ $+$ $+$ $+$
    or: $3+3+3+3+3$ $6 + 6 + 6 + 6$

We are easily reminded of the lower animals, consisting of only very few cells, or of the one-celled bacteria, which are only perceptible in the mass.

But there is also a great advantage in this indifference of structural rhythms to individuality: they may easily be linked with an organic, individual whole, in such a way as to support the character of the organism without opposing it in any way.

Thus they are suitable for putting life into thin areas of certain compositions; they have long been known as wallpaper patterns; and they lend neutral animation to the covers of books and portfolios.

Pure ornament is governed by primitive rhythmics (dividual or sometimes individual). It has no rhythmic relation to the inner creative drives of man.

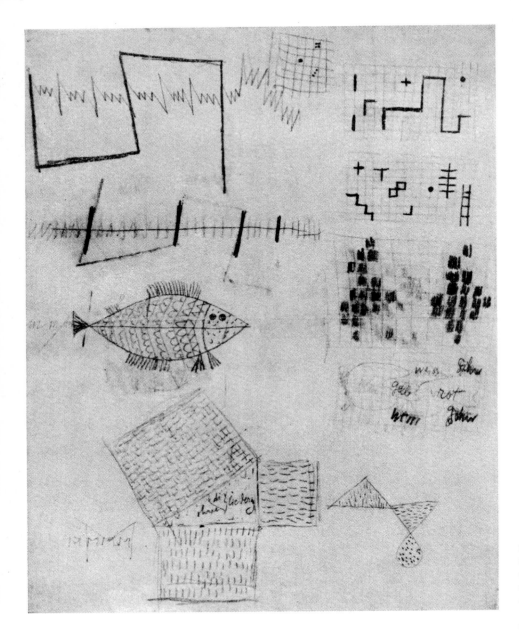

Examples of 'dividual structural rhythms' (characterised by repetition) and 'individual structures'. 'In part organically handled, so that one supports the other.' The accentuation of particular details gives rise to individual structures. In the present examples, individualisation is achieved through linear accent or with squares of colour. In the 'combination of structural and individual rhythms' the next degree of rhythm is reached by the 'intimate fusion of individual and structure' (an organic union of the two). The 'individual structure' is born.

For example: the fish.

Individual rhythms
(individual structures)

These cannot, on the other hand, be reduced to single or similar numbers, but inexorably only to ratios

such as   2 : 3 : 5
or   7 : 11 : 13 : 17
or   a : b = b : (a + b), Golden Section.

Special case of dissymmetry, the Golden Section: 3 : 5 = 5 : 8   8 : 13 = 13 : 21

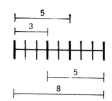

The smaller part is to the larger part as the larger to the whole: a : b = b : (a + b).

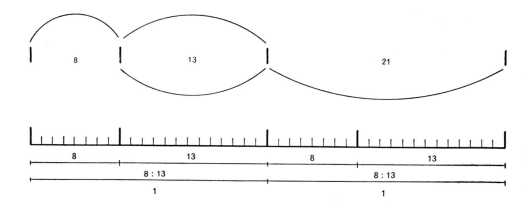

In a rhythmic individual whole, based on the Golden Section, the composite unit 1 = 8 : 13 is repeated.

231

1932/s 2: *City Castle of KR*. Oil.
Cf. analysis of movement, p.234.
The dividual structural characteristics (normative
units or basic form) alternate with the higher
units individualised by movement.

1. 'Constructive study of
   extensions of arcs. (F and F₁
   are centres of circles, drawn
   on the margins of whole
   numbers)'

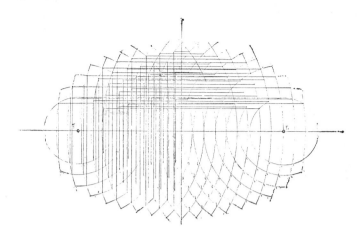

2. 'Point structure of 1'

3. 'Free structural variation on
   the theme (freely selected
   movements based on the
   constructive principles of
   1 and 2)'

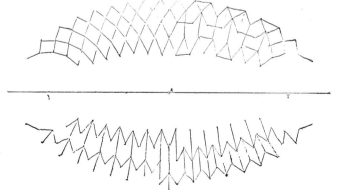

233

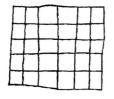
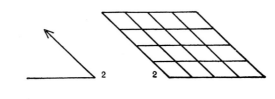
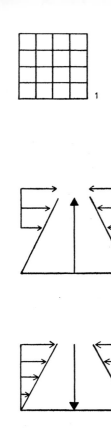

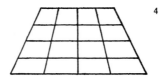
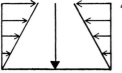
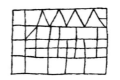

Analysis of movement in 1932/s 2:
City Castle of KR, p. 232.

'Basic design – this is the stage preceding
movement [1]. A simple principal
movement or angular movement.' [2].

'Twofold principal movement' [3].

'Twofold principal movement' [4].

Linear analysis of a part of *City Castle of KR*.
Seen in terms of ground-plan or elevation [5].
Spatial expansion through movement [6].

The structural characters are rhythmically joined
into an individual whole. Structural units with
two-dimensional emphasis alternate with others
projected into space.
'The movement of the subdivisions is organically
related to the principal movements.'
The movement in space and time is individual
in nature and determines the supra-rhythmical
character. 'Try to achieve the greatest possible
movement with the least possible means
(economy of means obtained by repetition of a
limited number of simple structural
characteristics).'

927/w 7: *Harmony of the southern flora.*
Watercolour [1].

927/w 1: *Thomas R.'s country house.*
Watercolour [2].

927/w 2: *Stratification sets in.* Watercolour [3].

Mass, weight and their movements

The picture plane with movement
intensified. Dividual-individual synthesis of
measure and weight.

'The norm is the usual state (state of rest)'. [1, p.234].
The notion of the norm provides a solid basis on
which to consider the action in the picture as a
whole and in its parts.
'Starting from the norm, freely chosen steps are
taken, leading to irregularity.'
Amplifications are achieved by movements
which lead to modulation of the strictly normal
formats (and norms). By expanding or contracting
movements of measure and weight (density and
extension). The direction of movement may be
generally progressive or regressive.

[1] 'The movement is unequivocal when,
among other things, the basic design
is both perceptible and locally defined.' The
movement grows (and is measurable) in relation to
the other, fixed dimension. The movement in the
realms of tonality and colour is based on
balanced masses. Individual colour actions
contrast with the dividual representation of
measurement. Static measurement – intensity of
colour movement. 'The colour actions advance
rhythmically or polyphonically. Keep the harmony
lively. The rise and fall start from points of
climax. In the vibrant dynamic realm, in the
realm of spirituality, of the complete circle and
whole movement, where pure colours make their
home, strong colour is the most powerful of
psychic energies.'
Movement and countermovement throughout the
colour plane lead to balanced movement. 'An
oscillating movement on the colour circle: hither,
thither, striving outward, returning home.
Uninterrupted movement stands higher than
direction.'
The basic measure (static) and the dynamic
discharge of tension are treated as
complementary in the realm of quality or colour.
'Here one thing is perceived acutely: the
distribution of roles.'
1927/w 7: *Harmony of the southern flora.*
Watercolour.
(Synthesis of dividual planar measure and
individual colour = quality.)
Similar colour action in:
1927/E 4: *Harmony of the northern flora.* Oil, p.506.

1938/H 20: *Oriental-sweet.* Oil.
Colour reproduction in Grohmann, p.331.
Cf. the peripheral colour movements, p.485.

[2] 'On the basis of symmetry, it
may be inferred that there has been a progressive
contraction which has changed the
dimensions of squares originally of
equal size. Assuming that the whole, taken field
by field, contained equal quantities of colour, the
colour diminishes when the dimensions are
increased, and increases when they are
diminished. As a result, the large fields are thin,
the small ones dense in colour.'
Simple and complicated movements seen as
increase and decrease of measure and weight.
Congruence of measure and weight results
in balance.
'Congruence of measure and weight should be
taken to mean that the highest density occurs on
the smallest surface. Large surfaces reduce the
density, lighten the weight of the given area, and
compensate for the reduced weight by an increase
in surface measurement. Thus balance prevails.
Theorem: Weight is the degree of density of one
element as against another.'
Where the picture plane is mobile, there is a
change in the regular projective relations,
corresponding to the greater mobility of the
basic proportions.
1927/w 1: *Thomas R.'s country house.* Watercolour.
(Simultaneous horizontal and vertical projection.)

[3] 'The dynamic is in the action. It moves in, it is
not static being, but action. Using normal
means, through articulation, or movement,
it is possible to capture the unique. There is
an organic connection between the main
movement and its subdivisions of movement.
Once you know what has stood fast and what
has moved, the pattern is clear.
'Principal lesson: accented factors take
precedence over unaccented factors.' If the
static relations are dynamically labilised, they
lose some of their fixity of place. Movement takes
the foreground. Movement and countermovement
become more and more intertwined or intermeshed
with the interpenetration of horizontals. Pressure
and counterpressure bring dislocation.
1927/w 2: *Stratification sets in.* Watercolour.
Cf. Structure with mobile base relations, p.252.
Warping of horizontals, p.311, and the relation
of fall to strata, p.414.

1929/s 9: *Old man reckoning*. Engraving.

The central opposition
Dividual-Individual[1]

The question as to whether a thing is dividual or individual is decided by the criterion of indefinite extension or definite measure. For where there is indefinite extension, arbitrary divisions can be made without changing the structural style. But where an individual has definite measure, nothing can be added or subtracted without changing it into another individual.

Symbol of dividuality: The structural as indeterminate number. The element may be either line (measurement) or tone value (weight).

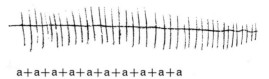

a+a+a+a+a+a+a+a+a+a

Indeterminate, dividual

Symbol of individuality: nothing is repeated, every unit is different from every other [1].
Indeterminate number, with individual stress (e.g. by difference in colour) [2].
Negative stress on the individual (gaps, elimination). Negative whole [3].
Additional possibility: positive and negative combined.

Note by Klee:
Structure: The question of the articulation, natural or otherwise, of matter. (Arrangement of the atoms in the molecule of a compound, expressed by the structural formula.)
Style: The question of the traces of the diverse manual movements. Where did these traces become visible?
Rhythm: The question of whether a number such as 2 or 3 (or possibly 1), 4 (as 2 + 2) or 6 (as 2 + 2 + 2) is repeated as the subdivision of a unit. If so, we have rhythm.
Dividual structure: The question of indeterminate extension of the units (dividual = divisible).
Individual structure is present when the concept is positively stated.'

1

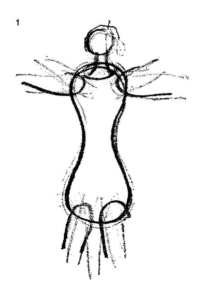

2

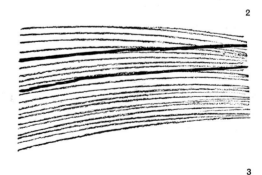

3

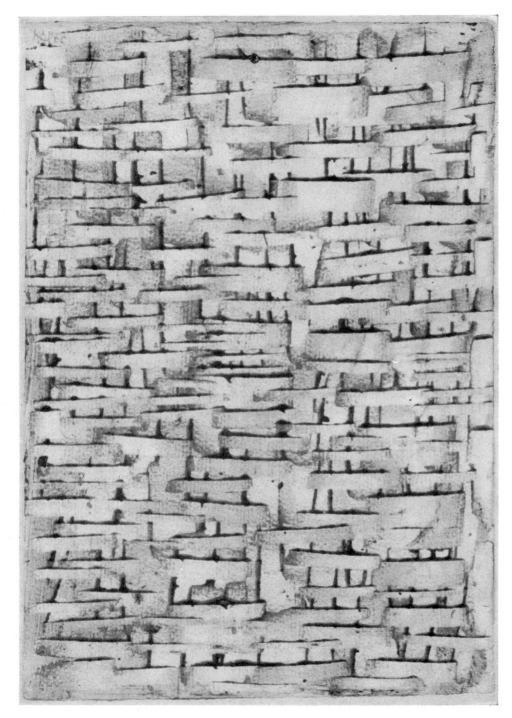

1933/E 13: *World harbour*. Paste and pigment
on paper.

Dividuality – Individuality

Dividuality:
indeterminate extension
of a two-part unit

Individuality: determinate extension

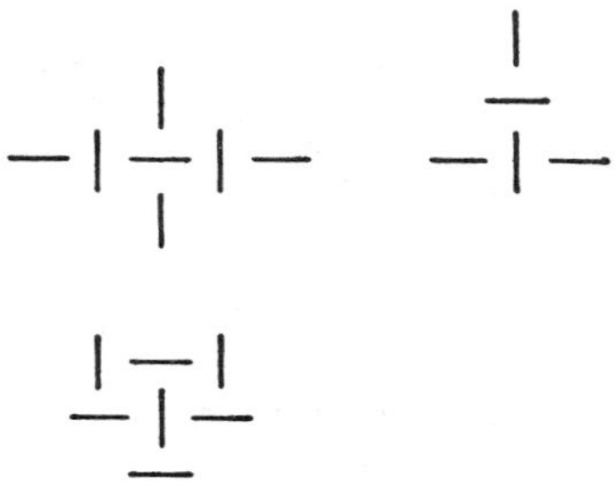

Rhythmic repetition, dividual

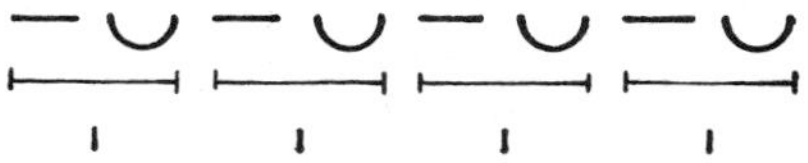

Rhythmic repetition '2',
heavy-light, dividual

Rhythmic repetition, '5', dividual

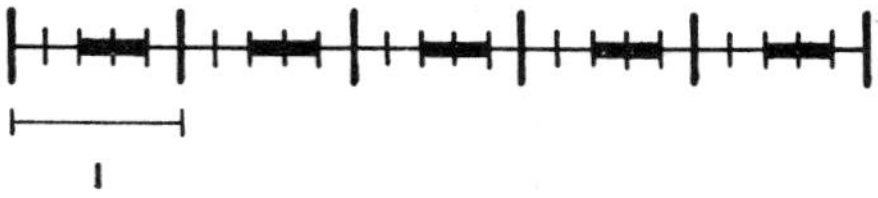

Two-part rhythmic unit, dividual

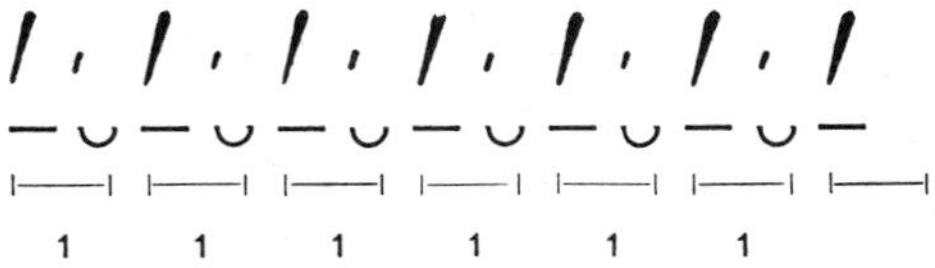

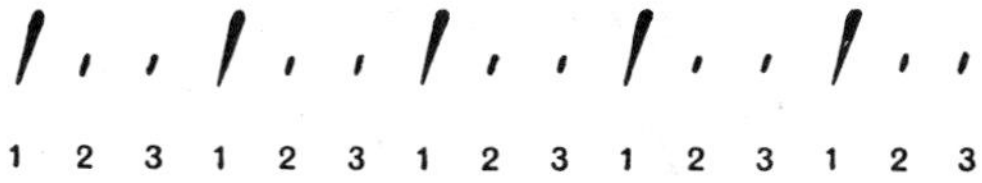

Three-part rhythmic unit, dividual. Qualitative accent: rhythm based on weight.

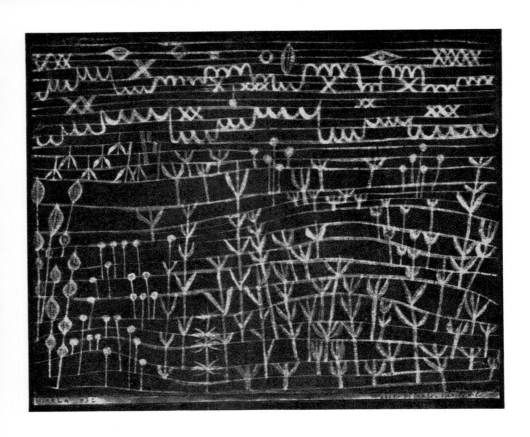

1924/132: *Hieroglyphic water plants*. Watercolour.

Examples:
1924/186 ARA: *Coolness in a tropical garden*.
Watercolour. Grohmann, p.394.
1925/8: *Vast (Harbour of roses)*. Watercolour.
1928/G 4: *Gardening*. Pen-and-ink.
1928/R 1: *Small units in layers*. Watercolour.
1929/UE 9: *Movements in sluices*. Pen-and-ink.

Other possibilities of dividual structure

Bending

Breaking

The mode of treatment depends on our feeling about the obstacles we are facing: are they hard or soft?

Combination of the two aggregate states solid and liquid

Liquid above solid below   Light murmur above, hard ring below

Slightly obstructed flow as of water over pebbles

Repetitive accent on units made up of higher and lower parts

'Gaseous', a refinement of liquid (evaporation). 'Cloudy'

1940/F 13: *Centipede in an enclosure*.
Pastel on cotton.

Examples:
1925/c 5: *Figure writing*. Pen-and-ink. Giedion, p.93.
1936/k 2: *Afflicted city*. Oil. Colour reproduction,
Giedion, p.139.
1938/8: *Animals in an enclosure*. Colour.
Grohmann, p.309.
1940/g 14: *Enclosure for pachyderms*. Oil
on burlap.
1940/ From Klee's estate: (*Captive*). Oil.
Grohmann, p.308.

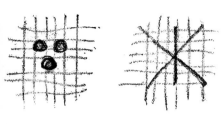

A small significant number keeps telling us that any division would destroy the character

The two structural types
dividual and individual combined

Formation of a higher intermediate unit by the overlapping of primary units.
3 = intermediate units

Change of structural character
coinciding with a
higher articulation

Formation of intermediate
units by structural overlapping
or interpenetration

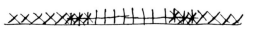

243

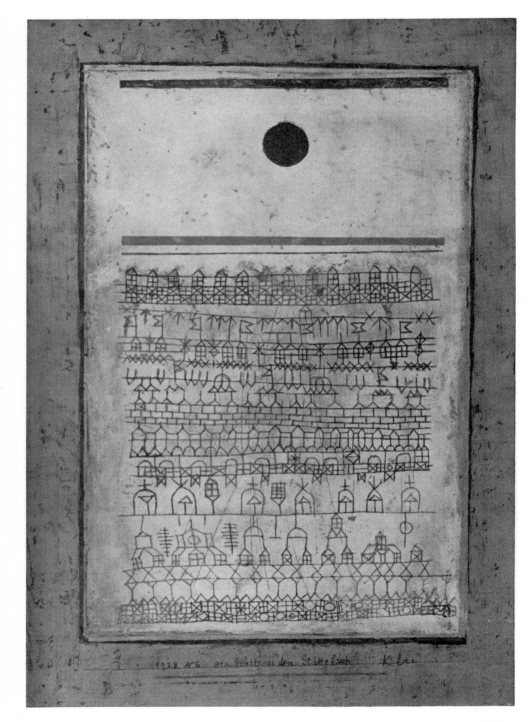

1928/N 6: *A page from the city records*.
Oil.

(*Cf*. 1927/K 10: *Pastoral* (*Rhythms*). Oil.
Grohmann, p.394.)

Fundamental possibilities of movement with dividual-individual structure
Types and directions of movement

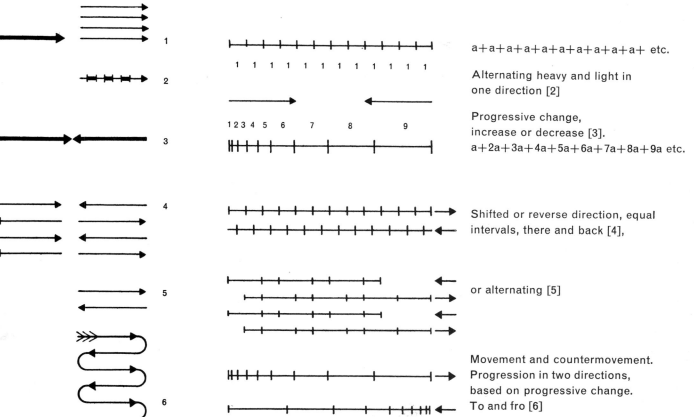

Symmetry is repeated. Linear-active, planar-passive, same measurement and direction.
Dividual, one-dimensional (purely linear) [1].

$a+a+a+a+a+a+a+a+a+a+$ etc.

Alternating heavy and light in one direction [2]

Progressive change,
increase or decrease [3].
$a+2a+3a+4a+5a+6a+7a+8a+9a$ etc.

Shifted or reverse direction, equal
intervals, there and back [4],

or alternating [5]

Movement and countermovement.
Progression in two directions,
based on progressive change.
To and fro [6]

Even or uneven movement, measured from a fixed limit (structural change), from an accented centre, or from the boundary of an individual unit [7].

Another possibility: movement from the inside out or from the outside in [8].
The whole is in movement, tending towards total fulfilment.

Number: indeterminate, dividual
(A special case of rhythm:
'one! one! one! one!')

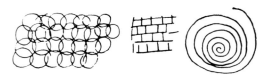

Determinate,
individual or rhythmic

|
| | | |
| | |
| |

Indeterminate number, dividual

Determinate number, individual

Free synthesis with change
of structure

Here two independent concepts meet: 'rhythm' and the distinction between dividual
and individual structure.

By way of clarification: the concepts are mutually independent in so far as both dividual
and individual formations can be rhythmic. Both can be rhythmic if their structure is based
on one of the numbers two, three, or four. It can also be a recurrence of a pure unit, or it
can be based on five. Or it may be based on 6, 8, 9, 12, if these higher numbers show
distinct caesuras indicating 2, 3 or 4.

The repetition of a composite unit is purely rhythmic; its subdivisions correspond in
principle to the numbers 2, 3, 4 (=2 × 2), 5 and 6 (=3 × 2 or 2 × 3).

Cf. 1927 L 1: *Artificial rock.* Oil. Grohmann, p.398.

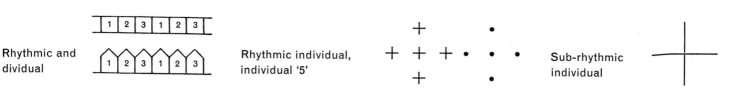

Rhythmic and dividual

Rhythmic individual, individual '5'

Sub-rhythmic individual

General structural concepts: The concepts of change, uniformity, multiplication, and displacement are general structural concepts that apply both to dividual and individual forms. Certain activities produce very definite structural forms which can observably become individuals. The individual is paramount. It is the higher structural character, even if it takes up less room. In this case its superiority lies in the quality or intensity of its special character, even if it seems limited in extension and inferior in position.

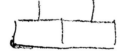

One brick on two bricks. The wall is a horizontal strip with alternate displacement of rows by half a unit.

1st half measure   2nd half measure   1st half measure   2nd half measure

Bricklaying – a double three-part rhythm (six-part time).

Criteria: The juxtaposition of like and unlike parts. Uniformity: like forms. Change: varying forms or the interpenetration of different forms.
The characters may be more or less independent of one another. Crucial are the positional relations between the units. Quantity determines the structural impression. The larger number, 'major', as an indeterminate number of structural units, constitutes the norm. 'Minor', the smaller, determinate number, appears as its opposite and tends towards individuality. 'Major-minor' are related in the same way as active-passive.

1934/L 5: *With the wheel.* Colour.

Organisation of structural characters. Decrease and increase of composite units.

The linear expression of structural ideas is not the only one. Planar formations can also be expressed in tonalities or colours, which may also serve to make the parts work towards the whole![1]

[1] Taking the primary colours as an example: 1=yellow, 2=red, 3=blue.

Square structuring can be accomplished in colour with two elements

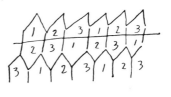

Progressive rows mean a change of position. Even or uneven movement on the plane (*cf.* the linear norms of motion p.245). Experiments using the smallest possible amount of means. See 1932/s 2: *City Castle of KR*, p.232.

Where planar units meet in a line a change of element is necessary. Where planar units touch in a point no change of element is necessary

The path to the individual from the confusing multiplicity of dividual units: certain units are accented and thus become dominant.[2] This leads to an organisation in which independent units are combined. The minor structure becomes truly individual in the figurative sense when its parts take on a character beyond the rhythm.

[2] Accentuation of colour or tone value. The major as predominating colour. The minor brought out by means of contrast.

Simple higher structures combined with rhythmic pattern

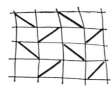

249

1924/128: *Mural*. Tempera on canvas.

'The question as to what is dividual and what is
individual implies the existence of a relation.
A field is delimited (a line here and a line there).
The organisation becomes truly individual in the
figurative sense when its parts take on a
character beyond rhythm.'
A 'composite unit' embodies progressive
rhythmic change: 'movement in long and short
steps, displacement, variation, uniformity, reversal,
increase, decrease of the structural elements'.
Mural shows a synthesis of dividual and individual
structuring. ('Planar effect with different types of
linear progression.') This higher unit leads to the
problems of proportion.

**Basic possibilities
of structural formation**
(linear-medial = planar-medial):

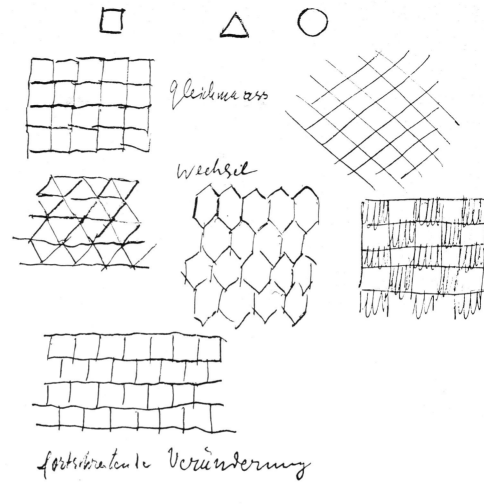

Uniformity

gleichmaass

Alternation

Wechsel

Progressive change

fortschreitende Veränderung

From the inside out
or from the outside in

251

Rhythmic structuring with flexible base. The spatial relationships between units: the question is, how do the units relate to each other and how can they be represented on a flexible base?

Figure on static base.
Constructive foundation

Regular grid and figure,
regular division as the norm

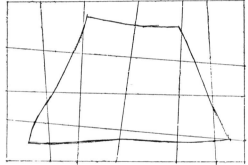

The grid lines
are somewhat displaced.
This is what happens to the figure

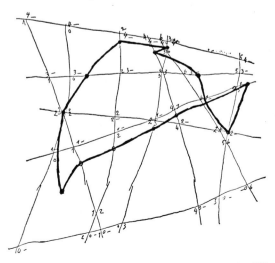

The grid lines are stretched and
squeezed into a perfect tangle.
This is what happens to the figure

Irregular projection on an uneven plane. Attempt to produce a rhythmically distorted structure while preserving regularity.
(Conversion by controlled change of proportion.)

Surface measurements
(with regular and irregular division).
Flat: two-dimensional.
Broken – planar angles; three-dimensional.
Bent – spherical on top: three-dimensional.
Broken on periphery, e.g. the top of a cube or sphere: three-dimensional.

Cf. 1934/19: *Mountain gorge*, p.361.

Rhythmically interpenetrating structure on a constructive base.
1931/T 19: *Model 106* (amplified).
Gouache [1]

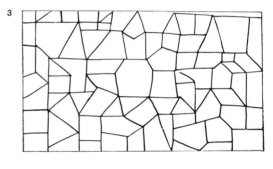

Irregular projection on an uneven surface. Where the base is flexible the regular projective relationships are modified (pulled out of shape) in proportion to the distortion of the base [2][1]

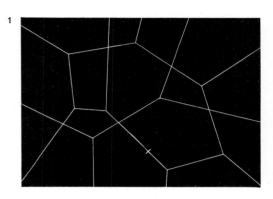

Projection on an uneven surface. Change of inner and outer forms. A certain rhythmic structure is added. Linear analysis from 1940/N 14: *Churches*[3].[2] (*Cf.* p.194)

Irregular projection with highly mobile (perhaps fluid) base [4]

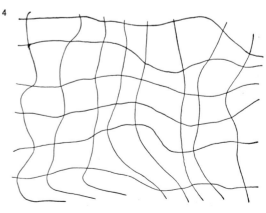

'Some of the forms move outward, some inward.'
Rhythmic structuring with simultaneous projection of base and elevation.
Note in Appendix.

1940/M 20: *Mountain game*. Gouache.
Cf. 1940/N 14: *Churches*, p.194
and 1940/N 16: *Double*. Gouache.
Colour reproduction in Grohmann, p.353.

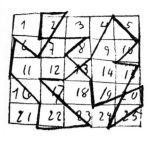

1

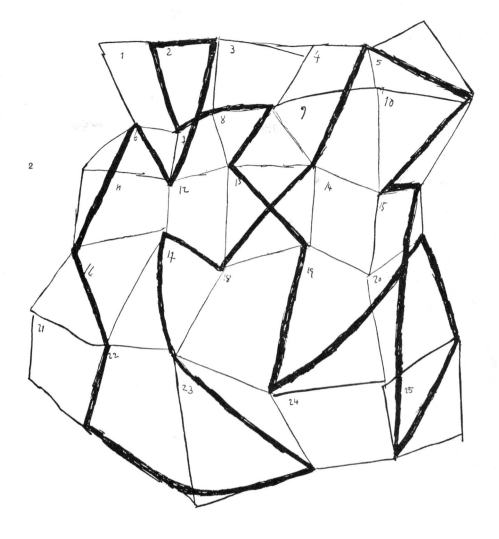

2

Increase in movement produces more fluid relations, e.g. in water or in air, the ideal dynamic media.

Flat projection: illustration on regular base 1–25 [1].
Irregular projection on uneven surface (1–25), 'pulled out of shape' by changes in the ground structure [2].

255

1920/109: *Flowers in a wheatfield*. Pen-and-ink.

Microscopic

Intermediate

Macroscopic:

A flower seen as three parts or as seven parts

individual,
indivisible, i.e.
the number cannot be
changed without changing
the character

Microscopic:
The material structure
of a flower, structural.
Division here and there
produces no essential
change in character.
Change not crucial, hence
divisible, dividual

By division
new structures

Macroscopic:
The meadow with many
flowers, general. Division
here and there does not
produce a crucial change,
hence divisible, dividual

By diminution
new structures

By increase
new structures

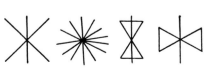

hence indivisible or individual

257

1939/JK 9: *Group of eleven*.
Paste and pigment on wrapping paper.
Cf. 1930/c 9: *Singers*. Watercolour.
Grohmann ,p.394.

Lower and higher individuals

Rhythmic-individual
one-two
with equal stress

In rhythmic individuals
one unit is
perceptibly repeated.
Uniform, three parts

Rhythmic individuals
repeated in two parts with
composite unit

Two parts disparate,
no longer rhythmic because
there is no repetition

Three parts disparate,
beyond rhythm

Two- and three- part
composite
rhythmic individuals;[1]

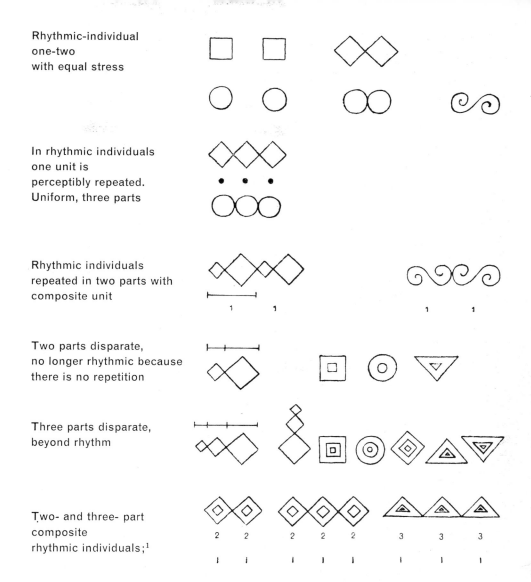

Two-part or three-part unit I, repeated.
Characteristic: repetition.

The smallest individuals are the simple rhythmic ones, then come the composite rhythmic
ones, and finally those that are not rhythmic (individual) or those that are beyond rhythm.

259

Dividual-Individual synthesis

Combination of two structures:
Individual '5'
(accented by use of different colour)

Means:
Accented or
unaccented line.
Individual characterised
by shift of position

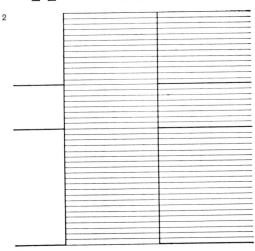

1   2

Individual minor
Number of units 3

Dividual major
Number of units 42

Simplest synthesis
Number of units
13 + 8 + 21

Examples of dividual–individual synthesis:
1929/o 8: *Huts*, p.25.
1929/o 4: *The cliff*, p.102.
1929/m 7: *Church and castle*, p.138.
1929/m 3: *Evening in Egypt*, p.146.
1929/s 2: *In the current of six crescendos*, p.212.
1929/s 9: *Old man reckoning*, p.236.

Analysis and synthesis, shown separately in
stages [2].

Example of synthesis.
Linear analysis from 1929/m 10: *Monument on the
frontier of the fruit country*. Watercolour [1].
Note in appendix.

Means of representation: Combination of possibilities

individual	– dividual
accented lines	– unaccented lines
tone value	– lines
colour	– tone value

The formation of organs with regard to their interaction in forming a whole

The usual cycle
(e.g. the water cycle)

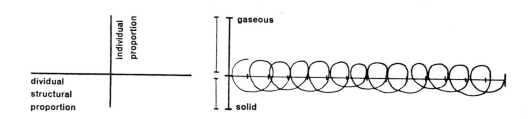

Polyphony: the teaching
of harmony.'

Three-part polyphony

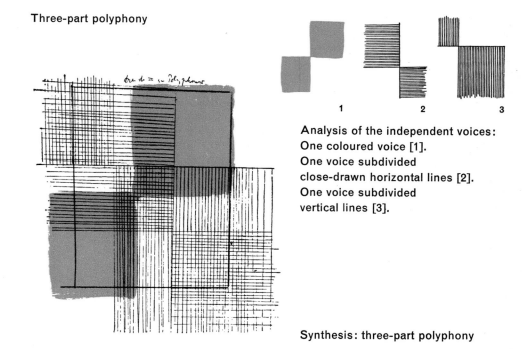

1   2   3

Analysis of the independent voices:
One coloured voice [1].
One voice subdivided
close-drawn horizontal lines [2].
One voice subdivided
vertical lines [3].

Synthesis: three-part polyphony

Klee to his students:
'Within the will to abstraction something
appears that has nothing to do with objective
reality. Free association supplies a key to the
fantasy and formal significance of a picture.
Yet this world of illusion is credible. It is
situated in the realm of the human.'

[1]*Cf.* the exercise on p.292: A composition made up
of I. individual and II. structural rhythms. They
must support each other in an organic whole.

262

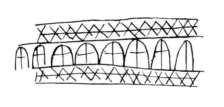

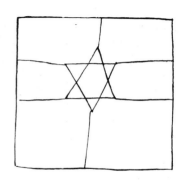

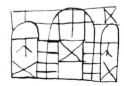

...inear analysis from a structural composition. The
...arts work together in a way that suggests the
...ultidimensional simultaneity of architectonic
...lements. Analysis from 1924/127:
...tructural composition. Colour drawing.

Cf. the polyphonic interpenetration of plan and
...levation: 1924/126: *Structural II*. Gouache,
...iedion, p.118 (synthesis of permuted squares
...n the ground plan and of the vertical structure).

...tructures in elevation, in part
...ransparent:
...927/2: *Beflagged city*. Watercolour. Colour
...eproduction in *Dokumentarmappe*
...lee-Gesellschaft, Benteli, Berne 1949.
...939/c 9: *Concert hall*. Watercolour. Grohmann,
...394.

263

The relation between the individual and the dividual belonging to it. In the higher unit the limit of the perceptible is always reached. Perceptibility does not go beyond this limit, but remains within the perceptible whole, entering into its parts, its dividual rhythms. Thus the lower is always the dividual.[1]

For example, the fish seen as an individual, breaks down into head, body, tail, and fins [1]. Seen dividually it breaks down into scales and the structure of the fins [2].

The individual proportion is determined by the relation between 1, 2, and 3 and cannot be essentially changed; in any case, nothing can be omitted. A few scales may be missing from the body, but we cannot do without the head, the eye, or any of the fins [3].

The dividual structure of this fish is variable in so far as it matters much less whether it has 330 or 350 scales than whether or not it has a head. Thus the distinction between dividual and individual involves a value judgment.

[1]dividual = lower, divisible structural unit.
individual = higher, indivisible unit.

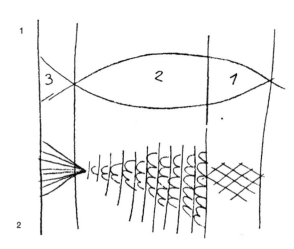

But is the fish always an individual? No, not when it occurs in large numbers, not when 'it's teeming with fish', as the saying goes [4].

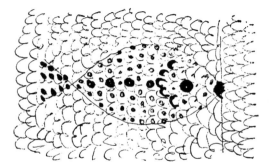

Fish with scales

Pond with fish

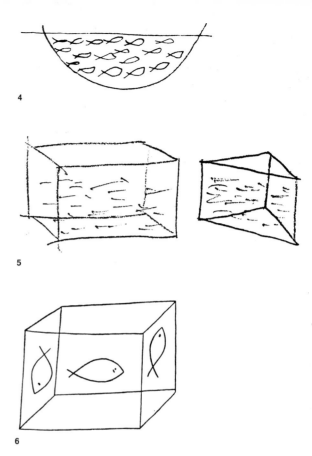

4

5

6

When it's teeming with fish, we have not one fish but many, we have a fish-pond or an aquarium [4, 5].
In this other fish-tank I must neither add nor subtract anything [6].

7

1 2 1 2

Exhibition of fish-tanks: many fish-tanks, arranged rhythmically, a cubical tank alternating with a spherical bowl [7].
The longer and more indefinite the series, the easier it is to add or subtract a few without making any essential change in the exhibit. In the same sense I can line up series of concepts (e.g. sound, syllable, word, sentence, etc.)

individual	and corresponding dividual
trunk	wood, fibres, wrinkles in the bark
tree	leaves, branches, twigs
forest	tree
forest region	particular forest

It depends on the way the zone is bounded (where the lines fall). For in every case we are dealing with a relationship.

Time division (pendular)

individual	and corresponding dividual
second	?
minute	second
hour	minute, second
day	hour, minute, second
week	day, hour, minute, second
month	week, day, hour, minute, second
year	month, week, day, hour, minute, second
generation, century	year, month, week, day, hour, minute, second
millennium	century, year, month, week, day, hour, minute, second
geological periods and so on down to eons	

12 hours – 1 day
7 days – 1 week
6 months – ½ year
3 years – etc.

Different time cycles on the basis of combined divisions within the circle. Growth through space and time (genetically from the inside out). 'What takes more time requires more space.'

The concepts lower (or dividual) and higher (or individual) are not absolute but mutually dependent; when I broaden the conceptual field, I create a higher perceptible whole.
It is good that in the course of time a certain elasticity has been achieved in regard to limits.
It has brought with it a certain relativity of division, which is a safeguard against absurdity. But in art we must eliminate this relativity by defining the scene of action with fixed limits.

Rhythms and rhythmic structures

We can perceive rhythm with three senses at once. First we can hear it, secondly see it, thirdly feel it in our muscles. This is what gives it such power over our organism.
The lowest rhythmical units:

Point of departure: the execution of acoustic rhythms by tapping with changing emphases. From quantitative expression without accent to qualitative with accent.

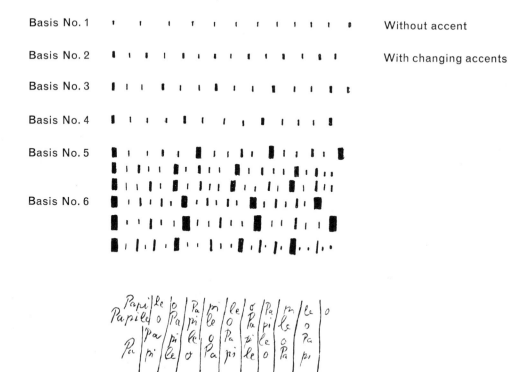

Another example of qualitative accent: Papileo.
The same unit with changing rhythmic emphasis.

Human rhythms

Man breathes in and out

A breath: in, out (one, two)

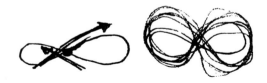

The rhythm of walking.
Dividual rhythm when the walk is of
some length.
The human trail,
e.g. footprints in the snow

In the pictorial realm the advance of
time brings with it a movement
of the picture plane.
Made into measures, a simple
rhythm of movement

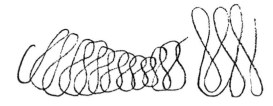

Physiological analysis of the
blood circulation

Purely liquid

Rhythms in nature.[1] Day and night

[1]Fundamental distinction: 'cosmic rhythms'
(e.g. the seasons, day and night),
'organic rhythms', and 'cultural rhythms'.

268

Structural rhythms in stanza form

Planar arrangement [1]

represented numerically [2][1]

Stanza form [3]

with the accent on colour [4]

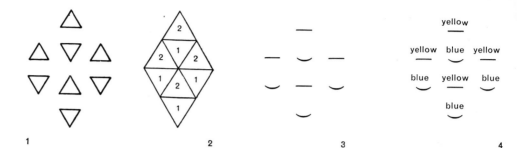

1

2

3

4

Further translations into the pictorial realm

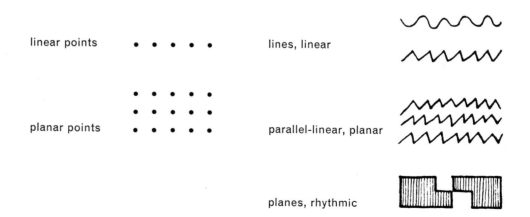

linear points

lines, linear

planar points

parallel-linear, planar

planes, rhythmic

Structural alternation of form or colour,
.g. 1 = red, 2 = yellow (with constructive
hoice of colour).

The main characteristic of rhythm is the repetition of small groups with or without evident division.

1920/41: *Rhythmic landscape with trees*. Oil.
The structural beat articulates the rhythm
of the landscape.

Cultural rhythms

I am going to reach out into the field of music. Here the basic structure lies in the beat. The ear hears the beat more or less subconsciously; but it is felt through the sound as a structural framework over which the quantities and qualities of the musical ideas move.

The basic beats are two and three

Two-part norm or two-part time

Three-part norm or three-part time

Variant of the two-part norm
A two-part measure with two-part
subdivision, or four-part time

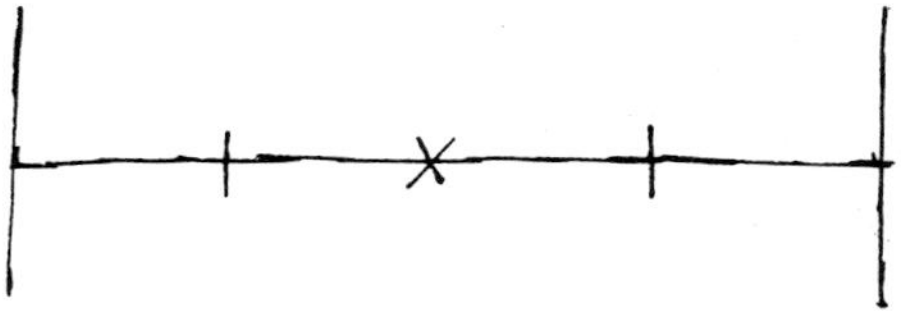

Variant of the two-part norm
with three-part subdivision or
six-part time

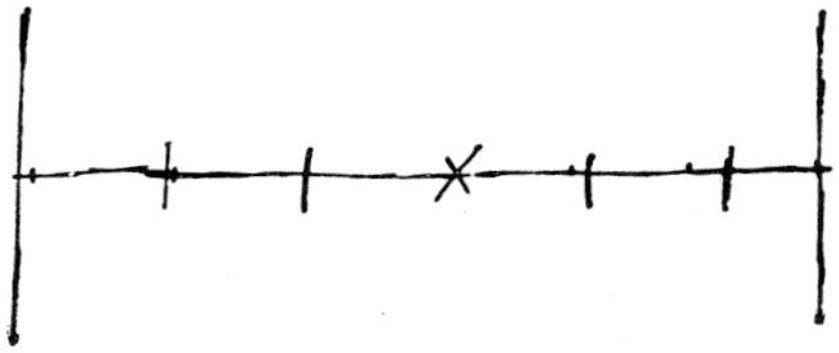

Variant on the three-part norm with
three-part subdivision or
nine-part time

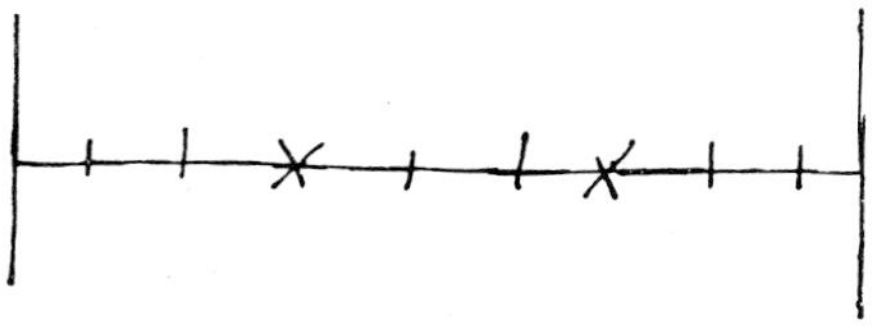

Variant of four-part time with three-part
subdivision of the quarters
or twelve-part time

271

1937/N 4: *Forked structures in four-part time*
Gouache.

We can obtain additional planar images of rhythm by watching a conductor.
We can learn from a quick glance at his baton.

In four-part time he strikes the first beat   downward

the second upward to the left,

the third from left to right,

and the fourth upward from the right

to the starting point of the first beat.   The general picture is:

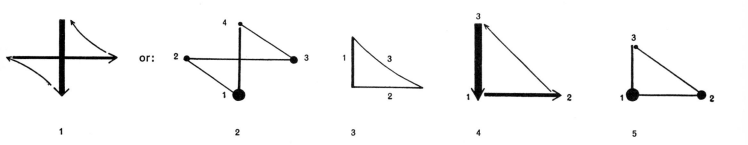

Picture of four-part time with a view to the dynamic [1].

Which fits in admirably with the special qualities of verticals and horizontals [2].

The picture of three-part time is equally attractive [3, 4, 5].

273

Among these cultural rhythms[1] the conductor's two-part time; the accented first beat appears as a downward vertical.

[1]Note by Klee: 'manual rhythms'.

In the pictorial field, the passage of time brings with it a movement of the ground-plane,

the movement of the conductor's two-part time is reversed.

Rigid

One-part time fluid. Two-part 'alla breve': Mozart, Don Giovanni. In this piece the rapid tempo blurs the two-part division that appears on the paper, and rhythmically one only feels the whole bars.

One-part time fluid

Two-part time loosely connected

274

This is how the conductor beats three-part time[1];

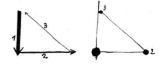

again the accented first beat is struck with corresponding emphasis, the horizontal is less important, and the third is again more like the first.

Variation with moving ground-plane

Rigid

Fluid

Three-part measures loosely connected

↑
Three- and four-part
time represented
schematically.
Possibility of coloured
polyphony

275

1927/E 9: *Sailboats in gentle motion.* Pen and ink.

Four-part time with varying accent 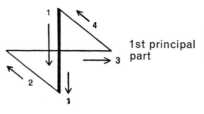 1st principal part | 2nd principal part | Subsidiary parts

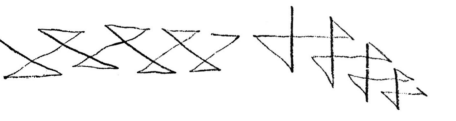

Variation with moving ground-plane or progressive direction of motion

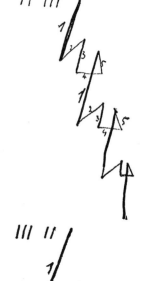

Five-part time with varying accent

277

1927/e 2: *Four sailboats.* Oil.
Articulation in varying times and types of movement
(spatio-temporal combination of movements).
Planar-rhythmical units on slightly mobile
ground plane with colour polyphony.

Spatio-temporal movement with
moving ground-plane

2×3

↑
1939/MN 9: *Fights with himself*.
Pencil and watercolour

Rigid (hard) 3×2

Fluid (soft)

Loosely connected (in two parts)

279

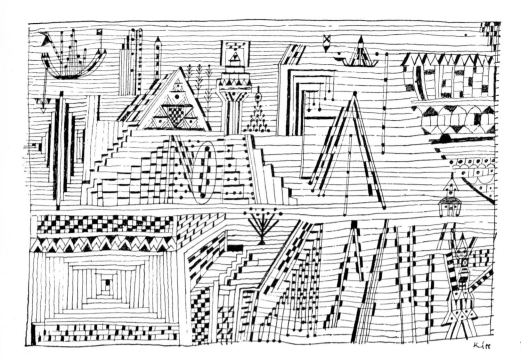

1927/o 1: *Beride (city by the water).* Pen and ink.

Constellation with inner structure. Schematic
excerpt from the watercolour:
1928/T 4: *Something freer in rigid garb.*

The limping rarities of five- and seven-part time are unevenly loaded two-beats:

2+3 or 3+2 (five) 3+4 or 4+3 (seven)

In representing rhythmic structure we take the quantitative view; absolute time measurements are transposed into absolute linear measurements (quantitative rhythm) [1]. The disadvantage is that the units of rhythm (designated by bars) are not strictly defined by linear measurements.

Where is the bar?

What do special symbols of this sort mean?

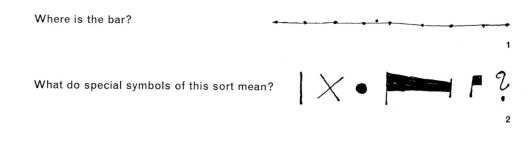

1

2

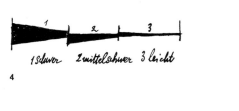

3

heavy   light

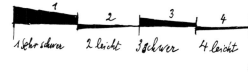

4

heavy   medium heavy   light

5

very heavy   light   heavy   light

¹Crossed out: 'of the qualities'.

They indicate different degrees of accent [2]. This points the way to another kind of picture that will do more justice to rhythmic structures and clearly bring out the quality of the measures. It consists in representing the relations between emphases,¹ in treating the rhythmic structures qualitatively (accented or dynamic rhythm) [3, 4, 5].

The form of four-part time, gently curved (factural rhythm)

Many beats in four-part time linked by rhythmic connections
(Dynamisation of the factural rhythm)

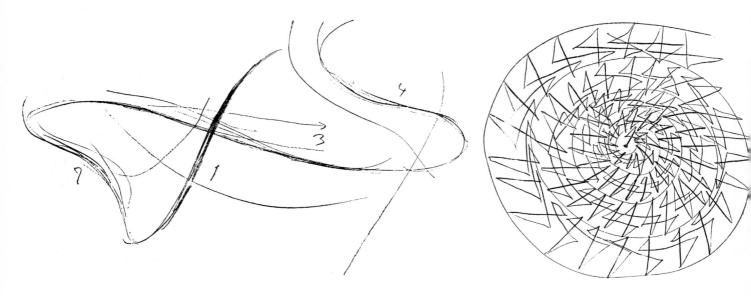

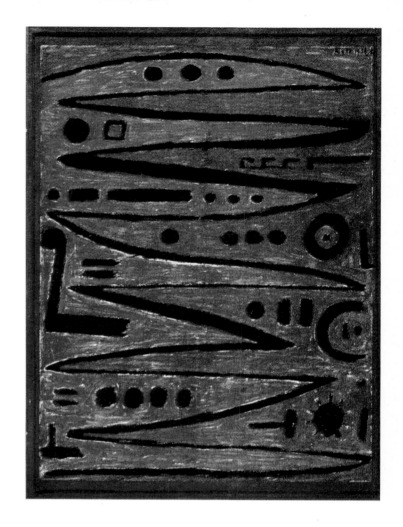

1938/1: *Heroic strokes of the bow*. Oil on plaster.

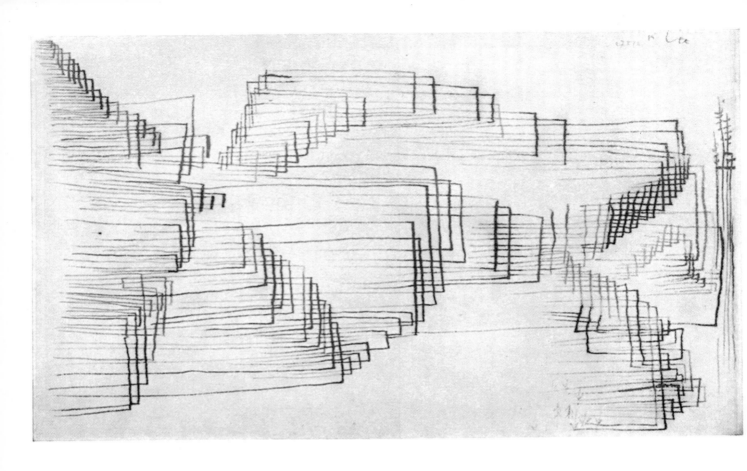

1927/D 8: *Slate quarry*. Pen and ink drawing.

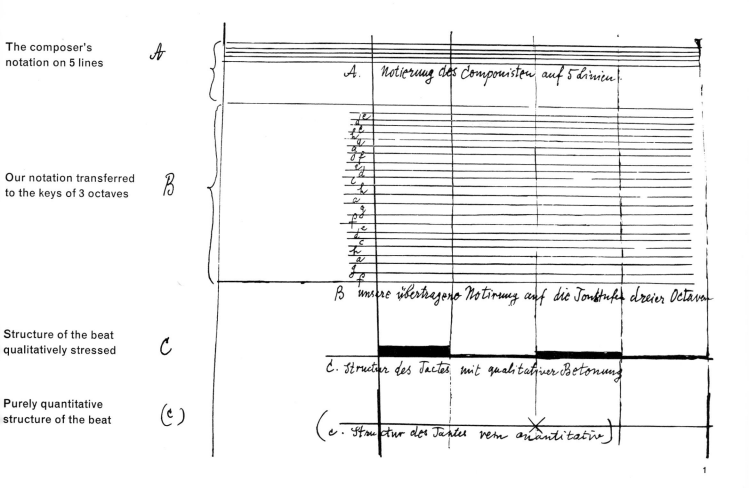

The composer's notation on 5 lines — A. — *A. Notierung des Componisten auf 5 Linien.*

Our notation transferred to the keys of 3 octaves — B — *B unsere übertragene Notirung auf die Tonstufen dreier Octaven*

Structure of the beat qualitatively stressed — C — *C. Structur des Tactes mit qualitativer Betonung*

Purely quantitative structure of the beat — (C) — *(C. Structur des Tactes rein quantitativ)*

On this foundation I can now try to execute a musical theme pictorially, whether in one voice or polyphonically.
I choose two bars of a three-part passage by Bach, and micro-copy it according to the following scheme [1].

Since music without dynamics sounds mechanical and expressionless, I select qualitative representation C and give the line more or less weight according to the tone quality, while the quantitative representation in B expresses itself in the vertical lines for bars and parts of bars.[1]

*Example from a three-part passage by Johann Sebastian Bach; folder attached to p.286.

285

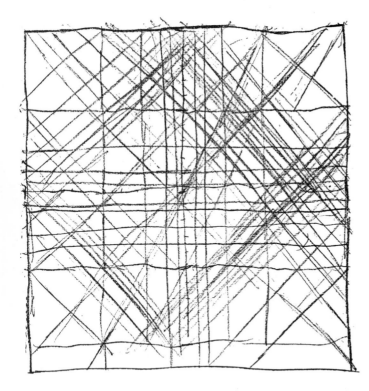

Key of Fes-is mur

Pencil drawing done on trip to Egypt in the winter of 1928–1929.

Rhythmic forms with many parts, gently curved.
Factural rhythms

A number of things may be learned from the example of the three-part passage (folder), which is an attempt to represent in simple pictorial form an object that is abstract and at the same time compellingly real.

First we learn that such representation is possible. Next we perceive the vertical and horizontal relations between the two or three 'voices'. And we see how they are related in respect of individualisation. Sometimes two, sometimes three voices sound at once (and there might be just one). The two voices (second and third voices) of the first measure are very different in individual quality. The lower one is clearly structural in character while the upper one is individual. Then the first voice comes in a little below the second, tries to jump over it, but does not succeed at first; only after the second voice has paused for a moment, does the first become dominant. With the individual entrance of the first voice, the second voice is reduced to a structural character and takes a register in harmonious contrast to the third, which descends a little at this point, so forming an arch beneath which moves the first, individual voice. After a resigned pause, the second runs parallel to the third. From the very start the third remains faithful to its structural character, up to the point where the second begins to run parallel to it: here we can discern a timid attempt at individuality.

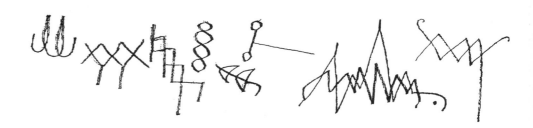

Detail from 1934/N 6: *A curtain is drawn.* Pencil drawing.

A glance at the quantities in the example (folder) also teaches us that the differences of measure are based on simple numbers near one another. If very small numbers were related to very large ones in this example, it would mean that the music contained ornaments,

¹Syncope: 'Cutting-together', i.e. rhythmic connection between two halves of a tone divided by bar, the shifting forward or backward of tones by half, rarely by a quarter, of their value, with parallel shift of accent. In pictorial terms: shift of structural rhythm; the shift between two structural values is connected or bridged over by a third (hovering bridges).

which, when used frivolously, are called flourishes.

Syncope:¹ temporally speaking: the accent is anticipated, moved from its normal position to the preceding unaccented note.
Positionally: one or more dividing lines are bridged over by longer tones (hovering bridges).

1932/m 1: *Plant hieroglyphics.* Colour.
Cf. 1924/132. *Hieroglyphic water plants*, p.240.

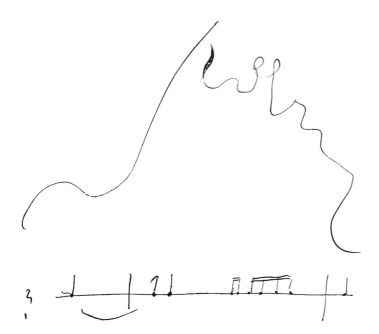

Two- and three-part time as elastic blows
Factural rhythms

Two-dimensional plan of
three- and four-part time

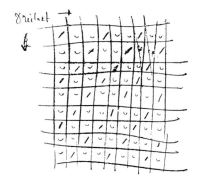
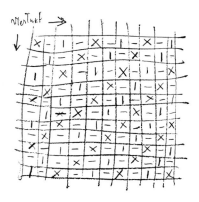

1937/R5: *The Rhine near Duisburg*. Oil on cardboard.

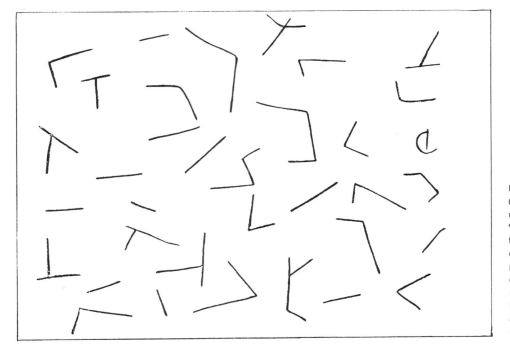

Freely chosen rhythms in fragmentary arrangement
(with interruptions). Dynamic shift of rigid
relations with free use of planar rhythms.
'Individualisation can be conceived in such a way
that several parts simultaneously rise to a
dominant position. The accentuation can be
positive or negative, obtained by means of accented
or unaccented lines; it can be more or less
markedly positive or negative. Negative accent
by means of elimination, gaps.' (Rhythms can
at the same time be regarded as angular
movements.)

ynamic shift of a static premise (labile
alance amplifying the static balance). Reciprocal
ovement with or without connection. Interaction
etween this side and that side of perpendicular
nd centre leads to a balanced movement.
Vhere there are open forms in the picture space,
ompromise occurs.' Basic process: 'Partially
onstructive reproduction of relationships. Several
artial analytical viewpoints combined with a view
dimensional synthesis.' In regard to 'combined
ovements', *cf.* spatio-temporal combination of
ovements, p.392.

We assemble objects but the relationship we create between them can be plausibly experienced only in fragments. Often it is suddenly interrupted; then we can no longer follow our idea of the object (or of the law). Memory, digested experience, yields pictorial associations. What is new here is the way the real and the abstract coincide or appear together. Often an organic context works with elements that can be read abstractly.

Wave-movement as two-part time

Wave-movement as one-part time

1938/v 2: *Interim near Easter*.
Oil on burlap.

23 January 1922

Exercise:

A composition of
I. individual and
II. structural rhythms.
Work the two together organically so
that they support each other.

Klee to his students:
'This formation is arrived at by a successive
singling out of parts of the total form.
Within a composition, one and one, line and line
or plane and plane, need not necessarily adjoin.
There can be a dual figuration expressing itself
in the independent contribution of plane and line.
Organic contrasting polyphony. But the parts
must move together and move apart organically,
harmoniously. There are many kinds of
composition. Among them we can distinguish
two that may be termed static and dynamic.
What leads to a standstill is the static, what
undergoes movement is the dynamic. There we
have an inner characterisation.
A synthesis of heaviness and movement can
result. The two forces must then make an artistic
pact that each will stand in its proper place. When
the structural takes on rhythmic variety, when it is
particularly conspicuous at certain points, we may
speak of a definite (i.e. individual) structural
proportion.'
Balance between statically and dynamically
accented structural parts and individual rhythms
(principle of complementarity). Space-time
relation experienced in fragments. Division and
connection as components of structural form
('loose separation and gathered separation').
Note in appendix.

III. The basic concepts of development
The figuration of movement. Emphasis on the processes that lead to form

Theory of figuration, combined with nature study
Tension between aim and method. Essence and appearance
Nature and abstraction

1937/R 6: *Terrace with flowers.* Oil.

'Amazing what happens when everything is cut off. When none of the virtual forms is fully present in the picture. This produces something remarkable in the way of expression. A tacit extension of the pictorial space, so that only a part of the whole is realised. One is enabled to put many many things into the picture without over-crowding. This tacit extension of the pictorial space provides a kind of liberation in brackets.

It is very interesting; let us look into the possibilities. The silence of the complements seems to express something sudden. Here you have a context in which limits and partial forms play a crucial role.

The decisive question is how the cutting out is done. The omissions might look accidental or capricious. That would be overdoing it. If this is not the case, we have the impression of being able to see only a part, that all the rest is silent, and that this silent part might be supplied. What is essential is that the most interesting and most important part of the whole is brought out.

Form may be characterised as static or dynamic. The static consists chiefly of the vertical and the horizontal on the basis of gravitation. The dynamic is more curved. There is also a possibility of combining the two; then the inside and the outside can coincide.'

1937/R 6: *Terrace with flowers.* Rhythmic structural characteristics in static-dynamic balance. Interrupted movements between weight and dynamic. *Cf.* p.393.

1. Different possibilities of movement
Types of rhythmic structure
Terrestrial and cosmic examples

Monday, 30 January 1922

**Combination of structural
and individual rhythms
Primal motion as norm
in the cosmos**

At our last meeting but one I pointed to repetition as the hallmark of structural rhythms. On the strength of a few elementary structural examples, we arrived, weighing or measuring, at series such as:

1 to 1 to 1 to 1 to 1 to 1   or 1+2 to 1+2 to 1+2 to 1+2
       or 11+10 to 11+10 to 11+10,

for which we substituted I to I to I to I, taking the Roman one to stand for a composite unit.

In the two-dimensional realm, on a plane, we arrived, in place of these series, at complexes such as:

In contrast to these types, we considered individual rhythms, and took as their basis numbers from which the repetitive factor is excluded. The prime numbers seemed particularly suitable:

3 to 5 to 7 to 11 to 13 to 17 to 19 to 23 etc.

In the following exercise which I called 'Combination of structural and individual rhythms' I warned you against calculating, for theory after all only means arranging things that are present in feeling and plays only a secondary role in the creative process, namely the role of criticism, which sets in afterwards.[1] A few solutions to this problem gave evidence of both talent and intelligence.

[1] *cf.* Analysis and examples, pp.303–305.

1931/L 4: *Three subjects, polyphonic.* Colour.

Polyphonic interpenetration of three individual rhythms (subjects).
In contrast to the linear illustration ([1], p.297) they are dynamically accented.

Klee on polyphony: 'There is polyphony in music. In itself the attempt to transpose it into art would offer no special interest. But to gather insights into music through the special character of polyphonic works, to penetrate deep into this cosmic sphere, to issue forth a transformed beholder of art, and then to lurk in waiting for these things in the picture, that is something more. For the simultaneity of several independent themes is something that is possible not only in music; typical things in general do not belong just in one place but have their roots and organic anchor everywhere and anywhere.'
Note in Appendix.

Below:
Study for drawing 1931/k 5: *Flight from oneself* (first version).

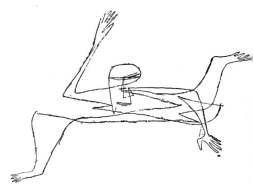

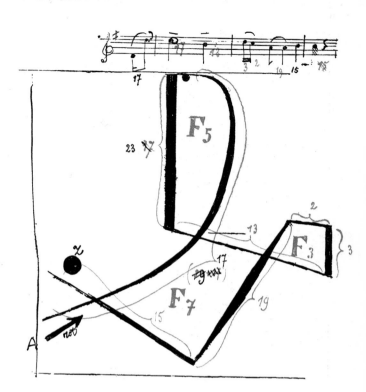

Some of your sketches showed an intimate fusion of individual and structure; the structure was the handmaiden, following the path of the individual, step for step.[1]

Let us suppose that Figure 1 represents the individual. Proof: there is no repetition. It begins like an upbeat at **A** with seventeen, then descends with the full force of twenty-three, bends off at an obtuse angle with thirteen, rises vertically with three, angles to the left with two, descends diagonally with nineteen, angles to the left with fifteen to the end point Z (and here I beg you not to take the numbers quantitatively but qualitatively). The results are three circumscribed planes of non-repetitive, that is, of individual character F_5, F_3 and F_7.

297

1927/f 4: *The tower stands fast.*
Indian ink drawing.

In Figure 3 the structural character is added. The fully weighted vertical breaks down into five times five (note the intersections!), the individual thirteen[1] breaks into a series of threes; a few twos, threes, sixes, etc. follow.

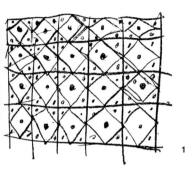

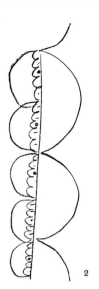

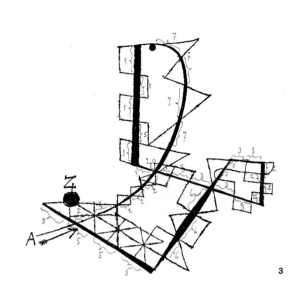

¹This way of writing '(line-) drawing' is intended to emphasise the act of 'drawing'. More emphasis on the individual movement than on the material line.

³Analysis of musical notation from J. S. Bach, folder opposite p.286.

Concerning the combined figure [3] this remains to be said: the measurements of the individual rhythm are greater than the measurements of the structure, and the individual (line-) drawing[2] is qualitative (or weighing) in comparison to the purely quantitative (or measuring) structure.

Not long ago I translated a musical figure into pictorial terms.[3] So now I can imagine the reverse and ask myself how our individual with its structure would sound as music. Purely melodic, for certain, with the subsidiary forms as pure accompaniment.

Five-part time in two-dimensional [1], and rhythmic-schematic form [2] (possibility of colour polyphony).

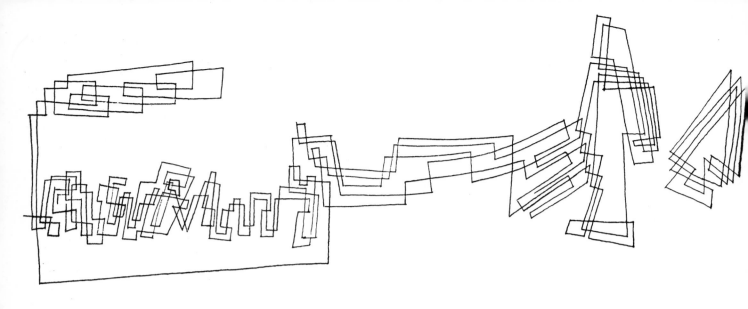

Klee

1   1927/F 2: *Symptomatic*. Pen and ink drawing.

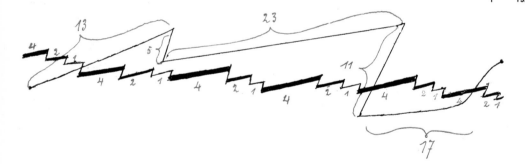

In this case [1] we may speak of a drawing in two voices. The individual theme is not cut off repetitively from the structural theme as before ([3] p.299), but only here and there, not even in every part. Thus we cannot deny that the structural theme has a certain independence. It is aware of this and takes on a dynamic character in the drawing. The individual feels exalted by its higher nature, requires no special bolstering of its ego, and runs along flute-like in quantitative silence, despite the companionship of the heavy structural instrumentation. The relation of the measurements in the two 'voices' corresponds to the relations of the first example ([1] p.297 and [3] p.299). The measurements of the individual rhythm contain the higher numbers.

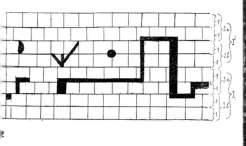

1927/Omega 10: *Green courtyard*. Oil on wood.

Example from the late work: 1938/H 20:
Oriental-sweet. Colour reproduction. Grohmann, p.331.

Cf. p.281. Representation according to the quantitative and qualitative view. The qualitative or accentual treatment of the theme is dynamised in comparison with the quantitative treatment.

In this new example [2] the structural part, if we disregard the verticals, may be analysed very simply as a continued relation of 1 to 1 to 1 to 1 to 1 to 1 etc. (horizontal parallels). With their slightly more highly developed rhythm the verticals add something new, namely alternation by pairs:

$$2a + 2b + 2a + 2b \quad \text{(vertical alternation)}$$

$$\underbrace{(1+1)}_{} \underbrace{(1+1)}_{I} \underbrace{(1+1)}_{} \underbrace{(1+1)}_{I} \quad \text{(horizontal parallels)}$$

or summed up: I   to   I

In this linear representation of structure, the expression is purely quantitative. If we imagine the squares alternating in colour, we must bear in mind that different colours signify the strongest (psychic) dynamism,[1] and in dealing with the individual, therefore, great restraint is recommended. The individual part of this example shows us a few divergent individuals without repetition. Where they are subdivided, the division is based on individual numbers. Here the expression is accentual (weight)[2] over against the purely quantitive expression (measure) of the structural part.

301

The main characteristic of rhythm is repetition.
Every accentuation of movement modifies the
regularity, tightens or relaxes, produces a positive
or negative emphasis on the dividual or individual.
'In the pictorial field the passing of time brings
with it a movement of the ground-plane.'
Articulation in time and in different kinds of
movement gives rise to different orders of
magnitude. In this 'identity of method and object'
movement is characterised by shift of position.
(Deviation from the repetitive norm. Varying
intensity of movement results in limitation or
amplification).

'Relations between planes are a result of forces.'
In individual terms: 'change of place', the road
travelled (measurement). The articulation of
movement and countermovement makes for
synthesis and balance.

In the tension between 'terrestrial' and 'cosmic'
the terrestrial structures are larger (nearer), the
cosmic structures finer (more distant).

1927/x 8: *Elected site*. Indian ink and watercolour.
Cf. Klee's notebooks for 1902 and 1914.
Note in Appendix.

302

Principles of movement:
repetitive rhythm, steady movement [1].

The regular accentuation of the rhythmic repetition
is modified by the intervention of a second active
influence which lends an irregular or individual
accent. Loosening and tightening, extension and
contraction with moving ground-plane. The new
movement brings a compromise between the
active and the passive [2].

In terms of space and time: shifts of measure and
weight, based on shifting centres [3].

Overlap with movement and countermovement
(e.g. back and forth) [4].
Excerpt from 1927/v 6: *Activity of seaside town.*
Pen and ink. Fully reproduced in Giedion, p.59. *Cf.*
the rhythmic structures on pp.277 and 279, and the
fundamental possibilities of movement with
dividual-individual structure, p.245.

blau	blue
braun	brown
dunkelgrün	dark green
rot	red
schwarz	black
violett	violet

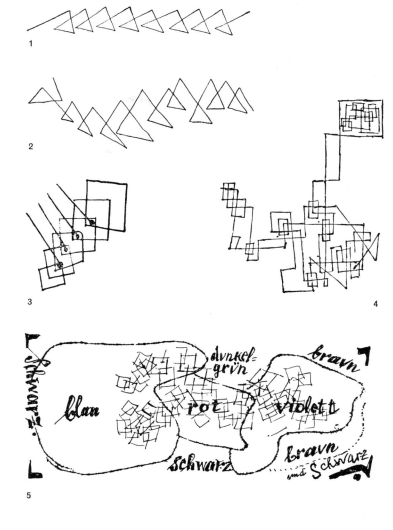

Examples:
1927/f 4: *The tower stands fast*, p.298.
1927/E 9: *Sailboats in gentle motion*, p.276.
1928/G 4: *Mechanics of a city neighbourhood.*
Pen and ink. Grohmann, p.76.
1927/Y 4: *City on Two Hills.* Pen and watercolour.
Colour Reproduction in Grohmann, p.263.

Comparison of the three examples: The first example ([3] p.299) was melodic with structural accompaniment,—a dominant individual; the second ([1] p.300) was thematic in two
voices with dynamic accent on the relatively structural part—a delicate individual (delicate
and pious); and the third ([2] p.301) is almost a symbol of the happy individual, or of
happy individuals, who can keep strictly to the structural law even over a wide area,
without doing damage to their individual character.
I find inspiration for an additional example in a very pretty little collage on glass that
came to my attention during our last exercise [5].

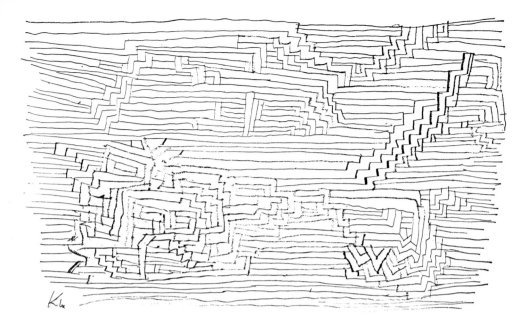

1934/qu 18: *Cliffs*. Pencil drawing.

Composition of I. individual and II. structural
rhythms: I. Rhythm with mainly rigid structure.
1934/qu 18: *Cliffs*.
II. Interchange of loose and rigid structure.
Polyphonic surface structure, individual; structural
rhythms, dividual; movement and tension in
different directions (individual structure
dynamised by structural rhythms).
1931/x 9: *Luxuriant countryside*.
III. In the main, a loosely articulated rhythm.
1934/qu 2: *Uphill and then what?*

1931/x 9: *Luxuriant countryside*. Pencil.

1   1934/qu 2: *Uphill and then what?* Pen and ink.

'Structural rhythm': Rhythms consisting of structural components of dividual and individual type. In a living 'structural rhythm' there is a harmonious balance between structural division (dividual) and individual rhythms.

It consisted entirely of square bits of paper ([5] p.303), which, freely disposed side by side or overlapping, their positions ranging from horizontal-vertical to diagonal, produced a lively structural rhythm.[1] Quite apart from their colour, the overlapping arrangement produced a dynamic extending from brightness to deepest dark. The collage was particularly rich in contrasts, because, as in the case of windows, the light was conceived as coming from behind.

Even in the deep dark tones there was a shift towards the individual. But the individual achieved its full dynamic expression in the rhythmic arrangement of the squares, organized according to their colour type: blue, red, violet, etc. The outcome was a highly dynamic individuality of colours, based on a tonal-dynamic structural rhythm. An additional possibility: A sweeping structural rhythm might be filled in with little individuals (individual-pessimistic) [1].

305

1939/ww 15: *Scene of fire.*
Oil and paste, waxed on burlap.

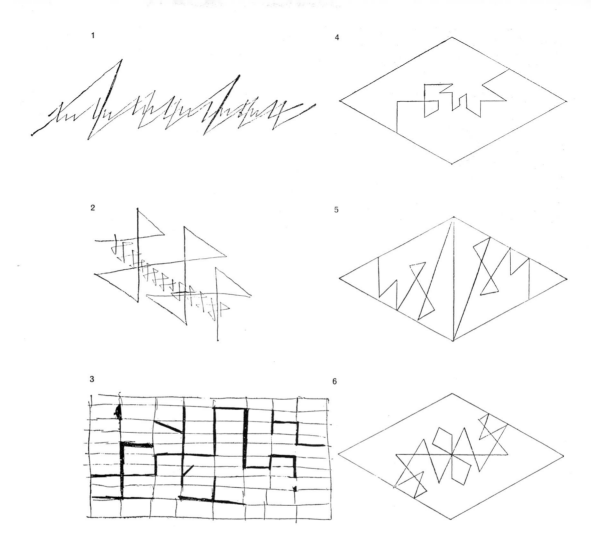

1

4

2

5

3

6

Additive formation:
Unit plus unit=sum (total form).
Multiplicative formation:
Factor times factor=product.

Example: 1939/ww 15: *Scene of fire.*

'Constructive representation links values in a
methodical way; impressionistic representation
provides a naïve joy of expression.'

Composite form:
Dividual-individual, connected by rhythmic structure [1, 2].
Individual structure on dividual base [3].
Partial construction in rhombus, set inside to good purpose [4].
Addition (a form combined with its reverse) [5].
Addition-multiplication[1] (the schema of the sum) [6].
It is easier to bring a complex process to life if one uses composite components.[2] Basic
possibilities: forms composed of two or three elements. Displacement, mirroring, rota-
tion with motifs of composite form.
Fully constructive, partially constructive, or impressionistic[3] (partially constructive
method: free choice of details).

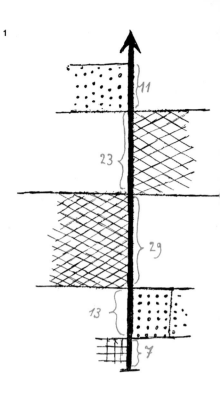

In conclusion, one more variant, in which an accented line borrowed from some individual is divided individually and where, in each segment, the structured plane and the structure-less plane face one another in such a way that the two types of plane alternate both horizontally and vertically [1] (lest anyone suppose that you have to work according to rules).

Thus far we have moved chiefly in the form world of culture. We have built on immanent-human premises such as our earthbound nature, the constraints on our movement, our physical limitations.

1922/176: *Little fir-tree picture*. Oil on gauze. In *Little fir-tree picture* the structural alternation is brought out by tone value and colour in contrast to the linear structure of the diagram [1].

937/qu 12: *Fragments*. Oil.

Memory enters and to some extent asserts itself. Now we have an organic context and elements that can be read abstractly. Meeting between the world of appearance and the abstract world. In themselves these degrees of contradiction are not unfavourable. It is possible that a picture will move far away from nature and yet find its way back to reality. The faculty of memory, experience at a distance, produces pictorial associations. In the creation of the picture an association is awakened which enters into the realm of life. It is all right for the fragmentary to appear, but it should not be inserted in another fragment. The relations between scene of action, structure, and composition produce a special effect when the expression remains definably within the function.' Separation and connection as means of rendering structural and individual relations.

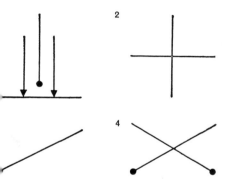

The main symbol of our activity has been the pair of scales; the horizontal dependent on the vertical attraction of the earth on which we are compelled to stand.

The simplest symbol for this 'force of attraction' is the plumbline, the simple vertical [1]. But the scales take the vertical into consideration; the vertical is their criterion for balance.
Thus we may say that the spirit of the scales is this cross [2].
Disturbances in the balance of the scales yield the diagonal [3].
And correction through counter-disturbances leads to this new cross, the diagonal cross [4].

1922/109: *Scene of calamity.*
Pen and watercolour.

Now where is the seat of this tremendous power of attraction? In the ground [1]:

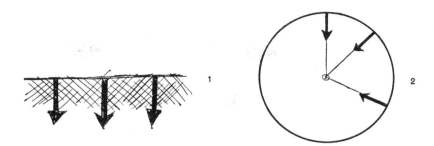

or, if we know that this ground taken as a whole has the form of a ball, it is in the middle of this ball, the centre of the earth [2].

Physically we cannot as a rule get away from it; everything that is earthly must reckon with it. In particular, every stone used for building is possessed by this force, the sustaining pillars as well as the bridges laid over them.

Consequently we shall keep running into problems of statics. And our own physical-human dependence on this earth force helps us to draw inferences about our fellow sufferer, the building, the physical object.

As we know, the surface of the earth grows and when we dig we can observe different layers that run parallel in a horizontal direction.

Pressure and counterpressure
lead to the formation of mountains

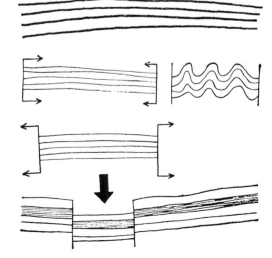

Or the opposite:
Relaxation of the pressure
results in dislocation

311

1923/217: *Severity of the clouds*. Pencil.

In practice our small physical size and our limited scope compel us to start from the part of the whole.

But this constraint, this limitation, should not deter us from knowing that things can also happen differently, that there are regions in which other laws are in force, for which new symbols must be found, corresponding to a freer movement and more mobile localities.

Earth, Water, and Air

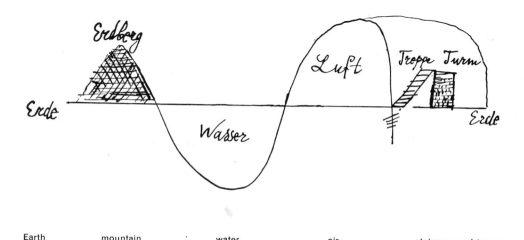

| Earth | mountain | water | air | staircase and tower |

The atmospheric zone, and its heavier sister the watery zone, can lend us a helping hand by which eventually to reach cosmic space. In water, as every swimmer knows, the new element and its increased weight make the earth's force of gravity work upwards, in the opposite direction.

But with a little effort a diver can master the depths of the water like a fish, or like the bird that masters the heights of the air.

He must also make intermittent efforts like a mountain climber or a man climbing stairs. But here the fixed points of adhesion, the footsteps, are eliminated. The rhythm of the swimmer's movements above or under the water is more relaxed, gentler, than the rhythm of walking on the ground or of climbing mountains or stairs. The swimmer in the air (the flier or glider) must become part of the machine and can, in conjunction with it, give

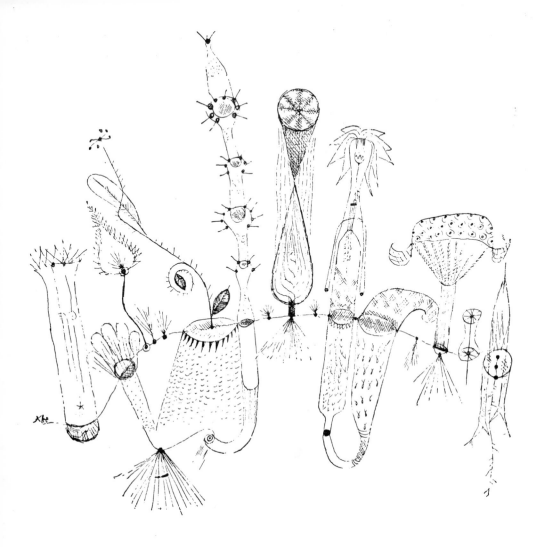

1920/205: *Sketch for realm of the plants, earth and air.* Pen-and-ink.

himself up to new kinds of movement. In a free balloon he doesn't do much. He entrusts himself to forces such as air currents or cool and warm air. The merging flow of air masses of different temperatures allows movement without resistance.

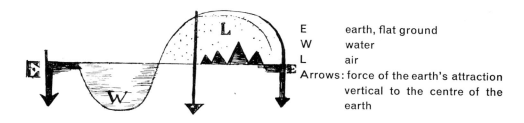

E   earth, flat ground
W   water
L   air
Arrows: force of the earth's attraction vertical to the centre of the earth

In cosmic space, finally, there are no longer either hard or soft caesuras. Here primal movement reigns, movement as norm. Everything moves. It is an illusion to suppose that we as earth[1] are standing still and the sun revolves round us. It is an illusion to suppose that the sun stands still and we on earth are the only ones moving.
The suns have moving orbits, the planets have orbits attuned to those of the suns. The whole thing moves.

[1]Crossed out: 'planet'.

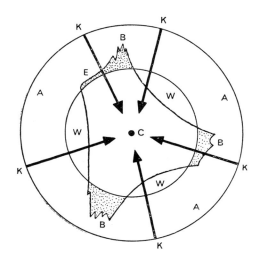

C   centre of the earth
W   water
E   level ground
B   mountains
A   atmosphere
K   force of the earth's attraction

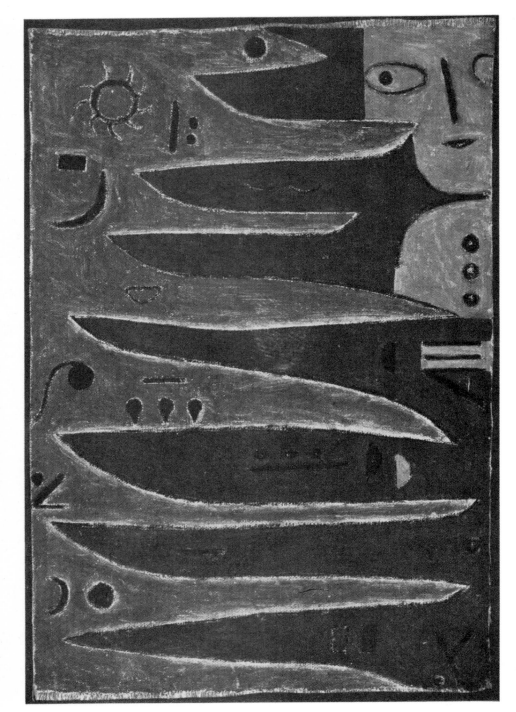

1938/J5: *The grey man and the coast.*
Oil.

'Give rigid rhythm to the individual and flowing rhythm to the structure, and let them work against each other.' The individual theme and the structural-rhythmic theme overlap. A similar rhythmic structure is shown in 1938/1: *Heroic strokes of the bow*, p.283.

Getting back to our physical existence, let us take up a few examples which lie somewhere between the two.

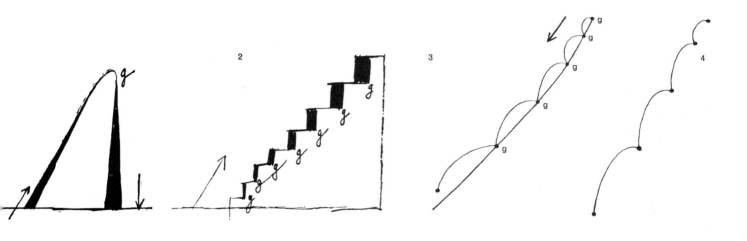

Air. A cannon ball fired up into the air at a steep angle rises with decreasing velocity, turns, and falls back to the earth with increasing velocity.
A two-part rhythm with flowing articulation: g [1].

Earth (mountain). A man climbing stairs with gradually increasing effort.
A rhythm with rigid articulation: g [2].
A stone rolls down a steep mountain slope with increasing leaps.
A rhythm with rigid articulation: g [3].

Earth (mountain) and air. Variant of example [3]. A rhythm whose articulation is partly flowing, partly rigid [4].[1]

Crossed out: whose articulation is 'simultaneously' flowing and rigid. If the accent is put on 'simultaneously', the sentence can be interpreted as referring to an interpenetration of the two types of articulation, partly rigid, partly flowing.

317

Klee

318

1934/qu 6: *Can't be climbed*. Pencil drawing

Movement in one direction, considered theoretically in relation to norm (N) and abnorm (A^n).

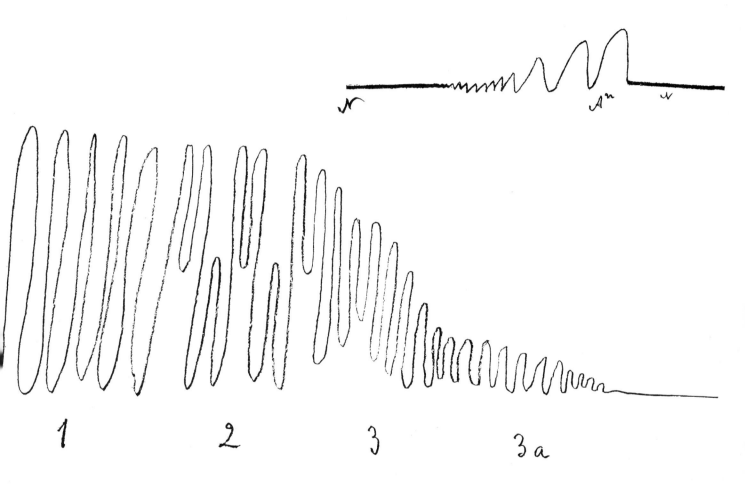

From the psychological point of view, primary contrasts side by side give a powerful expression. Primary contrasts with something between them move apart and the expression is toned down. Full leaps come from greater energy than do half leaps. Secondary contrasts, even baldly stated, lessen the power expressed. Elaborated, they weaken it by being over-rich and lessening the tension.

Curve of a development involving the concepts 'unalleviated primary contrasts' [1], 'elaborated' [2], 'secondary contrasts' [3 and 3a].

1934/s 7: *Spring in stream*. Pencil drawing.

1931/p 11: *Air currents*. Pencil drawing.

320

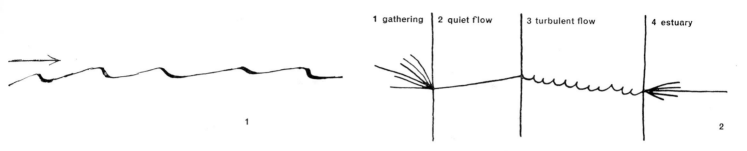

1 gathering	2 quiet flow	3 turbulent flow	4 estuary

1

2

¹ *Cf.* p.401 and *the water cycle*, p.402.

Water. The leg thrusts of a swimmer, a rhythm with loose articulation [1]. The watercourse. If I broaden my field of vision,¹ I create a perceptible whole at a higher level [2]. I give the drawing new, wider limits, or within the old limits I reduce the content.

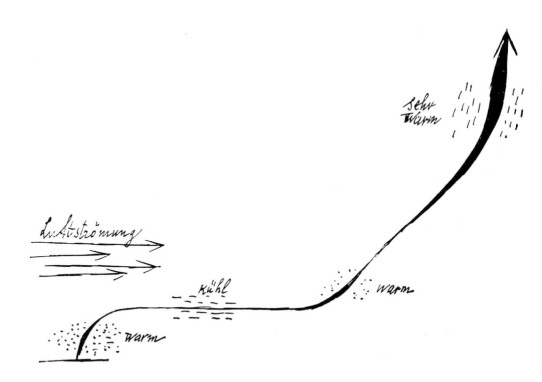

Air. In rising, a free balloon passes from a warm to a cool layer of air, then enters another warm layer, and finally a very warm one. A rhythm with loose articulation.

321

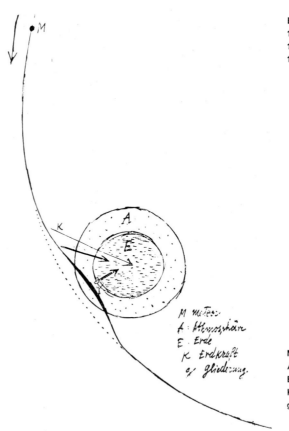

M mi:Teo:
A :Athmosphäre
E . Erde
K Erdkraft
g gliederung.

M   meteor
A   atmosphere
E   earth
K   earth's power of attraction
g   articulation

Examples:
1917/125: *Landscape with comet*, watercolour.
1918/58: *The Paris come.* watercolour.
1918/200: *A comet on the horizon,* watercolour.

Cosmic and atmospheric. A meteor describing its orbit comes close to the earth and is diverted from its orbit by the earth's attraction. For brief, critical moments it cuts through the atmosphere, and friction with the air turns it into an incandescent shooting star; just avoiding the danger of descending forever to earth, it goes on its way, cooling and losing its incandescence in empty space. A cosmic form with loose articulation: g.

Fluid-gaseous movement leads us to take short steps in the organisation of the picture (gliding succession of elements). Any longer step or jump approaches the realm of the solid, creates sharp boundaries that do not occur in the fluid-gaseous realm, except occasionally at the fringe, as at the edge of a pool of water, between mountain and sky, or on the horizon (symbol: the stairway).

The relevant movements and means of expression: dynamic-adjacent and static-contrasting.

322

Monday, 6 February 1922

Exercise: Combination of rigid and flowing (or loose) rhythms.
The ultimate result should be a composition.
The results of earlier exercises may be drawn in.

For example:
1. give rigid rhythm to the individual and fluid rhythm to the structural, or
2. give fluid rhythm to the individual and rigid rhythm to the structural, or
3. let two individuals work against each other, one fluid, the other rigid.

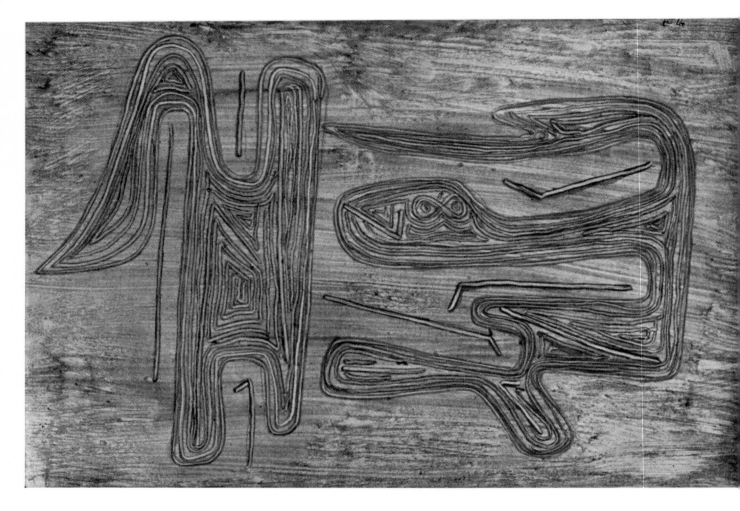

1934/12: *Temptation*. Gouache.

'There are also projections that cannot be explained, because the artist sometimes shows a faculty for projecting inner images in such a way that they become almost real or entirely so. You have to take care not to write the law simply and unimaginatively by itself, but to put yourself in motion round the law. Deviations from the strict law are movements that you feel: dimensional movements, kinematics, time, movements of change of place, alternation of inside and outside.' (On the combination of rigid and fluid rhythms into an organic whole, *cf.* pp.325–326.)

2. The natural organism of movement
as striving for movement and execution of movement
The function. Organic combination of two or three factors

Monday, 13 February 1922

Organic explanation of individual and structural articulation

I shall begin today by criticising a faulty solution of the last exercise. This doesn't mean that there were fewer good solutions than before, and I have no intention of finding fault with the author of the false solution. I merely wish to take his mistake as a basis for a discussion from which we can all learn and benefit.

The exercise was based on the preceding theoretical remarks on rigid articulation and loose articulation. It was:

Combination of rigidly articulated characters with loosely articulated characters into an organic whole (a composition).

Here I made a few suggestions:

First treat the rigid articulation individually and use the loose articulation to support that individual to which it is subordinated.

Or:

Second, restrict the loose articulation to the individual and (conversely) keep the rigid articulation structural.

In music these two ways of handling two characters are designated as melodic (solo voice and accompaniment).

Third, I suggested that you let the two types of articulation fight for equality; in music you would call this thematic treatment.

325

Or, fourth, treat both types of articulation equally, so that they do not conflict but complement each other in a friendly way, each in turn letting the other gain the upper hand. Another example of thematic treatment.

One of you chose very simple forms and, by the dynamic use of light and shade, rhythmicised on the one hand straight lines:

 and on the other hand circles:

1 2

Are these two characters appropriate examples of rigid and fluid articulation? To begin with the first character, what is this?

3

This is a plane verging on a straight line running in this ↓ or this ↑ direction.

And what is this?

4

This is the rigidly articulated growth and diminution of a series of planes verging on straight lines.

326

This growth and diminution develops in a horizontal direction thus → or thus ← and might also be represented as follows:

Thus the first character [1] fits in with the exercise. But what about the second one? Is the increasing and decreasing row of circles appropriate to the exercise?

Yes, for the articulation at a common point cannot be termed rigid, particularly as Figure 6 permits of other interpretations, as in Figure 7:

or as in Figure 8:

or their variants [9 and 10]:

327

Thus the row of circles as fluid or loosely articulated characters is quite in keeping with the problem. But how are the two characters related in the solution which I have questioned? If we had on one side an individual, on the other a structural character, we might know what to do with them; but here both characters are equally undeveloped.

My recollection is that they were related to each other like this:  or actually like this:  And what does that mean?

As far as our exercise is concerned, unfortunately it means nothing. In itself of course it could mean something, a unit with two or three parts; in everyday life perhaps a lamp with a base, a globe, and a cylinder

  or a pot-bellied vase:  or the pendulum of a clock: or just about anything:

The problem: 'Fusion of two characters' no doubt permits of many different kinds of solution, but fusion into a single thing is not possible in this case, for

 or is not an organic combination of circle and straight line!

Nor is the repetition of these themes a solution to our problem.

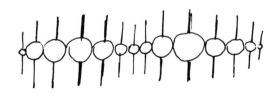

Perhaps we can appraise the situation more easily if we transpose our forms into matter. Then we might conceive of a row of unequal sticks, a bit like piano keys, each with the top of a tin lying over it.

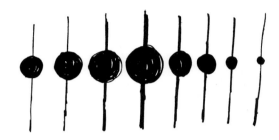

In this case we no longer have unified objects but rather two material items without visible relation between them, just one on top of the other, quite meaningless.

 In short: two unrelated
heterogeneous objects.

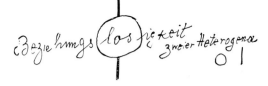

So we're back to nothing! What should we do to make something of it?
To go on with the material conception, let us keep our row of unequal sticks; but instead of the tin spheres let us set target discs or optical lenses or glass balls on top of them. And we shall have something 'visible', namely a pictorial expression of the relation between two heterogeneous objects ([1, 2, 3, 4] p.331).

1927/y 7: *Physiognomic lightning*. **Watercolour.**

Middle is
actively struck.

'The middle realm is actively struck.' Two
heterogeneous elements enter into relation with one
another; the tension between them brings out the
movement, in contrast to the 'adaptation by evasion'
in the examples [1, 2] on p.332. On the form of
lightning Klee notes, around 1927/28:
'The wonderful thing about lightning is the broken
form in the atmospheric medium.'

What sort of relations between the two characters have we here? Onslaught of the aggressive straight lines against the static circle [4], defeat of the straight lines as long as they are within the dangerous realm of their adversary. Struggle at the expense of the straight lines. Victory of the fluid over the solid character [1, 2, 3].

The following examples [5, 6] show another type of relation between two heterogeneous factors.

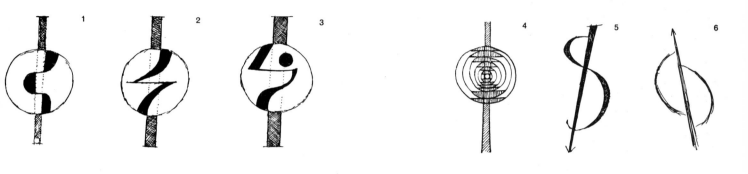

Intensely aggressive, the straight line becomes an arrow in flight and triumphs over the circle. The circle succumbs visibly [5, 6].

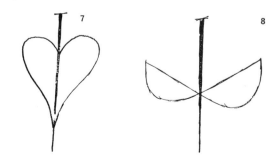

Again the circle is defeated [7, 8].

So much for types based on conflict. Let us go on to those showing adaptation.
Here the straight lines avoid battle. Adaptation by evasion; in the first case they go round on one side [1], in the other they split and go round on both sides [2].

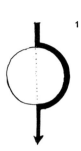

1

2

3

Or the circle avoids the battle by adapting itself to the straight line and becoming an ellipse [3].
And here, finally, we have a type in which both characters adapt themselves. Each meets the other halfway and changes its shape [4, 5].

4

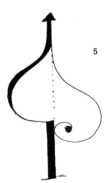

5

The circle is no longer a circle, the line is no longer straight. Further examples would contribute nothing essentially new; I shall limit myself to these few. According to the spirit of my composition, I accent one or the other of these typical motifs, to produce a figure of struggle or of friendship. The battle may be fought with varying intensity, and the friendship may be based on unilateral or mutual adaptation.

[1] Crossed out: 'compositional' process

[2] 'The straight-lines': relation of the straight lines to the circle.

Our interpretation of the constructive[1] process can become still richer in relationships if I call the straight line[2] masculine on the basis of its spontaneous activity and the passive circle feminine.

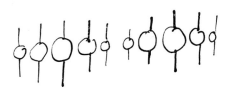

But, in the example we are criticising, both the themes and their compositional elaboration were so unrelated that one might say: the men are monks, the women are nuns, and though the two cloisters are right next door to each other, no life can spring from a representation of this sort.

So far my discussions of the structural concept have dealt with the most primitive structural type based on repetitive rhythms.

The concept of structure in nature

[1] Structural concept in nature: the grouping of the smallest bodies in matter, e.g. cellular or tubular bone corpuscles. 'Structural unit' designates a divisible (dividual) structural character. The simplest divisible unit is designated as a 'dividual structure'. A form is called a 'structural form' if it is composed of divisible units and does not reach the stage of an individually functioning organism. More highly developed than the structural unit is the individual structure (structural construction) of an indivisible organic whole (e.g. in a dynamic organism).

[2] Footnote in manuscript: 'A decomposed cabbage stalk and a piece of bone as an example.'

In our practical exercises I have often noted a structural unit[1] that rose above this simplicity. I found no reason to find fault with a structural individual of this sort if it were accompanied by, or subordinated to, a higher development. Here as everywhere else relativity, I said to myself.

As an introduction to the study of anatomy we usually start out by investigating the structure of the matter from which plants and animals are constructed. In this study we make use of a knife. By structure the anatomist means the grouping of the smallest particles of matter that can be seen with the naked eye or the microscope.

Similar structural designs are provided by matter which is exposed to destruction by decomposition. In a bone we can sometimes make out the rhythm of the bone corpuscles even with the naked eye; it takes the shape of a mass of cellular, tubular, or canal-shaped hollow spaces.[2]

333

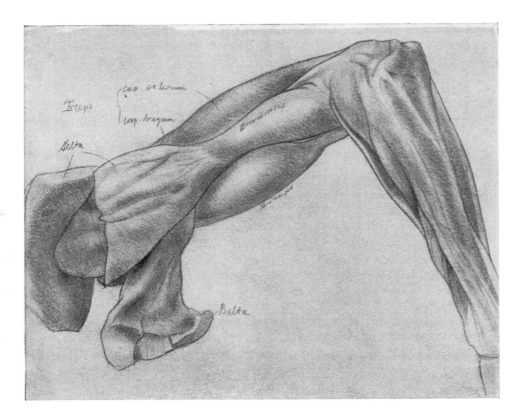

Anatomic drawing, pencil. Berne, November, 1902.

Diary notation, November 1902:
'Yes, I shall go on studying anatomy, but it is
more a means than an end.
I intend to limit myself more and more, dissect the
machine into its parts. I shall study anatomy along
with the medical students. Then, in the presence
of the living model, I shall make a new use of what
I have learned about the mechanical functions of
the body. I shall attend the evening life class at the
Kornhaus; along with the provincial painters I
shall sketch the hideous hetaera of the Matte in
Berne. I won't look down on the schoolmasters,
I'll make myself even smaller than they are, that will
surely leave me greater possibilities. If I still had a
shred of academic pride in me, I should have to
rebel against the corrections of one of those
well-meaning fellows.
But I'm not an academician. Let him say what he likes
On November 1, I started the course in anatomy.
A strange feast of the dead. Every morning I
work from 8.30 to 10.30 in the dissecting room. The
naked body is a thoroughly appropriate subject.
During the life classes I've inspected it a bit
from every angle. But now I no longer mean to
project some sort of diagram of it. I shall proceed
so that everything essential, even the essentials
that are obscured by optical perspective, show
in my picture.'

The grouping of the smallest particles of matter that can be distinguished with the naked eye or with the microscope [3].

1

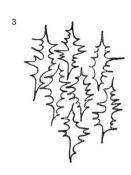

3

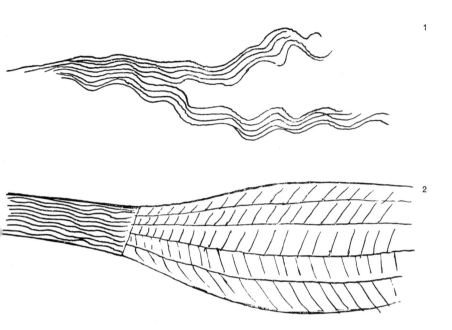

2

In a similar way we distinguish the structure of cartilages, ligaments, tendons, muscles, etc. The structure of the ligaments is a bundle of wire-like fibres [1].
The fibres of the tendons extend to the muscles and in the muscles a second striped structure is added across the first [2]. So much for the material structure, for the rhythm of the matter of which organs and the organism are made.

Material structures in nature: structure of ligaments [1], muscles [2], bones [3].

Let us from now on consider the organism as a motor in which the striving for movement and its achievement are interlocked; and let us build up from the servant to the master. In the whole field of action let matter be our premise. It should be everywhere. Now if first of all we consider the relationship between the bones which make up the skeleton, we notice at once that even in a resting position they require support from one another. The ligaments take care of this.

The ligaments connect several bones. They serve the bones [1]. Their function is of a lower order, they support by connecting, they are subordinate. Their function has a

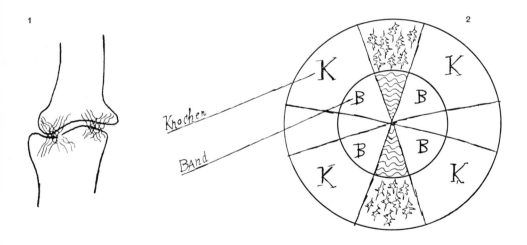

1

2

structural character in relation to the movement which is the higher function of the bones (one may speak of the structure of a function). Thus in the diagram I am drawing [2], I give the ligament (B) little space, but give rather more to the bone (K).

The natural motor organism: if in connection with the motor organism I consider the relation of bone to muscle, I perceive that the tendon here, in connecting muscle with bone [3], serves a mediating function similar to that of the ligament above.

And how is the muscle related to the bone? It can force it into a new position. Through its power of contraction, the muscle gives two bones a new angular relationship to one another (muscles have the ability to contract and thus shorten themselves).

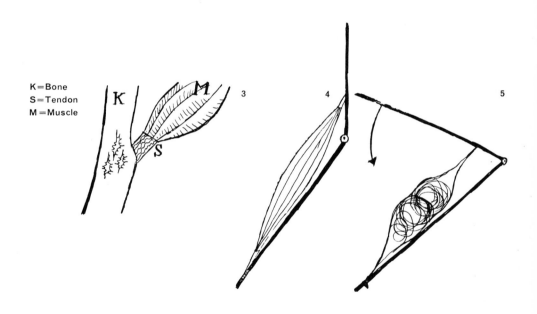

K = Bone
S = Tendon
M = Muscle

Ligaments and tendons help by holding the bones fast [4, 5]. The steps of motor organisation lead from the bone to the muscle; the tendon mediates between them.

The angle between bone and muscle must change because the muscle wills it. The motor function of the muscle is thus of a higher order than the motor function of the bone. The passivity of the bone is dependent on the activity of the muscle (the bone function is passive in relation to the muscle function). The bone function is 'structural' in relation to the muscle function.[1] It helps the muscle to carry out an order that has been received from somewhere. Thus in my diagram of the action of movement [1] I give the muscle the larger area and put the tendons between muscle and bone.

[1] The 'structural' is the subordinate function.

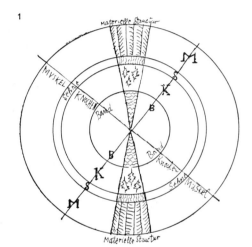

1

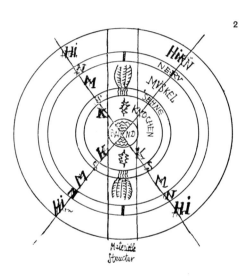

2

Hirn	Brain
Nerv	Nerve
Muskel	Muscle
Sehne	Tendon
Knochen	Bone
Band	Ligament

The muscles act independently of one another. Every muscle has a special task, one bends the organ, another stretches it, etc. Here again we note a higher functioning than in the bone, which can do nothing by itself but only in co-ordination with another bone.
But we have spoken of an 'order' or command. The muscle is self-sufficient only up to a certain point. It obeys when the command reaches it; it doesn't will to act but must act; at the very most, it has the will to obey. It obeys the brain's telegraphic command, which is communicated through the nervous system.
This means extending our diagram [2].

What do we learn from Figure 2? First of all we learn the relativity of serving and commanding, of structural and individual functioning. The whole is like a nest of boxes (box within box within box).

The functions are evaluated according to spatial or quantitative criteria: 'The more important a function is, the more space it needs.' The direction is eccentric [3]; the value, the importance, increases as we move from the centre to the periphery [2].

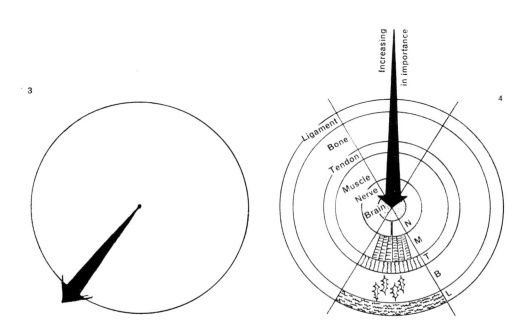

3

4

Progression of the function values
according to importance.
Qualitative representation,
with increase in value towards the centre
(concentric representation)

[1] The spatial or quantitative representation (eccentric) in Figures 2 and 3 contrasts with the qualitative representation (concentric).
A possibility: quantitative representation=linear and planar scale. Qualitative representation= weight scale (tonality and colour).
Note in Appendix.

The ideal view, on the other hand, starts with the brain; it attributes central importance and quality to this organ, which sends out rays of command on all sides. This view leads to a concentric or qualitative representation [4].[1]

The brain subjects the muscle to its will by means of the nerves; the muscle's command, sent through the tendon, gets to the bone, until the whole bundle of matter, despite its attachment to the earth, is set in motion.

'A linear figure takes time, and one must travel receptively the same road as one has taken productively. For example, things in motion, things that curve, things one has touched firmly, desultory things, are attached by a strong line and made into one. The longer a line, the more of the time element it contains. The purely linear always remains ideal. Distance is time, whereas a surface is apprehended more in terms of the moment.

A line contains energies that manifest themselves by cutting and by consuming time. This gives the linear element a mutual relation to imaginary space. For space is also a temporal concept.'

The course of the motor organism is indicated by arrows ('Identity of form and the method of its production'). *Cf.* the motor function, p.346 and cause and effect of concentric and eccentric forces, p.419.

Exercise for 20 February 1922

Weight scale:

I.

II.

III.

Problem: Organism in three parts:

I. Organ   active   (brain)
II. Organ   middle   (muscle)   or linear scale
III. Organ   passive   (bone)   instead of weight scale:

I.

II.

III.

340

1934/K 4: *Mister Zed*. Watercolour.

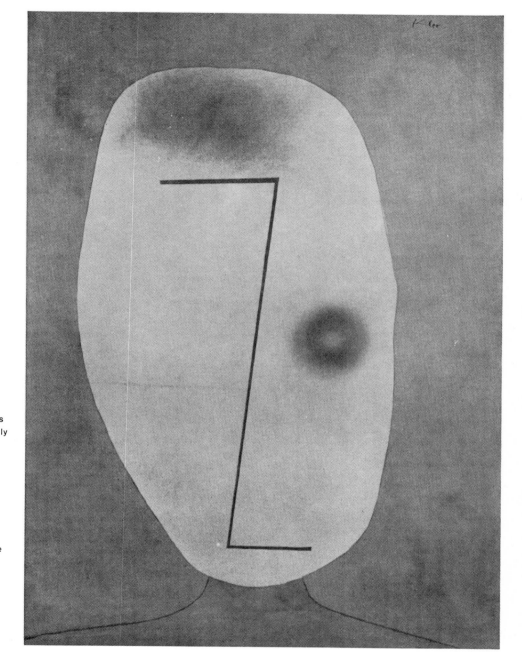

'The type symbol for the nature of pure line
is the linear scale with its innumerable variations
of length. The symbol for the nature of pure
tonality is the weight scale with its various degrees
of grey between white and black. Colour is primarily
quality. Secondly it is weight, for it not only has
colour value but also tone. Thirdly it is also
measure, for in addition to the above-mentioned
values, it also has its limits, its area and extent,
which can be measured. Thus we have formal
elements of measure, weight, and quality, which
despite the fundamental difference between them,
are related in certain ways. Each according to its
contribution, the three reference lines characterise
three realms which interpenetrate. They appear
in groups; first to a limited degree, then a little
more fully they combine into figures. Into figures
which in abstract terms may be called
constructions. The first constructive
combination of elements corresponds to
the dimension of form. Contradictions, contrasts,
are necessary if there is to be life in the picture.'
(On the 'specific dimensions' of measure (line),
of weight [tone value] and of quality [colour],
cf. pp.86–91.)

1939/UU 11: *On the Nile*. Oil on burlap.
On the appropriate choice, formation and
accentuation of the organs, *cf*. the example with
water wheel and flowing water, pp.343–349.

3. Movement is inherent in all change. The history of the work as genesis. The function of the work of art. The nature of real forms of movement and the organic connection between them

Monday, 27 February 1922

Appropriate choice, formation and accentuation of organs

Our problem last time was: the three-part organism.

> First organ, active character (brain).
> Second organ, middle character (muscle).
> Third organ, passive character (bone).

Brain, muscles and bones were not to be represented as such; rather, their position within the animal motor organism that I had discussed was to be characterised by a swift stroke or two.

The concepts active, middle, and passive can best be discussed in terms of linguistics:
When I say: I drive, that is the active form.
When I say: I am driven, that is the linguistic expression of the passive.
The middle form would be: I join, I integrate myself with, I make friends with.

Here it is worth recalling that the ancient languages formed the passive without an auxiliary verb, merely by using a special ending. I can even remember the pure middle form from the Greek, without any pronoun, expressed solely by the verb ending. The modern languages no longer express all these modes with the pure verb form, but employ various circumlocutions.
As to the rank of these three voices, active, middle, and passive, it will depend on the point of view. In an ideal order, the active would come first, because the impetus to movement begins in the brain, home of the thought that is father to all more highly developed action.

343

From a material point of view we should arrive at the opposite order and say that the solid matter of the bones takes the lead, because it first makes the movement concrete. But the two points of view need not be played off against each other. What is essential is the organic bond between the three parts as left, middle and right, or right, middle and left.

In view of the undoubted difficulty of the problem, I contented myself with solutions in which the organic context could clearly be seen, either in the shape of the organs themselves, or in the way these shapes were accentuated.

The appropriate choice, formation and accentuation of the organs, illustrated by the water mill.

A   Appropriate choice of the organs: ([2] p. 345).

1st organ:	the water course	active	brain[1]
2nd organ:	the connected wheels	middle	muscle
3rd organ:	the hammer	passive	bone

[1] 'The water course, active, brain.' By 'brain' one should understand the agent, the active, determining force.

B   Appropriate formation of the organs ([4] p.346). The main organ most individually structured, the others progressively less so.

1st organ:	the water wheel	(active)	the buckets	
2nd organ:	the wheel works	(middle)	of the big wheel	drive belt
3rd organ:	the hammer	(passive)	the spokes of the little wheel	

C   Appropriate accentuation of organs: ([11] p.349).

1st organ:	with main energy	active
2nd organ:	with intermediate energy	middle
3rd organ:	with subsidiary energy	passive

344

The Water Mill First example

Main organ: the water. Other organs: two wheels connected by a drive belt, one large, one small [1].

Criticism of Figure 1:

a) Formal mistake in the choice of the subsidiary organs. There is no organic three-part gradation relating them in the order of their importance to the principal organ.
b) Mistake in the form of the principal organ. At best its form is a conventional wave structure, 'the way you do water', not a striking representation of a principal organ.
c) Mistake of accent: the principal organ, the water, is not treated dynamically enough.

2

Correction to Figure 1:   A   The appropriate choice of organs: [2].

345

At this point the incongruity of Figure 3 from the point of view of form and accent must be obvious. The least probable event occurs; namely, that the intermediate organ becomes the most prominent.

3

4

Correction to Figure 3:
Water wheel and hammer [4].
B The appropriate formation of
the organs[1]   [1] with proper functional accent.

I.   The water wheel   active
II. The works   middle
III. The hammer   passive

Instead of extending the faulty example ([1] p.345) downwards by including the hammer in my choice of organs, I can extend it upwards. Then the hammer is omitted, the wheel becomes [III], the water becomes [II], and for my [I] I think up something new, which is all the easier as flowing water is hardly an original inspiration ([11] p.349).

5

We are familiar with the force of gravity

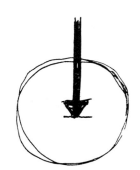

(towards the centre of the earth).

6

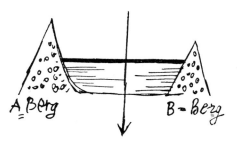

A Berg   B-Berg

We are equally familiar with the horizontal mirror of 'still' water [6];

7

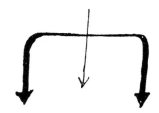

without Mountains A and B to hold it in, the water would flow off on both sides [7].

347

Berg	mountain
hindernde	obstructing
Schwerkraft	gravity
ursprünglicher	original
Wasserspiegel	water-level

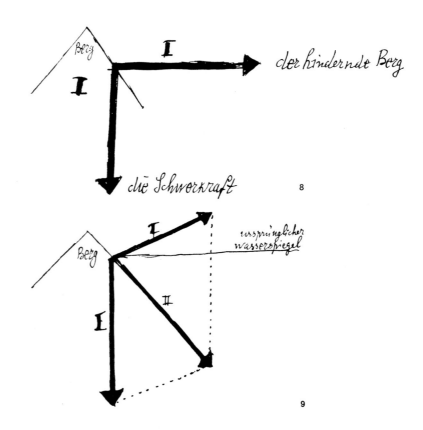

Berg · I · der hindernde Berg

die Schwerkraft

8

Berg · I · II · I · ursprünglicher wasserspiegel

9

But if we eliminate Mountain B and leave Mountain A in place, the water flows off only to the right [8].[1] Here two forces are at work, first gravity, second the obstructing mountain.

[1] 'the obstructing mountain B' ([6] p.347) is displaced or eliminated.

The diagonal in the parallelogram of forces will be the force of the flowing water, II [9].

10

With the accent misplaced  this variation looks like this.

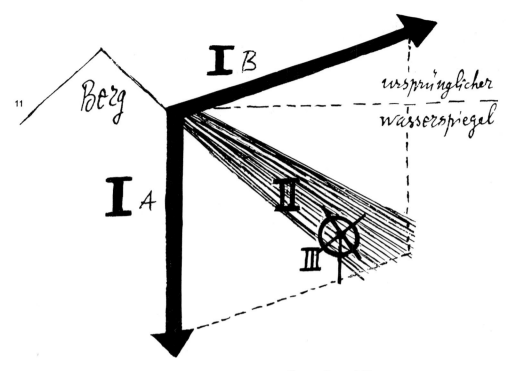

Berg   **I**B   *ursprünglicher wasserspiegel*

IA   II   III

Correction of Fig. 10: the water mill [11]

C   Appropriate accentuation of organs

I.   Principal energy   the two forces:
IA gravity, IB the obstructing mountain, active

II.   Middle energy   the diagonal of the parallelogram of forces, the force of the flowing water, II, middle

III.   Subsidiary energy   the wheel that is turned, III, passive

In terms of language:

I.   We drive   active

II.   I yield   but with the understanding that [I] is responsible in case anyone should suffer; middle

And as a matter of fact somebody does suffer:

III.   the wheel which says: I am turned, passive, III

349

1923/176: *Cosmic flora*. Watercolour.
Analysis p.343.

The Plant Second example

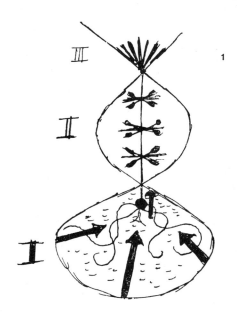

1

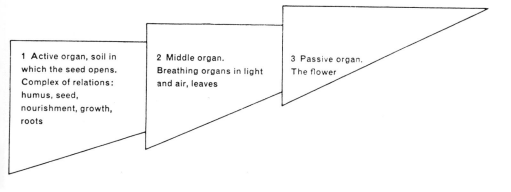

1 Active organ, soil in which the seed opens. Complex of relations: humus, seed, nourishment, growth, roots

2 Middle organ. Breathing organs in light and air, leaves

3 Passive organ. The flower

Misplaced accent

I. Let the active force be the soil in which the seed opens: The complex: soil, seed, nourishment, growth, roots, which produce the form [I].

II. Rising into the light and open air the breathing organs form: one or two tiny leaves, and then more leaves and more leaves.

III. Result, the flower. The plant is full grown.

Variant of the plant example: reproduction.
With the function of the flower begins the sexual episode which serves for reproduction.
Here our three-part schema takes the following form:

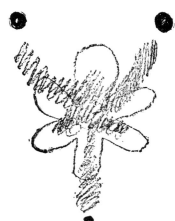

I. Active organ: stamens and pollen
(male organs)

II. Middle organ   the insects as intermediaries

III. Passive organ: the fertilised seeds
(female organs, fruit)

Representation of natural growth in longitudinal section and cross-section: A longitudinal section of growth does not give us a total picture of the expansion, but only of the action in a single direction. Synthesised, it leads to the total centre, while in cross-section growth leads to all sides, away from the centre. Figuration starting from the centre in progressions, i.e. movements in the smallest parts and in the whole (see p. 354).   Note in Appendix.

Material and ideal statics and static-dynamic synthesis

Analysis of 1923/176: *Cosmic flora*, p.350.
(*Cf.* Material and ideal statics, pp.182–183.)

In regard to material and ideal statics Klee notes: 'Seen in cosmic terms the earth provides the basis for a static-dynamic synthesis. On this basis the earthly creature arrives at a cosmic-ideal, static view of the world and at a terrestrial-cosmic view.'

When material statics (terrestrial relationships) are combined with ideal statics (cosmic relationships), the tension between the centre of the earth and the horizon incurs new limitations.

In ideal statics height is unlimited, in material statics it is absolutely limited. In the pictorial field a combination of the two leads to two different horizons:

The horizontal divides

above
_____
below

Ideal statics in pictorial space

Material-static

a
b

Material statics

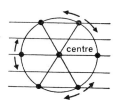

Dynamic tension and horizontal planes of varying height

Ideal-dynamic accent

Static-dynamic tension. Possible displacement from the centre (upward and downward $\updownarrow$)

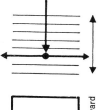

On combined bases, a composite form:
(a) Back section; (b) front section produce horizontal planes of different heights.
(*Cf.* [1, 2, 3] p.162.)

From the standpoint of the norm, combination of the ideal and material view (*cf.* p.185) increases the possibility of transcending terrestrial (static) limitation.

'The cosmic is the higher point of view, away from mere earthliness to something more comprehensive.' In practice the deviation from static accent on the horizontal (horizon) is achieved by 'a particular kind of deviation in the choice of method'.

(a) 'By wider choice with reference to neighbours;
(b) by shifting the whole (cut off the top, begin at the bottom. By a reversal of causality);
(c) by varied conversion and progressive restriction;

(d) By changes in centres of gravity, dense and loose;
(e) by rotation round an irregular angle;
(f) by composite form. Representation of the line as dividing or unifying.'

Where one is free to choose, the step towards specific action is determined psychologically. 'Fundamentally style is the human attitude both towards immanent and transcendent problems. Between the static-classic and the dynamic-romantic there lies an intermediate realm where statics yearns for the freedom of dynamics.'

353

We have before us, therefore, two opposing principles of movement. We might call them masculine and feminine.

In questions of movement we thus distinguish two sexes. There is an absolute means of representing directed movement: with the help of major-minor; and a relative means based on the sex, or gender, of the movement. If you judge not from part to part but as a whole, the question of movement and the inclination to choose a definite movement appear in another light. Then the form stands before our eyes as an undivided whole and takes on an aggressive tendency: sharp and cutting.

Volumes growing on all sides: feminine, growth in partial cross-section [1, 2]. longitudinal section [3]

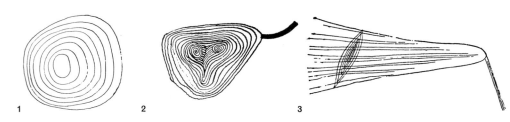

Aggressively advancing but regressive lines: masculine

One-sided progressive increase, growing in longitudinal section[1]

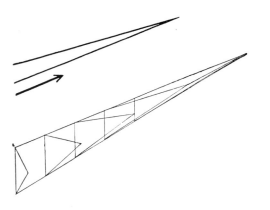

A Cycle   Third Example

Our anatomical studies might also be extended from the realm of voluntary movement to that of involuntary movement. Voluntary movement, as the name indicates, occurs at the command and according to the need of the authority that we call the brain. It seldom extends to the whole motor apparatus but only activates certain couplings[2] (in a part of it). This part of the animal motor machine is subject to fatigue; here fatigue, slackness, and temporary discontinuity (in sleep) are the norm.

[1] 'Longitudinal sections are typically static and cross-sections typically dynamic pictures.' *Cf.* growth in partial cross-section and longitudinal section on p.23. Examples:
1927/ue 2: *Ardent flowering*, p.20.
1927/Om 6: *Times of the plants*.
Oil and watercolour. Grohmann, p.228.

[2] 'Coupling': Combination, things that work together. Meaning of the sentence: 'It seldom extends to the whole motor apparatus, but only brings alive certain relationships in a part of it'.

354

The involuntary movements of the other part of the machine: the heart, the lungs, the alimentary tract—these involuntary movements are continuous as long as we live. Here one does not reckon on fatigue, slackness, or temporary stoppage.

     I. The heart pumps (active).
       III. The blood flows through the arteries, is moved (passive).
      II. The lungs purify, they participate by purifying (middle).
      III. The blood flows passively back towards the heart.
    I. The heart pumps again (active).
      III. The blood is again set in motion and returns to the part of the heart where the cycle started (passive).

    I. Heart
   II. Lungs
  III. Blood of the arteries and veins

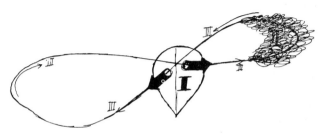

So much as a supplement to our last exercise. You have probably noticed the schematic succinctness of my representation, which on the one hand makes for clarity and simplicity, and on the other hand leaves you free to treat the formal concepts and formal relationships we have been discussing in the most diverse ways.

Movement caught in the work

But to figure the formal relations (even further narrowed in our exercise) which constitute movement (in our case only movement which is induced, translated, and forced), and to bring these relations back to nature through abstract analysis, for all this we need more than a clearly thought out diagram.
In the first place, what do we mean by movement in the work? As a rule our works don't move. After all, we are not a robot factory.
No, in themselves our works, or most of them, stay quietly in place, and yet they are all movement. Movement is inherent in all becoming, and before the work is, it must become, just as the world became before it was, after the words, 'In the beginning God created', and must go on becoming before it is (will be) in the future.

355

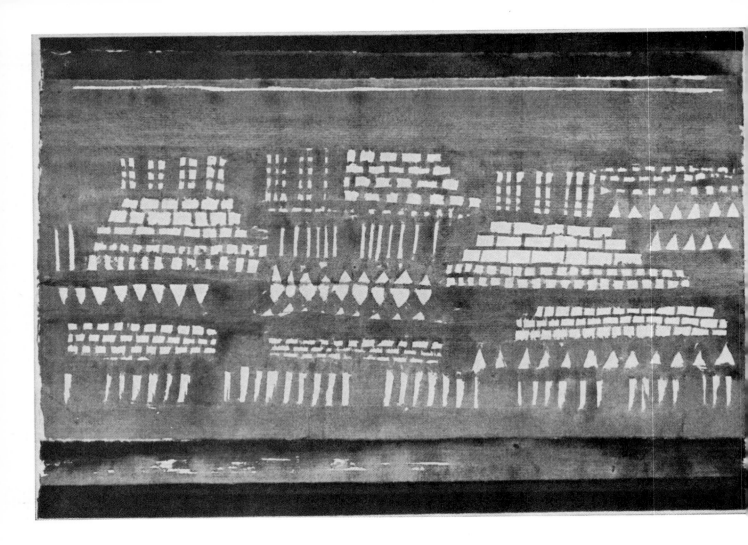

1928/q 5: *Foundation walls of K*. Watercolour.

356

Productive and receptive movement

The work grows 'stone on stone' (addition)

Or out of the block: 'Piece from piece' (subtraction)

plus 1
plus 2
plus 3
4

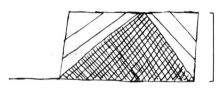

4 minus 1
3 minus 1
2 minus 1
equals 1

Both processes, building and cutting down, take place in time. The work as human action (genesis) is movement both in a productive and a receptive sense.

This is the initial productive movement, the creator's first action. Even this first move is temporal, whether it remains flat or leads to space: it takes time.
Shortly after the first productive movement the first countermovement sets in, a receptive movement. In plain English: the creator looks to see what he has achieved so far (and, says the Bible, it was good).
Another occurrence in time. Only the smallest of all things, the intrinsically dead point is timeless. When it becomes movement and line, that takes time. Or when the line shifts to form a plane, or when planes move to produce volumes. From the cosmic point of view, movement is the primary datum, an infinite power that needs no extra push. In the terrestrial sphere matter obstructs this basic movement; that is why we find things in a state of rest. It is a delusion to take this earthbound state as the norm.
The history of the work, which is chiefly genesis, may be briefly characterised as a secret spark from somewhere, which kindles the spirit of man with its glow and moves his hand; the spark moves through his hand, and the movement is translated into matter. The work as human action (genesis) is movement both in the productive and the receptive sense.
Productive movement depends on the creator's manual limitations (he has only two hands).
The step from dividual articulation or structure to workmanship or craft: we may speak of craft when a unit of dividual structure coincides with the action of the hand that makes it, e.g. stone to stone.

material craft

spiritual craft

The receptive process. The 'receiver', or viewer, who may be the creator himself, moves as it were in the opposite direction. But he too moves wholly in time. First physically: even on the simplest surface the eye does not in any one moment perceive everything with equal intensity. Of this it is physically incapable, because the retina does not register the whole image with maximum sharpness, but only Part I which is in the neighbourhood of the point that lies on the straight line through the focus of the lens and the

Sehnerv = optic nerve
Netzhaut = retina
Zentrum der Sehschärfe = centre of sharp vision
Linse = lens
Dreiteiliges Objekt = three-part object
unscharfe Aussenbezirke = blurred outer zones

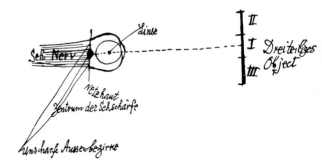

retina's centre of sensitivity. If the eye wishes to see Part II of the object sharply, it must turn upward; if it wishes to obtain a clear image of Part III, it must turn downward.
The eye muscles turn the eye in this direction and that, from left to right, from angle to angle, round in a circle, and the successively registered parts are gradually integrated in the brain. The brain has the ability to store up images and to make a whole of them; the eye has the ability to return time and again to a spot for verification and confirmation. We know of course that the image is actually reversed in the eye, but this makes no essential difference in the process.

(below) Muskel zur Senkung = muscle for lowering
Muskel zur Hebung = muscle for raising
Richtung Gehirn = towards the brain
Richtung Objekt = towards the object

First stage

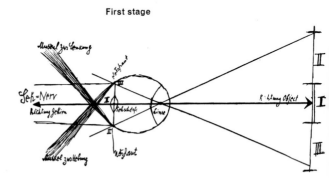

1st Stage: The viewer takes in the middle zone, Part I. Parts II and III produce a blurred impression on the retina. The muscles for lifting and lowering the eye remain passive, they play no part.

uskel zur Hebung aufgespannt, contrahiert=
uscle for raising tense, contracted
uskel zur Senkung=muscle for lowering

2nd Stage: The eye obeys the viewer's desire to obtain a sharp image of the upper region. The lower muscle becomes active, contracts until the eye is brought into a new position where the sharp zone of the retina, the focus of the lens, and Zone II of the object are in a straight line.

Zone I is still perceived, but less sharply, whereas III, which was previously blurred passes out of the field of vision.

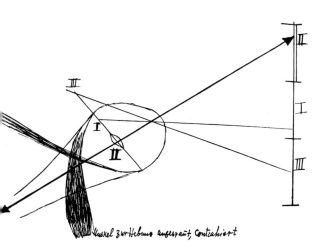

Second stage

Third stage

3rd Stage: Now the viewer wishes to obtain a sharp image of the lower zone. The muscle for lowering the eye contracts and the eye follows until the retina's zone of clear vision, the focus of the lens, and Part III of the object are in a straight line. Part I remains visible (though not sharply), while II passes out of the field of vision. Thus the eye, like a grazing animal, feels out the terrain not only from top to bottom but also from left to right and in all directions for which it feels the need. It travels the paths laid down for it in the work, which itself came into being through movement and became fixated movement.

359

It travels these paths in different ways, according to the organisation of the work. If the work is built solidly and clearly, with successive development of values, the eye moves, grazing from the values that attract it to other values that attract it after the first values have been 'grazed over' [1].

If the work is formally firm and clear, yet governed by strong value contrasts, the eye moves more in leaps, in the manner of an animal hunting [2]. Or more rhythmically [4]. But if the formal values of the work are not firm and clear, but fluid, if they themselves are movement and flow, the eye drifts casually about in the current like a boat, or it sails as a (light) cloud does in a gentle breeze or a storm [3].

Works with mobile forms involve greater activity

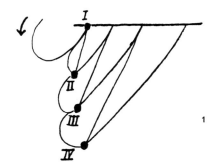

1

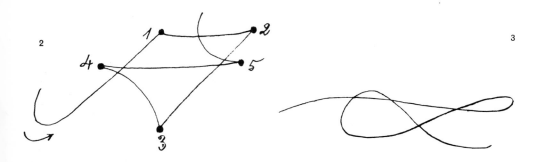

2

3

360

a: Example with radial auxiliary lines and intensified dynamic activity
b: Example with ordered development of values.

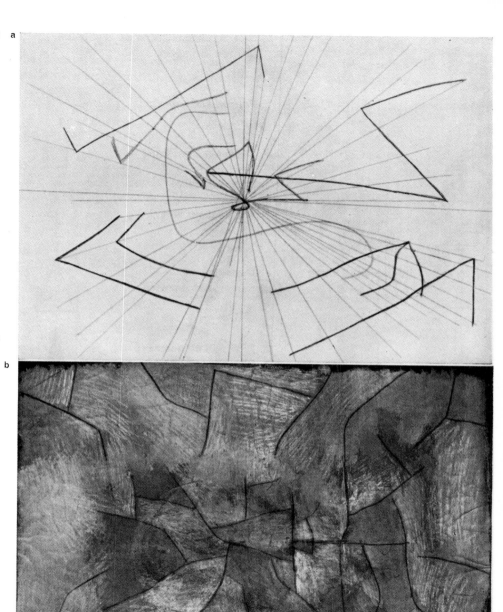

In composition main accents may be so chosen that a contact is made; it catches the eye, which can rest on it. But there is also the possibility of attracting the eye in a mobile way, without fixing it on a point. In this case we should let the eye move freely (in physical terms we should speak of 'relaxation'; but the physical context is imaginary). Here again we have harmonisation. The force of attraction can be preserved by the accentuation of proportions. Whenever you bring different things together, the question of proportion comes up, the relation between things and their position. Proportion is not only a question of actual measurements, but also of the forces at work in the measurements. It can be extended to produce local density, simplicity, or complexity. In a composition, one and one, line and line, or plane and plane need not always join. There can be a dual procedure in which plane and line operate independently to produce an organic counterpoint.

From the point of view of the motif, the landscape does not stand there in itself; because we are moving, it must at least take on a countermovement. Man has made the landscape able to move.

The mobile forces, as it were, of man's relation to the landscape. This is the mobile attitude we can take towards the landscape. What is close to us passes quickly; what is far away goes along with us' (remains within our sphere of vision).

Cf. The activity of works with mobile forms [1, 2, 3, 4] p.360.

1934/19: Mountain gorge. Colour.

Now let us apply what we have learnt
to a few examples.

First example:

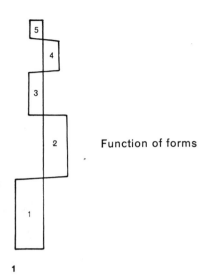

Function of forms

1

Formal statement:

Overall design: firm

Plan: vertical

Articulation: firm

Development:
progressive increase

Direction of increase:
from top to bottom

Ideal statement:

The idea of the weight of matter.

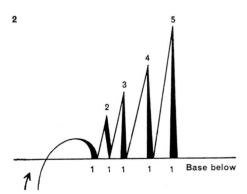

2

1 1 1   1   1   Base below

Receptively modified function:[1]

The eye of the viewer
seizes at once on the juiciest spot in
pasture No. 1, compares it with No. 2,
which it compares with No. 3 etc.
Base below [1, 2].

[1] *Cf.* Productive and receptive movement, p.357,
and pp.369–373.

362

Second example: **Formal statement:**

3

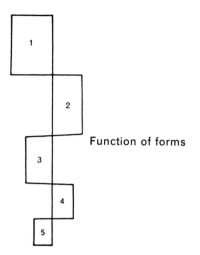

Function of forms

3

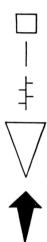

Overall design: firm

Functions: design vertical

Structure: firm

Development:
progressive increase

Direction of increase:
from bottom to top

Ideal statement:

Overcoming material gravity.

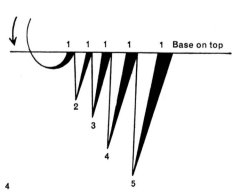

4

Receptively modified function:

The viewer's eye heads for the part
of the pasture where the grass grows
thickest, No. 1, compares No. 2, and
then No. 3, No. 4, and No. 5.
Base on top [3, 4].

Third example:

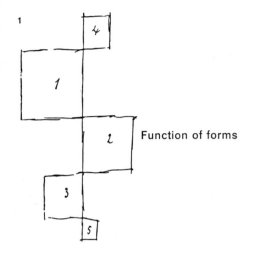

Function of forms

Overall design: firm

Plan: vertical

Articulation: firm

Development: progressive increase   and progressive decrease

Direction of increase: downwards to the middle
                                upwards to the middle
Direction of decrease: from the middle upwards
                                from the middle downwards

Ideal statement:

Combination of the material   material
and the idealistic interpretation   ideal

Receptively modified function:

The viewer's eye is attracted mainly
by values 1 and 2, vacillates between
1 and 2, compares 3 and 5 with 1 and 2,
and finally compares 4 as well.
Base in middle [1, 2].

364

Fourth example:

Formal statement:

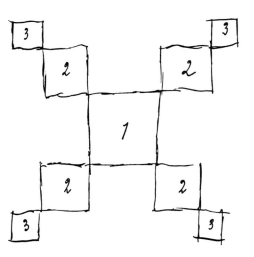

Function of forms

3

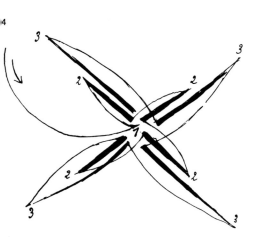

4

Overall design: firm □

Plan: diagonal ✕

Articulation: firm +++✕

Development:
increase and decrease

Direction of increase:
from outside to inside

Ideal statement:

Overcoming of gravitation.
It is replaced by centrifugal force
(*Cf.* [2] p. 377).

Receptively modified function:

The viewer's eye is most strongly
attracted by the main weight 1, because
this main weight also occupies the central
position, then it shifts round in a circle
among the four 2's and in a new circle
among the four 3's [3, 4].

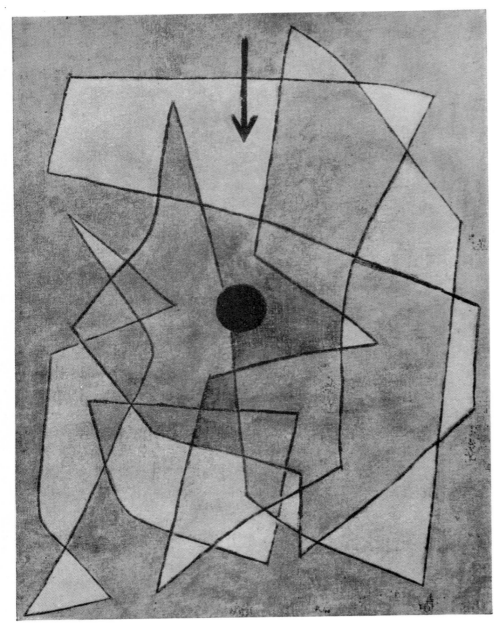

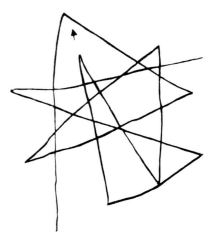

Linear diagram from 1933/K 11: *The will*.
Colour.

In *Tragedy* the primordial, self-contained centre is
threatened by the accented activity of the arrow
pointing from outside. Energies opposed to the
natural unfolding from within. On progression
Klee notes: 'Proof of the meaning and truth of
figuration from within: progression from the centre
is alive, progression towards the centre kills.
Possible positive-negative alternative: sacrifice-
life.' In *Tragedy* freely chosen movement with
shifting ground relations leads to
interlocking actions.

 From the inside out

 From the outside in

By contrast, the figuration of movement striving for
extreme liberation, in *The Will*. As a variation on
the theme, the same formal development in mirror
image (drawing on transparent paper) bears the
title 1934/p 19: *Forced issue*. *Cf.* 'the combination
of the material and ideal views', p.364.
'Concentric and eccentric forces', p.415.

366

This teaches us that the movement of a picture need not be stressed as such. For as you have seen, even the most static, rigid work has movement. Nevertheless, the question as to the nature of real forms of movement, of really moving form, is very much alive. It can lead us into new and richer realms of form.

Monday, March 13, 1922

Exercise:

I. Pasture of a grazing animal, functions of this part [1, 2]

II. Hunting ground of a beast of prey, functions of this part [3, 4]

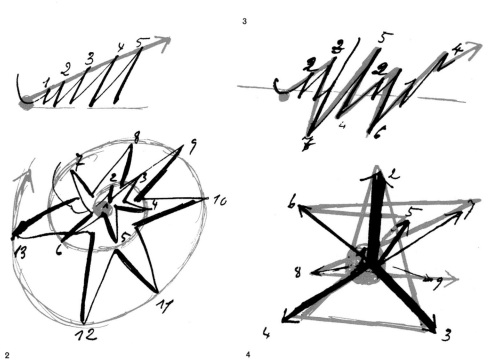

Figures 1 and 3: The foundation of the movement is relatively static (*cf.* pp.362–364).

2

4

Figures 2 and 4: Radiating from a centre, the movement is, to various extents, given dynamic emphasis
(*cf.* [2] with p.377).

III. Possible combinations of I and II; one character is subordinated to the other or the two are given equal weight

1927/i 1: *Many-coloured lightning*. Oil.

'Seventeen nodal points inside the square. Nodal points are points of support for the different parts of the picture and for the free space of the picture as a whole.' [1]→

'Movements chosen on the basis of the 17 nodal points inside the square. Each constructive point of support serves as a new jumping-off plac Organic lightning in square [2]→ drawn according to point schema [1]. (Movements chosen within strict norm).'

4. Succession, or the temporal function of a picture
Movement as action and form

The real forms of movement

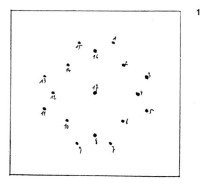

1

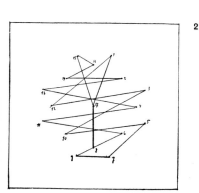

2

By the function of a picture we mean the way in which the movement of the picture's genesis gets to the eye, and the way in which the movement inherent in the picture communicates with the eye and with the mind behind it.

This brings up the old story of 'effect', but in view of our emphasis on the character of movement in each particular picture, we shall be speaking not of effect in general and as such, but of the specific effect of each particular picture.

To distinguish and classify these varieties of effect amounts to a classification of the pictures themselves.

As we saw at our last meeting, every work, even the most succinct, moves in time, not only as it comes into being (productively), but also as it is apprehended (receptively). Our eye is so constructed that it must take time to explore what it perceives.

Weary of the familiar nature and culture surrounding it, the eye seeks out new charms. If it looks for them in a picture, it is first attracted to the region marked by the most intense development of pictorial energy.

An attraction of this sort is always relative. If we have a white surface (my sheet of paper on the blackboard) that has aroused the curiosity of the eye, a deep black on it will have intense energy compared with the white. Or suppose a green surface has lured us to examine it more closely. Here a strongly contrasting red would be the special energy.

And similarly with white on black, warm on cool, lively on tranquil, or the other way round, higher on lower, stronger on weaker, harder on softer. Or active on static, not to mention all the other contrasts that can captivate the eye in a picture.

I have a feeling (which the results of our last exercise seem to substantiate) that I haven't made myself quite clear enough. Let us start by going back a little.

1923/62: *Architecture (yellow and violet graduated cubes).* Oil.

[1] In the pictorial sense the 'product' is a representative or additive action (combined by addition). Figure 1 with three values or stages (*cf.* p.357). The recept represents the function corresponding to a product, i.e. a picture. 'Recept' (receptive movement) designates the way in which a form is perceived by the eye.
'The deficiency of the eye is its inability to see the whole of even a small surface, all at once with equal sharpness. The eye must graze over the surface, sharpen one part after another, transmit one after another to the brain, which gathers the impressions and stores them in the memory.'
The diagrams on p.360 show the itineraries of the eye. The accent is on the movement. Every work moves both productively and receptively in time. Both in product and in recept the eye needs time to work. *Cf.* pp.357–365.
Note by Klee: 'productive-accusative = the question where to? Receptive-ablative = the question where from?'

I should like to show you once again how both product and recept[1] move in time. As my product I choose a very simple figure. But rudimentary as it is, it cannot come into being all at once even if I work with both hands.

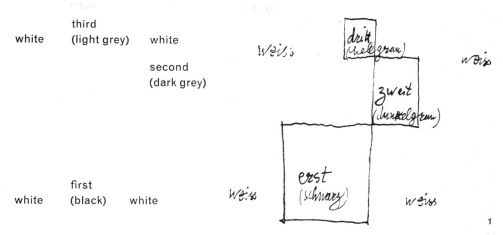

white	third (light grey)	white
	second (dark grey)	
white	first (black)	white

1

Product Figure 1

This figure [1] consists of the factors 'first', 'second', and 'third'. As we see, this product did not come into being all at once, since it took time. And, notwithstanding its extreme compactness, it cannot be perceived all at the same instant.

No: the stimulated eye leaps 'first of all' to the strongest energy,

with which it compares the 'second',

and with it in turn the 'third'. This once again means succession, a movement in time.
[2, 3, 4] Receptive process in connection with Figure 1

2

3

4

This receptive process, or 'recept' for short, represents the function of the product in Figure 1. Now we have before us: [1] the product, a planar form, and the 'recept' [2, 3, 4], a linear form. In one case active planes, in the other, active lines that are functionally connected.

1927/v 1: *Ships after the storm.*
Crayon drawing.

In the one case active planes,[1] in the other active lines,[2] which are not (it goes without saying) dependent on each other in the same way (described above) as the passive lines are dependent on this active plane: or as here where the plane is the result of lines, hence passive:

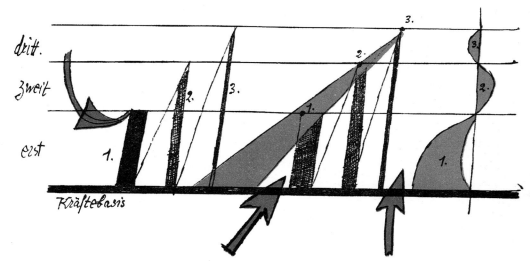

Recepts A, B and C, correspond to the product in Figure 1, p.371.

Looking more closely at the recept we see a movement getting smaller as it moves away from the energy base, or the successive devaluation of the principal values.
These red forms diminishing in energy are the expression of the three values of our product ([1] p.371). At the same time the new form is a picture in itself, and as a matter of fact it is a picture whose form is one of pure movement. We shall make this last insight still clearer with the help of a new product.

373

1930/x 10: *Polyphonic setting for white*
Watercolour.

Polyphonic setting for white illustrates the
elementary form shown in Figure 1, p.375.
'Polyphonic' refers to the interpenetration of
several tonalities or colour values. The picture is
centric in character with transparent illumination.
The transparency, the 'pervasive light', increases
towards the centre.
As contrast: light falling from above; illumination and
shadow accumulating towards the centre. The eye
moves slowly from the centre 1 to the successively
weaker values 2, 3, 4, 5, 6 (movement), then leaps
back to the strongest energy (countermovement).

In schematic form:

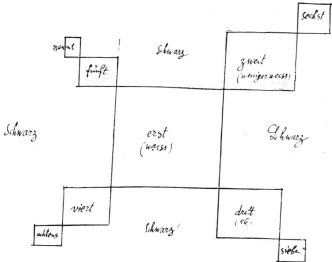

erst	1st
zweit	2nd
dritt	3rd
viert	4th
fünft	5th
sechst	6th
siebent	7th
achtens	8th
neunt	9th
Schwarz	black
Weiss	white
weniger weiss	less white

The new product consists of nine graduated values, which for the sake of simplicity I have distinguished only quantitatively [1]. A gradation of tone value or colour value would of course bring out both expression and function still more vividly.

In view of the centric character of this product, I find that in drawing the recept I shall have to schematise the gradation of values as nine concentric circles [2].

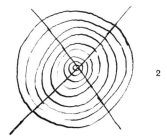

2

The diagonals should also be considered. The stage is set for the receptive action.

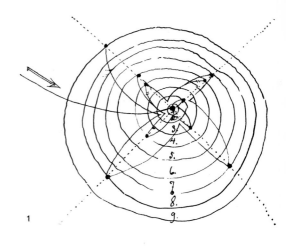

1

1932/v 17: *Helical flowers I.*
Black and white watercolour.

Before taking up the product, let us consider the following little prologue. We have been moving about in nature for some time and are tired of its out-of-doors impressions. It seems a blessing to enter a dark house.

The room in which we find ourselves is pitch dark, empty and black. The next room we enter is also black except for a painted wall. Here our eye, intensely stimulated, leaps at the pure white spot I have marked 'first'. Then at the still very bright 'second' and then on to the other, increasingly dark values [1].

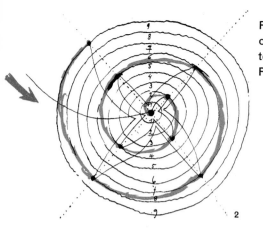

Recept corresponding to Product, Fig. 1, p.375

1926/R 2: *Spiral flowers*. Oil on canvas.

Spiral flower: genetic movement from the inside out (growth).

In this way the eye's path runs in a spiral round the central white through the various stimulus points [2]. The stimulus points move farther and farther away from the centre but preserve their relation to it.

The product ([1] p.375) consisted of solemnly rigid and static forms; its recept [2], the function of this rigid figure, is the purest conceivable form of movement, a spiral. And in every further attempt to represent the functions of a picture we shall always acquire forms of movement; the closer we come to the essence of the function, the purer will be the forms of movement.

377

'Discontinuous arrangement of values, physically loose-knit. No mobile contact between the scattered and fragmentary and the clear relation that brings things together (formal reconstruction necessary). "Divisive figuration" divides the picture in a diminishing or negative sense. The product must be divided. The part is something divided from the rest. The part (quotient) can stand by itself or can be recomposed into a whole that deviates from the product. **Possibility of impressive dissection.**' The formal tension of values in *Outburst of fear* is brought into agreement with the inner statement, the discontinuously moving inner tension.

378

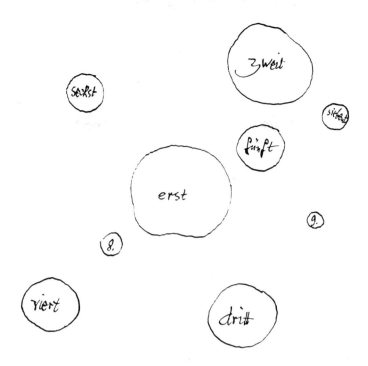

In comparison with those preceding, this new product shows a more irregular arrangement of values [1]. The previous pastoral of the grazing cow has turned into the hunting ground of a beast of prey, as will be clearly shown by the corresponding function picture.

Receptive preparation: For my first diagram of this function I choose a rather epic system to be read from left to right. On it I note the values, not in the order of rank, but, in accordance with the irregular displacements of the product, from bottom to top in the following order: third, fourth, eighth, ninth, first, fifth, seventh, sixth, second. The special position of first at middle height should be kept in mind. The sequence and order of rank are not identical (Recept, Diagram I, p.381).

379

1930/OE 5: *Polyphonic-abstract*. Watercolour.
Note in appendix.

For my second diagram I choose something more dramatic. The main value is inside; thus we have a central arrangement. The values are grouped according to their relation to the centre of the product:

Recept, Diagram I

second	
sixth	
seventh	
fifth	
first	●
ninth	
eighth	
fourth	
third	

↑

● first (centre)
eighth
fifth
ninth
fourth
seventh
sixth
third
second

Recept, Diagram II

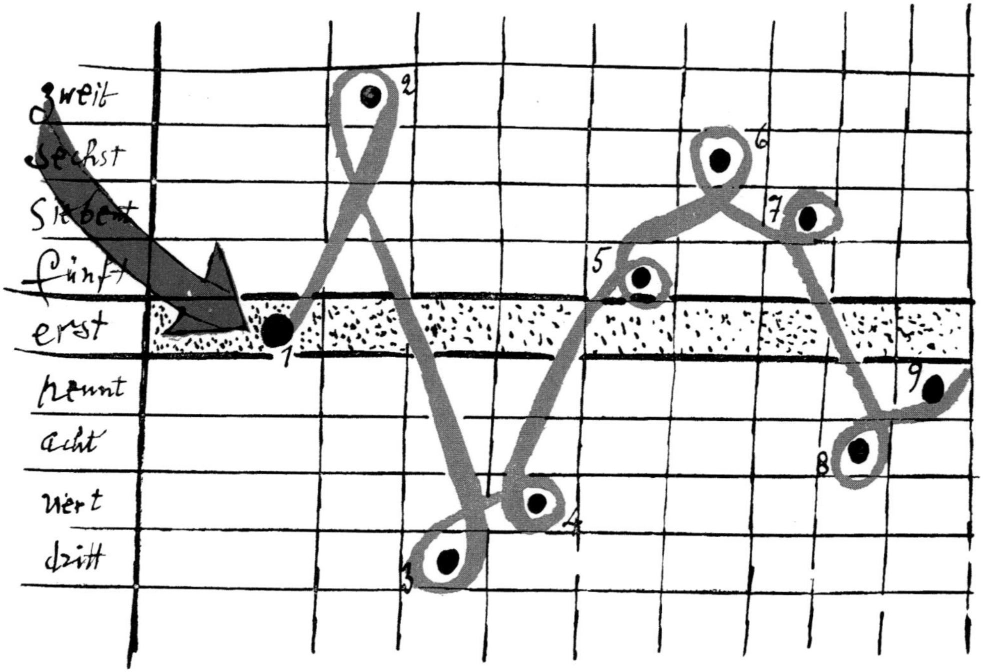

Receptive action. In both diagrams I put my notations in the position corresponding to the situation of the values in the product, and by connecting them in the order of their rank obtain two different recepts which intrinsically of course are almost exactly alike.

[1] Recept according to Diagram II
corresponding to Product Figure 1, p.379

[2] Free movement on
constructive foundation

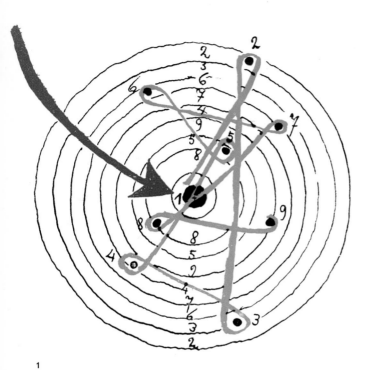

1

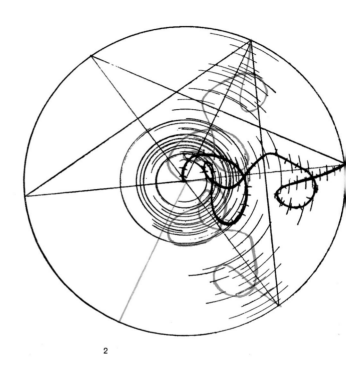

2

Now that we have come to the mobile form, let us first make a slight distinction.
The movement by which a formal element develops into a new formal element does not
necessarily produce a dynamic form. The movement of a point into a mathematical
straight line · ——— is indeed an act of movement but not a dynamic form. The same line,
when it shifts to form a plane, is not a dynamic line, because it is then no longer any
line at all, but a plane.

1931/m 7: *Figure.* Colour.

On the question of 'how to represent things',
Klee notes: 'Representation according to
essence, contrasted with representation according
to appearance or with physical and spatial
penetration. Accent on the processes leading to
the form.' Unlike the example of free movement on
constructive foundation, this 'figure' (Latin: *figura*)
indicates interpenetration of outward form and
inner nature. 'The core of the matter is a liberated
feeling for new possibilities transcending the
realm of the static. Once realised, the idea of
dynamic construction from the inside perceives
the specifically human content of this form from
within.' The organism is figured from within, on the
basis of its essence. 'Inwardly full of form.'
'Individual' figural proportion is taken into account.
Cf. 1931/L 4: *Three subjects, polyphonic,* p.296.
The linear-polyphonic example of p.84.
1932/y 4: *The fruit,* p.6, Endotopic-exotopic, p.51
and Interpenetration, pp.129–31.

383

Nor does the plane produced by the line's act of movement necessarily show dynamic character. A visible dynamics is created only by successive growth or diminution in respect of the quantity or quality of the energy employed. You remember the part played by the scales when we were still rigid and static, weighing the values on this side and that side against each other. But of what use are the scales when we want to measure moving values? How are we going to weigh things that won't stand still? Perhaps some comfort will be found in the following conception:

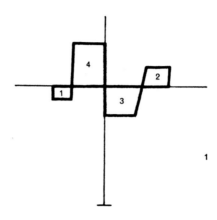

Is this little edifice with its one small foot expected to stand? That will not be so easy. So out with the scales, and this time let them be the gold scales! The weights are right: 4+1=2+3.

But in practice the thing still looks rather questionable. What shall we do? Let us, since we ourselves are, after all, edifices made to stand on small bases without falling over, try to get the feel of it. What do we do to prevent ourselves from falling? What do we do if we have not succeeded in balancing the weights inside ourselves, and have failed to achieve internal static equilibrium. We first move one leg (enlargement of the base) and perhaps a moment later the other. And in the end we walk; that makes balance easier. We have become moving form and feel rather relieved about it.
But our little edifice on one foot can't walk.
No, it can't walk, but perhaps there is another kind of movement that suits it. We shall not enlarge its base; on the contrary, we reduce the base to a point and set it spinning.

384

Symbols of the figuration of movement

The top. A visible dynamic is created by successive increase or decrease in the quantity or quality of the energy employed. No matter how accurately the weights are divided, the standing scale supported by the earth at one point only will totter and fall [2].

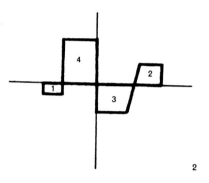

2

Set spinning
about itself, it will
be saved from falling.
Then it is called a top

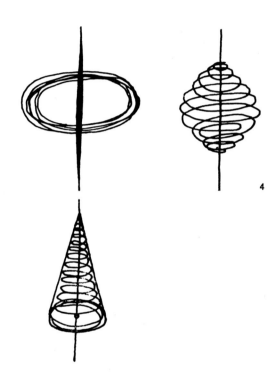

3

4

5

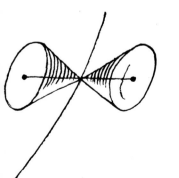

6

Every child knows that a top does not fall as long as it remains in motion, as long as it spins [3, 4, 5]. We can derive equal comfort from a rolling wheel, a child's hoop, or even a diabolo, the double top on a tense cord [6], which knows how to walk tightrope without falling.

But there are other paths from plane to volume by rotation round a common vertical axis. Result: sphere, cylinder, and cone, and perhaps a double cone.

Comforted in principle by such thoughts, let us look further for a substitute for the 'obsolete' pair of scales.

385

The pendulum. A very interesting little instrument is the pendulum consisting of a little lead weight and a hair which swings back and forth from a fixed point p; p is the centre of a circle, the hair acting as a radius.

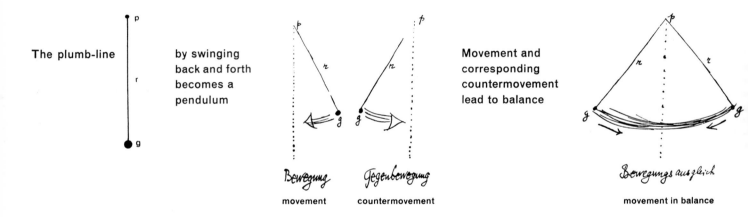

The plumb-line

by swinging
back and forth
becomes a
pendulum

Bewegung

movement

Gegenbewegung

countermovement

Movement and
corresponding
countermovement
lead to balance

Bewegungs ausgleich

movement in balance

Essential here is the concept 'back and forth', i.e. the pendulum's characteristic ability to register the compensating interaction of movement and countermovement.

In the swing of the pendulum new forces appear, which under certain circumstances shatter the domination of gravity. Then statics is suspended and dynamics takes its place.

386

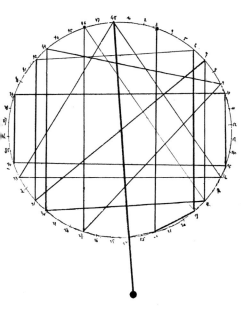

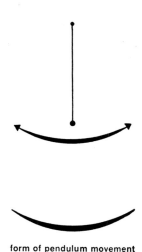

form of pendulum movement

The miraculous pendulum.'
The pendulum is an expression of temporal unity, a compromise between movement and counter-movement, the symbol of mediation between gravity and momentum. 'Drawing of double parallelism between static rest and rightward pendular movement.' Balanced movement in 48-part circle.

In between, between statics and dynamics, lies an intermediate realm, whose symbol, the pendulum, represents a compromise between the two realms.
One may say that, when a pendulum begins to swing, the force of gravity is suddenly suspended, replaced by momentum. When the movement and countermovement proceed from a fixed point, the balance between them leads to the form of the pendulum's movement.

Between gravity and momentum

Gravity and momentum are closely related

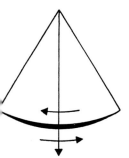

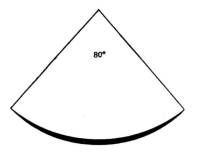

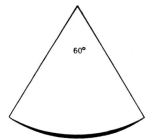

387

1934/qu 7: *Agitated*. Pencil.

Through the combination and intensification of movement and countermovement the tension or charge passes into a 'neighbouring realm of dynamic movement'. The balance of movement (excess movement annulled by excess in the opposite direction) extends the static analogy in the chapter on balance (p.211).
The synthesis of construction and balanced movement points to the intermediate realm 'between statics and dynamics'.

[1] Klee frequently attended *Pelléas et Mélisande* at the Weimar Opera.

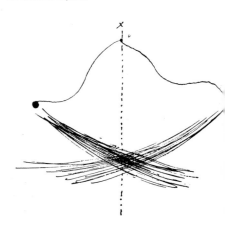

But this one instance of balanced movement and countermovement is not the only possibility. We can conceive of a less mechanical form, even of a highly sensitive manual movement.
Let us take a very long hair (one of Mélisande's[1]), attach the lead weight, and let the hair hang slack.
Handled in this way, the lead will describe both movement and countermovement independently.

Analysis of the dynamic function in 1922/159:
Oscillating balance, p.390.

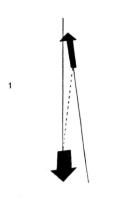

1

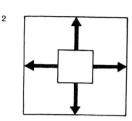

2

The main tensions move in two directions,
upward and downward: gravitation ↓
and as countermovement, momentum ↑ [1]
(*cf.* 'Formal and ideal statement', pp.362–365.)

Measured by the norm of an equal movement on all
sides of a square (from the inside out) [2],

energies move in different directions from the
ideal centre: a free balance of energies results in
static-dynamic shift, balance expressing mobile
calm or calm movement that demands
expression [3].

If we take the parallelogram of forces into
consideration, the balancing action looks like
this [4] (cf. pp.210–211).

In a more dynamic picture [5] (with accent on the
momenta) the balancing action is conceived in the
form of a pendulum on a moving pivot, or the
ground-plane is moving; *cf.* [2], p.391.

Movement and countermovement

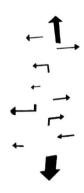

3

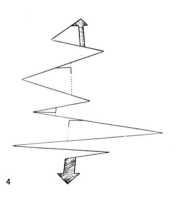

4

5

Starting from symmetrical balance as the
norm, we have asymmetric oscillation, wholly
subservient neither to gravity (static) nor to
momentum (dynamic). Oscillation should be taken
as compromise between gravitation and
momentum (along the upward or downward path
followed by the eye). The deviations from pure
statics point to the realm of
'pictorial mechanics': that is, 'to forms of

movements in the intermediate realm between
statics and dynamics'. Gravitation and
momentum add up to earthly cosmic-tension.

Cf. 'Static-dynamic tension', p.393.
'Gravitation and momentum', p.395,
and the pictorial schemata on the first and second
laws of Statics, building-up and falling-down, p.414.

1922/159: *Oscillating balance*. Watercolour.
Analysis p.389.

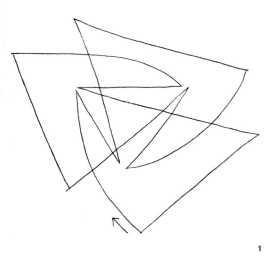

1

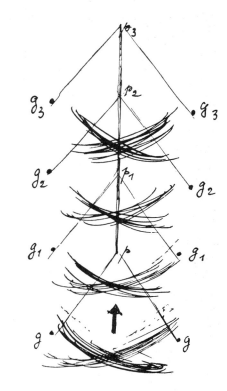

2

[1]'Sum of instantaneous movements with extended shifts. [1] (energetic theme in tonic and dominant).'
Examples:
1927: *Little jester in trance*, p.130.
1927/f 4: *The tower stands fast*, p.298.
1929/n 6: (Little) *jester in trance*, p.130.
1930/J 7: *Twined into a group*, p.340.
1934/qu 2: *Uphill and then what?* p.305.
1927/J 2: *Allegoric figurine*. Oil. Grohmann, p.230
1930/h 6: *The mocker mocked*. Oil. Giedion, p.153.
1931/Y 7: *Diana*. Oil. Colour reproduction in Grohmann, p.279.

We can go still further, from the loose manual stroke to the perceptible displacement of the central point p, and the pendulum writing becomes a transcribed expression of each displaced form ($p \rightarrow p_1 \rightarrow p_2 \rightarrow p_3$).

Here for example the pendulum writing is a dynamic expression of vertical straight lines and we arrive at a dynamic variant of the static figure [2]. We can also draw the straight form so that it seems to follow a winding path or any other form we please [1][1]. Or at any given moment we can relax the drawing completely by dropping the form. The pendulum becomes a gentle sling, writes like this, and like the countermovement of the fixed pendulum the countermovement of the sling is easy to feel and complete. The implications of the shifting centre are carried over to the extended forms of movement.

Temporal and spatial movement combined.[1]
Dynamic shift of a static premise.
Irregular lines in circle with constructive nodal points as jumping-off points (freely chosen movement). Twelve-part circle with six parallels in six directions.

[1] In connection with the section on irregular internal divisions of the circle, Klee notes: 'Remember the elastic tempo'.

¹ Notation by Klee on 'pictorial mechanics'.
'Subordinate to mechanics: statics: theory
of balance. Dynamics: theory of forces in a state
of motion. Kinematics: theory of movement.
Dynamic processes are relevant to art in so far as
they balance one another, in other words
where they partake of statics.'
(*Cf.* static-dynamic tension and position of
balance, pp.178–181).

Static-dynamic tension.[1] The pendulum is a symbol of mediation between statics and dynamics, between gravity and momentum, between rest and movement. If the motor force weakens, gravitation reclaims its right. The pendulum also expresses a unit of time.

↑
Linear analysis from 1937/R 4: *River trip.*
Oil. Note in Appendix.

Static tension passive

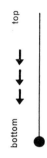
top
bottom

Static tension active

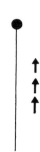

Static-dynamic tension
falling down ↓ building up ↑

Dynamic tension centre

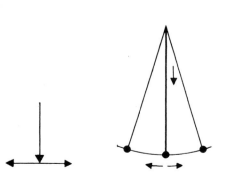

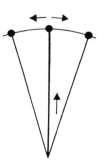

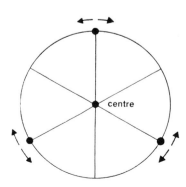
centre

393

1921/3: *Inscription*. Watercolour and pen and ink.

Gravity and momentum

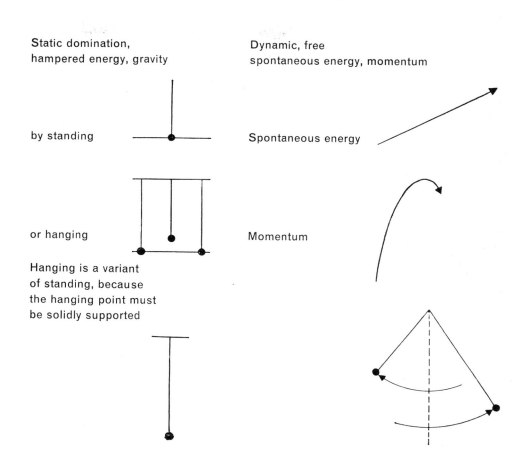

Static domination,
hampered energy, gravity

by standing

or hanging

Hanging is a variant
of standing, because
the hanging point must
be solidly supported

Dynamic, free
spontaneous energy, momentum

Spontaneous energy

Momentum

The hanging pendulum is inclined
to wander into the dynamic
realm and swing back and forth.

Anything on earth that shows dynamic
will seeks to overcome its gravity by
momentum; but whatever is purely
dynamic or transcendent, has normal
power of movement; it is mobile and
without heaviness. Its freedom
of movement is not obstructed
by any attraction as on earth.

395

1937/T 9: *Sextet of geniuses*. Pastel.

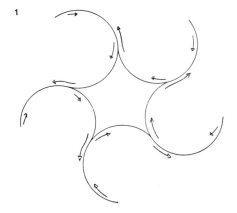

1

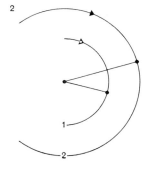

2

[1] 'Constructive foundation: inner extension of the natural dynamics of the circle. The fivefold curve. Dynamic gesture on the basis of free circular movements.'

[2] 'Combined time in relation to movement:
1   uniform tempo advancing, faster.
2   uniform tempo retarding, slower.
Partial movements on curves with flexible tempo.'

396

The circle. But something new happens when, as the pendulum[1] swings quietly back and forth, we suddenly think away the force of gravity [1]. Or if we swing the pendulum with so much force that gravitation is overcome. In either case the bond with the earth is broken and the cosmic form of motion sets in forthwith: the pendulum begins to swing round in a circle, which is the purest of dynamic forms [2].

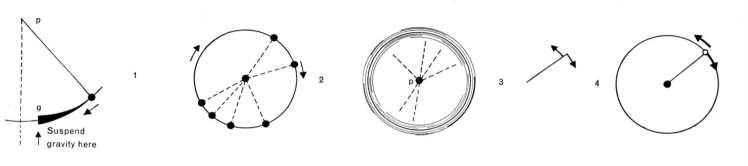

p

1

g

Suspend
gravity here

2

p

3

4

Circular movement of pendulum [3].
In this closed, endless movement, the need for countermovement disappears, and actually the pendulum abandons it under the new conditions. The purest form of movement, the cosmic form, arises through the elimination of gravity, of our bond with the earth. The circular form remains the same whether the movement is to the right or to the left. In the circle the dominant power is in the centre. The circle results from the primordial dynamics of a point connected with a dominant centre (by the power of constraint) [4]. All positions are possible; that is the symbol of dynamics.

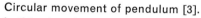

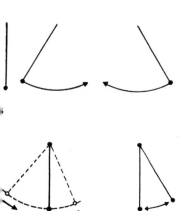

Yet the force of gravity is still at work. There is no perpetuum mobile. If we confine the eros of the pendulum to a special case—the arc of a circle—the plumb-line on the horizontal is still a fundamental symbol. A kind of compromise occurs. More and more, the line loses importance [5].

When the movement is jerky, tension makes the steady state mobile, and things that are already mobile are disturbed by its constraint. As a result we get irregular curves and spirals.

397

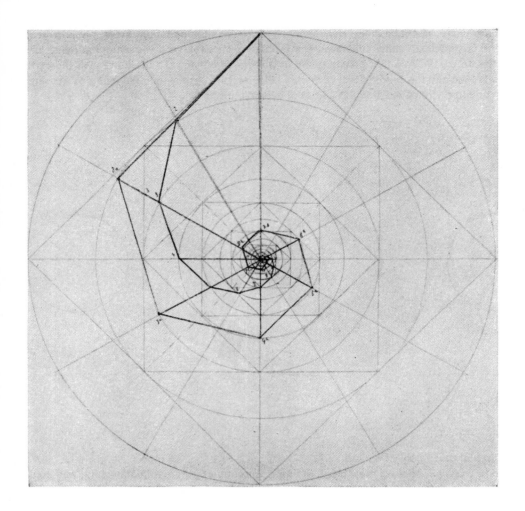

From progression or regression of the radius to the spiral.
Concentric squares each at an angle of 45° to the last. As you see, each new square is smaller than the one preceding. Now we describe a circle round each square. The radius of the innermost circle is twelve or, if you will, six times smaller than that of the outer circle. We connect the points thus obtained (12-part circle and square or 6-part circle and square).

The spiral. Thus we have made the acquaintance of a new force, which I call centrifugal as opposed to the force of gravitation. The pendulum swinging in a circle can describe new shapes if the central point is set in motion or if the movement begins with the radius, which either lengthens, producing larger and larger circles, or shortens, making the circles smaller and smaller, until our little drama suddenly jerks to a stop in the point [3].

Variable radius length combined with peripheral movement transforms the circle into a spiral. Lengthening of the radius produces the living spiral; decrease of the radius makes the circuit smaller and smaller [1, 2].

1

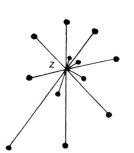

2

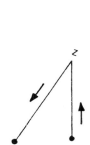

3

This last figure tells the story of the spiral. Its movement is no longer endless and self-contained; the problem of direction comes up again. We have to know the direction, because the lengthening or shortening [2] of the radius raises a question that is vital from the standpoint of physics. The question is: Am I being released from the centre in a movement that is becoming more and more free? Or: Are my movements more and more bound to the centre, which in the end will swallow me up entirely?

It is the direction that decides whether we are being released from the centre in a movement that is ever freer or whether we are becoming more and more attached to a centre that will ultimately destroy us [3].

Either: movement of the radius away from C Or: movement of the radius towards C. C=Centre

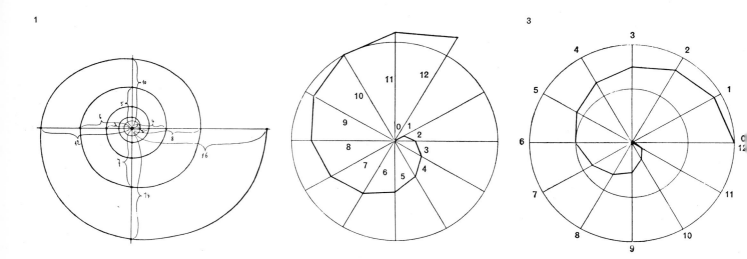

The question means nothing less than life or death.[1] Movement of the radius in relation to the centre: progressive, 'towards life', regressive, 'towards death'. And the decision rests with the little arrow.

We'll speak of the arrow next time, when we shall also take a look at my fine collection of arrows.

1. Radius movement (progression) from the inside out. Constructive picture (1 2 4 8 16 32 64 per revolution).
2. Twelve-part circle with arithmetic progression for twelve-fold increase or decrease of radius.
3. Spiral. Development during a single rotation.

[1] Crossed out: 'freedom' (or death).

Cf. 'two broken spirals', p.415.

400

Monday, 27 March 1927

Exercise in movement: 'the fountain', not the appearance of the fountain, but its nature. The hydraulic forces considered as design but above all as dynamic function. Sketch of solution:

* (Lösungs-Schema der Aufgabe)

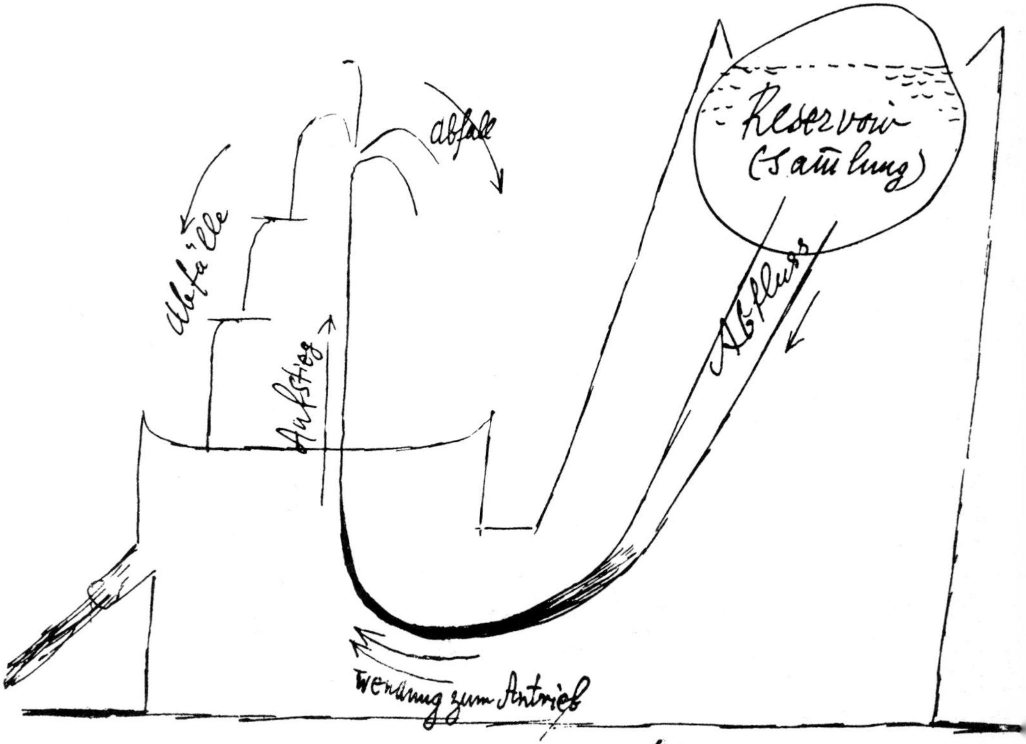

Abfall *or* Abfälle = fall
Wendung zum Antrieb = stream turns upward
Aufstieg = rise
Abfluss = downward flow
Lösungsschema der Aufgabe = solution of problem

'If I broaden my concepts, I create a higher perceptible whole. I give my picture new, wider limits.'

The water cycle

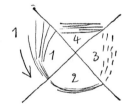

'Our epic has neither beginning nor end. This can be remedied by inserting a connective. But to connect beginning and end of a finite temporal process is to create a cycle. The water comes from the sky in the form of rain and rises up to the sky in the form of vapour. Thus I guide my curve upwards and complete the circle in the clouds.'

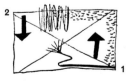

1 gaseous towards the sky
2 liquid away from the sky

5. Cause, effect, and the figuration of dynamic forces
The organism of movement and the synthesis of differences with a view
to producing a whole characterised by mobile calm and calm movement
The solution of endless movement

Monday, 3 April 1922

The arrow

In regard to duration and direction of energy the arrow is a precise projectile. The very simplest weapon developed from the need to extend our limited human reach: e.g. the cudgel, prolongs the arm and increases its striking power, providing (direct) contact with the target and satisfying our desire to attain this target that is beyond our reach without loss of time or other resources: with it I hit the otherwise inaccessible target without stirring from where I happen to be standing.

A weapon of this sort with a longer range is the stone we throw. It strikes its target; dispensing with direct contact, it reaches the distant object through the air. In order to reach the object with some effect, it must, during its brief journey, preserve its force and direction, direction as far as the target, and force even beyond.

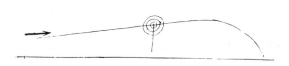

It was not so much the inaccuracy of this weapon as the effort the thrower had to make, that led to the development of better projectiles.

Beyond a doubt the invention of the sling shot provided such an improvement. I remember how as a boy we cut hazel switches and picked up 'projectiles' in a nearby potato field. We spitted the potato-projectiles on the switches; then we set the apparatus in centrifugal motion, increasing it till the very moment that the projectile flew off the switch.

The effect was amazing. We no longer had to swing our whole arm as in throwing stones; the switch relieved us of most of the effort; all that was needed was an energetic snap of the wrist, extending to the forearm for barely a moment at the end.

In regard to the saving of energy, we had made great progress; the potato flew over several houses, and landed ten, or even twenty times further away then we could throw a stone. And we weren't the least bit tired afterwards. But the accuracy was very questionable, and in secret we admired the accomplishment of David the shepherd boy, who had hit Goliath in the middle of his forehead which could not have been very big.

We needed more accuracy, and we were also able to obtain it.

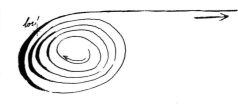

This time we cut forked branches in the woods and fastened rubber bands

to the ends, which

could be pulled far back. When released they gave the projectile considerable force and the direction could be regulated. We further improved our accuracy by exchanging the stone for a kind of arrow that we made out of a hairpin.

A little tassel of coloured wool served as a rudder, a handle, and also as an ornament. Related to this device was the bow and arrow, which of course we also learned to use.

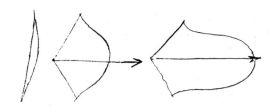

Economy of energy and improvement of aim had been achieved. Both considerations had exerted a determining influence not only on our little contrivance but also on the shaping of the projectile which, because of its length, created little friction, while its straightness made it easier to aim. The arrow had been born: the arrow consisting of shaft, tip, rudder.

The arrow consists of   shaft

tip

and rudder

The bow with the further refinements of an aiming device, a contrivance to pull the string, and a trigger to release it, is called a crossbow. The body is relieved of effort, one can concentrate on aiming. William Tell's shooting of the apple is of interest only because of the emotional complications. If he had not been so upset, there would have been no difficulty in hitting the target with so perfect an instrument.

Our modern firearms reach far back to the blowpipe, which is known to every boy. But an important innovation is made in the arrow, which we still atavistically call a ball or bullet: its two-dimensional movement.

1922/30: *Mural from the temple of
yearning*↘ *thither* ↗. Watercolour.
Cf. the exercise: 'Balanced structures in the plane',
p.149.

The lines in the rifle barrel give the projectile a rotary motion. One might call this modern projectile a screw arrow or a drill arrow, because the two-dimensional forward movement reminds one of a screw or a drill.

(Note: the motion of big steamships and torpedoes is based on the same principle.)

The father of every projectile, whether fired or thrown, hence also of the arrow, was this thought: how shall I increase my range in that direction? Across that river, this lake, this mountain?

Whither?　　　　　　　　　　　　　　　*dorthin?* ⟶

Common to the arrow and all its offspring are: the linear motion and the length of the trajectory in relation to the size of the projectile. The father is all spirit, all idea, all thought. Its motion can be mathematically straight, unaffected by obstacles, without friction because it has no body; it can be as long as it pleases, finite or infinite. Man's ability to measure the spiritual, earthbound and cosmic, set against his physical helplessness; this is his fundamental tragedy. The tragedy of spirituality. The consequence of this simultaneous helplessness of the body and mobility of the spirit is the dichotomy of human existence.

Man is half a prisoner, half borne on wings. Each of the two halves perceives the tragedy of its halfness by awareness of its counterpart.[1]

[1] First version of the sentence: 'Man is half a prisoner, half borne on wings. Each of the halves perceives the tragedy of his halfness through awareness of his "opponent".'
Cf. etching 1905/38: *Hero with wing* (Grohmann, p.108) and this entry in Klee's diary:
'Berne, January, 1905. The tragicomic hero with the wing, a modern-antique Don Quixote. Unlike the divine creatures born with only one angel's wing, this man is forever trying to fly. He keeps breaking his arms and legs, but that does not prevent him from clinging to his idea of flight. I wished to capture the contrast between his monumental-solemn attitude and his already ruinous state.'
New version written after 1922: 'The source of man's tragedy is the contradiction between his physical weakness and his ideal ability to measure both the earth and the cosmos at will. This conflict between power and weakness is the dichotomy of human existence. Man is half a prisoner, half borne on wings.'

[2] The concept of 'terrestrial cosmic tension' (terrestrial-static, cosmic-dynamic).

The idea as intermediary between earth and cosmos[2]

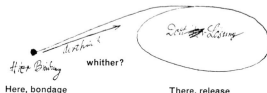

Here, bondage　　　whither?　　　　　There, release

The longer the journey from here to there the keener the tragedy. But it begins in the very fact of the starting point, in the need for release from bondage, in the need for becoming mobile if one is not just to be and remain so. Thus there is tragedy in the very beginning. And correspondingly in the continuation of the process: how can the arrow overcome the obstacle of friction? Will the movement persist (certainly not indefinitely, but at least that far), a little farther than possible, than usual?

In parentheses: And so ye arrows, let yourselves be winged, lest you tire too soon; let yourselves be shaped so that you strike home, even if you do weary and do not strike home!

407

1937/L 5: *Labile pointer*. Watercolour on blotting paper.

Dynamic shift of a static premise.
'An amplification of the rigid, static analogy in the chapter on static balance.'

'The psychology of the figuration of definitely directed movement: Productive: Question, where to? Receptive: Question, where from? In both cases the same direction, direction united by the differently formulated question "where to?" or "where from?" Activity or passivity towards the arrow changes nothing in the actual direction of its motion.'

Examples:
1922/79: *Separation in the evening*, p.11.
1922/109: *Scene of calamity*, p.310.
1922/159: *Oscillating balance*, p.390.
1927/d 10: *The ships set sail*, p.80.
1929/s 7: *Arrow in garden*, p.56.
1929/3h 43: *Mixed weather*, p.402.
1930/s 10: *Hovering before rising*, p.172.
1937/qu 17: *The way to the city castle*, p.166.
1936/k 2: *Afflicted city*. Oil. Colour reproduction in Giedion, p.139.

A genuine African arrow of this sort¹ consists of shaft, tip and rudder.

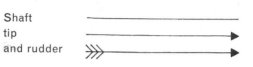

Shaft
tip
and rudder

The tip should not only cut sharply through the air, but should penetrate the target as deeply as possible, and cling with the help of a barb.
The rudder or vanes of such an arrow should add to its steadiness of direction, help it to keep its path.
Our symbolic arrow differs somewhat from the African arrow. The shaft is replaced by the concept of 'trajectory' and the tip by the concept of the 'tip rudder'. Thus the tail rudder of the African arrow is no longer needed.

The symbolic arrow is trajectory

tip and rudder
combined into tip rudder (aiming power)

And so our arrow looks like this:

The two lines forming the tip are equal in length and form the same angle with the horizontal shaft; this results in a horizontal trajectory.

Provided that a＝b and angle α＝angle β, the result will be the horizontal trajectory C.

409

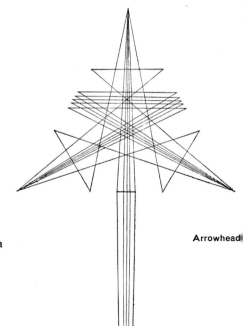

Arrowhead

The parallelogram of forces. Unequal length and angles of the tip lines result in a trajectory deflected upwards or downwards.

$a > b$ $\alpha > \beta$
results in rising trajectory

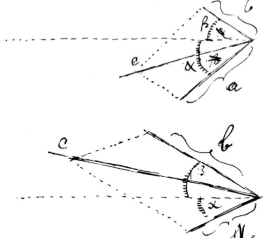

$b > a$ $\beta > \alpha$
results in falling trajectory

The underlying principle is the parallelogram of forces, which is excellently illustrated in so far as it concerns direction.

Two forces *a* and *b* working in different directions result in a new force *c* which proves to be a diagonal of the parallelogram formed by forces *a* and *b*.

On the parallelogram of forces
cf. 1930/s 10: *Hovering before rising*, p.172.
1930/W 5: *Braced planes*. Oil. Grohmann, p.400.
1932/t 10: *Lift and flight (glider flight)*. Oil.

If the two sides, or vanes, of the tip rudder stand in the same relation to the horizontal, the trajectory remains horizontal. If their relation to the horizontal is dissimilar, the trajectory is deflected by the vane with the greater deviation from the horizontal.

In synthetic representation, this tip

will result in this picture:
the bigger the ascending vane,
the more pronounced will be the rise

Or this tip

will result in this picture:
the larger the descending vane,
the more pronounced will be the fall

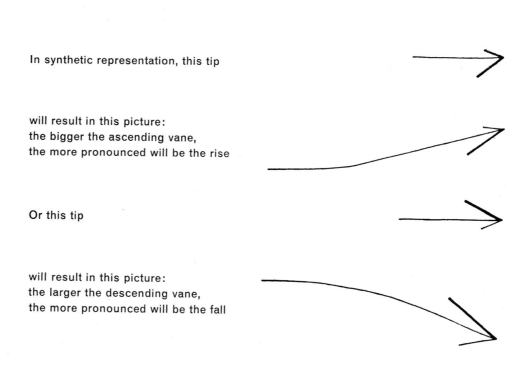

The larger the ascending vane, the more sharply the trajectory will rise; the larger the descending vane, the more sharply it will fall. In earthly reality it is this latter which always occurs after a short while, for as the velocity is reduced by friction and interference, the attraction of the earth grows dominant and makes the descending vane more and more important ([1] and [2] p.413.).

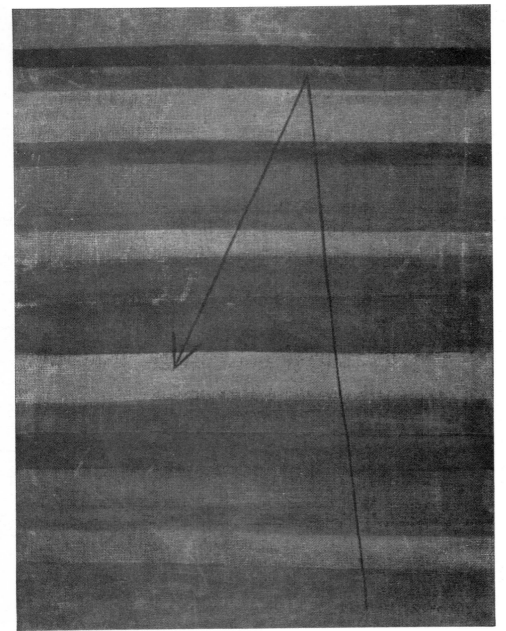

1932/1933: (*Descent*). Oil on burlap.

Change of direction (rising and falling) in the realm of horizontals. 'Horizontals develop from differences of weight in gravitational movement; they represent total subjection to the law of the plumb-line. The absolute domination of this power of the plumb-line is the death of spontaneous movement (stratification). All vertical straight lines are abstracts of the first law of statics, the law of gravitation.'

In earthly terms horizontals (as a fixed dimension without independent movement) are the result of gravitational forces in one direction. 'The movement becomes unequivocal when the ground is concretely present and locally defined.' Movement (rise and fall) increases and decreases in relation to the dimensions that remain fixed. The increase and decrease in the height of horizontals point to the amount of time that passes. Movement in a definite direction:

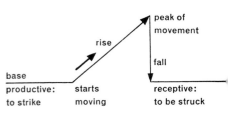

On the 'psychology of the phenomenon' Klee notes 'An arrow is an arrow, activity or passivity towards it has no effect on its actual direction of movement. I strike with the arrow, the observer is struck. The productive individual strikes with the arrow, the receptive individual is struck by the arrow.'

412

Thus the terrestrial curve appears as finite movement [2, 3];

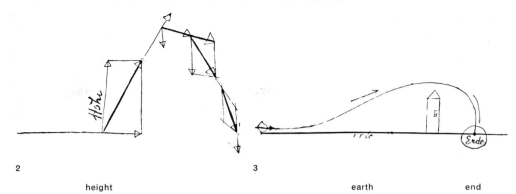

2   3

height   earth   end

in practice the end occurs at the surface of the earth, in theory at the centre of the earth [4].

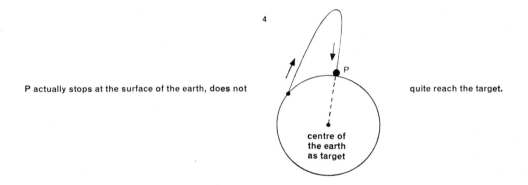

P actually stops at the surface of the earth, does not   quite reach the target.

centre of
the earth
as target

One of the principal forces in nature is attraction. We call it gravitation. The notion of weight is connected with it. In our gravitational realm of experience, the earth (or, actually, its centre) always wins.
Falling is for us an empirical, terrestrial business. These processes take place directly on the earth. The falling body tends to continue towards the centre of the earth. (Prematurely completed fall: a common occurrence on the crust of the earth.)

The straight trajectory (rise) undergoes a transforming influence. Here velocities play an essential role. Through this influence the straight line, temporarily at least, is transformed into a curve, deflected (attraction of the earth) [4]. In earthly reality it always begins to fall after a certain time. Then the trajectory runs straight again. When the descending vane becomes more and more predominant, the curve ends as a straight line (with the centre of the earth its goal) [4].

413

Static movements

Pictorial schemata of the 1st,
2nd, and 3rd laws of statics
(The possibility of compensation)

1. Falling leads to the centre of the earth but stops on the first available horizontal shelf.
2. The displacements leading to balance: building is the prevention of falling, either by a
raising or by a contrary movement of the main ledge. When constructed things fall, they
end as horizontals, and the same is true of fallen man or beast. The pair of scales is a
horizontal on a built-up point.
Static bodies are of their nature constructed to cling to the earth. The animal as horizontal,
man as upright construction. Contrastingly, dynamic bodies are constructed to hover
and glide (their innermost essence, the bubble).

The laws of statics translated   plumb-line, falling   counterforce, building   [1] For example: see note in appendix.
into pictorial abstraction[1]

All straight lines that run vertically are schemata of the first law of statics (gravitation).

Straight lines that run horizontally are schemata of the second law of statics (horizontals,
stratification as consequence of gravitation).

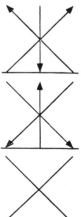

Possible compensation in the case of
falling

Possible compensation in the case of
building

The compensating diagonals are the   third law of statics.

414

Concentric and eccentric forces. In contrast to this[1] we have the cosmic curve moving away from the earth ad infinitum; i.e. becoming a circle or at least an ellipse [1].

At these heights developments are also conceivable, even if one knows nothing about the changing orbits of the stars. One can conceive of such a circling as the growing thread of a screw [2].

Which in flat projection becomes a spiral with positive movement [3].

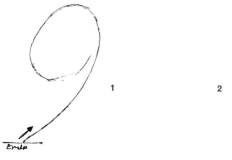

1

2

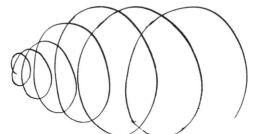

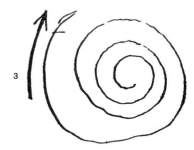

3

But if we suppose conversely that a circling star comes too close to a larger star, so that its circles become increasingly smaller, we arrive symbolically at the death spiral, whose curve of movement becomes smaller and smaller, leading deceptively to nothing. What is deceptive about this picture is the terrifying rhythmic acceleration towards the end. The concentric vane of the arrow's rudder becomes increasingly dominant as the catastrophe approaches [1] p.417.

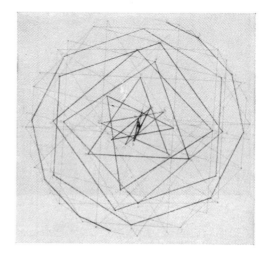

'Two broken spirals (based on a progression in the 24-part circle). The fragments first increase towards the centre, then decrease; they become feverish before dying.'

415

1938/J 18: *Timid Brute*. Oil.

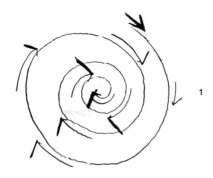

1

Anyone who would like to experience this need only imagine that he is a round ball, in centrifugal motion round the inner wall of a funnel. The curves grow narrower and narrower, the rhythm faster and faster as he approaches the bottom of the funnel, the dead point. There is no escape unless a gate opens somewhere, unless a new repelling or attracting force makes itself felt as it does here:

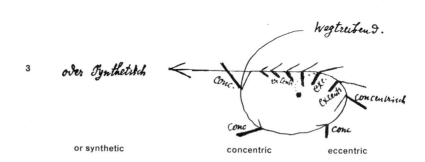

2

attracting

repelling

The beginning of movement in Figure 3 is concentric (towards the centre). In the course of the movement an opposing eccentric force makes itself felt (driving away from the centre). Force and counterforce (of the concentric and eccentric vanes) unite in a synthesis that determines direction.
Cf. Cause and effect [1], p.419.

3

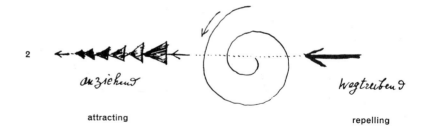

or synthetic   concentric   eccentric

where through the appearance of a new force the concentric rudder vane cedes its position of dominance to the eccentric vane [2, 3].

417

1938/c 7: *Torture*. Oil.

With this phenomenon in mind, let us pass from the symbol to the composition shown in the diagram [1].

Ursache=cause   Wirkung=effect

1

As you see, I distinguish between cause and effect. For the purpose of my diagram, the causes, treated analytically, are concentric forces A_1 and A_2 and eccentric force B; the effects, taken synthetically, are the negative spiral A and its emergency exit B. I assume that the arrow, considered in itself, is itself a synthesis of cause and effect.

The two lateral vanes, or the two sides of the parallelogram of forces, may be taken as the causes of direction [2]. The diagonal may be considered as dependent on them, that is, as the direction resulting from them. [3].

2   3

But we find a new relation between cause and effect as soon as we turn to the overall compositional synthesis of cause and effect.

Then, seen from a broader point of view, the concentric forces A_1 and A_2, the forces that would like to lead the spiral movement ad absurdum to the point C (centre), may be regarded as the causes (hostile to movement), while, in relation to these causes, the trajectory of the deflected spiral arrow is only an effect (Effect A_1, Effect A_2 and Effect B).

Examples:
1932/y 4: *The fruit*, p.6.
1932/v 17: *Helical flowers I*, p.376.
1938/R 14: *In itself*. Drawing. Grohmann, p.8.

419

One of the first exercises in movement I shall give you after Easter will be:

Determine the causes of this effect, and represent them in a free drawing:

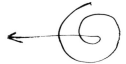

Assuming that you have understood what I mean, I shall now pass from the schematic composition to the delineation of moving forces. How, for example, I ask myself, can one represent Cause A_1?

1939/MN 5: *Fleeing woman looks back.*
Pencil drawing. Synthesis of cause and effect.
Definite direction of movement.

Examples:
1930/J 7: *Twined into a group*, p.340.
1931/p 11: *Air currents*, p.320.
On causality see note in Appendix.

The creation of moving forces

In our diagram, Cause A_1 had roughly this form:

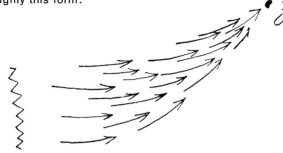

It had the shape of a horn, broad as it emerged lower left, ending in a point z (centre) upper right.

Or if I unite the moving particles, this form:

The black arrow

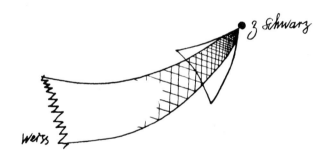

The movement of tone value (from white to black). This means a development or increase of energy along a curve from lower left to upper right. In the present picture it means a development or increase of black energy starting from the underlying, 'given' white. A black action emanating from neutral white. If this order of energy is clear, the direction of the movement will be so compelling that the symbol of the arrow can be dropped.[1] The given white is seen everywhere, one is accustomed to it; the eye takes little interest in it. But in response to the more particular contrast our perception increases in intensity as it moves towards point z.[2]

This extraordinary increase of energy or, receptively speaking, of energic fare, is compelling in regard to direction.

Or, to go beyond black and white:

[1] Note by Klee: 'The receptive process confirms this assumption.'

[2] The first version of this sentence was: 'But the eye rushes towards the contrasting particular, rushes towards point z.'

421

Contrasts in colour temperature (cold and warm colours).
The hot arrow: heating. Given water; enter fire. Here is the scene: [1]. Or in the realm of colour. The green-red arrow: Given green; enter red [2].

Table of colour heating (from cold to warm, chiefly from blue to orange). A movement of this sort is called 'heating'. Here is our heating table in the form of an arrow, starting from the given 'cold' [3].

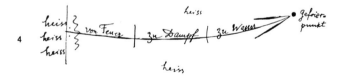

Wasser	water
Dampf	steam
Feuer	fire
kalt	cold
heiss	hot
Gefrierpunkt	freezing point
Glühpunkt	point of incandescence
von	from
zu	to
rot	red
Rotgipfel	red peak
orange	orange
gelb	yellow
grün	green
blau	blue
violett	violet
grau	grey

The cold arrow: cooling.
The opposite movement, starting with 'burning hot', is known as 'cooling' [4].

Table of colour cooling (from warm to cold, chiefly from orange to blue). Given fire; enter water. At first it produces steam; then the water gets the better of the fire, until the partly burned house is entirely under water (the fire is out) [5].

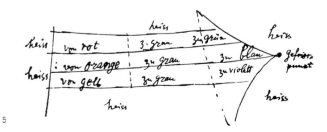

422

The movements of colour tonality. Let us briefly touch on the movements of colour tonality: increase of red. Given: lack of red, i.e. very little red.

The red arrow

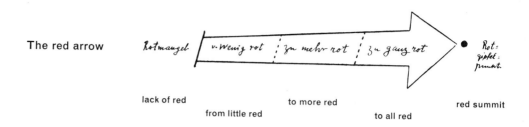

lack of red   to more red   red summit

from little red   to all red

Or the other way round, reduction of red, and all the other possibilities of crescendo or decrescendo. Long leaps are the result of greater energy than half leaps. Secondary contrasts, even directly contiguous, soften the expression of energy. This gives us an abundance of possibilities. We need only avail ourselves of them in accordance with our inner need, and the details of composed movement will lend themselves to figuration.

Synthesis of tonality-movement and temperature contrast. Tonality moves back and forth between the poles of white and black. The 'given' white is the light as such. For the present all resistance is dead and the whole is without movement. We must introduce black and encourage it to fight; to attack the formless domination of the light. We are equally dismayed by the formless preponderance of a black surface, on which our source of light casts no waves, either big or little. In this case we ally ourselves with white and employ this kind of energy.

We must organise a war game, flowing visibly in both directions; we must make energetic use of both poles. Every vital expression in the realm of tonality is in some way connected with the two opposite poles, black and white. It is they that lend tension to the play of forces on the black-white scale.

The dimension of tone value: the concept of illumination is situated in the 'up-down' dimension: uppermost the light, the sun; right at the bottom, the concept night [1].

1

Without action

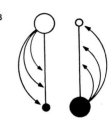

2

3

The dimension of temperature contrasts: the concept of temperature moves in the 'left-right' dimension [2].

The movement from light to dark and dark to light, up and down with variable time scale. Where white is the premise, black is the agent, or vice versa [3].
The movement from white to dark gives an idea of the vast distance from one pole to the other, the distance from the very source of visibility to the last limit of the barely visible, or the clash of the two extremes in open battle.
Seen in partial actions: where the span is large, the full swing of the pendulum from black to white gives force to the action; where the span is smaller, the radius of the swing is lessened, the rift between the opposites is made less severe.

4

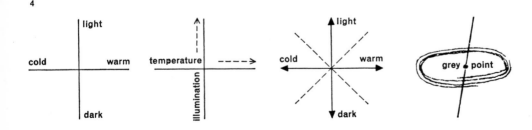

If a colour action is added to the light-dark dimension (up-down), the schema is broadened by the dimension of temperature contrasts (left-right). The two dimensions combined give two directions for movement and countermovement. As the combination of these two is increased and decreased we find, in addition, the dimension 'back-front'. It suggests a top made of a plumb-line and a disc. [4].

5

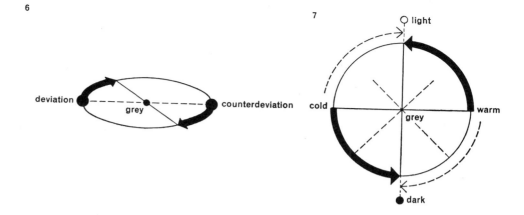

6

7

The temperature contrast would be easy to see if we really had a colour sphere in front of us and set it gently moving about its black-white axis [5].
The sphere fulfils itself at least as the shell, the outward surface of this synthesis of light and temperature.

The reciprocal movement of the arrows is a symbol for balance between movement and countermovement [6]. Spatial balance arises through the combination of balanced motion in depth and height. Spatial balance means: meaningful and forceful position in the whole realm of colour and tone values.

8

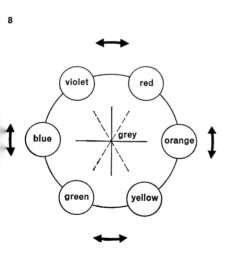

Visible movement is created by an increase or decrease in the quantity and quality of the energy employed. Through tension, the state of rest is changed to movement. Movement and countermovement give rise to dynamic balance or the purest of dynamic forms, the circle.
In the circular line a closed, endless movement is effected, there is no longer any need for countermovement.
Movement and countermovement combine into a centrifugal swing of the pendulum [7].

The belt with the colours of the spectrum is the equator so to speak [8]. The black and white points are the poles [7]. The grey point is equidistant from all five basic elements: white, blue, yellow, red, black.
The colours are on the left-right, back-front plane, purest at the edge of the circular line. The purest colour relations are found on the periphery. The last limit of total balance is grey, harmony without life.

425

1938/J 12: *Source of fire*. Oil on canvas.

Examples:
1931/n 18: *In flames*. Colour.
1933/g 20: *Hot place*. Colour.
1940/G 12: *Death and fire*. Oil on burlap.
Colour reproduction in Grohmann, p.361.

426

The development of movement

The development of movement, that is, the composite (simultaneous) operation of organic parts in an independent whole, characterised by calm movement and mobile calm; a statically dynamic or dynamically static whole, which can be achieved only when movements are joined by countermovements or when we find a solution whose movement has no end.

Part of this text is in mirror writing. From right to left: hot, from warm, to medium, to cold. Klee wrote with his right hand, but drew and painted with his left. He did mirror writing with his left hand. This is particularly evident in the titles or legends of his early etchings, which he inscribed on the copper plate in mirror writing.

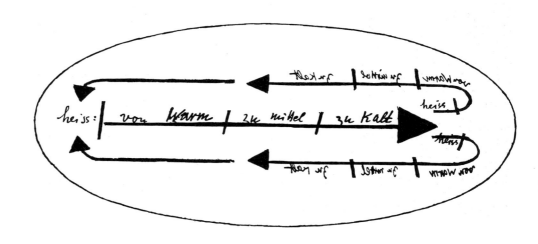

(in mirror writing): to cold   to medium   to warm
                                                  hot

hot: from warm to medium   to cold
                                        hot

(in mirror writing) to cold   to medium   to warm

Struck out: 'Every higher organism depends on the synthesis of differences.' *cf.* p.429.

Our attention is called once more to the swing of the pendulum (p.386): dynamic compensation of errors or overshooting by errors and overshooting in the opposite direction.[1] More about this static analogy may be found in the chapter on static balance (pp.209-211).

Infinite movement
The colour circle

At last we approach the centrifugal swing of the pendulum (p.397), the infinite movement in which direction becomes irrelevant. First of all I omit the arrow. Thus I obtain a combination of heating and cooling. Pathos turns to ethos which, as you will see, unites and encompasses forces and counter-forces.

So we drop the arrow. The movement may be from left to right → or from right to left ←.

A centre emerges, central grey.

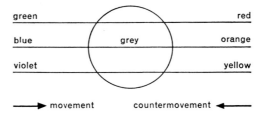

As this becomes purer, so the grey becomes smaller and smaller. In theory it even shrinks to a point. For to the left of the grey point

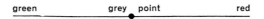

green is still dominant and to the right of the point, red. Through purification of the grey the green-red and violet-yellow scales of movement are bent. But if I let the purity of the grey complete (unify) itself in the point, the two scales will inevitably be transformed into diagonals.

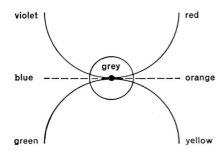

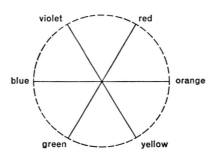

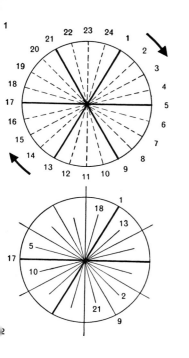

1	red
2	red-red-orange
3	red-orange
4	orange-orange-red
5	orange
6	orange-orange-yellow
7	yellow-orange
8	yellow-yellow-orange
9	yellow
10	yellow-yellow-green
11	yellow-green
12	green-green-yellow
13	green
14	green-green-blue
15	blue-green
16	blue-blue-green
17	blue
18	blue-blue-violet
19	blue-violet
20	violet-violet-blue
21	violet
22	violet-violet-red
23	red-violet
24	red-red-violet

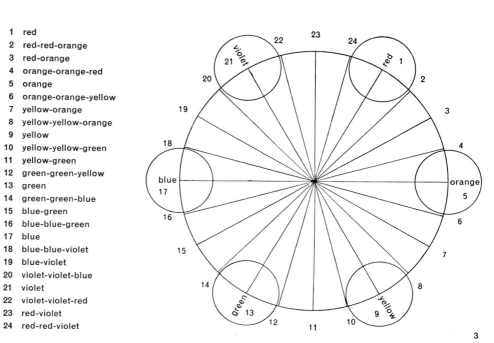

2

3

2] By carefully balancing the movement and countermovement of colours on the colour circle we neutralise them all. The result is grey.

This brings us to the colour ethos, the colour circle.
The flat topography of the spectral colour circle (in segments).

The spectral colour circle is a rainbow, gathered in and crushed.
The arrow is gone; we no longer say 'that way', but everywhere, which includes 'over there'.
Every higher organism is a synthesis of differences.

429

1938/J 16: *Shattered key*. Oil on canvas.

'A picture can often be compared to something. Then it becomes a symbol, and symbols by their very nature mean many things at once. Then perhaps one is reminded of something else. Something poetic, poetic I say, not literary, something that also seems to speak symbolically, a though a certain diffidence stopped it from putting things the way they are. To write poetry means to choose words and arrange them in such a way as to produce balance and impressive images. To this is added the freedom of creating. The connection is no clearly defined, but also has a symbolic character.'

IV. The articulation of the pictorial whole
The development of movement
Types of articulation and their evaluation
Subjects and parts

1932/Y 6: *Shattered labyrinth*. Oil and watercolour on paper prepared with oil on canvas.

'In certain pictures you can interpret one thing or another in relation to its form, or prototype. Sometimes the things are far removed from the prototype. So many steps have been taken in converting the experience. Often, on the other hand, there is more unity, because there is no tie with definite concepts. We frequently see forms that can be interpreted in simple terms: leaflike, flowerlike, animal-like, human, constructed, artificial forms, or technological, earthly, airy, solid ones. Or two tendencies appear, the one more, the other less exact. A mixture full of logos and eros. This produces a character, a certain reconstruction of the prototype. The distance from the prototype can be so great that we put strange things together. Sometimes we can distinguish the parts quite easily, sometimes with greater difficulty, and sometimes not at all. Along with the distant prototype the "I" is still present – the active "I", which enters into a relation with the prototype and sometimes brings in experiences gathered elsewhere. Something intrudes which, unless it is given artistic form, will perhaps be regarded as a foreign body. If the conflict between the prototype and the "I" is justified, we have an active process. Then perhaps it will be best not to let the last thread of content snap. It is often better to preserve some thread of connection with the prototype. Even in the most abstract pictures we can detect the thread of connection with the prototype. To be sure, one needs a special kind of experience to be able to appreciate this. Sometimes you can guess the prototype of an abstraction at a glance, but sometimes the connection is more circuitous and ceases to be discernible.'

Cf. 1939/U 9: *Labyrinthine landscape*. Watercolour and 1939/U 11: *Labyrinthine park*. Watercolour.

1. Not the work that is, but the work in process
The building up of multiplicities into a unity. The development of the whole
Repetition

1st Exercise: Monday, 15 May, 1922

My last word: Every more highly developed organism is a synthesis of differences. We arrived at this insight by the analytical method, that is, through critical examination of the differences (the parts) in themselves and in relation to each other and the whole. I tried to give the differences some sort of face, some sort of meaning that would be more than formal. Of course, our practical solution of the problems that came up had first to be formal, in accordance with our craft. But the underlying idea was expected to give a natural character to the component features, so that the composition could find its own nature. We were determined to avoid formalism, the new academy.

At the beginning of last semester[1] I started with the simple, self-contained movement of the line:

then I showed by a few examples how this melody can be 'accompanied' or transposed so that it spreads out (filling or determining the surface). Then I attached the line to a number of points,

giving it this succinct, restricted character.

[1]Cf. the note on the six exercises, p.437.

1932/z 19: *The step.* Oil on burlap.
Synthesis of basic formal diversities.

A man walking is a combined application of the rules of locomotion, which as we have seen are rules of statics. This spontaneous movement of the man walking is a shifting of weights. His balance is a movement away from the vertical, always compensated by a corresponding counter-movement. Construction combined with a lateral shifting of weights. "First this way" and "then that way"! These notions can be represented abstractly through the contrast between the active (the particular) and the already accomplished (the inactive).'

Then I took the step to the first basic formal difference by carrying the line back to its starting point:

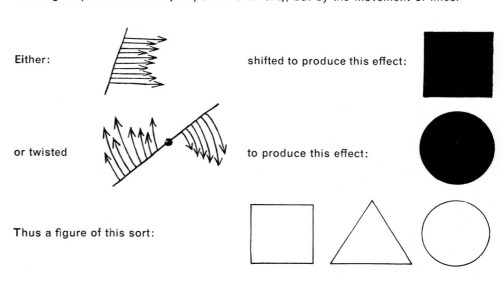

free: ◯   restricted: ▢   △

Here there can no longer be any question of elementary linear effect; the effect is planar. The free circular plane and the constrained square and triangular planes. But these are not elementary planes either. For you do not produce elementary planes by circumscribing a space with lines (i.e. point movement), but by the movement of lines.

Either: shifted to produce this effect:

or twisted   to produce this effect:

Thus a figure of this sort:

from an elementary point of view is neither line nor plane, but some sort of middle thing between them. The production is linear, the movement of a point, but the result is the illusion of a plane.

¹Cf. Active, middle, passive, pp.115–116.

Thus we may distinguish three characters:[1]

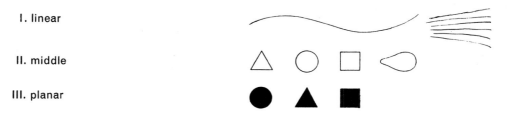

I. linear

II. middle

III. planar

² Cf. p.120.

I and III are elementary characters, II is an intermediate character, a hybrid. The characteristics meet only in the middle zone[2] (Fig. 1, p.438).

435

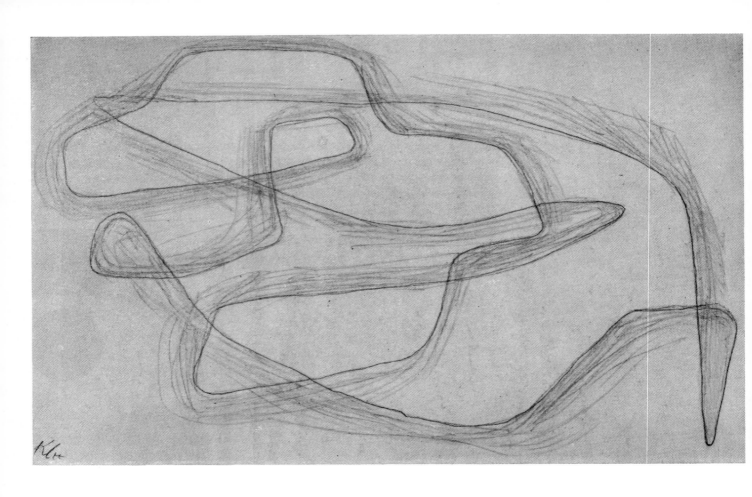

1931/M 18: *Entwined curve with positive-negative plane formation*. Pencil drawing.

938/y 11: *Tale of the three fishermen.*
Gouache.

Six hours of the summer semester of 1922 were
set aside for recapitulation. They were devoted to
problems and ideas from the 'Contributions to a
theory of pictorial form'.

1st exercise: Monday, May 15, 1922, pp.103–120.
2nd exercise: Monday, May 22, 1922, pp.421–427.
3rd exercise: Monday, June 12, 1922, pp.427–429.
4th exercise: Monday, June 19, 1922, pp.197–214.
5th exercise: Monday, June 26, 1922, pp.217–235,
343–402.
6th exercise: Monday, July 3, 1922, General review.

In certain of the exercises, the problem is to combine
two or more pictorial elements into a synthesis.
These problems are more than review exercises;
they are also devoted to the analysis of form,
productive method, structure, and organisation
of parts into a higher pictorial whole. The accent
is on a broader outlook that will make for natural
harmony in the work, on content as opposed to
calculation and formalism. Klee's formulations of
the problems are brief and epigrammatic. He calls
for a freer method of work. 'Please do not',
he writes, 'take our diagrams as models in regard
to form, but only in regard to meaning. Work
naturally, from within, so that your pictures will
come alive.' According to an inner logic, not by
calculation. In the general review one sentence
assumes central importance: 'But no work is
just a result, not a work that is, but first
and foremost genesis, work that is in progress.'

437

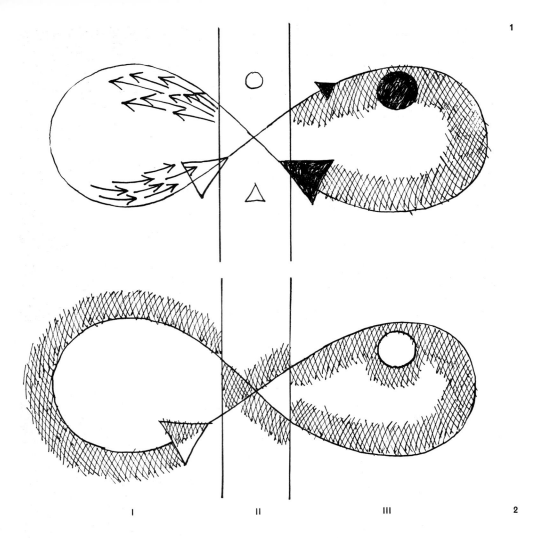

Basic relations in positive-negative plane
formation (and treatment of relief):
I   Exotopic accent
II Change of border contrasts (middle zone)
III Endotopic accent.

In spatio-plastic treatment (mutual penetration or
mixture) the accent is alternately endotopic and
exotopic. Balance between active and passive,
heavy and light. Further examples: mutual
penetration, three-dimensional interlocking,
transparent and polyphonic overlap.

438

1931/r 9: *Stakim*. Oil.

1931/p 13: *Bull's head*. Colour.

439

1940/N 13: *Still life on 29th February*.
Oil.

'In conclusion, one more variant in which an
accented line borrowed from some individual is
individually divided and in which the structured
plane and the structureless plane (or tonalities) of
every segment are so related that the two kinds of
plane alternate both horizontally and vertically.'

1940/M 19: *After the act of violence.*
Coloured paste on paper.
Positive-negative plane formation.

1939/CD 15: *O the rumours!* Tempera and oil on burlap.

Linear-active action. The plane as middle zone between light and dark, blurred and clear (intermediate character). Content: interpenetration of essence and appearance.

1st exercise:
Summing up: Simple static line movement. Line with restricted character. The basic formal differences: active, passive, middle. An underlying idea should give the component differences a natural character. Syntheses of differences into a higher organism.

The exercise calls for an attempt at composition with the three elements: line and plane fully clear, the middle zone blurred (in practice, tone-value movements or colour tonality).
Examples:
1932/x 10: *View over the plain*, p.8.
1932/k 9: *Tendril*, p.104.
1931/S 18: *Mosaic from Prhun*. Colour. Grohmann, p.401.
1931/T 16: *Steamers and sailboats towards evening*. Colour, Grohmann, p.401.
1932/K 2: *At anchor*. Oil. Colour reproduction, Grohmann, p.313.
1932/x 14: *Ad Parnassum*. Oil. Giedion, p.132.

1938/E 7: *Stormy mise-en-scène*. Colour.

'Even if you try for effects and by some indirect process obtain them, you should also hope for a corresponding action and function. You must demand that the illusion express something definable in the function. It should be possible to say: this is an opposition which is not resolved, which does not make use of its power. A play of forces. An expression of it might dominate the whole picture.

To represent light by means of bright colour is old stuff. Light as colour movement begins to be something new. I try to show light simply as the unfolding of energy, to accent the light psychologically, in those places where the mind needs it, not where nature sets her highlights.'

2nd exercise:
Figuration of dynamic forces. Development and increase of energy with movement in a single direction. Functional values or increase of energies should be characterised first of all quantitatively (extension, measure) but weight (tonality) should be included. Keep these two elements in mind:
Measure: line, plane and weight: tone value (movements of colour or tonality).
Pathos: impetuous-expressive. 'According to appearance', not 'according to essence'.

Examples: measure and weight structures (chess-board). Material structures in nature: bones, tendons, muscles. Plant examples, the cycle and its function. Organic and useful connections. What we want is the appropriate choice of organs in their spatial (measured) order. Tonality movements: lighting, temperature contrast.

2nd Exercise: Monday, 22 May, 1922.

A movement in colour or tonality with definite direction, possibly with countermovements, with a view to balanced composition. Pathetic character, yearning in that direction perhaps the goal comes to meet you, or at least you take a few comforting looks back over the path taken.

443

1939/P qu 11: *Arrogance*. Coloured paste and oil;
yellow wrapping paper on burlap.

3rd exercise.
Ethical character of movement. Qualitative
characterisation of the action. 'We are striving for
a crystallisation of the accidental. Inclusion
of the concepts of good and evil creates an
ethical sphere, to which corresponds the
simultaneous conjunction of forms, movement,
and countermovement, or to put it more naïvely,
representational contrasts (in the realm of colour,
use of decomposed colour contrasts as by
Delaunay). Every element demands a complement
if it is to attain a state of self-contained rest,
above the play of forces. From abstract formal
elements a formal cosmos is created, transcending
their assembly into concrete beings or abstract
things such as numbers or letters.' According to
Klee, ethical means: more according to the essence
than according to the appearance, causally real,
inward. Qualitative representation of the
functional or dynamic character. Quality=colour.
In the realm of colour, combination of heating and
cooling, movement and countermovement, leads
to endless movement, the spectral colour circle.
Movement towards a goal must be based not only
on its effect but also on its cause.
'According to your inner need.' Qualitative colour
differences: temperature (warm-cold), illumination
(light-dark).

[1] Note in diary: 'There is an ethical force
in such colour.'

3rd Exercise, 12 June, 1922.   Problem: the ethical character of movement[1]

The development of movement, that is, the composite (simultaneous) operation of organic
parts in an independent whole characterised by calm movement or mobile calm, can be
achieved only when movements are balanced by countermovements, or when we find a
solution whose movement continues indefinitely.

At last we approach the centrifugal swing of the pendulum, endless movement in
which direction becomes irrelevant. First of all I omit the arrow. Thus I obtain a combination of heating and cooling. Pathos turns to ethos which unites and encompasses forces
and counterforces. So we drop the arrow. The movement may be from left to right – or
from right to left (=spectral colour circle, Ed.).
Every higher organism is based on the synthesis of differences.

'This new energy is probably a little heavy at first,
it pulls things too much to the left. I shall have
to put in a considerable counterweight on the right,
in order to restore the balance. And he keeps
adding a bit on this side, a bit on that side until
the scale is balanced. And he is overjoyed if his
pure construction of a few good elements needs
only to be a little shaken up to provide those
contrasts and contradictions essential to a
lively picture.'

4th exercise.
The sensation of balance as a pictorial element.
Static construction rigid. Weight and
counterweight lead to a balance of measure
(plane) and weight (tone value). Measuring and
weighing as a pictorial process. Representations
of balance and balanced structures in two
dimensions. Balance of forces: quantity and
quality and their relativity.

4th Exercise:
Problem: Static construction rigid
(no figuration of movement).
Balance of organic parts
evenly distributed

Scenen im Waarenhaus

Maass und Gewicht		reine Qualität (imponderabel)
Kunde: 1. Kaufmañ gib mir einen Eimer voll von dieser Waare! Der Kaufmañ misst und verlangt 100 Mark. KU: (gut) 2. Nun Kaufmañ, gibt mir den selben Eimer voll von dieser andern Waare. Der Kaufmañ misst und es kostet 200 Mark. KU: (warum doppelt soviel?)	KA: Weil diese andere Waare doppelt so schwer ist. (Der Kunde sieht ein und bezahlt) KU: 3. Nun Kaufmañ gib mir ebenso schwere dritte Waare! Der Kaufmañ wägt und es kostet 400 M. KU: (warum doppelt so viel?)	KA: Weil diese dritte Waare doppelt so gut ist. haltbarer, viel schmackhafter, begehrter, schöner (Der Kunde schwankt.)
trifft ins Gebiet der Linie. lineare Wertung: länger, kürzer, gröber und feiner.	trifft ins Gebiet des Ton (helldunkel) Tonale Wertung: heller, dunkler schwerer, leichter.	trifft ins Gebiet der Farbe. Farbige Wertung: Begehrter, schöner, besser, zu sättigend zu schön! zu süss, zu herb, zu heiss, erkältend, hässlich.

446

MASS   and   WEIGHT   PURE QUALITY
(Imponderable)

Customer:
1) Give me a bucketful of this stuff.
The merchant measures it out and says it costs 100 Marks.
2) Now, salesman, give me the same sized bucketful of this other stuff.
The merchant weighs it and says this costs 200 Marks.
Customer: (why does this cost twice as much?)

Merchant:
Because this other purchase is twice as heavy. (The customer agrees and pays him).
3) Customer:
Now give me an equally heavy amount of this third material.
The merchant weighs it and says it costs 400 Marks.
Customer:
(Why is it double the price?)

Merchant:
Because this third selection is double the value, keeps longer, tastes better, is more sought after, nicer to look at. (The customer is undecided).

Falls into the sphere of
LINE
Linear value:
longer, shorter,
coarser and finer

Falls into the sphere of
TONE (tonality)
Tonal value:
brighter, darker,
heavier, lighter

Falls into the sphere of
COLOUR
Colour value: more desirable,
more beautiful, better, too deep,
too beautiful, too sweet, too bitter,
too hot, chilling, ugly.

MASS	and	WEIGHT	PURE QUALITY
			(Imponderable)

Customer:

1) Give me a bucketful of this
   stuff.
   The merchant measures it out
   and says it costs 100 Marks.
2) Now, salesman, give me the
   same sized bucketful of this
   other stuff.
   The merchant weighs it and
   says this costs 200 Marks.

Customer: (why does this cost
twice as much?)

Merchant:
Because this other purchase
is twice as heavy. (The
customer agrees and pays him).

3) Customer:
   Now give me an equally
   heavy amount of this
   third material.
   The merchant weighs it and
   says it costs 400 Marks.
   Customer:
   (Why is it double the price?)

Merchant:
Because this third selection is double
the value, keeps longer, tastes better, is
more sought after, nicer to look at.
(The customer is undecided).

Falls into the sphere of	Falls into the sphere of	Falls into the sphere of
LINE	*TONE* (tonality)	*COLOUR*
Linear value:	Tonal value:	Colour value: more desirable,
longer, shorter,	brighter, darker,	more beautiful, better, too deep,
coarser and finer	heavier, lighter	too beautiful, too sweet, too bitter,
		too hot, chilling, ugly.

1938/B 14: *Coarser and finer.* Pen and ink.

'But the notion of "coarse and fine" is also dependent on scale. And scale itself is dependent on distance from the beholder. Coarse and fine are relative and should not be represented as though coarse and fine could be measured with an instrument. One day you might feel inclined to the coarse. If it means anything, both fine and coarse work will take on a particular expressiveness.'

1938 B-4   größer und feiner

5th exercise. Scenes in a store.
The problem is to combine three dimensions in a composition. To arrive at an organic combination of
measure = (line, plane)
weight = (tonality, tone value)
quality = (colour, qualitative characterisation of the values);
to show an understanding of the function of movement and of the organic relation between the elements. Scale points to the developing balance of forces, the action. Accent on action.

Measuring and weighing can appear as structural rhythms (dividual). Linear and planar measure make it possible to include the concept of time.

Cf. p.217; also the organic combination of two and three factors, p.325; and the three-part organisms with active, passive, and middle functions, pp.336–55.

5th Exercise: Monday, 26 June, 1922

Scenes in a store

Problem: Organic treatment of two (or three) components.
1. Measure and weight and 2. Quality (colour).
Coloured qualities which cannot be weighed enter into relation with the measurable and weighable lines and tone quantities.
Thus the evaluation of colour is not definite and set but purely imaginary. If it is too hot, one longs for green-blue; if it is too cold, one longs for yellow-red. The demand can change, the taste can change.

447

1939/A 5: *Child's game*.
Coloured paste and watercolour on cardboard.
'When an action is expressed, it makes a
difference whether it is development or a
single moment that is caught.'
On the organism of movement, *cf.* pp.325–40.

2. The organisation of differences into unity
Subject and parts
General review

6th Exercise: Monday, 3 July, 1922

The aim of our theoretical work is always, in one form or another, the organisation of differences into unity, the combination of organs into an organism.

For example: every day, every hour, we look at human bodies. We see a body either as a whole (in short, as a man) or as an aggregate of head, trunk, arms, legs.

When we see it as a whole, that is the synthetic view; when we see it as an aggregate of parts, that is the analytic view. The end result is the same: a man, but the approach is different.

The analytical approach is useful to us because it makes us familiar with the parts and the way they work together. A work, however, is not primarily a product, a work that is, but first and foremost genesis, work in progress. No work is predetermined; every work begins somewhere with a motif and outgrows its organ to become an organism.

Likewise structure, which is what we are aiming at here, does not spring up ready-made' but is developed from interior and exterior motifs into its parts and thence into a whole.

Like a man, a picture has skeleton, muscles, and skin. We may speak of a specific pictorial anatomy. A picture of the object 'nude man' should follow the dictates not of human, but of pictorial anatomy.

First we build the scaffolding. How far beyond the scaffolding we get is an open question; the scaffolding itself can produce an artistic effect deeper than that of the surface alone. Higher than books and verbal leagues of nations, I value the single living word that wakes. Of course there must be someone to listen. There are many gaps which must be present in the word, at least implicitly. Books are made of split words and letters, split time and again until there are enough of them. The professional journalist may have time enough for that. But the truly creative person works with the lapidary quality of language, not with its multiplicity.

'When bodies touch, a certain thirst for adventure arises. If this be not so, they must keep apart. This distance between them should remain harmonious.

The coming together and the moving-apart must be organic, harmonious.

We must be especially careful in places where complications arise from the mixture of similar things. Here lies the possibility of freedom, derailment, or supreme artistic development. The cause of failure may be that the action or values of the alien things that confront each other are not properly selected. Especially when they are superimposed or side by side. There can be richness even in simplicity.

This may give us the courage to be simple. Simplicity makes possible a general view of the things themselves, their order, and the way in which they appear. Let the mind make much out of little.'

1939/FF 13: *Mountain under compulsion.*
Oil on canvas.

Nature can afford to be lavish in all things; the artist must be thrifty in every detail. Nature is loquacious to the point of confusion; let the artist be silent and orderly. Never work towards a ready-made pictorial impression. Give yourself entirely to the development of the part you are painting. Reduce the whole to a very few steps, let the general impression rest on this principle of economy.

Will and discipline are everything. Discipline in respect to the whole work, will in respect to its parts. In this connection, will and ability are largely the same; without ability you can have no will. From these parts the work is made, through discipline directed toward the whole.

If my pictures sometimes make a primitive impression, it is because of my discipline in reducing everything to a few steps. It is only economy, or if you like, the highest professional sensitivity; in fact the precise opposite of true primitivism.

Having gained new strength from my naturalistic studies, I can venture to return to my original field of psychic improvisation. Now that I have only the most indirect ties with a natural impression, I can venture once more to express whatever happens to be weighing on my soul; to record experiences that might be transposed into line even in the darkness of the night. This possibility of new creation has long been with me, interrupted only by the anxiety of isolation. Now my true personality will speak, now it can move in perfect freedom.

451

1938/x 1: *Fragmenta veneris.* Oil.

From the very beginning, and with time more and more clearly, I have seen that my task here is to communicate the experience acquired in my own work of ideal figuration (drawing and painting). This experience concerns the building of multiplicities into a unity. I communicate it to you partly in syntheses, that is, I show you my works; and partly in analyses, that is, I divide the works into their essential parts. I let you play with them and if you break these toys to see how they are made, you have my approval.

For the most part, we deal with combined forms. In order to understand combined forms, one must dismember them. In nature for example: at first glance you do not perceive how the natural law works. You must first look for it, investigate. For nature does not pursue a single aim, but many. The scientist takes his knife and dissects; he is thus enabled to measure the relations between inside and outside. He finds that for internal reasons, as with us in art, something is concealed, overgrown with various other things, so to speak. From the inside, you can understand it biologically. And it is only afterwards that you turn to the visible cloak or to the covering.
In art we follow such an aim, just as in nature, but we are not able to free ourselves entirely from this example.
Our work is given form in order that it may function, in order that it may be a functioning organism.
To achieve the same as nature, though only in parallel. Not to compete with nature but to produce something that says: it is as in nature.
This means of course that those who work receptively have little to learn from us.

The form is the centre of interest. That is what we are striving for. It is the first consideration of our craft. But it would be a mistake to conclude that content is secondary.

No doubt one can make a picture for the sake of the law. But there is no artistry in that. You must take account of everything that transcends the law. The actions that transcend the law play a different role from the others.

To produce form demands less energy than to determine form. In both kinds of formation, the ultimate result is form. From the methods to the goal. From the action to the perfect. From the truly living to the inactive.
In the beginning, the male role, the dynamic impetus. Then the carnal growth of the egg. Or: first the flashing lightning, then the raining cloud. Where is the spirit at its purest? In the beginning.

453

Accordingly, do not think of form but of formation. Hold fast to the path, to the unbroken connection with the original ideal. Thence carry the formative will onward with the force of necessity, until it permeates the particles and parts. Step by step, carry it from the smallest to the larger, press forward until you have penetrated the whole; keep the formative line in hand, hold fast to the creative stroke.

As in all theory, theoretical exercises are an aid in clarification. Exercises differ from theory, they partake of practice. In essence they are not deeds but potential actions which repeat the integral form, and rehearse the step into action.
The wide variety of these exercises indicates the importance of the domain; the results which extend into the realm of art, at first a primitive, intuitive kind of art, but subsequently rounded out, enriched, developed into a spiritual art.

I myself have carried out many experiments with laws and taken them as a foundation. But an artistic step is taken only when a complication arises. Thus we have made a number of successful sallies into the realm of art without any self-conscious thought of art.

In summing up we may say: Something has been made visible which could not have been perceived without the effort to make it visible. Yes, you might see something, but you would have no exact knowledge of it. But here we are entering the realm of art; here we must be very clear about the aim of 'making-visible'. Are we merely noting things seen in order to remember them or are we also trying to reveal what is not visible? Once we know and feel this distinction, we have come to the fundamental point of artistic creation.

The picture has no particular purpose. It only has the purpose of making us happy. That is something very different from a relationship to external life, and so it must be organised differently. We want to see an achievement in our picture, a particular achievement. It should be something that preoccupies us, something we wish to see frequently and possess in the end. It is only then that we can know whether it makes us happy.

1937/w 17: *Successful exorcism.*
Paste with black pigment on paper.

'The calligram is "medium" writing, an inward drawing to manifest the typical character of the handwriting. In this connection China comes to mind. The Chinese do not look on painting as a technique, a craft, but liken it to calligraphy. In the Chinese view the essence of calligraphy consists not in the neatness and evenness of the handwriting, which can easily lead to stiffness, but in the endeavour to express as perfectly as possible and with the greatest economy of means. To bring out this calligraphic character in drawing or painting is a part of the artist's craft. Hence an additional aid in clarification.
The more capable our handwriting is of writing, the more sensitive become its signs.'

455

1938/J 3: *Animal monument*. Oil.

Field and parts:
Under the cloak. Man: representation according to essence and appearance.
Palaces. Buildings, simultaneous base and elevation.
Animal monument. Synthesis of two thematic dimensions.
Cf. 1939/FG 8: *Animal and landscape combined*. Drawing.

Subject and parts. In my striving for content, in my striving to avoid calculated formalism, I gave many different names to the relationship between the parts, the way in which they work together to form a whole. With a view to deeper understanding, I explained it on the basis of many different concepts.

But obviously the thing can't be done with precepts; like nature it has to grow. The way to *Weltanschauung* is productive, it builds up spontaneously with time. The more often it is travelled, the plainer becomes the trail.

Genesis as formal movement is the important thing in the work. In the beginning the motif, injection of energy, sperm.

The work formed in the material sense: proto-feminine.

The work as form-giving sperm: proto-masculine.

1940/K 16: *Palaces*. Colour.
1938/F 16: *Under the cloak*. (Original title, crossed out: 'Exact man in cloak').
Paste with black pigment on paper.

Gebiet		Teile		
Musik	1.	Melodie		Begleitung
	2.	erste Stimme	zweite Stime	dritte Stime
			in selbständiger Führung	
	3.	Choral		figuration · höhere Polyphonie
Perspective	4.	Hauptgrad: Vertical	zweiter Grad: Horizontal	Nebengrad: Diagonal
Statik	5.	Gleichgewicht als Gegebenes	Störung	Gleichgewicht als Korrektiv Wiederherstellung
Mathematik	6.	Individuen aus höheren Zahlenverhältnissen		dividuelle Rhythmen generelle Zahlencomplexe od. structurale Chaktere
musikalisch – mathematisch	7.	Thematische Gebilde		Taktrhythmen
Naturgeschichte	8.	Formen der festen Sphäre (irdisch)	Formen der flüssigen oder der (medial) · Athmosphäre	Formen der kosmischen Sphäre (Kosmsd.)
	9.	Geologisch	aerologisch, hydrologisch	astrologisch

bewegt geformt	intuitive	Gebiet	field
Begleitung	accompaniment	Gebilde	construction
Drang	urge	Gehirn	brain
dritte	third	generelle Zahlencomplexe	general numerical complex
Erlösung	solution	Gleichgewicht als Gegebenes	balance as norm
erste	first	Hauptgrad	main direction
festgeformt	deductive	höhere	higher
Formen der festen Sphäre (irdisch)	forms of definite realms (terrestrial)	in selbständiger Führung	conducted independently
Formen der flüssigen oder der Athmosphäre	fluid forms (atmosphere)	Individuen aus höheren Zahlenverhältnissen	individuals from higher relationships of numbers
Formen der kosmischen Sphäre	formative cosmic realms	Knochen	bone

Philosophy in the extended sense of *Weltanschauung* (Wagner, Bach, Beethoven, Mozart) and in the restricted sense: logical, psychological, rational, irrational, etc.

Gebiet		Teile	
(Naturgeschichte)	10.	anatomisch aktive Funktion: Gehirn	anatomisch mediale Funktion: Muskel	anatomisch passive Funktion: Knochen
Sprache (Philologie)	11.	aktiv ×	medial ×	passiv
Kunstgeschichte	12.	Festgeformt produktiv		bewegt geformt receptiv
	oder			
Litteratur	13	Inferno	purgatorio	paradiso
	14	Dostojewsky	Voltaire	Laotse
Philosophie	15	statisch		dynamisch
	16	logisch		psychologisch
	17	pathetisch		ethisch
	18	tragisch		orphisch darüber Don Giovani
	19	"	komisch	" Gott Zauberflöte
	20	Mensch	Titan	
		Rich Wagner }	Bach / Beethoven }	Mozart }
	21.	Drang		Erlösung
	22	Ursache		Wirkung
	23	quantitativ		qualitativ
	24	rational		irrational
	25	ponderabel		imponderabel

komisch	comic	Störung	disruption
Kunstgeschichte	history of art	Gleichgewicht als Korrektiv	equilibrium as corrective
Mensch	man	Wiederherstellung	readjustment
Naturgeschichte	natural history	Taktrhythmen	rhythmic beats
Nebengrad	subordinate direction	Teile	parts
pathetisch	emotional	Ursache	cause
ponderabel	appraisable	Wirkung	effect
Sprache	language	zweite	second
Stimme	voice	zweiter Grad	secondary direction

'The disembodied figure needs no support. It
hovers. How? Where? Access to it can be
reconstructed imaginatively. In the course of the
metamorphosis a new reality is created. The
picture is purely psychic, signs that have sprung
directly from internal agitation. The cleavage
between the real and imaginary is clearly
discernible. If one can distinguish between real
things and those that partake more of the realm of
appearance, it is a matter of the proportion
between the disjointed parts.
The cleavage is not hard and fast; certain
tangible things merely become more remote.
Some forms are rendered in their entirety; others
partly, scarcely, or not at all. Naturally a form
defined in full is more conspicuous than one that
is less definite.
In this realm we cross a boundary line of reality.
There is no copying or reproducing, but rather
transformation and new creation. If we surrender
to it, a metamorphosis occurs, something which,
if healthy, is always new. This is perfectly
permissible, possible, and natural. The sum of our
experience of nature constitutes our knowledge.'

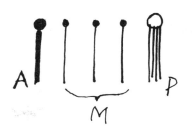

New example of this:
A comes jostling,
A and M fall jostling,
P lies jostled[1]

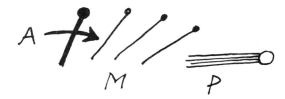

This, of course, is not to be learned by heart. Everybody will feel at home somewhere in this table (pp.458–59). Perhaps it will fit in with the picture you are now working on; if so you can analyse it for me, both as to form and content.

We should not hesitate to follow our bent, but when it comes to the result, in the absolute sense, that is, there has to be a solution. If a picture is good, one must be inwardly satisfied even if one disregards what it represents.[2]

Everything passes, and what remains of former times, what remains of life, is the spiritual. The spiritual in art, or we might simply call it the artistic. In everything we do, the claim of the absolute is unchanging.

Beauty, which is perhaps inseparable from art, relates not to the object but to the pictorial representation. That is why art overcomes ugliness without evading it.

461

1938/k 5: *Forest witches*.
Oil with wax on coated newsprint
on burlap.

Title in Klee's own hand on the back of
the picture; the title 'Earth witches' used
in the literature on Klee is incorrect. Klee
is quoted as explaining that the picture
refers to the witches in Macbeth, and
particularly to the line in Act I, Scene 1:
'Fair is foul and foul is fair'

We leave the immanent world and build into a transcendent one that can be all affirmation. Abstraction. The cool romanticism of this style without pathos is astonishing. The more horrible the world is (as today) the more abstract art will be, whereas a happy world produces a realistic art.

It is interesting to observe how real the object remains in spite of all abstractions. One can often feel a difference in abstract art. Does the abstraction go so far that the real disappears, is dematerialised, or not? There are times when something almost seems to be painted after nature, from a model so to speak: a wire model or something of the sort. This kind of abstraction seems to excite our curiosity. But is it abstract? The whole thing need not always be clear, but if you work through it lucidly, you may ask yourself: how is that? what is that? You can imagine a mixture of the clear and unclear, which will be convincing if the proportions are right. Then it has to mean something. Abstraction in a picture is absolute, and perhaps can only be recognised as such by psychic feeling. Just as the abstractness of a piece of music or a poem is not in the theoretical structure but exists and is felt for itself. Thus it may be a mistake to speak of abstract art. This kind of abstractness is constructed, made. It's not a question of adding or subtracting; either something is there, or it is not there.

In abstraction, reality is preserved. We find a bridge to the experience of reality. A way of mastering the conflict that is the stuff of life with all one's senses, of tracking down its meaning, while striving for supreme development.

I have been trying to instil more life into your work. So much for that. The power of creativity cannot be named. It remains ultimately mysterious. What does not shake us to our foundations is no mystery. Down to our finest particles we ourselves are charged with this power. We cannot formulate its essence but we can, in some measure, move towards its source. In any case we must reveal this power in its functions, just as it is revealed to us. Probably it is only a form of matter, but one that cannot be perceived with the same senses as the kinds of matter we are used to. Still, it must make itself known through the familiar kinds of matter and be at one with them in function. Merged with matter, it must enter into a form that is alive and real.[1] And it is thus that matter takes on life and order, from its smallest particles to its subsidiary rhythms and its higher structures.

Creation lives as genesis under the visible surface of the work. All those touched by the spirit see this in retrospect, but only the creative see it looking forward (into the future).

[1] Cf. p.17.

463

1937/T 8: *Children's playground.*
Pastel and red chalk.

464

This is an alphabetical glossary of words
and phrases, mostly relating to colours, which
occur in diagrams between pages 465 and 511.

N.B. Colour mixtures and colour tones are indicated by
compound words, e.g. Gelb-grün for yellow-green, Hellblau
for light blue.

Basis	base
Blau, blau(e)	blue
blaufreie Strecke	arc free of blue
bläulich	bluish
Centrum	centre
dunkel	dark
Gelb, gelb(e)	yellow
gelbfreie Strecke	arc free of yellow
gelblich	yellowish
Grau	grey
Grün	green
grüne Erde	earth green
hell	light
Kadmium	cadmium
Karmin	carmine
kein	no
Kobalt	cobalt
Königsblau	royal blue
Krapplack	rose madder
Krapplack purpur	purple madder
Kreis	circle
kühles Rot Ende	cool end of red
mittel	medium
oder (od.)	or
Orange	orange
permanent Grün	permanent green
polar	polar
preussisch Blau	Prussian blue
Punkt	point
Reinrot	pure red
Rosa	pink
Rot, rot(e)	red
Rotgipfelpunkt	red peak
Schwarz, schwarz(e)	black
schweinfurth Grün	emerald green
spectral	spectral
stumpfgrüne Töne	dull green tones
Summe	sum
Terra de Siena gebrannt	burnt sienna
Ultramarin	ultramarine
Umbra gebrannt	burnt umber
Umbra natural	umber
Violett, violett(e)	violet
warmes Rot Ende	warm end of red
Weiss, weiss(e)	white
Zinnober	cinnabar
Zinnoberrot	vermilion

This is an alphabetical glossary of words
and phrases, mostly relating to colours, which
occur in diagrams between pages 465 and 511.

N.B. Colour mixtures and colour tones are indicated by
compound words, e.g. Gelb-grün for yellow-green, Hellblau
for light blue.

Basis	base
Blau, blau(e)	blue
blaufreie Strecke	arc free of blue
bläulich	bluish
Centrum	centre
dunkel	dark
Gelb, gelb(e)	yellow
gelbfreie Strecke	arc free of yellow
gelblich	yellowish
Grau	grey
Grün	green
grüne Erde	earth green
hell	light
Kadmium	cadmium
Karmin	carmine
kein	no
Kobalt	cobalt
Königsblau	royal blue
Krapplack	rose madder
Krapplack purpur	purple madder
Kreis	circle
kühles Rot Ende	cool end of red
mittel	medium
oder (od.)	or
Orange	orange
permanent Grün	permanent green
polar	polar
preussisch Blau	Prussian blue
Punkt	point
Reinrot	pure red
Rosa	pink
Rot, rot(e)	red
Rotgipfelpunkt	red peak
Schwarz, schwarz(e)	black
schweinfurth Grün	emerald green
spectral	spectral
stumpfgrüne Töne	dull green tones
Summe	sum
Terra de Siena gebrannt	burnt sienna
Ultramarin	ultramarine
Umbra gebrannt	burnt umber
Umbra natural	umber
Violett, violett(e)	violet
warmes Rot Ende	warm end of red

V. The order and nature of pure colours
Topology of colour relations
Finite and infinite movements of colour on the plane
Partial colour actions and colour totality

1940/k 8: *Glass façade*. Oil.

1. Order in the realm of colours
The finite colour series and the infinite blending of colours
Diametric and peripheral colour relations

Tuesday, 28 November 1922

The rainbow as
a finite colour series
The pure colour scale
The spectral colour circle
[1] Note in Appendix.

Diary entry, Kairouan, April 16, 1914: 'Colour
has me. I no longer need reach out for it. It has
me forever and knows it. That is the meaning of
this happy hour. Colour and I are one. I am a
painter.'

I shall try to tell you a few useful things about colours. In this I shall not limit myself to my own observations, but in order to tell you these useful things, I shall not hesitate to draw on specialists in the field and others. Goethe, Philipp Otto Runge, whose colour sphere was published in 1810, Delacroix, and Kandinsky, author of *Concerning the Spiritual in Art*,[1] to mention only a few.

The first part of my undertaking is to set up a kind of ideal paint box, in which the colours are arranged on sound principles, a kind of tool kit if you like.
Nature is full of ideas about colour. The world of plants and animals, mineralogy, the composition that we call the landscape; all give us something to think about and to be thankful for.

But there is one colour phenomenon that rises above all the rest as a symbol of all use of colour, all mixing and blending of colours. As far as its purity of colour goes, we may call it abstract. I am referring to the rainbow.
Quite significantly, this exceptional phenomenon, this pure colour scale is to be found not on the earth but in the atmosphere, the intermediate realm between earth and outer cosmos. We may therefore expect it to have a certain degree of perfection, but, since it is only half transcendent, not yet the highest.

But here again our creative faculty enables us to transcend the inadequacy of appearances and to arrive at a synthesis, at least, of transcendent perfection.
We assume that what comes to us only imperfect as appearance exists somewhere without any imperfections; the artist's instinct in us must help us conceive the form of this flawless state.

467

But what is the flaw in the rainbow as we see it? . . . Someone picked out a series of colours, seven of them with the names

and people were very pleased with the number 7. After all, they said by way of confirmation, there are also seven tones in our musical scale.

But much as the number 7 appeals to me in certain respects, I have no faith in it here. For red-violet and blue-violet, or indigo, as it is called in the schoolbooks, is a rather subtle division!

We all of us know that green, orange, and violet differ in kind from red, yellow, and blue; I can anticipate this much without spoiling the surprise that is in store for us. But what about red-violet or blue-violet or indigo?

The first important point is that the arrangement of the colours in the rainbow is linear. We must not forget that in the rainbow a yellow point marches along in a line, side by side with a green one, and a green point side by side with a yellow one, etc. [1].

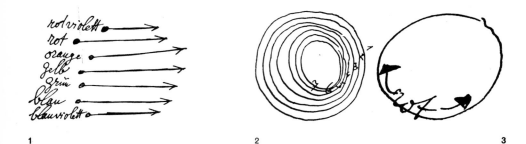

1   2   3

We must not forget that when we extend the arc into a circle we still do not have a complete colour circle; what we have are seven coloured circles, one within the other [2].

A linear representation of a plane, in this case of a circular plane, has a drawback. A circle formed from a red line is not yet a red circle [3].

For, as we have said before, such a representation of a plane is not active but only 'middle'. This red or blue or yellow line does indeed convey a planar impression, but it is not itself a plane; it remains a line.

468

Thus we can safely call the rainbow a linear representation of colours; we can also say that as a colour chart it is inadequate. We learn very little from it, and about the relation between the colours nothing at all. That is perfectly clear.

But the main flaw consists in the finiteness of this colour series. The pure colours are transcendent. The intermediate realm of the atmosphere is kind enough to communicate them to us, but in an intermediate form and not in their transcendent form, which must be infinite.

The discrepancy of the two violets becomes more interesting (important) when we learn from the scientists that there's something queer about the ends: there is something beyond the red, something that behaves like heat, and the blue end also has its secret, which is manifested as a chemical effect.

In our frantic thirst for colours we might be tempted to conceive of two additional pure colours to which our eye is not attuned. But we shall not be so rash.

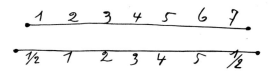

We shall simply say this: that we are dealing with two halves, that the two halves should become a whole, the two violets *one* violet, and that the two mysterious ends of the one string should be tied together at infinity (endlessness).

And the thing without beginning and end that results looks like this:

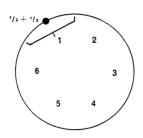

The six colour tones
of the spectral colour circle
(the rainbow seen as a ring)

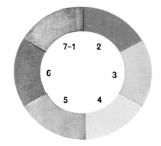

1	red-violet
2	red
3	orange
4	yellow
5	green
6	blue
7–1	blue-violet

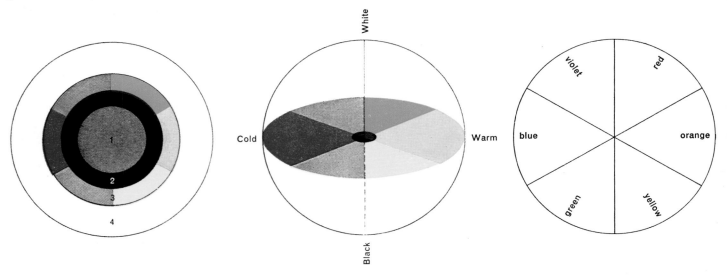

3

1

2

White

Cold — Warm

Black

violet / red
blue / orange
green / yellow

1

2

3

4

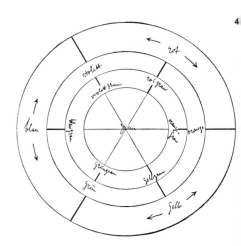

4

1. The spectral colour circle as a horizontal disc passing through the equator of the colour sphere.

2. The spectral colour circle as a disc (flat topography of the colours on the spectral circle).

3. The colour disc as colours in ideal order:
   1 grey circle   2 black circle   3 spectral circle   4 white circle

4. Situation of the primary, secondary, and tertiary colours on a cross-section through the colour sphere; the grey circle is taken into account.

Now we no longer have to oscillate, swinging from 1 to 7 and, with the countermovement that replaces infinity, back again from 7 to 1, searching here, searching there, trying to get away, returning home. Instead:

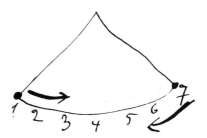

We leave the human realm, the realm of the higher animal, the realm of pathos and striving, of the spirit-body, the half-static, half-dynamic intermediate realm symbolised by the triangle, where the pure colours are only half at home. We free our pendulum from gravity, we let it fly to the divine, dynamic realm, the realm of the spirit, of complete rotation and whole movement, the realm symbolised by the circle, where pure colours are truly at home. Now 1 and 7 coincide, and the place we were worrying about is simply called violet.

The spectral colour circle

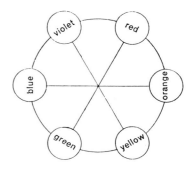

This cosmic concept of pure colours has found its appropriate representation in the circle. The rainbow, the terrestrial manifestation of pure colours, was a mere reflection of a hitherto unknown totality, the transcendent whole that we have now produced by synthesis. The colour circle is now before us.

Or in reverse we may see violet as the breach made by the power which humanises and transforms the things of God to show them to us. This assault was made on the colour circle at violet. The colour circle stretched and tore; a column of coloured points marched off, and that was the rainbow.

If we look more closely at this new system, the colour circle, we shall be interested to see how much more it can tell us about the relationships between the colours.

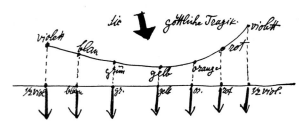

The Divine Tragedy

First of all, the riddles of the finite colour series are solved or cease to exist. We are no longer baffled when the scale comes to violet, and we are no longer faced with such problems as infra-red and ultra-violet. The new movement along the circumference of the circle—I should like to call it peripheral movement (scale)—lends itself perfectly to endless interlock and flow.

That is one aspect of the novelty. The other is disclosed in the three diameters with which we can connect the six colours, dividing them into three colour pairs.

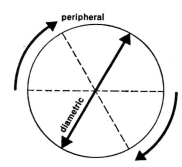

Thus we have on the one hand a peripheral movement and on the other hand movements across the diameters.[1]

[1] *Cf.* the summary 'on the nature of pure colour' pp.87–88.

2. The relations between the colours
Diametric colour relations
The true and false colour pairs

The true colour pairs

This second aspect of our new discovery is very promising. The three diameters connect first red and green, second yellow and violet, third blue and orange. All three intersect at one point, the centre of the circle.

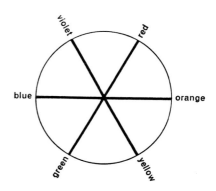

The picture looks suggestive. Surely there is a deeper meaning behind it. What can it be? Experiment shows that if we expose our eye to red for a while and then suddenly look away, an astonishing after-effect is produced: we see not red but green. Or when we expose the eye to green for some time, the after-effect will be red.

By the same magic, yellow and violet alternate, as do blue and orange.

Anyone can determine the three colour pairs in this way and convince himself of the phenomenon of complementary colours. Another little experiment will teach us a second lesson:

We divide a strip of white paper into seven fields. Except for Field 7 we coat it with thin, pure red water-colour. After the red coat has dried, we coat the strip (except for Field 1) with thin, pure green water-colour. When the two coats are dry, we perceive a reddish Field 1 and a greenish Field 7. In between there are five colourless fields 2–6.

We now enhance the rather feeble effect of these first two steps by continuing the operation. Alternately we add red from above and green from below, first five red fields from above and five green fields from below; then four red from above and four green from below, then only three red from above and three green from below. And so on, each time less red (from above) and less green (from below).

In the language of painting this way of mixing colours is called glazing. Separate coats are laid on at intervals. At each step something is added: from left to right less and less, from right to left more and more. The result, or rather the sum, remains the same.
By the gradation of our coats we obtain a precisely graduated movement from red to green-red to green, or the other way round.

1 all red in the 1st field:	6 parts red, no part green
7 all green in the 7th field:	no part red, 6 parts green
4 green-red in the 4th field:	3 parts red, 3 parts green, in between 2 red and 2 green gradations
2 in the 2nd field:	5 parts red and 1 part green
3 in the 3rd field:	4 parts red and 2 parts green
5 in the 5th field:	2 parts red and 4 parts green
6 in the 6th field:	1 part red and 5 parts green

$$I_R + I_g + II_R + II_g + III_R + III_g + IV_R + IV_g + V_R + V_g + VI_R + VI_g = \text{Summe } R + g$$

'Movement and countermovement (red and green).
A centre is in the making, median grey.
Sevenfold gradation of true colour pairs mixed
by glazing.'

Cf. 1922/79: *Separation in the evening*, p.11.
and 1921/102: *Red-green gradation*. Watercolour.
Giedion, p.99. (Title in catalogue of works:
'Abstract red-green gradation'.)

It is easy to see how the red and green diminish towards the middle and balance each other
out in the fourth red-green or grey field (although thereafter the colours increase again).
Towards the middle both colours diminish in hue as the quantities of red and green
approach equality. No direct use of grey has been made and yet (pure) grey has been
created in the fourth field where the colour quantities are equal.
This median colourlessness decreases both to left and right, to the left in favour of
increasing red, to the right in favour of increasing green.
This reciprocal red-green scale reminds us of the movement and countermovement of
our pendulum.

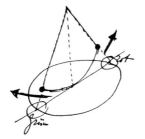

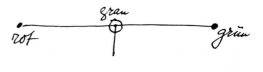

It also reminds us of the mobile scale which finally comes to rest at the grey intersection,
but this should not be taken to mean that red and green lend themselves to static

475

treatment with all red on the left and all green on the right. That would hardly give us a picture of their reciprocity. Both green and red would have to jump back and forth (form-building!).

In summing up I can say this about the green-red pair:
1. Each colour calls forth the other in the eye.
2. Between the two colours stands grey.

I could make the same demonstration with the two other sets of diametric colours, yellow-violet and blue-orange. But for the sake of variety I shall give you a more geometrical illustration,[1] which is applicable to all three diameters of the colour circle.

[1] Note by Klee: 'Check by measuring the lines. A point=zero.'

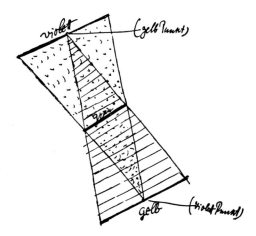

In this case we have at one end a violet, at the other a yellow base. Violet has its greatest extension on top where yellow can be perceived only as a point, that is, it cannot be measured. At the bottom yellow has its greatest extension while violet is only a point. If I now connect the yellow point with the yellow base I get a yellow triangle; and if I connect the violet base with the violet point I get a violet triangle. The triangles interpenetrate. Each in itself expresses the diminution of its colour with distance from the base. Now I divide the two bases, into 12 parts let us say. At any point on a line parallel to the base, I can now measure the yellow and the violet content, and the effect will be roughly the same as before when we added coats of watercolour.

476

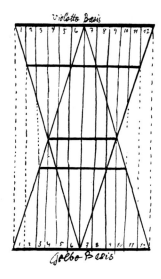

12 parts violet, no part yellow

10 parts violet, 2 parts yellow

6 parts violet, 6 parts yellow

8 parts yellow, 4 parts violet

12 parts yellow, no part violet.

Measurement on the violet base shows 12 parts of violet and none of yellow. On the yellow base 12 parts of yellow and none of violet. In the middle 6 parts of violet and 6 of yellow (hence grey). On the violet side near the base, 10 parts of violet and 2 of yellow. On the yellow side near the middle, 8 parts of yellow and 4 parts of violet.

Concerning yellow and violet I can thus say: between them lies grey. Observation of blue and orange would show the same thing. In practice the best way would be to start with a colour that seemed very pure to us, to let an effective quantity of it work on our eye for an effective time, then ascertain the complementary colour by a quick look at a white surface, prepare the complementary colour at the same intensity, and obtain colourless grey by mixing the two in equal quantities in a bowl or on a piece of paper.
If this second test for colour pairs were to fail, we should have to admit that we had not found pure complementaries. Then we should either have to correct one of the complementaries or, as often happens, make a virtue of a mistake and get a richer effect by using consciously false pairs. We shall have more to say of this later on.

For the present let us return to our colour circle and see how well its mathematical character meets our needs.

477

The radius (half a diameter, that is) cuts the circumference just six times. Through the points of intersection corresponding to the six colours we can draw the six diameters corresponding to the principal colour pairs. The diameters meet in the centre, the grey point common to all colour pairs.

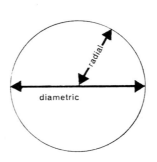

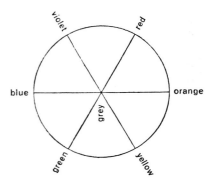

In addition to these three diameters, of course, we can draw as many more as we please; they will be no less correct than those discussed, but will mean something different. The slightest rotation of the diameter round the fixed grey point indicates new colour pairs, which will be correct but less important.

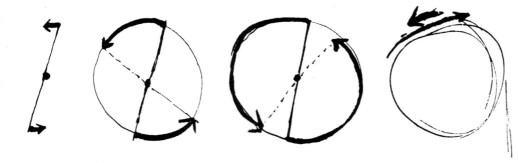

In such a search for new colour pairs simultaneous movement and countermovement gradually develop into endless movement and we arrive at colour relations in which endless movement makes the direction of the arrow uncertain (cancels it out), something which had already been suggested by the simultaneity of movement and countermovement.

The reciprocal movement of the arrows is a graphic representation of balanced movement and countermovement (movement of a colour pair towards the poles).

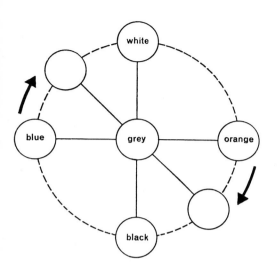

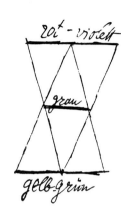

¹The spectral colour circle turning diametrically.

Let us first rotate our diameter¹ to the exact spot between red and violet or between yellow and green. This gives us the new colour pair red-violet × yellow-green.
The grey effect of this colour pair is necessarily composed in equal parts of red-violet and yellow-green. Red-violet itself is composed of equal parts of red and violet, and yellow-green of equal parts of yellow and green.
Thus the grey effect is composed in equal parts of four components, red, violet, yellow, and green. In my diagram I am free to arrange these four components in any way I please.

If I combine them crosswise:

In this arrangement I first recognise our old friend red-green and then yellow-violet. Each pair produces grey by itself, and the addition of two (nota bene) half-greys does not contribute an atom of colour. The grey effect is demonstrated and with it the authenticity of the colour pair red-violet × yellow-green.

479

This is how it looks algebraically: ½ red + ½ violet + ½ yellow + ½ green = (½ red + ½ green) + (½ violet + ½ yellow) = ½ grey + ½ grey = grey.

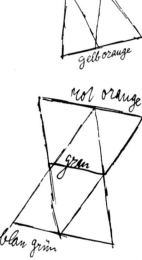

With an additional rotation of the diameter round the grey point I run into a new colour pair:

blue-violet	yellow-orange
blue	violet
yellow	orange

Blue, violet, yellow and orange read crosswise:
blue-orange=grey and yellow-violet=grey.
Or algebraically: blue+violet+yellow+orange
=(blue+orange)+(yellow+violet)=grey.

A third diametric rotation stops
on the one hand exactly between the peripheral colours
red and orange,
on the other hand exactly between blue and green,
and we have another true colour pair:

red-orange	blue-green
red	orange
blue	green

Red, orange, blue and green, crosswise:
red-green=grey and blue-orange=grey,
or: red+orange+blue+green
=(red+green)+(blue+orange)=grey.

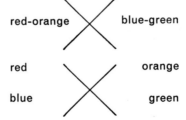

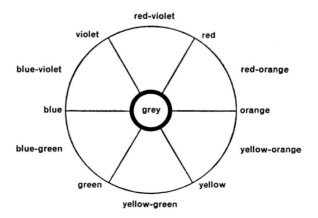

Thus the authenticity of three new colour pairs is proved. Sum of the peripheral colours=grey.

The false colour pairs

But if, as I suggested above, we make some mistake (or mésalliance) in pairing our colours, we shall have trouble with our proof of grey. But it will be worth our while to take a closer look at this kind of deviation from the true colour pair, for there is no reason to suppose that colour composition must be limited to complementary colours.

For example, I cannot connect green with orange on the colour circle by a diameter but only by a chord [1]. The orange base and the green base do not run parallel but will soon intersect somewhere [2]. In calculating the result of a mixture of green and orange, I start from the fact that green is exactly half-way between yellow and blue, while orange is exactly half-way between yellow and red. Accordingly, green+orange=yellow+blue+red+yellow. From this I can make certain inferences, both upward and downward:

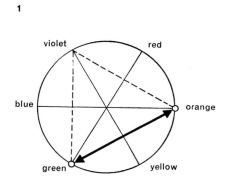

1

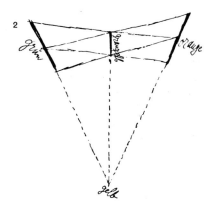

2

Hence:

$$
\begin{array}{l}
\text{grey} \quad +\text{yellow} \\
\overbrace{\text{green} \quad +\text{red}+\text{yellow}} \\
\text{Green}+\text{orange}=\underbrace{\text{yellow} + \text{blue}}+\underbrace{\text{red}+\text{yellow}} \\
\text{yellow} + \text{blue}+ \underbrace{\text{orange}} \\
\text{yellow} + \quad\quad \text{grey}
\end{array}
$$

First result: grey+yellow
(yellowish grey)

Second result: yellow+grey
(yellowish grey)

$$
\text{Green-orange} = \begin{matrix} \text{blue} \\ \text{yellow} \\ \text{yellow} \\ \text{red} \end{matrix} = \begin{matrix} \text{yellow} \\ \text{yellow} \\ \text{blue} \\ \text{red} \end{matrix} = \left. \begin{matrix} \text{yellow} \\ \text{yellow} \\ \text{violet} \end{matrix} \right\} \text{grey}
$$

Third result: yellow+grey
(yellowish grey)

The result of this mixture is not a pure colourless grey but a yellowish grey, because yellow is contained both in green and in orange and because the two bases are not parallel but tend to intersect at yellow. Our proof has failed; green-orange is not a true colour-pair.

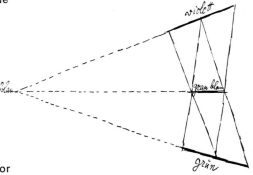

Another false colour pair, as a glance at the colour circle shows, is violet-green. For green and violet is the same as yellow+blue+red+blue.

Green+violet =

	grey	+blue		First result:	grey+blue
	yellow+ violet	+blue			(bluish grey)
	yellow+blue+red	+blue			
	green	+red+blue			
	grey	+blue		Second result:	grey+blue
					(bluish grey)

Green-violet =

blue	blue	blue	blue			
yellow ⎫		= orange =	blue	⎫		
red ⎬				⎬ grey	Third result:	blue+grey
blue	blue	orange	⎭		(bluish grey)

The result of the mixture is a bluish grey, for blue occurs in both colours, the violet and the green bases are not parallel but tend to intersect at blue.

The third colour pair of this sort is violet-orange.

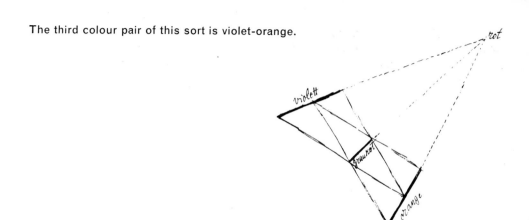

$$\text{Violet}+\text{orange} = \begin{array}{l} \text{red}+ \qquad\quad \text{grey} \\ \text{red}+\text{blue}+\quad \overbrace{\text{orange}} \\ \text{red}+\text{blue}+\text{yellow}+\text{red} \\ \underbrace{\text{violet}}\ +\text{yellow}+\text{red} \\ \underbrace{\text{grey}} \qquad\quad +\text{red} \end{array}$$

First result: red+grey
               (reddish grey)

Second result: grey+red
               (reddish grey)

$$\text{Violet-orange} = \left.\begin{array}{l}\text{blue}\\ \text{yellow}\\ \text{red}\\ \text{red}\end{array}\right\} = \left.\begin{array}{l}\text{green}\\ \text{red}\\ \text{red}\end{array}\right\}\text{grey}$$

Third result: grey+red
               (reddish grey)

---

[1]Examples:

1922/57: *Flower faces, green-orange gradation.* Watercolour.

1922/59: *Three houses, green-violet gradation.* Watercolour.

1922/61: *Mask, orange-violet gradation.* Watercolour.

1922/71: *Orange-violet-green gradation, orange vanishing.* Watercolour.

1922/73: *Structures in orange and green, black half moon in the distance.* Watercolour.

The result is a reddish grey. Red occurs in both component colours. The two bases, violet and orange, are not parallel but tend towards a point of intersection on the red side. I think this is enough for today. It will all sink in a little deeper in our practical exercise next week, and then no doubt it will take on more life and expression for you.

The application can be conceived in different ways. Last summer I myself tried out the partial colour actions we have been discussing, one after another in separate pictures.[1] It should not worry us that individual works of this sort are lacking in total effect. We still strive for totality and that in itself produces new things. Smaller or larger groups of partial actions coalesce in a greater whole.

483

As an application to the Bauhaus, or rather to the building of houses, I suggest that you try this: First choose graduated tones of the three real colour pairs for three different rooms. Each room will provide a part of the general effect, which is based on red, yellow, and blue. The onesidedness of each individual room will arouse a desire for a compensating onesidedness which will be reflected in the treatment of the next room. The onesidedness of the different rooms will have the advantage of setting us in motion towards the other, complementary rooms. An impression of wholeness will result if all the rooms are 'modulated' both in the pictorial and the real sense.

And another time try this: paint three connected rooms in such a way that the tone of each one corresponds to one of the three false colour pairs we have mentioned. Then a feeling of excess yellow will come over us in the first, of excess blue in the second, and of excess red in the third. But since we have 'modulated' all three rooms, the three one-sided impressions will be combined into a total impression of red-yellow-blue.

I have borrowed this idea from our next lecture. We have had a good deal of theory today and I'd like to leave you on a livelier note. However, we shall have to speak more seriously about this idea of a three-colour totality.

Tuesday, 5 December 1922

(Exercise at five o'clock)
Bring along:

1. Paper that takes water but is not too absorbent.
2. At least two clean bowls.
3. The colours of the periphery; try to avoid opaque colours.
4. Let each coat dry by the stove.

Exercise: Practise the seven-step scale of the real colour pairs according to the indications on pp.473–480. In the peripheral dimension it is important to find the right localities, that is, to find the green corresponding to the red you have chosen, etc.[1] and in the diametric direction it is important to measure your qualities carefully; that is, not too much blue, not too much violet.

[1] See example p.475.

Tuesday, 12 December 1922

Exercise

Problem: Seven-step gradation of false colour pairs.

I think we all of us got some fun out of our theoretical and practical treatment of the diametric movement and gradation of colours at our last meeting. We made certain practical discoveries, particularly in regard to the order of the colours. We learned to place various (indefinite) intermediate tones that had long been known to us. Though we did not always succeed in defining the colour pairs exactly, we at least learned, precisely because it was so difficult and because grey is no more than a point on a large plane, that these relations are extremely delicate—in both dimensions. In the diametric dimension we found difficulty in making the ends equal in hue. In the peripheral dimension the difficulty lay in determining the exact point corresponding to another point on the circumference, that is, half a circle away from it. Putting it crudely we should say: don't take too much or too little of any colour and don't pick the wrong colour. The science of optics, it seems, has to meet these two conditions if it is to prove itself in experiment. But we are concerned with other criteria which are only partly related to those of science. And we gain just as much experience even if the result is not the ultimate in perfection.

Peripheral movement along the circumference of the circle.

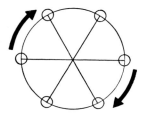

Today I shall first take up the peripheral movement of colour, the movement that leads along the circumference of the circle. In contrast to oscillating diametric movement, this movement is endless. It has no ends, no pairs; all its transitions are fluid. There are no interruptions, every beginning is also an end. Uninterrupted movement is above direction. This clock can run backwards too.

Whereas the diametric movement could rise above direction only by breaking off and shuttling back and forth.

But this is not to say that the peripheral movement is without character or that it lacks articulation. The qualitative differences along even a short arc are already too great [1]. In the neighbourhood of red, for example, the difference in character between violet and orange is overwhelming.

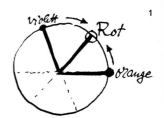

And yet red is contained in both colours. How enormous must the difference then be between red and a colour that contains no red!

In line with modern thinking I shall not ask: What *is* red? I prefer to ask: what does it *not* mean? That is, where does it cease to be effective? What is its scope? And here we shall hardly go wrong if we say that its scope amounts to two-thirds of our circumference [2].

Last time we saw that it definitely did not mean green, for red and green nullified each other as colours.

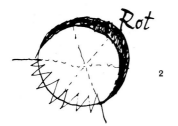

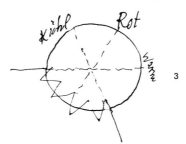

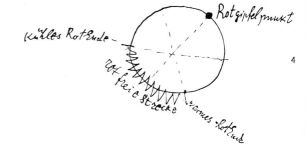

There is a yellowish red (so-called warm red) and also a bluish red (so-called cool red) [3]. But from the stand-point of red, bluish and yellowish mean a weakening. Thus we must note a diminution of red in two directions or conversely an increase of red from these two sides towards red.

This increase from two sides naturally leads to a peak, to the culmination of red.
Thus I can locate three points on our periphery:
1. the red peak, 2. the warm end of red, 3. the cool end of red [4].

These three points divide the periphery into a red arc measuring two-thirds and an arc free from red, which measures one-third and lies opposite the red peak.

I could consider the blue and the yellow zones in the same way:

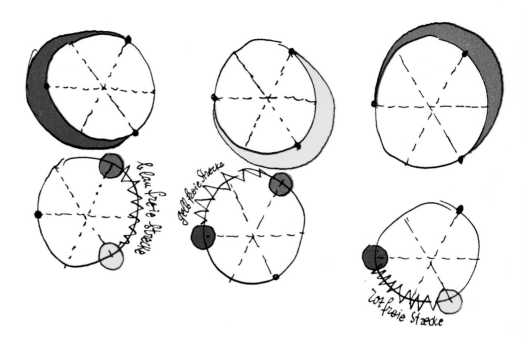

But I shall make my words rather brief and simply read from my sketches: Blue, as well as yellow and red, has an arc measuring two-thirds of the circumference. The last third is always free: free of blue, free of yellow, or free of red. The third that is free of blue is between the yellow and red peaks; the third that is free of yellow is between the blue and red peaks; and the third that is free of red is between the blue and the yellow peaks. Thus each peak, each culminating point, remains for a moment free from the influence of its neighbour peaks. I am now in a position to say not only that red is not green, but also that red is not blue and not yellow, even though it can be bluish or yellowish. In the same way blue can reach out towards red and towards yellow, but never can it reach their peaks. And yellow can tend towards blue and red, but it can never be blue or red.

This is an illustration of these sentences which are as important as they are simple; one might call it the chain of totality.

487

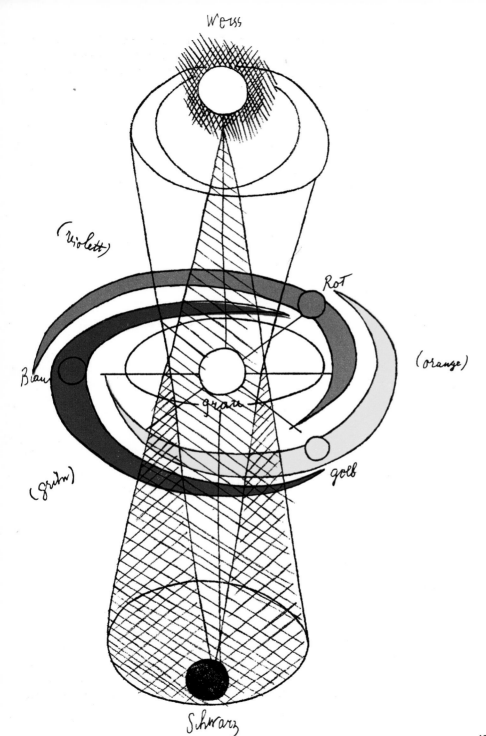

Weiss

(violett)

Rot

(orange)

Blau

grau

(grün)

gelb

Schwarz

The canon of totality.

488

Every colour starts ever so gently from its zero, that is its neighbour peak, rises to its own peak, and from there descends again slowly to its zero, that is, the next neighbour peak. It is immaterial whether I give this crescendo and decrescendo its naturalistic form or its exact form or an artificial, graduated form (though there must be some exact basis of course).

Naturalistic, natural

exact

artificially graduated

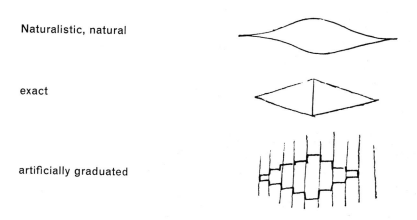

But now something else comes in: The colours on this circle do not sound in unison as the chain might lead one to suppose, but in a kind of three-part counterpoint.

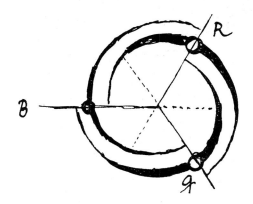

This combined diagram permits us to follow the three-part movement. The voices come in successively as in a canon. At each of the three main points one voice reaches its climax, another voice softly begins, and a third dies away. One might call this new figure the canon of totality.

489

1921/69: *Fugue in red*. Watercolour.
Rhythmic articulation combined with tonal
movement in the realm of colour.

'The repetitive factor characteristic of structures
is here the concept of increase or decrease which
is repeated at every step. If the naturally ordered
movement perceived with the ears instead of the
eyes is comparable to the movements of natural
tones, the artfully ordered movement is reminiscent
of the structured division of tones we find in
musical scales.'

490

And now, just as we did last time, I should like to prepare the way for practical attempts at measurement. To this end I must once again unroll the circumference. Then our canon assumes the following form and the notation of a musical canon makes its appearance. The main bars are situated at nodal points in the rotation, namely the points where recurrence or repetition begins.

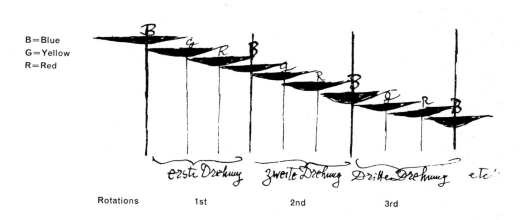

B = Blue
G = Yellow
R = Red

Rotations   1st   2nd   3rd

.Note: In the oscillation of the colour pairs it was different. We had to retrace our steps to get back to the starting point.

This is how it would be in writing: *(zigzag figure)*   a zigzag.

But now we roll ahead in rhythmic circles.

This is how it would be in writing: *(spiral figure)*   a spiral movement.

But not in unison; in several voices.

What comes now will remind you at once of my charts of the relations between red and green[1] and black and white,[2] except that this time we are dealing with blue and yellow. Then I shall show you yellow and red and then red and blue, which brings us back to the starting point. This time there will be only five (arithmetical) steps.

The only satisfactory and practical way of representing the peripheral colour movement follows the arithmetical table. For if increase, culmination, and decrease are not taken into account, we obtain mixtures that are too dark in relation to the pure colours (in watercolour particularly, where the white background plays an important part, our pure colours will be too light and our mixtures too dark.)

[1] Cf. p.474.
[2] Cf. pp.9–10.

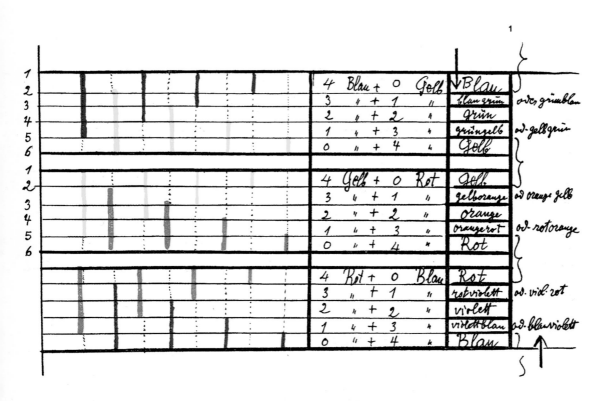

To the left the plan ([1] p.492) of the operation, in the middle the computation of the direct content, to the right the verbal characterisation of the mixtures, the indirect result of the operation. Thus green is the indirect result of blue and yellow in equal parts, and orange and violet are similarly related as effects to their causes, yellow-red and red-blue. And so we are justified in assigning different ranks to the colours that appear on the right. Primary, secondary, tertiary colours.

A geometrical picture of the whole process will make it still clearer [2].

Primary, secondary and tertiary colours

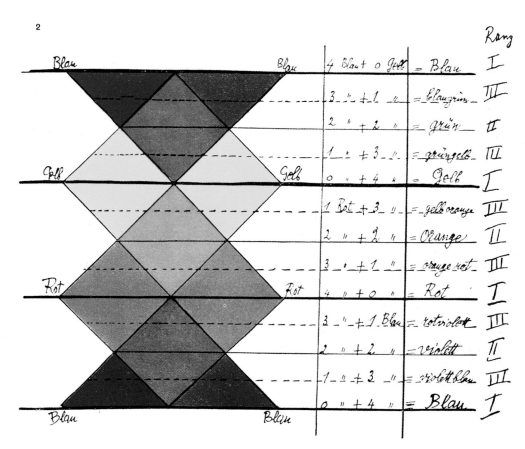

I primary colours
II secondary colours
III tertiary colours

Now the secondary character of the three mixtures is obvious. Their position in relation to the blue, yellow, and red movement could not be brought out more clearly ([2]p.493). The causal character of the three primary colours is brought out, and the dependent character of the three secondary colours, according to the relationship of cause and effect, is made clear. And now we begin to suspect that there is more to our canon than the range of its notation.

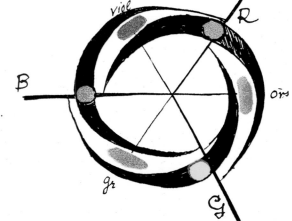

This is the drawing that I called the 'canon of colour totality'.

It circles round in three parts, determined by the three peaks of the primary colours. At each of these peaks the two other primary colours, which do not culminate at this point, begin and die away. But between the three culminations, at the meeting place between the voice that has just culminated and the voice that has just begun, the secondary colours appear, another in each segment of arc. Now in order to represent the inferiority of the secondary colours as simply as possible, I can connect the three culmination points of the primaries in a different way that departs from the circle.

At its peak the pure red should contain neither blue nor yellow; it should neither be bluish-cool nor yellowish-warm. But in view of the natural circular movement that is fed by fluid transitions between increase and decrease, this can be true only for an instant. The same is true of the brief pure instants on the blue and yellow hills. The characteristic sign for an instant is the point[1] ([1] p.496).

[1] Crossed out: The characteristic 'concept' for an instant is the point.

Painting on black
background, 1940
(untitled). Oil on canvas.

495

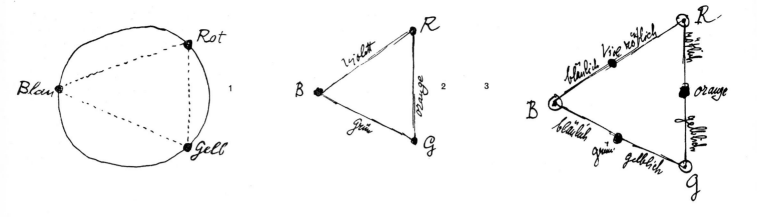

By connecting the three points I obtain the equilateral triangle blue-yellow-red [1]. But the sides of this triangle are not instants: they are gliding lines corresponding to the varying character of the secondary colours [2]. I advise you not to imagine any top and bottom to this triangle; otherwise I should have set it solidly on one side. Think of it as lying flat on the ground (you will soon see why).

If it lies flat on the ground, I can get inside it. If I turn towards red, I have a figure before me which represents the red hill exactly as it is.

If I turn to B, I see before me a pyramid resembling a blue mountain (there actually are such mountains), and turning towards G, I see the yellow mountain. Thus the triangle is a good form for our purposes (but we must really assume that it is flat). We can reach each peak of these mountains from two sides, and there are two paths leading down again. But having come half-way, we reflect for a moment that whether we are headed up or down, we now have half the distance behind us. On every side of our flat triangle these half-way points are neutral points. Here the secondary colours are pure, that is, they contain the two adjacent primary colours in equal parts. Thus the sides of the triangle break down each into two halves, bluish and yellowish, yellowish and reddish, and reddish and bluish [3].

496

Thus I obtain a new picture of the peripheral movement. One advantage of the triangular representation is that it distinguishes clearly between the primary and secondary colours. Blue, yellow, and red are placed in dominant positions; green, orange, and violet are dependent on them. This is the advantage of the triangle over the circle.

But that is not all. The triangle can also give us a more graphic picture of the sections we have called diametric movement. For example, the red-green section perpendicular to the green side is highly informative. The perpendicular strikes the neutral green point [4].

Complementary movement and component movement

This neutral green point is in turn illuminated by the flanking components of green, blue and yellow [5]

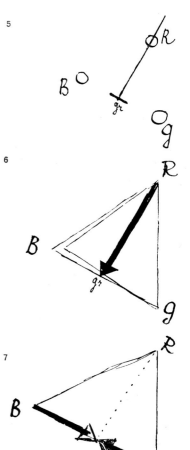

Here we have the movement of the red-green section or complementary movement [6]

And here we have the blue-yellow peripheral movement or component movement [7]

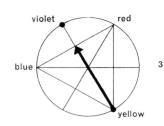

1

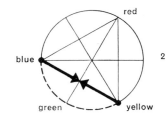

2

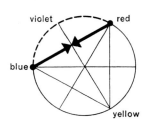

3

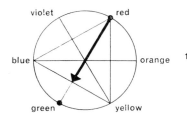

4

If we consider the construction as a whole, the red vertical runs into the green side (complementary) [1], and the green side is flanked by the blue and yellow points (components) [2]; the yellow vertical runs into the violet side (complementary) [3], and the violet side is flanked by the red and blue points (components) [4]. The blue point faces the orange side (complementary) [5], which is flanked by the yellow and red points (components) [6].

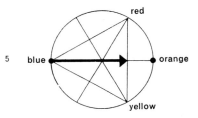

5

Complementary movements [1, 3, 5]
Component movements   [2, 4, 6]

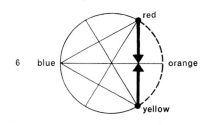

6

To sum up: The complementary diametric movements of the primary colours: blue, yellow, red (complementary movements) [7].

The component movements designate the components of the secondary colours: green, orange, violet [8].

But the three complementary diameters (the plumb-lines) intersect at the well-known grey point [9, 10].

7

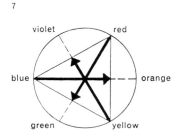

8

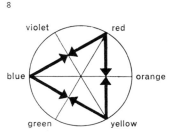

9

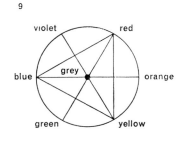

10

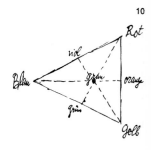

4. The law of totality on the colour surface

[1] The reading in quotes crossed out: . . . which tries to 'translate' the naked law into the 'person'.

Before I go into the three-dimensional, let us catch our breath and move about a little on this surface. There are so many clever people and there always have been. The contrapuntal relation between blue, yellow, and red, the fact that they formed a balanced totality, was recognised long ago. We hear it said that none of the three voices should be absent, that there should be neither too much nor too little of any one. This is a law well worth taking to heart, provided that you guard against the schematism which tries to put the naked law into the actual work.[1] Such misunderstandings lead to construction for its own sake. They haunt the minds of narrow-chested asthmatics who give us laws instead of works. Who have too little air in their lungs to realise that the laws should only be underneath in order that flowers may grow from them. That we look for laws only in order to find out how a work deviates from the natural works around us, land, animals, and people, but without getting foolish about it. That laws are only the common foundation of nature and art.

People have been heard to say such things as: Don't use any grey, but only the components of grey, the complementary colours. Grey is already contained in them. Grey arises by itself. Or: Only use the three primary colours blue, yellow, and red, in their most perfect purity. And in their most perfect balance. For they contain all the other colours. Then all the other colours arise by themselves. Such people make a principle of jumping like goats. Once in a while you will want to take a jump like that. But only if it meets some need, never out of principle.

Examples to p.498:
1921/144: *Combined gradations: orange-blue. red-green, yellow-violet.* Watercolour.
1921/48: *Perspective in yellow-violet.* Watercolour.
1922/16: *Landscape in green with red qualities.* Watercolour.
1924/24: *Exercise between blue and orange.* Watercolour.

And so I should like to warn you against the impoverishment that comes of taking the law too literally. I should not like you to misunderstand what I have been teaching you. Such a misunderstanding might lead you to end up with nothing but grey, on the ground that it is the centre of the whole and contains all the colours, blue, yellow, and red. And black and white for that matter.

The result would be to outlaw all colours, even black and white. Only grey would be permissible, and only the one median grey. And the result? Would the world be grey on grey? No. Worse than that. It would be one single grey, one nothing.
Yes, simplicity can be carried to such absurdity, the ultimate impoverishment, the end of life.

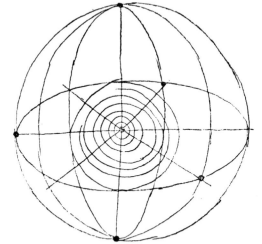

The grey point as total centre

Grey for its own sake

The dominant importance of the three primary colours permits me to characterise their presence as the law of totality in the realm of colour. A few examples will show what this law covers and how I find out if it is fulfilled.

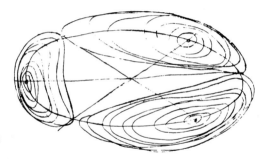

Blue, yellow, and red
in three-dimensional centric representation

500

1. The confusion of the law with the work, of the foundations with the house, of the formula with the operation, can be illustrated by the symbol of the three points. They provide the formula of the triangle •⋮

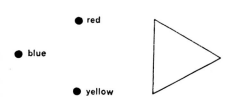

The triangle flat

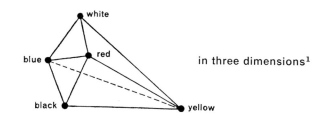

in three dimensions[1]

[1] Seen three-dimensionally as a polyhedron of totality.

2. The triangle itself means far more. The three sides symbolise the whole colour movement that takes place on them, the whole periphery.

3. Complementary sectional movements are also triangular in a sense, though the triangular character is somewhat obscured by the fact that the secondary colour takes the place of its two component primary colours. Thus a complementary movement is quite close to colour totality.

Complementary sectional movement

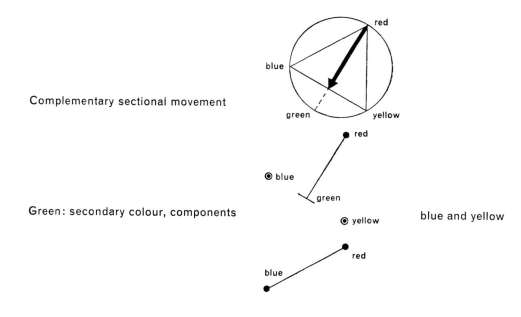

Green: secondary colour, components

blue and yellow

4. The partial peripheral movement blue-red is designated by a symbol inferior to the triangle. The law of totality is only two-thirds fulfilled (two points instead of three).

501

5. The movement between false colour pairs is supratriangular, that is, it goes beyond the triangle.

Green-orange=

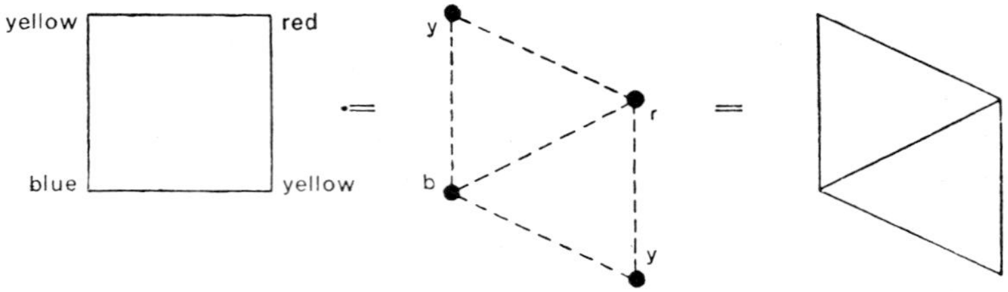
yellow
red
blue
yellow
=
y
r
b
y
=

= rectangular or bitriangular

Green-orange is supratriangular, it has a yellow point too many. Hence the excess of yellow.

Violet-orange=

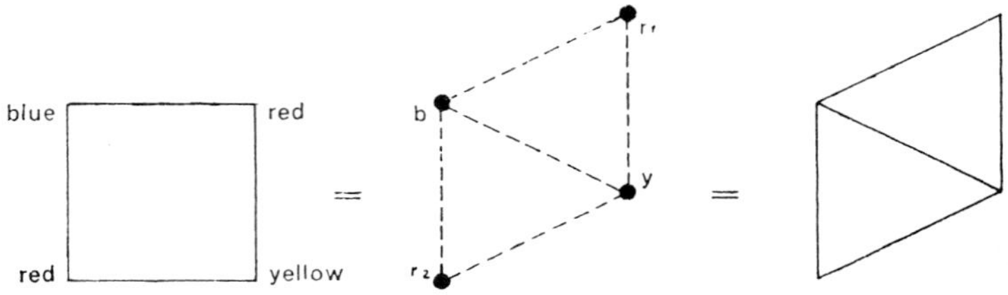
blue
red
red
yellow
=
b
r1
y
r2
=

Violet-orange is also supratriangular, bitriangular or rectangular. This movement has a red point too many, hence the excess of red.

Green-violet=

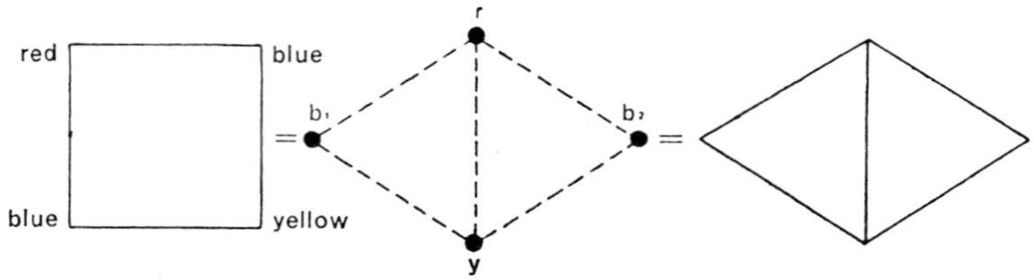
red
blue
blue
yellow
=
r
b1
b2
y
=

Green-violet is supratriangular, bitriangular or rectangular. It has a blue point that exceeds the formula of totality, hence the excess of blue.

These colour actions, as you see, do not always comply with the law of totality. Some omit a point, some give one of the three points too much weight. Such actions are not total but may be designated as partial.

Should they be condemned for this reason? Certainly not. From the point of view of totality they are in need of amplification but they also lend themselves to it.

As I explained in an earlier lecture, time is an essential factor in the pictorial field. Even partial actions take place in time. Hence if a partial action is successful in some respect, if it is well-organised as a part, it should not be abandoned. It can be rounded out later into totality; time makes it possible to catch up with totality, as I recently explained by the example of the three rooms.

[1] Cf. Section 4, p.501.

For example, the two-point partial action blue-red[1] might be even shorter than it is; even if it extended only from blue to violet, it could still be rounded out into totality:

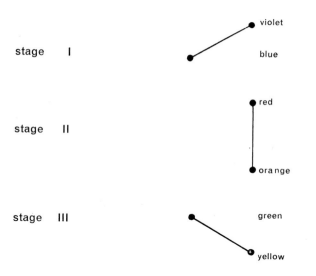

stage   I

stage   II

stage   III

Combination of the three stages brings total satisfaction, both as to number and as to weight.

[2] Cf. [8], p.498.

Number and weight[2]

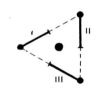

1937/T 5: *Overland*.
Paste with pigment and pastel on burlap.

¹ *Cf.* Section 3, p.501.

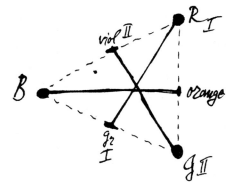

Or shown in a different form,
the complementary partial action
might be rounded out
this way into totality[1]

² *Cf.* Section 5, p.502.

I totalise the rectangular partial
actions according to their weight[2]

1st stage:
green-orange

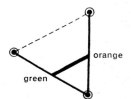

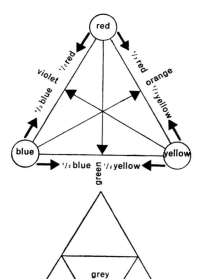

2nd stage:
violet-orange

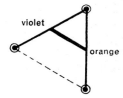

3rd stage:
green-violet

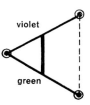

Or represented in a different way:
the three main colour elements
and grey, the total equilibrium

1st, 2nd, and
3rd stages
combined

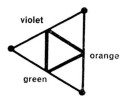

505

1927/E 4: *Harmony of the northern flora.*
Oil on cardboard coated with chalk.

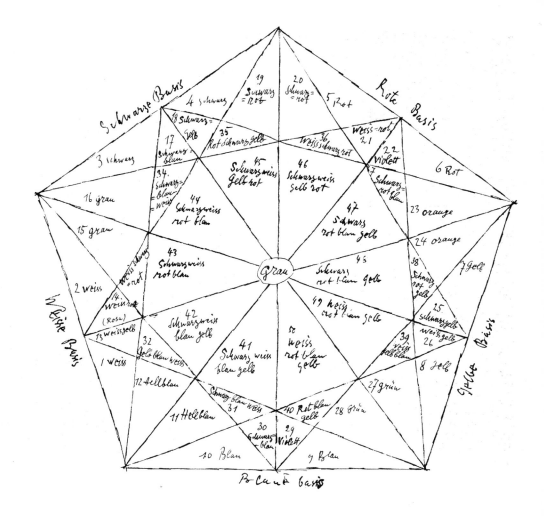

The star of the colour elements or of colour totality. The polarity lines join at grey, the common equilibrium.

507

So much for flat colour photography. I have established and explained all the positions in terms of the surface.
A final effort brings us to a three-dimensional synthesis which takes in the strongest points, the totality points white, blue, red, yellow, and black, and defines the whole geography of pure colour.

Orientation according to the cardinal points of the colour globe:

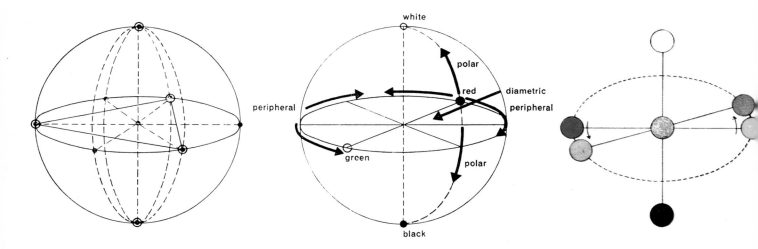

The topography of the colours extended into space:

I ⊚ white, blue, red, yellow, black
II ● grey, orange, green, violet

The three colour movements, e.g. red
a) peripheral (either towards blue or towards yellow)
b) diametric (towards green)
c) polar (towards white or black)

Movement of a colour pair
on the spectral circle

The three-dimensional equilibrium supplies powerful and significant orientation in the total field of colour and tone value. The complementary colours move round the main points white, blue, red, yellow, and black. They move in all three dimensions, while two-dimensional equilibrium only provides significant orientation on the spectral plane.

508

5. The position of the pigments on the colour circle

It is customary in this country to limit the scientific aspect of the question to a mathematical-logical proof of correctness. Thus the psychological aspect is neglected, by Ostwald for example. The psychology of the colourist demands the division of the circle into three or six parts ($\frac{1}{6}$ is more closely related to the circle than $\frac{1}{8}$!).

The definition of pure red is more difficult than that of the other colour elements. Thus since pure blue and pure yellow are more readily determined than pure red, attune your pure red so that it gives a good violet when mixed with pure blue and a good orange when mixed with pure yellow. You will already have accomplished a good deal.
The diametric contrasts should be determined by experience, by testing the effect on the eye of a colour and its counterpart. If in relation to red for example you should establish a green which is not the perfect green between yellow and blue, this is less unfortunate than the division of the circle into four or eight. That really hurts!

The metallic tones: gold is a vibration between saturated yellow and a dazzling white. Its definition is variable. Silver vibrates between dark and very bright; its definition is also variable. Copper is a vibrato between red-orange and bright light. The metallic tone values must be considered as extraordinary pictorial means.

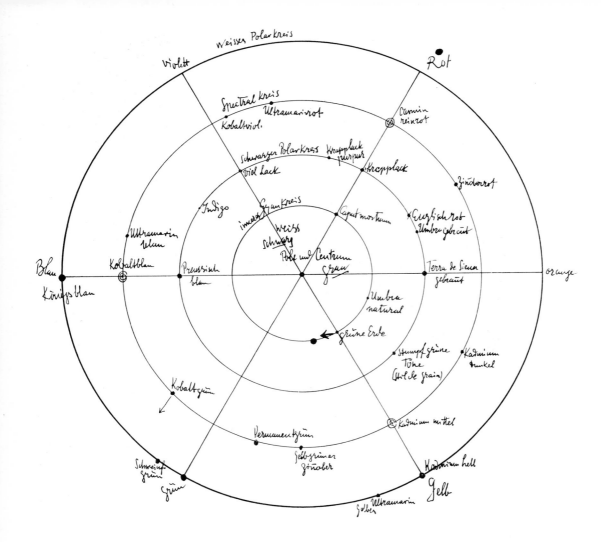

The circle contains the following handwritten labels (German):

Weisser Polarkreis · Violett · Rot · Spectral kreis · Ultramarinrot · Kobaltviol. · Carmin reinrot · Schwarzer Polarkreis · Krapplack purpur · Viol Lack · Krapplack · Zinoberrot · Indigo · innerer Graukreis · Caput mortuum · Englisch rot · Umbra gebrant · Ultramarin blau · weiss · schwarz · Blau · Königsblau · Kobaltblau · Preussisch blau · Pole und Centrum grau · Terra de Siena gebrant · orange · Umbra natural · grüne Erde · Stumpf grüne Töne (stille farain) · Kadmium dunkel · Kobaltgrün · Kadmium mittel · Permanentgrün · Gelbgrüner Zinober · Kadmium hell · Schweinf grün · Grün · Gelb · Gelber Ultramarin

Position of the pigments
in relation to the spectral
circle with shifted poles
and centre

From the inside out:
Poles and centre
Inner grey circle
Black polar circle
Spectral circle
White polar circle

510

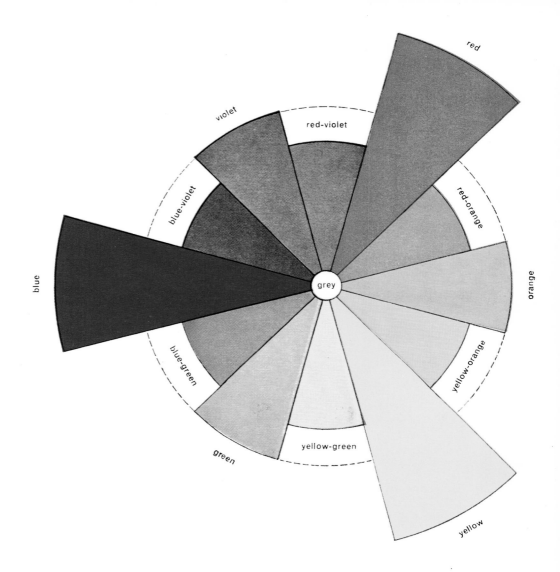

red

red-violet

violet

blue-violet

blue

blue-green

green

yellow-green

grey

red-orange

orange

yellow-orange

yellow

The position of the pigments on the 12-part circle according to Klee. The importance of blue, yellow, and red as primary colours is emphasised by the space they occupy. Psychological experience is taken into account since, in view of their superior energy, the most important diametric contrasts or complementary pairs occupy a larger area than the other pairs (quality).

511

Appendixes

Notes

Page 28

On the subject of 'organically harmonious plasticity'
Klee said to his students:
'The ultimate harmony would be attained if one
approached things from the tiny spot they have
in common, the centre. When they met there, a kind
of tranquillity would set in, which would amount
to a complete standstill. Such a harmony has its
meaning and is valuable as an example. But since
it would achieve but a neutral, or impersonal,
harmony, it would be dead, an inactive harmony.
What we need is an active harmony. This requires
deviation. We can deviate in different ways, by
holding the central point fast in the imagination
but deviating from it in practice. By deviations we
can achieve an active harmony. Not the ultimate
harmony, but an active one. There are certain
dangers in deviation. The nucleus is displaced.
These are just a few notes about the organic law
underlying the pictorial art. It is often possible to
draw compelling inferences about the organic
development of a picture; the conditions of the
pictorial art must be satisfied harmoniously and
organically. Many things come together, but reason
demands that they move apart again. This
moving-together and moving-apart must be organic
and harmonious. A symmetry that is too dominant
can be tedious, but variation can enliven it.
Well-composed pictures produce a
wholly harmonious effect. But the layman is
mistaken when he supposes that in order to
achieve such a general harmony one must form
each part harmoniously. The effect would be
weak. For once a first part is brought into harmony
with a second part, no third part is required. Only
if there is a tension in the relation between one and
two, is there a need for three, to transform the
tension into harmony. This new three-part
harmony will be much more convincing. But one
must proceed responsibly, so as to produce
human harmony; then the harmony will be
powerful. In our search for harmony or pictorial
totality we are dealing not only with a problem
of form and colour; the problem of psychic
wholeness also remains to be solved.'

Page 78

In the first printed edition of the 'Creative Credo',
which appeared in 1920, the first section of
Chapter V differs from the manuscript version:
'Formerly artists depicted things that were to be
seen on earth, things people liked to see or
would like to have seen. Now the *reality* of visible
things is made manifest...'

The manuscript version quoted in our text says
what Klee meant. It runs:
'Now the *relativity* of visible things is made
manifest...'
As early as 1902 Klee noted in his journal:
'I no longer mean to project a diagram ... but to
proceed so that everything essential, even the
essentials that are obscured by optical
perspective, show in my picture' (*cf.* p.334).
Notes from the Bauhaus period bring out the same
basic idea, *cf.* 'Ways of Nature Study', pp.63–66, and
the following lines from the 'General Review'
(p.454): 'Here we must be very clear about the aim of
"making-visible". Are we merely noting things seen
in order to remember them or are we also trying to
reveal what is not visible? Once we know and feel
this distinction, we have come to the fundamental
point of artistic creation.'

Page 159

Examples of the basic types of irregular projection.
(The different types often merge; our distinction
between them is to be taken more as a basis of
comparison than in strict application to the
individual work.)
Representation of the surface,
i.e. more according to appearance than to essence:
1925/T 4: *The last village in the valley of Ph.*, p.25.

Interpenetration of endotopic and exotopic:
1919/199: *House interior*, p.154
(three-dimensional transparent).
Spatial-transparent and transparent-polyphonic:
(in transparent treatment of bodies or
interpenetration of inside and outside, essence
and appearance are represented simultaneously).
Constructive drawing *Nodal points in space*, p.68
(simultaneously inside and outside).
1928/P 6: *Italian city*, p.42.
1928/D 7: *Perspective of a city*. Watercolour and
pen and ink. Grohmann, p.219.
1929/c 4: *Uncomposed objects in space*, p.140.
1929/g 10: *Santa A at B*, p.54.
From the standpoint of the base:
1934/19: *Mountain gorge*, p.317.
1939/M 8: *Houses close together*, p.160.
From the standpoint of simultaneous base and
elevation:
1921/125: *Chorale and landscape*. Oil. Grohmann,
p.393.
1930/y 1: *House, outside and inside*, p.48.
1930/w 9: *Polyphonic architecture*. Oil.
Giedion, p.100.
1932/x 16: *Little cliff town*, p.160.

Succession or interpenetration of perspective visual points:

1918/93: *With the net fisherman.* Watercolour, Giedion, p.89.

1923/11: *Town square under construction,* p.153.

1923/131: *Houses in projection,* p.152.

1927/L 7: *Excavation site.* Oil. Colour reproduction in Grohmann, p.261.

1932/v 11: *Small town,* p.150.

Shifting or variable viewpoint. Several viewpoints combined. Synthesis of spatio-plastic treatment and movement:

1919/156: *Composition with B.* Oil on cardboard. Reproduced in colour, Giedion, p.97.

1919/191: *City plan with green steeple.* Watercolour.

1919/193: *New fortress.* Colour. Grohmann, p.389.

1922/29: *Arabian city,* p.156.

1922/42: *Castle in the air.* Watercolour and oil and gauze sized with plaster.

1924/39: *Houses in landscape,* p.186.

1925/f 9: *Houses in the country,* p.168.

1928/p 7: *Little week-end house,* p.142.

1930/s 1: *At seven over rooftops,* p.164.

1930/s 10: *Hovering before rising,* p.172.

1937/qu 17: *The way to the city castle,* p.166.

1940/N 14: *Churches,* p.194.

On the synthesis of spatio-plastic treatment and movement, *cf.* the stages of development from the Bauhaus period to the late work:

1924/39: *Houses in landscape,* p.186.

1932/x 16: *Little cliff town,* p.160.

1937/qu 17: *The way to the city castle,* p.166.

1940/N 14: *Churches,* p.194.

Page 213

Klee discussed some of his works at the Düsseldorf Academy. A remark has been preserved about 1930/y 4: *Daringly poised,* watercolour.

'Daringly poised: I have been told that this is an example of optical illusion, that the dark spot is made to look light by the zone round it (some of the students present agree that this is so). This seems to spring from the physiology of the eye. I was not aiming at such an effect. Optical illusion is psychological and therefore different for each individual. Perhaps the individual structure of the eye has something to do with it too. I have never used this method consciously. We had better leave the study of optical illusions to the psychology of perception.' (Turning to a student: 'I didn't mean to say that you shouldn't have asked. Always ask.')

Page 215

For Klee letters and figures had an expressive value of their own. (The 'Creative Credo', pp.76–77, refers to the relation between formal signs and outward experience.)

In connection with letters and numbers Klee inquired into the 'causal principle', the essence and appearance of the written sign. He investigated the origin of the letters of the hieroglyphic and sign languages and finally the alphabets of various cultures. Letters and numbers are not only vehicles of experience but also carry their own history in their forms.

Klee's library included: Karl Weule, *Vom Kerbholz zum Alphabet, Urformen der Schrift.* Kosmos, Stuttgart 1915.

Page 227

The variations on the chessboard structure (heavy-light) and composite units should not be taken as an interpretation of something ready-made, but as a movement and development of form. 'Constructive representation', he notes, 'provides regular relations between values. Constructive methods of composition are norms and guiding lines for the treatment of the pictorial elements.' Within any one norm, 'a movement of productive form' develops according to the means employed. Next comes 'impressive treatment', a free, creative application of the insight gained by the constructive principles. . . . If we follow the gradual unfolding of a primitive simple work, we shall obtain a closer view of two things: first the phenomenon of formation, . . . formation bound to the conditions of life, . . . This phenomenon was discernible in the very earliest craft, when form in the smallest sense (structure) first made its appearance. . . . As the creative process continued, as the way grew longer, the danger of monotony became apparent. For the way, . . . It must rise higher, branch out excitingly, rise, fall, digress; it must become by turns more or less distinct, broader or narrower, easier or harder. And the sections must fall into a definite structure; . . . The different segments of the way join into an articulated whole . . . The different modes of interaction produce works of different kinds. (*Cf.* the complete text, pp.168–169). 'In this realm we cross a boundary line of reality. There is no copying or reproducing, but rather transformation and new creation. If we surrender to it, a metamorphosis occurs, something which, if healthy, is always new. This is perfectly permissible, possible, and natural. In the course of the metamorphosis a new reality is created.'

Page 253

Examples mainly with emphasis on base:
1931/s 11: *Ground plan* (sketch). Pencil.
1931/s 12: *Moving form on ground*. Pencil.
1931/c 5: *Active articulation*. Pencil drawing.
1933/A 7: *Pathways on the edge of the village*. Oil.
1939/M 8: *Houses close together*. Colour sketch, p.160.
1940/Z 10: *Rearranged town*. Colour sketch.
Grohmann, p.398.

Simultaneous base and elevation (with varying
accent on the projection of base and elevation):
1927/W 9: *Côte de Provence I*. Colour. Grohmann,
p.399.
1932/x 16: *Little cliff town*, p.160.
1937/qu 17: *The way to the city castle*, p.166.

Rhythmic structuring, accent on elevation (spatial-
plastic accent obtained by structuring of planes):
1929/s 6: *Castle hill*, p.158.
1929/D 2: *Fairy tale*. Oil. Grohmann, p.398.

Page 260

On dividual-individual synthesis:
1929/R 10: *Main path and side paths*. Oil.
Giedion, p.129.
1929/N 1: *Monument in the land of fruit*.
Water-colour. Giedion, p.130.
1929/s 1: *Necropolis*. Gouache. Colour reproduction
in Giedion, p.131.
1929/n 1: *Surveying*. Watercolour.
1930/R 2: *Individualised altimetry of horizontals*.
Colour sketch. Colour reproduction in
Grohmann, p.277.

Page 291

Concerning structural formation and the synthesis
of individual and dividual characters see the
later work:
1934/P 5: *Secret script picture*. Paste with pigment.
Grohmann, p.401.
1938/D 17: *Boundary*. Paste with pigment.
1938/D 18: *Law*. Water-colour and paste with
pigment.
1938/E 2: *Poster for Comedians*. Paste with pigment.
Grohmann, p.297.
1938/J 16: *Intention*. Paste with pigment on
newsprint on burlap. Colour reproduction in
Giedion, p.175.
'Lower and higher individuals organically joined.
Loose-knit and separate (physically loose-knit),
but brought together by a clear relationship.'

Page 292

Examples illustrating the exercise: 'Composition
of I, individual and II, structural rhythms. To be
developed organically, the one supporting the
other.' As a solution to the problem Klee cited
'The fish', pp.297 and 264. Examples from
the theory of structure facsimile pages 58 and
230.

Examples of diverse structural foundations:
1920/109: *Flowers in a wheatfield*, p.256.
1924/128: *Mural*, p.250.
1924/126: *Structural II*. Colour drawing.
Giedion, p.118.
1926/2: *Castle to be built in the woods*.
Colour sketch. Grohmann, p.226.
1926/3: *A garden for Orpheus*. Pen and ink.
Grohmann, p.368.
1927/D 9: *Difficult journey through O*, p.106.
1927/N 2: *Air-tsu-dni*. Pen and ink. Grohmann, p.259.
1929/p 6: *Village in the rain*, p.45.
1931/x 9: *Luxuriant countryside*, p.304.
1934/qu 18: *Cliffs*, p.304.
1935/L 15: *Ostentatious defence*, p.262.
1937/Q 16: *Cool weather sets in*. Oil. Grohmann, p.294
1938/B 14: *Coarser and finer*, p.403.

Synthesis of rigid and fluid structural and
individual rhythms:
1924/132: *Hieroglyphic water plants*, p.240.
1934/qu 2: *Uphill and then what?*, p.305.
1937/R 5: *The Rhine near Duisburg*, p.290.
1938/J 5: *The grey man and the coast*, p.316.

Light and colour energies as dividual rhythms,
individual accent on the active character of the line:
1931/T 16: *Steamer and sailboats toward evening*.
Colour. Grohmann, p.401.
1931/V 8: *The light and various things*. Oil.
Grohmann, p.241.
1932/15: *The landscape of UOL*. Colour drawing.
Grohmann, p.401.
1932/K 2: *At anchor*. Oil. Colour reproduction in
Grohmann, p.313.
1932/k 9: *Tendril*, p.104.
1932/x 10: *View over the plain*, p.8.
1932/x 14: *Ad Parnassum*. Oil and casein on canvas.
Giedion, p.132.

Page 296

Comparison of the three pictures on pp.291, 294,
and 296 reveals three fundamental principles of
composition. Klee distinguishes the possibilities:

1. 'Physically loose-knit (partially constructive reproduction of relations, or free irregularity)'.
2. 'Brought together through clear relationships.'
3. 'Unbroken contact.'

1937/U 11: *View in red*, p.291. Labile balance from a static premise. Partial representation of the conception 'physically loose-knit'.

1937/R 6: *Terrace with flowers*, p.294. Static-dynamic synthesis. Balance between gravitation and momentum. Parts 'brought together by clear relationships'. In contrast to this, partial actions with interrupted connections in a composition with static and dynamic elements.
1938/v 2: *Interim near Easter*, p.294.

1931/L 4: *Three subjects, polyphonic*, p.296. Dynamically accented rhythms, polyphonic and colour-transparent, in 'unbroken contact'.
In *Three subjects, polyphonic*, the additional differentiation according to the criteria of statics and dynamics provides an intensification of movement, progressing rhythmically from the shifted balance of the elements of synthesis to full dynamic polyphony. On polyphony see the note to p.380.

Page 302
From the notebooks of Paul Klee:
1902: Finally back to N., now a silent sowing of lights at my feet. Oh, the overflowing confusion, the displacements, the bloody sun, the deep sea full of crooked little sailboats. Matter on matter. I could dissolve in it. Oh, to be a man, in ancient times, naïve and insignificant, but happy! May the day of evidence dawn and reconcile the opposites! To express the many sides of things in one word. The city is a moving army of spots. The blocks of houses are planes of light and shade; white streets, solemn-green parks.
April 7, 1914. Later on, the first Arab city was clearly discernible. Sidibou Saïd, a hillside with the white shapes of houses growing on it in strict rhythm. As real as a fairy tale, but not yet within reach; far away, quite far and yet very clear. The sun darkly powerful. The coloured clarity of the country is full of promise. The colours are more glaring and are a little darker. The Arab city at night. Matter and dream united and a third party, I mean I, myself, surely, in the very midst of it. Something good must come of this.
April 8. My head is full of the experiences of last night. Art, nature, myself. Went to work at once

and painted water-colours in the arab quarter. Attacked the synthesis: city architecture=picture architecture.
April 12. The evening is indescribable. On top of it all the full moon rises. L. is prodding me. He wants me to paint it. I say: it won't be any more than an exercise. In the face of such nature I am bound to fail. And yet I know something more than I did before. I know the road from my failure to nature. That is an internal affair to keep me busy for the next few years. It doesn't trouble me one bit. No use hurrying when you want so much. This evening is deep inside me – for ever. Many a blond northern moonrise, like a muffled reflection, will remind me time and time again. It will be my bride, my alter ego. A spur to find myself. I myself am the rising southern moon.
April 14. Arrived at Hamamet; it is still a little way from the city.
The city (Tunis) is marvellous, right by the sea, jagged and rectangular and then jagged again. Now and then I get a look at the city walls. Painted a good deal and dawdled. At a café in the evening a blind singer and his boy beating the drum. A rhythm that will stay with me for ever.
April 16. (Kairouan.) First a great turmoil. No particulars, only the whole of it, and what a whole! Extract of Arabian Nights with 99 per cent reality content. What an aroma, how penetrating, how intoxicating and at the same time clarifying. Order and intoxication. An evening of delicate yet sharply defined colour. I'm going to stop work now. Something so deep, so gentle is entering into me; I feel it and that gives me a feeling of certainty, without effort. Colour has me. I no longer need to reach out for it. It has me forever and knows it. That is the meaning of this happy hour; colour and I are one.
April 19. First, preparations for my departure. Lots of watercolours and all sorts of other things. Most of it inside me, deep inside, but I'm so full that it keeps bubbling out.

Page 339
Cf. the new view of structure in biology as well as the scientific study of 'inwardness' as a world of qualities.
Adolf Portmann, 'Die Wandlungen im biologischen Denken', in *Die neue Weltschau*, International discussion concerning the dawn of a new anti-perspective age. Technical High School, St Gallen Vol.I, Deutsche Verlagsanstalt, Stuttgart 1952.

Page 352

Starting from premises similar to those of Klee, Hans Kayser investigates the idea of harmonic form in the development of plant forms, relating them to the causal phenomena of the tone scale. Basic form, leaf form, ramification, the leaves as a whole, and the flower. His investigations show that the function, life, sex, nutrition, and growth of plants are summed up in the harmonic forms of the plants: discontinuum, stages, rhythm, polarity, symmetry, spiral, etc.
Hans Kayser, *Harmonia Plantarum*. Benno Schwabe & Co., Basle 1943.
One of Kayser's chief works (*Der hörende Mensch*, Lambert Schneider, Berlin 1932) has the sub-title: 'Elements of an acoustic view of the world'. Kayser's ideas on harmonics in the plant world often come close to Klee's conceptions of pictorial harmony. Klee's library included Kayser's *Orpheus, morphologische Fragmente einer allgemeinen Harmonik*, Berlin 1924.

Page 366

1932: *Tragedy*. Oil. The picture was given the English title of 'Tragedy' when reproduced by Karl Nierendorf, *Paul Klee, Paintings, Watercolours, 1913 to 1939*, ed. by K. Nierendorf, intro. by V. V. Sweeney, OUP, New York, 1941.
There is no corresponding title in the catalogue of Klee's works.

Page 380

The watercolour *Polyphonic-abstract* is called 'polyphonic movement' in the manuscript version of the œuvre catalogue. 'Polyphony: the study of harmony, the theory of simultaneous sounds. Simultaneity of several independent themes. Polyphony as a simultaneous multi-dimensional phenomenon.'
'Colour polyphony: harmony of several colour voices.' On the figuration of colour polyphonies Klee says: 'They must be complete in order to be heard. Polyphony should be constructive-linear and also carried through in the colour values, or else you are likely to get a somewhat unpleasant mixture of freedom and constraint.' Criteria of differentiation: Purely linear, linear and planar, or predominantly colour-polyphonic. Statically or dynamically accented style.

Static polyphonic
Linear:
The key of Fes-is-mur, p.286.

1927/D 8: *Slate quarry*, p.284.
1929/o 4: *Rock*, p.102.
1929/o 8: *Huts*, p.25.

Linear-planar and colour polyphonic:
Three-part polyphony, p.261.
1927/E 4: *Harmony of the northern flora*, p.506.
1933/H 7: *A little room in Venice*. Pastel. Grohmann, p.399.
1937/qu 18: *Architecture in the evening*, p.184.
1938/H 20: *Oriental-sweet*. Colour reproduction in Grohmann, p.331.

Colour polyphonic:
1923/62: *Architecture (yellow and violet graduated cubes)*, p.370. Colour reproduction in Grohmann, p.201.
1923/102: *Colour trinomial from A, B and (A+B)*. Water-colour. Grohmann, p.395.
1927/w 7: *Harmony of the southern flora*, p.235.
1932/x 13: *Polyphony*. Oil.

Exception: transparent-polyphonic:
1930/y 1: *House, outside and inside*, p.48.
1930/x 8: *Pyramid*. Watercolour.
1930/x 10: *Polyphonic setting for white*, p.374.

Intermediate realm between statics and dynamics
Linear
Diagram of two-part polyphony, p.300.
1927/F 2: *Symptomatic*, p.300.

Colour:
1923/67: *Intensification of colour from the static to the dynamic*. Grohmann, p.395.
1930/w 9: *Polyphonic architecture*. Oil. Giedion, p.100.
1934/T 19: *In bloom*. Oil. Colour reproduction. Giedion, p.101.

Dynamic polyphonic
Linear:
Illustrations pp.62 and 84.
1930/J 7: *Twined into a group*, p.340.
1930/a 7: *Twins*, p.118.

Linear-planar and colour-polyphonic:
1928/F 4: *Dramatic landscape*. Colour drawing. Grohmann, p.399.
1929/OE 4: *Illumined leaf*, p.65.
1931/L 4: *Three subjects, polyphonic*, p.296.
1931/m 7: *Figure*, p.383.
1932/y 4: *The fruit*, p.6.

1935/P 15: *Lady demon*. Oil.
Colour reproduction, Giedion, p.163.
On the subject of polyphony, Klee noted in 1917:
'Simple movement strikes us as banal. The time
element must be eliminated. Yesterday and
tomorrow treated as simultaneous. In music this
need was partly met by polyphony. The quintet in
Don Giovanni is closer to us than the epic
movement of Tristan. Mozart and Bach are more
modern than the nineteenth century. If in music
the time factor could be overcome by a step
back acceptable to our consciousness, a late
flowering might still be possible ... Polyphonic
painting is superior to music because its time is
more spatial. The idea of simultaneity comes out
more richly. The reflection in the side windows of a
moving tram car gives an idea of the backward
movement I have in mind for music. Delaunay
tries to follow the example of a fugue and put the
pictorial accent on the time factor – this he does
by choosing an immensely elongated format.'
(*Cf.* Klee's note on polyphony, p.296.)

Page 393

Cf. in connection with the form of the
pendulum movement:
1938/1: *Heroic strokes of the bow*, p.283.
1938/J 5: *The grey man and the coast*, p.316.
1938/J 12: *Source of fire*, p.426.

In connection with the static-dynamic synthesis,
Klee notes:
'The pendulum expresses a unit of time. It is a
symbol of mediation between rest and movement,
gravitation and momentum. In the static the accent
is on the vertical and horizontal, which are based
on gravitation. The dynamic stresses the curve,
which is based on momentum. There are
possibilities of combining the two. An
amplification of the rigid static analogy in the
chapter on balance.'

Simple example:
Linear analysis from 1937/R 4: *River trip*.
Oil, p.393.
Higher examples with mixed accentuation of
gravity and momentum:
1931/Y 7: *Diana*. Oil. Colour reproduction in
Grohmann, p.279.
1937/R 6: *Terrace with flowers*, p.294.
1937/qu 10: *Harmonised disturbances*. Charcoal
and watercolour on burlap.

1937/U 6: *Harmonised battle*, p.178.
1937/U 12: *Stage landscape*. Pastel.
Colour reproduction in Grohmann, p.323.
1937/T 5: *Overland*, p.504.
1937/U 8: *Blue night*. Tempera and pastel on canvas.
1938/E 7: *Stormy mise-en-scène*, p.443.
1938/J 8: *Capriccio in February*. Oil.
Grohmann, p.403.
1938/J 16: *Shattered key*, p.430.
1938/J 17: *Aeolian*. Oil. Grohmann, p.405.
1938/v 2: *Interim near Easter*, p.292.
1939/P qu 11: *Arrogance*, p.444.
1940/x 1: *Eyes in the landscape*, p.96.
Cf. Ideal and material statics, pp.182–5. and
Gravitation and momentum, p.395.

Page 414
Examples of the pictorial schemata of the first,
second, and third laws of statics.

Simple examples:
1923/138: *Tightrope walker*, p.196.
1927/v 1: *Ships after the storm*, p.372.
1929/m 3: *Evening in Egypt*, p.146.
1929/M 4: *The sun grazes the plain*, p.163.
1929/o 4: *Rock*, p.102.
1929/o 8: *Huts*, p.25.
1929/s 2: *In the current of six crescendos*, p.212.
1930/N 1: *Scaffolding of building under
construction*, p.209.
1935/qu 15: *Will you be seated?*, p.206.

More complicated examples:
1924/39: *Houses in landscape*, p.186.
1924/189: *Collection of signs*. Watercolour and
pen and ink. Grohmann, p.177.
1927/om 9: *Variations (progressive motif)*, p.28.
1931/V 8: *The light and so much else*. Oil.
Grohmann, p.241.
1932/v 11: *Small town*, p.150.
1935/M 17: *Signs in the field*, p.198.

Synthesis in the late work:
1937/M 17: *Under the viaduct*. Colour.
Grohmann, p.407.
1937/Q 7: *Comments on a region*. Colour sketch.
Grohmann, p.405.
1937/qu 12: *Fragments*, p.309.
1937/qu 17: *The way to the city castle*, p.166.
1937/qu 18: *Architecture in the evening*, p.184.
1937/R 2: *Temple festival*. Colour. Grohmann, p.405
1937/R 5: *The Rhine near Duisburg*, p.290.
1937/U 6: *Harmonised battle*, p.178.

1937/U 10: *Signs in yellow*, Pastel, Grohmann, p.404.
1937/U 11: *View in red*, p.291.

Page 420

On the causality behind the figuration of
concentric and eccentric forces and their
syntheses, *cf.*
The examples of 'Rhythms in nature', p.268.
The rhythmic structures, pp.275, 279, and 282.
The formal statement and recept picture, p.365.
The function of form (recept), p.377.

Examples:
1926/R 2: *Spiral flowers*, p.377.
1932/v 17: *Helical flowers I*, p.376.
1932/y 4: *The fruit*, p.6.
1939/A A 2: *Fama*. Oil on canvas.

Page 467

Klee on the colour theories of Goethe and Runge:
'As we all know, there are many colour theories.
We have Goethe's theory of colours, which he
probably worked out in order to refute Newton's
assertions. Goethe's work is the most detailed
discussion of the physiological, physical, and
chemical colours of his time. He also treats the
sensory-ethical effects of colour. We find earlier
traces of a colour theory and a theory of painting
in general in Leonardo, Dürer, and others. Today
still other colour theories have been devised.
Two of them in particular are discussed from
time to time, those of Hoelzel and Ostwald.
But here we are neither a paint industry nor a
chemical dye house. We must be free and have
access to all the possibilities. I believe that the
theory of Philipp Otto Runge, which to be sure was
taken over from others, is closest to us painters'.

Philipp Otto Runge.
Klee is referring to Runge's *Farbenkugel oder
Konstruktion des Verhältnisses aller Mischungen und
Farben zueinander und ihrer vollständigen Affinität.*
(*Cf.* Philipp Otto Runge, *Schriften, Fragmente,
Briefe,* ed. Ernst Forsthoff, Berlin 1938.
Otto Böttcher, *Philipp Otto Runge. Sein Leben,
Wirken und Schaffen,* Hamburg 1937).
Unlike Klee, Runge does not stress the movements
on the colour circle. He was mainly interested in the
relation between the quality and quantity and the
mechanics of colour relations. In Klee the relations
of three-dimensional equilibrium on the colour
circle (or sphere) have been amplified by
functional mobility. He took from Runge the

concepts of 'absolute unity' (totality) and the
tension between 'finite and infinite', which in his
writing becomes a tension between the earthly
and the cosmic, the immanent and the
transcendent (*cf.* the example of the rainbow).
A passage in one of Runge's letters, dated 1809,
suggests that his view of the world was very close
to Klee's: 'The analogy between vision . . . and
hearing gives great promise of a future union
between music and painting or between the
tones and colours.'
On the same problem Klee says:
'Today a synthesis between the worlds of sound
and appearance seems to be a possibility.'

Wassily Kandinsky.
Kandinsky's contributions to the theory of colour
are contained in the following works:
Kandinsky: *Über das Geistige in der Kunst* (1912).
*Wirkung der Farbe, Formen- und Farbensprache,
Theorie.* Fifth edition, Benteli, Berne 1956.
English translation: *Concerning the Spiritual in
Art and Painting in Particular.* G. Wittenborn Inc.,
New York 1947.
'Die Grundelemente der Form, Farbkurs und
Seminar' (1923), 'Analyse der primären Elemente
der Malerei' (1928) in: Kandinsky, *Essays über Kunst
und Künstler,* ed. Max Bill, Stuttgart 1955.
Kandinsky, *Punkt und Linie zur Fläche, Beiträge zur
Analyse der malerischen Elemente* (1926).
Bauhausbücher No.9, Third edition, Benteli,
Berne 1955.
Klee describes his relation to Kandinsky in a
testimonial on his sixtieth birthday:
'In addressing a word to Kandinsky, I shall try to
remain in the background . . . At the beginning of
the century our ways crossed for a moment at the
Munich Academy, but neither of us attached deep
importance to the meeting. Then, a dozen years
later, our first real meeting took place at a time
when Munich, unofficially at least, was a lively
place, the crossroads of the European trends
which produced the *Blaue Reiter.* He was more
advanced in his development than I; I could have
been his pupil and in a certain sense I was, for
some of his words managed to encourage,
confirm and clarify my striving. It goes without
saying that these words were backed up by actions
(Kandinsky's early compositions). Then came
something we believed we did not need, the
shattering reality of the European conflict and
with it, after a brief meeting on a neutral island, a
protracted physical separation. But the work went

on quietly, for him abroad, for us others here.
The current of feeling between us remained
unbroken but indemonstrable, until Weimar
fulfilled our hope of a new meeting enriched by
our common pedagogic activity. Which is now to
be continued in Dessau.
Today we are on the eve of a great occasion, his
sixtieth birthday. But there is nothing sombre
about that for one who has followed his *œuvre* and
knows him personally.
Some complete their work quickly (like Franz Marc),
others in their fifties are still taking resolute steps
into new territory and building richly on the ground
they have conquered. This is not twilight.
The richness and perfection of such acts,
whether performed early or late in life, seldom or
more frequently, sets them above the life span of
the artist and even above the time in which he lives.
This is what happened yesterday, and it can happen
tomorrow in his sixties. It is a work in which all
tensions are concentrated. Today I say: good
morning, and coming from the west, I move a little
closer to him. He takes a step towards me and my
hand rests in his.
Germany in the year 1926.'

Wilhelm Ostwald.
On Ostwald's theory of colours Klee has the
following to say in a letter to Hans Hildebrandt
(first published in 'Die Maler am Bauhaus',
Katalog der Ausstellung. Munich 1950):
'When I read Ostwald's Colour Theory some time
ago I understood the distaste of most painters for
the scientific study of colour. But I decided to
wait a little while to see whether some benefit might
not remain from my reading after all. And actually
a few little oddities have stayed with me. One such
item is the assertion that the science of acoustics
promoted musical production. It is not so
mistaken to draw a parallel between Helmholtz
and Ostwald, to say that they had the same
negative relation to the arts. But that is not how the
comparison is meant. Scientists often find
something childlike in the arts. The present case
permits us to return the compliment. A number
of other things are also childlike, such as the
idea of a Potsdamer Platz with automobile horns
tuned to the C-major chord. Aside from the
murderous effects of such harmony, it is ridiculous
to claim that this sort of tone painting free from
dissonance is musical. We find the same freedom
from dissonance in his ideas about colour harmony;
the resulting chords would be comparable to the

yodler and the Gstanzerl. For it is an old story
that beautiful with beautiful soon gets dull. Another
remarkable opinion is that the tempering of the
clavichord was a scientific achievement. I can only
regard it as a practical aid, like the colour scale of
the chemical paint industry. Of course we have
been using it for a long time, but we don't need a
theory of colour. All their interminable mixing will
never give you a simple emerald green, fire red,
or cobalt violet. For us a dark yellow is not mixed
with black, because that would make it veer towards
the green. And besides, with all their learned
whitewashing they don't pay a moment's attention
to such things as transparent mixtures (glazes).
Not to mention their utter ignorance of the
relativity of colour values. They regard the
very possibility of producing a universal norm by
the harmonisation of equivalent tonalities as a
trespassing on the preserves of psychology.
I ask you!'

Bibliography

1. Writings of Paul Klee

Essays, Lectures, Poems

'Die Ausstellung des modernen Bundes im Kunsthaus Zürich.' In: *Die Alpen*, Vol.6, No.12. Berne 1912.

'Über das Licht.' An essay by Robert Delaunay, translated from the French by Klee.
In: *Der Sturm*, Vol.3, No.144–145. Berlin 1913.

'Schöpferische Konfession.'
In: *Tribüne der Kunst und Zeit*, a collection of writings edited by Kasimir Edschmid. Vol.XIII, with contributions by Beckmann, Benn, Däubler, Hoelzel, Marc, Schickele, Schönberg, Sternheim, Unruh and others. Erich Reiss, Berlin 1920.
Reproduced in part in: Wilhelm Hausenstein: *Kairuan oder eine Geschichte vom Maler Klee und von der Kunst dieser Zeit*. Kurt Wolf, Munich 1921.
Reproduced in part in English in: *Paul Klee*, 2nd ed. Museum of Modern Art, New York 1945.

Klee's biography based on information supplied by the artist.
In: H. von Wedderkop: 'Paul Klee', *Junge Kunst*, Vol.13. Klinkhardt & Biermann, Leipzig 1920.
Reprinted under the title 'Eine biographische Skizze nach eigenen Angaben des Künstlers', in *Der Ararat*, second special number, 'Paul Klee', (Catalogue of the 60th exhibition at the Galerie Neue Kunst – Hans Goltz). Goltzverlag, Munich 1920.

'Über den Wert der Kritik.' A questionnaire to artists. In: *Der Ararat*, Vol.2, p.130. Goltzverlag, Munich 1921.

'Wege des Naturstudiums.'
In: *Staatliches Bauhaus Weimar, 1919–1923*.
Published by the Staatliches Bauhaus, Weimar and Karl Nierendorf, Cologne. Bauhausverlag, Weimar and Munich 1923.

Pädagogisches Skizzenbuch (Bauhausbücher No.2), edited by W. Gropius and L. Moholy-Nagy, Albert Langen, Munich 1925. English edition: *Pedagogical Sketch Book*, translated by Sibyl Peech. Nierendorf Gallery, New York 1944.

'W. Kandinsky.' In: *Katalog der Jubiläumsausstellung zum 60. Geburtstag von W. Kandinsky*. With contributions by Dreyer, Grohmann, Fannina Halle, Klee, Galerie Arnold, Dresden (1926).

'Emil Nolde'. In: *Festschrift zum 60. Geburtstag von E. Nolde*. Neue Kunst Fides, Dresden 1927.

'Exakte Versuche im Bereiche der Kunst.'
In: *Bauhaus, Vierteljahrzeitschrift für Gestaltung*, Vol.2, No.2/3. Dessau 1928.
Reprinted, under the title 'Paul Klee spricht', in the Bauhaus prospectus *Junge Menschen kommen ans Bauhaus*, Dessau 1929.
Reproduced in part in English under the title 'Paul Klee speaks' in *Bauhaus 1919–1928*, Museum of Modern Art, New York 1938.

'Aussprüche und Aphorismen.' From the notebooks of a student (Petra Petitpierre) at the Staatliche Kunstakademie, Düsseldorf.
In: *Die Tat*, Vol.5, No.274. Zürich 1940.

Über die moderne Kunst. (Prepared as a lecture on the occasion of an exhibition at the Jena Kunstverein, 26 January 1924.) Benteli, Berne-Bümpliz 1945. English edition: *On modern art*, translated by Douglas Cooper. With an introduction by Herbert Read. Faber and Faber, London 1947.

8 Poems.
In: *Poètes à l'écart*, edited by Carola Giedion-Welcker. Benteli, Berne-Bümpliz 1946.

'Die Stimme Paul Klees.' Extracts from the journal 1902–1905, from the article 'Die Ausstellung des modernen Bundes im Kunsthaus Zürich' and from the Jena lecture, brought together by Carola Giedion-Welcker.
In: *Du*, Vol.8, No.10. Zürich 1948.

Dokumente und Bilder aus den Jahren 1896–1930. Part 1 (Text of the writings, letters and journals from Klee's literary estate) edited by the Klee-Gesellschaft, Berne. Benteli, Berne-Bümpliz 1949. This contains, under the title 'Gedanken über Graphik und über Kunst im allgemeinen', extracts from the draft for the 'Schöpferische Konfession' (1919).

'Karl Jahn als Lehrer.' Klee's obituary notice for his violin teacher in Berne. A single column notice of 52 lines in an unidentified Berne newspaper (date not yet established).

Aus der Malklasse von Paul Klee.
Edited from the shorthand notes of a student Petra Petitpierre. Benteli, Berne 1957.

Gedichte. Poems edited by Felix Klee. Arche, Zürich 1960.

Extracts from the journals

Tagebücher von 1898 bis 1918. Edited by
Felix Klee. 2nd ed. Du Mont Schauberg,
Cologne 1960.

Entries from the journals 1902–1905. In:
Leopold Zahn: *Paul Klee: Leben, Werk, Geist.*
Gustav Kiepenheuer, Potsdam 1920.
Partly reproduced in English in: *Paul Klee.*
Translation by Mimi Catlin and Greta Daniels.
2nd ed. Museum of Modern Art, New York 1945.

Extracts from the journals, translated by Jean
Rousset. In: *Lettres*, edited by Pierrette
Courthion. No.4, Geneva 1945.
Some of these journal entries have not been
published elsewhere.

Quotations from Klee's journal and the
1929 Bauhaus prospectus ('Paul Klee spricht').
In: Robert Goldwater and Marco Treves:
Artists on art. Pantheon Books, New York 1945.

Entries from the journal, 1912. In: *Der Blaue
Reiter. Der Weg von 1908–1914. München und die
Kunst des 20. Jahrhunderts.* Catalogue of the
exhibition in the Haus der Kunst, Munich,
edited by Ludwig Grote, Munich 1949.

Documents

Felix Klee: *Paul Klee. Leben und Werk in
Dokumenten.* Diogenes, Zürich 1960.

Felix Klee: *Mein Vater Klee.* Diogenes, Zürich 1960.

Carola Giedion-Welcker: *Paul Klee in
Selbstzeugnissen und Bilddokumenten.* Rowohlt,
Hamburg 1961.

Letters

Three quotations from Klee's private
correspondence. In: *Catalogue of Paul Klee
Memorial exhibition.* Museum of Art,
San Francisco 1941.

Extract from a letter to Galka Scheyer, Weimar
10 January 1924. In: *The Blue Four; Feininger
Jawlensky, Kandinsky, Klee.* Exhibition catalogue.
Buchholz Gallery, New York 1944.

Extracts from Klee's letters (as well as Kandinsky's
and Schlemmer's) to Hans Hildebrandt. In: *Die
Maler am Bauhaus.* Catalogue of the exhibition
held at the Haus der Kunst, Munich.
Prestel, Munich 1950.
Reprinted under the title: 'Aus Briefen von Paul
Klee an Hans Hildebrandt'. In *Paul Klee, Gemälde,
Aquarelle, Zeichnungen und Graphik*, published
by Lothar-Günther Buchheim-Militon,
Frankfurt a.M. 1950.

2. Works cited in the text

Pierre Courthion: *Klee.* Vingt reproductions en
couleur. (Bibliothèque Aldine des Arts, Vol.27.)
Fernand Hazan, Paris 1953.

Carola Giedion-Welcker: *Paul Klee.* Viking Press,
New York 1952; Faber and Faber, London 1952;
Gerd Hatje, Stuttgart 1954;
Arthur Niggli and Willy Verkauf, Teufen/St Gallen
1954.

Will Grohmann: *Paul Klee.* 2nd edition.
W. Kohlhammer, Stuttgart 1954; Harry N. Abrams,
New York 1954; Lund Humphries, London 1954.

Daniel-Henry Kahnweiler: *Paul Klee*
(Collection Palettes), Ed. Braun, Paris 1950.

W. Kandinsky: *Über das Geistige in der Kunst.*
Munich 1912.
English translation: *Concerning the Spiritual in Art
and Painting in Particular*, Wittenborn, New York 1947.

List of works reproduced

1902	Anatomic drawing	Pencil	Klee-Stiftung, Berne	Page 334
1915/83	Blossom	Pen and ink drawing		72
1918/207	Inscription	Pen and ink	Felix Klee, Berne	210
1919/14	Oh-oh, you strong man!	Lithograph		31
1919/113	Meditation (self-portrait)	Lithograph		20
1919/115	Landscape with gallows	Oil on cardboard	Galerie Ferd. Möller, Cologne	77
1919/199	House interior	Watercolour	Dr R. Jucker, Milan	154
1919/260	Artist's picture (self-portrait)	Pen drawing	The Pasadena Art Institute, California	92
1920/41	Rhythmic landscape with trees	Oil	Edgar Horstmann, Hamburg	270
1920/109	Flowers in a wheatfield	Pen and ink		256
1920/205	Sketch for realm of the plants, earth and air	Pen and ink	Klee-Stiftung, Berne	314
1921/3	Inscription	Watercolour and pen and ink	Rolf Bürgi, Belp/Berne	394
1921/24	Perspective of room with occupants	Watercolour	Klee-Stiftung, Berne	144
1921/69	Fugue in red	Watercolour	Felix Klee, Berne	490
1922/29	Arabian city	Watercolour and oil on gauze prepared with plaster	Privately owned	156
1922/30	Mural from the temple of yearning ↖ thither ↗	Watercolour		406
1922/79	Separation in the evening	Watercolour	Felix Klee, Berne	11
1922/109	Scene of calamity	Pen and watercolour	Klee-Stiftung, Berne	310
1922/159	Oscillating balance	Watercolour	Klee-Stiftung, Berne	390
1922/176	Little fir-tree picture	Oil on gauze	Kunstmuseum, Basle	308
1923/11	Town square under construction	Watercolour	Staatliche Kunstsammlungen des Landes Nordrhein-Westfalen, Düsseldorf	153
1923/62	Architecture (yellow and violet graduated cubes)	Oil	Hermann Rupf, Berne	370
1923/79	Assyrian game	Oil on cardboard on wood	Werner Allenbach, Berne	38
1923/131	Houses in projection	Watercolour		152
1923/138	Tightrope walker	Lithograph	Klee-Stiftung, Berne	196
1923/176	Cosmic flora	Watercolour	Klee-Stiftung, Berne	350
1923/179	Landscapely-physiognomic	Gouache	Privately owned, USA	128
1923/217	Severity of the clouds	Pencil	Felix Klee, Berne	312
1924/21	Village in blue and orange	Oil on paper prepared with chalk	Klee-Stiftung, Berne	191
1924/39	Houses in landscape	Colour		186
1924/128	Mural	Tempera on canvas	Klee-Stiftung, Berne	250
1924/132	Hieroglyphic water plants	Watercolour	Lyonel Feininger Estate, New York	240
1925/c 9	Profile of head	Relief-like painting Oil on plaster	Felix Klee, Berne	7
1925/f 9	Houses in the country	Oil	Privately owned, Basle	168
1925/T 4	The last village in the valley of Ph	Colour on paper		25
1925/y 1	Exotic bird park	Pen and ink		35
1926/R 2	Spiral flowers	Oil on canvas	Galerie Beyeler, Basle	377
1926/E 0	Reworked in 1946. Fish in circle	Oil	Felix Klee, Berne	46
1926/T 7	Two boats near path	Crayon drawing	Felix Klee, Berne	18
1927	Little jester in trance	Oil print		130

The picture titles and designations of works are for the most part taken from the originals; where this was not possible, they have been taken from Paul Klee's own Catalogue of Works. Pencil drawings, pen-and-ink drawings, and pictures done in watercolour or gouache mixed with paste are on paper where there is no indication to the contrary. Works in mixed technique (oil and watercolour) are for the most part on a surface prepared with chalk or plaster.

1927/k 3	Artist's portrait	Oil		208
1927/m 9	Pagodas by the water	Pen and ink		12
1927/o 1	Beride (city by the water)	Pen and ink	Klee-Stiftung, Berne	280
1927/o 8	City of Cathedrals	Pen and ink drawing		12
1927/o 9	Rain	Pen and ink	Klee-Stiftung, Berne	12
1927/D 8	Slate quarry	Pen and ink drawing	Felix Klee, Berne	284
1927/D 9	Difficult journey through O	Pen and ink	Felix Klee, Berne	106
1927/d 10	The ships set sail	Oil on canvas on wood	Werner Allenbach, Berne	80
1927/e 2	Four sailboats	Oil	Galerie Beyeler, Basle	278
1927/E 4	Harmony of the northern flora	Oil on cardboard coated with chalk	Felix Klee, Berne	506
1927/E 9	Sailboats in gentle motion	Pen and ink	Privately owned, Berne	276
1927/F 2	Symptomatic	Pen and ink drawing	Felix Klee, Berne	300
1927/f 4	The tower stands fast	Indian ink drawing	Privately owned, Berne	298
1927/i 1	Many-coloured lightning	Oil	Staatliche Kunstsammlungen des Landes Nordrhein-Westfalen, Düsseldorf	368
1927/i 3	Figurine 'The jester'	Oil on canvas	Privately owned, USA	130
1927/v 1	Ships after the storm	Crayon drawing	Felix Klee, Berne	372
1927/w 1	Thomas R.'s country house	Watercolour	Felix Klee, Berne	235
1927/w 2	Stratification sets in	Watercolour	Felix Klee, Berne	235
1927/w 7	Harmony of the southern flora	Watercolour		235
1927/x 8	Elected site	Indian ink and water-colour		302
1927/y 7	Physiognomic lightning	Watercolour		330
1927/ue 2	Ardent flowering	Watercolour	Rolf Bürgi, Belp/Berne	20
1927/om 9	Variations (progressive motif)	Oil on canvas		28
1927/om 10	Green courtyard	Oil on wood	Dr Forell, Munich	301
1927/3h 4	About to take a trip	Pen and ink drawing		26
1928/k 2	Three phantom ships	Pen and ink drawing	Klee-Stiftung, Berne	36
1928/k 5	Horn perceived in tent	Pen and ink		31
1928/k 9	Overtones	Pen and ink drawing	Privately owned, Berne	31
1928/N 6	A page from the city records	Oil	Öffentliche Kunstsammlung, Basle	244
1928/P 6	Italian city	Watercolour	Felix Klee, Berne	42
1928/p 7	Little week-end house	Oil	Staatliche Kunstsammlungen des Landes Nordrhein-Westfalen, Düsseldorf	142
1928/q 5	Foundation walls of K.	Watercolour	Ida Bienert, Munich	356
1929/m 1	Houses at crossroads	Watercolour	Felix Klee, Berne	50
1929/m 3	Evening in Egypt	Watercolour	Privately owned, Berne	146
1929/M 4	The sun grazes the plain	Watercolour	Klee-Stiftung, Berne	163
1929/m 7	Church and castle	Pen and ink drawing	Felix Klee, Berne	138
1929/n 6	(Little) jester in trance	Oil on canvas		130
1929/o 4	Rock	Pen and ink	Felix Klee, Berne	102
1929/o 8	Huts	Pen and ink drawing	Felix Klee, Berne	25
1929/p 6	Village in the rain	Pen and ink drawing	Felix Klee, Berne	45
1929/s 2	In the current of six crescendos	Oil	Galerie Beyeler, Basle	212
1929/s 6	Castle hill	Oil	Privately owned, Zurich	158
1929/s 7	Arrow in garden	Oil	Daniel-Henry Kahnweiler, Paris	56
1929/s 9	Old man reckoning	Engraving		236
1929/c 4	Uncomposed objects in space	Watercolour	Privately owned, Berne	140
1929/g 10	Santa A at B	Pen and pencil drawing	Klee-Stiftung, Berne	54

526

1929/y 2	Propagation of light 1	Watercolour	Galerie Rosengart, Lucerne	41
1929/OE 4	Illumined leaf	Watercolour	Klee-Stiftung, Berne	65
1929/3H 26	Collapse	Watercolour	Felix Klee, Berne	176
1929/3h 43	Mixed weather	Oil	Felix Klee, Berne	402
1930/N 1	Scaffolding of building under construction	Colour	Kunstmuseum, Berne	209
1930/R 2	Planes measured by their heights	Pastel with paste	Klee-Stiftung, Berne	41
1930/U 9	Spatial study (rational connections)	Pencil drawing	Klee-Stiftung, Berne	54
1930/w 8	Twins	Oil on canvas	T. Kneeland, Hartford, Conn.	118
1930/x 4	Six species	Watercolour	Felix Klee, Berne	116
1930/x 10	Polyphonic setting for white	Watercolour	Klee-Stiftung, Berne	374
1930/y 1	House, outside and inside	Watercolour	Hermann Rupf, Berne	48
1930/y 4	Daringly poised	Watercolour	Klee-Stiftung, Berne	213
1930/A 1	Abundance in village	Pen and ink	Felix Klee, Berne	214
1930/a 7	Twins	Drawing		118
1930/C 3	Jumper	Varnished watercolour on cotton and wood	Felix Klee, Berne	30
1930/e 8	Brother and sister	Oil on canvas		118
1930/e 10	Ad marginem	Oil	Kunstmuseum, Basle	74
1930/s 1	At seven over rooftops	Tempera and watercolour, varnished	Galerie Louise Leiris, Paris	164
1930/s 10	Hovering before rising	Oil on canvas	Klee-Stiftung, Berne	172
1930/J 7	Twined into a group	Pen and ink drawing	Klee-Stiftung, Berne	340
1930/OE 5	Polyphonic-abstract	Watercolour	Hermann Rupf, Berne	380
1931/k 5	Study for flight from oneself (first version)	Drawing	Klee-Stiftung, Berne	296
1931/L 4	Three subjects, polyphonic	Colour		296
1931/M 1	New things on old soil	Colour	Privately owned, Paris	38
1931/m 7	Figure	Colour		383
1931/M 18	Entwined curve with positive-negative plane formation	Pencil drawing	Klee-Stiftung, Berne	436
1931/p 11	Air currents	Pencil drawing	Felix Klee, Berne	320
1931/p 13	Bull's head	Colour	Privately owned, Berne	439
1931/r 9	Stakim	Oil	Galerie Louise Leiris, Paris	439
1931/u 15	Variation on 'Circuit through 6 planes'	Coloured ink on paper	Klee-Stiftung, Berne	163
1931/w 18	Landscapely-physiognomic	Colour		66
1931/x 9	Luxuriant countryside	Pencil drawing	Felix Klee, Berne	304
1931/y 3	Chess	Oil	Galerie Beyeler, Basle	216
1932	Tragedy	Oil	Galerie Beyeler, Basle	366
1932/k 9	Tendril	Oil	Felix Klee, Berne	104
1932/m 1	Plant hieroglyphics	Colour	Klee-Stiftung, Berne	288
1932/s 2	City Castle of KR	Oil	Dr R. Doetsch-Benziger, Basle	232
1932/t 5	Garden rhythm	Oil	Felix Klee, Berne	323
1932/U 12	Deceased melancholic	Black and white watercolour		445
1932/v 11	Small town	Colour	Felix Klee, Berne	150
1932/v 17	Helical flowers I	Black and white watercolour		376
1932/x 10	View over the plain	Oil on wood	Staatliche Kunstsammlungen des Landes, Nordrhein-Westfalen, Düsseldorf	8
1932/x 16	Little cliff town	Oil	Klee-Stiftung, Berne	160

1932/y 4	*The fruit*	Oil	Mies van der Rohe, Chicago	6
1932/z 19	*The step*	Oil on burlap	Felix Klee, Berne	434
1932/1933	*(Descent)*	Oil on burlap	Felix Klee, Berne	412
1933/L 4	*Dominated group*	Watercolour	Felix Klee, Berne	176
1933/z 6	*Scholar (self-portrait)*	Oil on canvas on wood	Rolf Bürgi, Belp/Berne	20
1933/D 20	*Bust of a child*	Oil	Klee-Stiftung, Berne	89
1933/E 13	*World harbour*	Paste and pigment on paper	Felix Klee, Berne	238
1934/12	*Temptation*	Gouache	Klee-Stiftung, Berne	324
1934/19	*Mountain gorge*	Colour	Felix Klee, Berne	361
1934/K 4	*Mister Zed*	Watercolour	G. David Thompson, Pittsburgh	341
1934/L 5	*With the wheel*	Colour	Felix Klee, Berne	248
1934/N 6	*A curtain is drawn*	Pencil drawing	Felix Klee, Berne	287
1934/N 17	*Avenue with trees*	Pencil	Felix Klee, Berne	100
1934/qu 2	*Uphill and then what?*	Pen and ink	Klee-Stiftung, Berne	305
1934/qu 6	*Can't be climbed*	Pencil drawing	Felix Klee, Berne	318
1934/qu 7	*Agitated*	Pencil	Felix Klee, Berne	388
1934/qu 10	*Heavily fructified*	Pencil drawing	Galerie d'art moderne, Basle	26
1934/qu 18	*Cliffs*	Pencil drawing	Felix Klee, Berne	304
1934/s 7	*Spring in stream*	Pencil drawing	Felix Klee, Berne	320
1934/s 11	*Calix abdominis (Belly bud)*	Pen and ink		25
1934/U 2	*Fear*	Oil on burlap	Nelson A. Rockefeller, New York	16
1934/U 17	*Snake-paths*	Oil	Rolf Bürgi, Belp/Berne	85
1934/U 19	*Botanical theatre (1924–1934)*	Oil on wood	Rolf Bürgi, Belp/Berne	94
1935/L 15	*Ostentatious defence*	Colour	Klee-Stiftung, Berne	262
1935/M 17	*Signs on the field*	Watercolour		198
1935/qu 15	*Will you be seated?*	Charcoal and red chalk	Klee-Stiftung, Berne	206
1937/L 5	*Labile pointer*	Watercolour on blotting paper	Felix Klee, Berne	408
1937/N 3	*Germinating*	Pencil drawing	Felix Klee, Berne	124
1937/N 4	*Forked structures in four-part time*	Gouache	Felix Klee, Berne	272
1937/P 17	*Peach harvest*	Colour		122
1937/qu 12	*Fragments*	Oil	Galerie Louise Leiris, Paris	309
1937/qu 14	*Little seaport*	Oil	Galerie Louise Leiris, Paris	200
1937/qu 17	*The way to the city castle*	Oil	Galerie Louise Leiris, Paris	166
1937/qu 18	*Architecture in the evening*	Oil	Galerie Beyeler, Basle	184
1937/R 1	*Superchess*	Oil	Kunsthaus, Zürich	222
1937/R 5	*The Rhine near Duisburg*	Oil on cardboard	Heinz Berggruen, Paris	290
1937/R 6	*Terrace with flowers*	Oil	Galerie Louise Leiris, Paris	294
1937/R 11	*Harbour with sailboats*	Oil	Galerie Louise Leiris, Paris	108
1937/T 5	*Overland*	Paste with pigment and pastel on burlap	Felix Klee, Berne	504
1937/T 8	*Children's playground*	Pastel and red chalk		464
1937/T 9	*Sextet of geniuses*	Pastel		396
1937/U 6	*Harmonised battle*	Pastel	Klee-Stiftung, Berne	178
1937/U 11	*View in red*	Pastel	Felix Klee, Berne	291
1937/w 17	*Successful exorcism*	Paste with black pigment on paper		455
1938/1	*Heroic strokes of the bow*	Oil on plaster	Nelson A. Rockefeller, New York	283
1938/D 16	*(Landscape) with the two who are lost*	Gouache on newsprint	Kunstmuseum, Basle	192

1938/E 7	*Stormy mise-en-scène*	Colour		443
1938/F 16	*Under the cloak* (Original title crossed out: *Exact man in cloak*)	Paste with black pigment on paper	Felix Klee, Berne	457
1938/g 10	*Dancing from fright*	Watercolour	Klee-Stiftung, Berne	114
1938/J 3	*Animal monument*	Oil	Galerie Louise Leiris, Paris	456
1938/J 5	*The grey man and the coast*	Oil	Felix Klee, Berne	316
1938/J 12	*Source of fire*	Oil on canvas	Rolf Bürgi, Belp/Berne	426
1938/J 16	*Shattered key*	Oil on canvas	Rolf Bürgi, Belp/Berne	430
1938/J 18	*Timid brute*	Oil	H. Arnold, New York	416
1938/k 5	*Forest witches*	Oil with wax on coated newsprint on burlap	Fritz Gygi, Berne	462
1938/k 6	*Lady and fashion*	Oil	Staatliche Kunstsammlungen des Landes Nordrhein-Westfalen, Düsseldorf	451
1938/T 19	*Le rouge et le noir*	Oil	Rolf Bürgi, Belp/Berne	14
1938/v 2	*Interim near Easter*	Oil on burlap	Staatliche Kunstsammlungen des Landes Nordrhein-Westfalen, Düsseldorf	292
1938/x 1	*Fragmenta veneris*	Oil	Privately owned, Zürich	452
1938/y 11	*Tale of the three fishermen*	Gouache		437
1938/B 14	*Coarser and finer*	Pen and ink	Felix Klee, Berne	447
1938/c 7	*Torture*	Oil	Felix Klee, Berne	418
1939/M 4	*Outburst of fear III*	Colour	Klee-Stiftung, Berne	378
1939/M 8	*Houses close together*	Colour		160
1939/w 11	*Violin and bow*	Pencil drawing	Felix Klee, Berne	121
1939/Y 6	*Shattered labyrinth*	Oil and watercolour on paper prepared with oil on canvas	Klee-Stiftung, Berne	432
1939/A 5	*Child's game*	Coloured paste and watercolour on cardboard	Felix Klee, Berne	448
1939/FF 13	*Mountain under compulsion*	Oil on canvas		450
1939/UU 11	*On the Nile*	Oil on burlap	Privately owned, Basle	342
1939/ww 15	*Scene of fire*	Oil and paste, waxed on burlap	Felix Klee, Berne	306
1939/CD 15	*O the rumours!*	Tempera and oil on burlap		442
1939/JK 9	*Group of eleven*	Paste and pigment on wrapping paper	Klee-Stiftung, Berne	258
1939/LM 18	*Accident*	Tempera and crayon on white underpainting		40
1939/MN 5	*Fleeing woman looks back*	Pencil drawing	Felix Klee, Berne	420
1939/MN 9	*Fights with himself*	Pencil and watercolour	Felix Klee, Berne	279
1939/Pqu 11	*Arrogance*	Coloured paste and oil; yellow wrapping paper on burlap	Klee-Stiftung, Berne	444
1939	*From Klee's estate No.017* (Untitled)	Watercolour	Felix Klee, Berne	460
1940	*Painting on black background* (Untitled)	Oil on canvas	Felix Klee, Berne	495
1940/x 1	*Eyes in the landscape*	Oil	Dr E. Friedrich, Zürich	96
1940/N 13	*Still life on 29th February*	Oil	Klee-Stiftung, Berne	440
1940/N 14	*Churches*	Colour	Klee-Stiftung, Berne	194

1940/M 19	*After the act of violence*	Coloured paste on paper	Felix Klee, Berne	441
1940/M 20	*Mountain game*	Gouache		254
1940/k 8	*Glass façade*	Oil	Klee-Stiftung, Berne	466
1940/K 16	*Palaces*	Colour		457
1940/F 13	*Centipede in an enclosure*	Pastel on cotton	Klee-Stiftung, Berne	242
1940/F 20	*Assault and battery*	Paste with black pigment on paper		461
1940	*From Klee's estate* (Untitled)	Paint mixed with paste, on paper	Privately owned, Berne	5
1940	*From Klee's estate No.028* (Untitled)	Watercolour mixed with paste on burlap	Felix Klee, Berne	202
1940	*From Klee's estate No.034* (Untitled)	Pigment mixed with paste on paper	Felix Klee, Berne	18

87 Properties and application of three lines of reference. Logical to handle them all with same precision. Distinguishing symbols of pure line (linear scale), pure tone (weight scale), and pure colour (colour circle)

88 Picturing the chief scenes in the drama of colour relations. The emergence of the elements in a new order, producing a figure called form or object

89 Motif and theme. Every complex structure lends itself to comparison with familiar forms in nature. Associative properties

90 Justification of an objective concept in a picture. The formal elements singly and in their special context; their appearance in groups.
A further dimension: that of content

91 Contrasts and subtle variants on them

92 Dimension of style.
Static and dynamic aspects of pictorial mechanics (impulses of energies and force of gravity). Classicism and romanticism.
Composition.
Distortion of natural forms. Image of creation as genesis

93 Journeying along the paths of natural creation is an excellent school of form.
Scientific knowledge:
For purposes of comparison, only with a view to mobility, and in freedom.
From prototype to archetype.
Not only to reproduce things seen, but to make secret vision visible

95 The cultivation of the pictorial elements, purification and use in pure state. Benefit from association between philosophy and craftsmanship. A work of vast scope spanning element, object, content and style

538